THE FARMER'S *Bride* COLLECTION

DiAnn Mills

Kimberley Comeaux, Susan K. Downs, JoAnn A. Grote, Ellen Edwards Kennedy, Debby Mayne

BARBOUR
PUBLISHING

Print ISBN 978-1-62416-231-2

eBook Editions:
Adobe Digital Edition (.epub) 978-1-62416-449-1
Kindle and MobiPocket Edition (.prc) 978-1-62416-448-4

Published by Barbour Publishing, Inc., P.O. Box 719, Uhrichsville, Ohio 44683, www.barbourbooks.com

Our mission is to publish and distribute inspirational products offering exceptional value and biblical encouragement to the masses.

Member of the
Evangelical Christian
Publishers Association

Printed in Canada.

CONTENTS

ONE LITTLE PRAYER

by Kimberley Comeaux

Chapter 1

One minute James Edward Larabee, a former captain of the Confederate Army, was riding on his horse through the woods, the next minute he was flat on his back. Stunned, he could do nothing but lie there for a moment, before his soldier instincts kicked in and he began taking quick inventory of himself and his surroundings.

The first thing he noticed was that his leg was covered in blood. Then, the most horrific pain he'd ever felt in his life exploded throughout his bloody limb, causing him to cry out. He'd been shot, he realized. But that couldn't be. The war was over; it had been over for nearly two and a half years. Why would someone shoot him?

The snap of a twig, then a movement out of the corner of his eye, caught his attention. He looked up and saw a hazy figure running away from him. He could barely make out the blue and black clothing, as the person darted through the trees.

"Hey! Come back! I need some help here!" he called several times, but the person just kept going.

It must have been the person who shot him. But why? It couldn't be an outraged Yankee who decided to use him for target practice. He no longer wore the gray pants trimmed in gold that were a sign of his involvement with the Confederate Army. If only he'd gotten a better look at the person who shot him. What kind of man would leave another to bleed to death? Or maybe it was a woman, he just couldn't tell.

Helplessness poured over him as he struggled to sit up. How was he supposed to get help? He had no idea where he was. And to top it all off, his horse had run off with all his belongings and money.

But he'd have to address that problem later. If he didn't get the wound bandaged, they would be finding a dead man instead of a wounded one.

Almost methodically, he took off his jacket, then pulled his shirt off, leaving only his long johns top, and began wrapping the shirt around his thigh, just as he'd done to wounded soldiers in the war. And as he pulled at the sleeves of the shirt, tying it tightly, he thought that it was ironic that he'd managed to escape the bullets during the war, only to be brought down on his way to start a new life. Had God forsaken him again?

The January wind cut through his clothes, and he stared at the sky peeking through the tree branches. He thought briefly of saying a prayer but decided that it wouldn't do any good. Had God listened when he'd prayed that his father and brother would return from the war? Had He listened when he prayed that their plantation would still be intact?

No. His father and brother died in the war and their plantation in Dothan, Alabama, had been burned to the ground. His faith had died along with them.

The one saving grace had been the money that his father had buried in the family cemetery before they went off to fight. Daddy had put ten thousand dollars at the foot of Mama's grave. That cash was going to buy him a brand-new life out West. He'd made plans to purchase a saloon in San Francisco. All he had to do was show up, sign the papers, and hand over the money.

But now here he lay, probably bleeding to death, his horse missing. . . suddenly those plans seemed very far away. And though the pain in his leg seemed to lessen, the pain in his soul became worse. Bitterness ate at his gut as he silently laid one more accusation at God's door. What was next? Was he to die here? All he knew was that he was in the middle of a forest, somewhere in north Louisiana. There might not be anyone for miles.

But the sound of footsteps coming his direction quickly banished that notion. As it came closer, though, he realized it was a horse's gallop that he heard. He breathed a sigh of relief. His horse had obviously come back to him. If he could manage to get on the animal's back, perhaps he could find a doctor or at least someone who could remove the bullet.

He raised himself on his elbows and watched as the horse came into view. His eyebrows suddenly lowered and he frowned at what he saw next. Though it was his horse that was coming toward him, it was being ridden by. . . well, he couldn't really tell what was on Rebel's back.

When the horse was reined to a stop, the most strangely dressed little girl he'd ever laid eyes on looked down at him. For a moment, he could do nothing but gape at her attire. On her thin shoulders she had draped an old faded sheet tied at her neck. Her chest was decorated with pieces of tin sewn carefully to her thick brown blouse. But it was what she wore on her head that got his greatest attention. Sitting pertly on her golden curls was a uniquely carved-out. . .gourd!

After studying him for a moment through narrowed, suspicious eyes, she whipped out a wooden stick, holding it like a sword and pointing it at him. "What army are you with, sir?" she demanded in a high, extremely Southern-sounding voice.

He couldn't help but chuckle at her serious face. As if irritated, she jabbed him with the stick, hitting him in the chest. "Are you English or French?" she asked as she went to poke him again.

He quickly grabbed the stick before it reached him and yanked it out of her hand. "Listen, little girl, you've stolen my horse and poked me with sticks and I'm getting a little tired of—"

"How dare you address me as 'little girl'! I am Joan of Arc, and I've seized your horse! Now, give me back my sword so that I may slay you." She lifted her chin and held out her hand so regally that James couldn't help but admire her.

Suddenly the costume made sense—of course Joan of Arc would be dressed as a soldier. He quickly searched his mind, trying to remember whether Joan was French or English. "Uh. . .I'm French?" he tested carefully. He couldn't figure out if the little girl was playing a game or if she actually believed she was Joan of Arc.

She withdrew her hand and put it on her hip. "Well, in that case, I'll let you live."

He moved and then winced as his leg began to throb again. In her child's play he'd forgotten all about his wound. "Joan, I'm not going to live if you don't run and get me help. Someone shot me in the leg," he told her gruffly as he adjusted his makeshift bandage.

Suddenly Joan's eyes filled with horror as she noticed all the blood that she seemed to have missed before. "Goodness gracious, Mister! You're bleeding like a stuck pig!" she said, falling out of character.

She jumped down from the horse, her tin clanging as she ran to him and knelt down. He saw that she wore trousers under her skirt, and he put her age to be about nine or ten. Clearly old enough to understand how to get help.

"Yes, Joan, and that's why I need for you to—"

"That bullet's gonna have to come out!" Joan interrupted.

"I know that. I—"

"Someone must have thought that you were a deer! Don't you know not to go traipsing through the woods this time of year?"

James closed his eyes and took a deep breath, then opened them again. "Joan, could you just—"

"And here you are all dressed in brown just like a deer. Nope, that wasn't too smart!"

He narrowed his gaze at her. "If it's too dangerous to be in the woods, what are you doing here?"

She just smiled and pushed the gourd back off of her forehead. "'Cause these are my woods! Ain't nobody gonna shoot me!" she exclaimed, looking at him as if he were the dense one. "And my name's not really Joan."

"Well, whatever it is, could you just—"

"My name's Louanne Wise. But you can call me Victoria."

He knew that he shouldn't ask but... "Why do you want me to call you Victoria, if your name is Louanne?"

"Because Louanne is so plain! Victoria is more. . . noble sounding, you know, like Queen Victoria! But it seems I am doomed to live out my existence with the name I was born with." She finished with a long-suffering sigh.

She then looked at him with renewed interest. "What is your name? You're not a robber or outlaw or anything like that, are you? Because if you are, I'm not supposed to be talking to you. Actually, I'm not supposed to be talking to anyone who doesn't live in Wiseville. I'm a Wise, you see, and practically everyone around here is kin to me one way or another; so it's all right if I talk to them. But I don't believe that I've ever seen you before!"

It was he that took the breath after that little speech. It made him tired just listening to her.

"My name is James Larabee of the Alabama Larabees, and I promise you that I'm not an outlaw. But I am going to pass out if I don't get this blood stopped," he grumbled, then added, "You know, Joan of Arc wouldn't allow a man to suffer out in the wild."

She thrust her chin up and adjusted the bed sheet around her shoulders. She was back in character. "Of course not. Joan of Arc can do anything!" Then she was quiet for a moment. "Except, of course, she didn't save herself from being burned at the stake. She should have come up with a better plan," she added with a frown.

"Louanne, honey, please. . . ," he groaned. "Get help."

"Okay." She jumped up and looked at his horse. "Can I take your horse?"

"If it'll help you get help faster, by all means take him."

With the skill of one who had been raised around horses, Louanne climbed on the back of the brown animal and took off.

As she galloped toward home, she thought about the man she'd left behind. He sure seemed like a nice person, even if he was just a little grumpy. She hoped that his leg would be all right. One of her uncles had come home from the war with one of his legs cut off at the knee. She didn't want that to happen to Mr. Larabee.

It seemed strange to find a man who wasn't kin in her woods. Strangers just didn't pass through Wiseville that often.

Then she got another idea. What if God had brought Mr. Larabee to her? She had been praying for God to send her a daddy, since He had her real daddy in heaven. Mama had told her to make a prayer list, and that was one of the first things she prayed for everyday, though Mama wasn't aware of it.

One of her many uncles was the preacher in town, and he always said that God worked in mysterious ways. Well, finding a shot-up stranger in her woods was the most mysterious thing that she'd ever come across! Surely, that must mean that he was the answer to her prayers! It made perfect sense!

As her house came into view, however, she wasn't sure that her mother would go running to help a man that she didn't know. Since Daddy's death, two years before, gentlemen had been flocking around her mama, asking for her hand in marriage. Mama never seemed very interested. She was always telling them that it just wasn't proper to come calling out at her house, since she and Louanne had no menfolk who lived with them to make it proper. She would allow only the cousins and uncles to visit. Louanne wished that her mother would marry someone. The man in the woods was as good as any of the men who'd come calling. If only Louanne could find some way to get her mother to meet him. Suddenly, an idea came to her. It was in the form of a lie. She got off the horse and ran to where her mother was coming out of the chicken coop.

"Mama! Come quick! I just found a man in the woods, and I think he's. . .dead!"

James realized that he had dozed off, when a sound startled him and shook him out of his slumber. He saw that it was a small wagon being pulled by a horse, coming down the wooded trail.

The little soldier had done it! She'd gotten him help. He relaxed and closed his eyes again, waiting for them to reach him. He wondered if she had brought her parents with her. He hoped that she at least had gotten her pa. A woman would have a hard time lifting him into a wagon.

He heard the clatter of the wagon. He opened his eyes and saw a beautiful woman dressed in blue calico, getting down from the wagon. But other than the little girl and the woman, there was no one else. He shifted his weight to sit up but accidentally hit the wound against a rock on the ground. The pain was so intense he couldn't cry out; instead, he felt himself blacking out. He fought it, trying desperately to hold on to consciousness.

"You're right, Louanne. I think he's dead," the woman said.

Dead? He wasn't dead. . .was he?

"Why don't you listen to his heart, Mama?"

There was a pause, then the woman said, "Alright."

He heard a rustle of fabric, then the scent of honeysuckle flooded his senses and the touch of her soft hair brushed against his chin. He opened his eyes and saw her press her ear to his chest.

"My, you smell pretty," he said in his best Southern drawl, despite himself.

Her head reared and whipped around. Startled blue-green eyes flew to his face. "You're alive!" she charged and scrambled back. But in doing so, she lost her balance and tumbled to the ground.

He managed to lift himself to his elbows. "Of course, I'm alive. Didn't Louanne tell you that I needed help?"

The woman pushed herself upright and smoothed her skirts modestly over her ankles, while she sat a small distance from him.

"She said that you were dead!" she told him, sending Louanne a warning glare that future retribution was soon coming her way. Louanne began to play with the tin on her chest.

"Ma'am, please, I've been shot, and I need to get this bullet out of my leg. . . ."

"Oh, my goodness! You're not an outlaw or something, are you?" Her hand was over her heart, a horrified expression on her pretty face.

Was everyone in this family suspicious of outlaws?

"Momma, someone shot him thinking he was a deer," Louanne chimed in helpfully.

An understanding look came over "Momma's" face. "Oh, dear. I'll bet that's what happened. You are bleeding pretty badly," she said carefully, as if trying to make up her mind about something.

Suddenly, she hopped up and clapped her hands together. "Well, I guess we need to get you aboard this wagon, don't we?" She looked at him as if measuring him up, then she glanced at the wagon. A worried expression overtook her face.

James grabbed a stick beside him. "Ma'am, if you can help me, I can lift myself up with this." He lifted one arm, while gripping the branch with the other. "My name is James Larabee, by the way."

The woman reached down to clutch his arm, and together they managed to bring him to his feet. He put his arm around her and leaned heavily on her shoulders. She, struggling to hold his weight, turned toward him. James found himself no more than a half an inch from her face.

As he stared into her eyes, his pain didn't seem nearly as bad. She seemed to feel it, too, because she stared back.

Before the war, James Larabee had courted some of the most beautiful young women around Dothan, but none of those compared to the petite angel who was looking into his eyes at that moment. None had the silky-smooth, soft peach skin nor the long brown eyelashes that framed her ocean-blue eyes. And, though most of her hair was wound loosely in a knot on top of her head, the rich chestnut color gleamed in the soft light of the woods.

"You never told me your name," he said to her, but he wished he hadn't spoken.

As if she'd suddenly become aware of their situation, she blushed hotly and looked away. "My name is Mrs. Tessa Wise," she told him, emphasizing the title.

James's heart sank, and he could feel the pain again in his leg as the euphoric feeling he felt at her nearness began to melt away. She was married. He was ashamed that he'd embarrassed them both.

But as she helped him slide into the back of the wagon, he reminded himself that it didn't matter—he wasn't in the market for a wife. Saloon owners didn't marry. That was no life for a family.

And besides, he had lost too many loved ones. He would not make himself vulnerable to those feelings ever again.

They set off in the wagon. The pain in his leg throbbed as he was jostled about, and he blamed his delirium for making him think of love. Tessa Wise was going to take out his bullet and perhaps let him bunk down a few days in her barn. Then he'd leave.

A whole new life was waiting for him, and he wasn't going to allow anything to stand in the way.

Yet, the whole time he repeated the words to himself, he couldn't get rid of the picture of those beautiful blue-green eyes.

Chapter 2

More than once on the journey back to her house Tessa Wise wondered what she had gotten herself into by offering to help James Larabee. She and her daughter were alone, and having a man at her house, injured or not, just wasn't seemly.

Of course, he'd just have to stay in the barn. But, then again, the barn was so drafty, and it was January, just a week after the New Year. Already this winter was proving to be a rough one and was predicted to be even worse later in the month.

She sighed and chewed on her bottom lip as she worried over her situation. Mr. Larabee was injured and he needed help. What would God think of her if she left an injured man to bleed to death? He was, after all, shot on her property!

That thought caused her to start chewing on her lip again. Who had shot him? Had they really mistaken him for a deer? And if so, why had they not come to him, seen their error, and helped him?

Tessa had the sinking feeling that it was one of her late husband's young cousins or maybe one of their friends. It would be just like them to shoot impulsively, get scared, and run away.

"Isn't he handsome, Mama?"

That little whisper from Louanne broke Tessa out of her fretting in a big hurry! "What did you say?" she demanded, also speaking in a whisper.

Louanne smiled and got closer to her mother's ear. "He is so handsome. Riding up and finding him just lying there in the forest was like something out of a fairy tale," she said dramatically while putting her hand over her heart.

"Oh, Louanne, I don't want to hear any of your nonsense! This man is not a prince, and if he was, he wouldn't be tromping through our woods in the dead of winter!"

Actually, her daughter did have a point. The man was quite nice-looking. He had dark, wavy brown hair that was slightly longish and curled at the collar. His nose was straight, but not too long, and his cheekbones were prominent, his jaw square and manly. But that doesn't matter, she told herself, shaking herself from the picture that she'd just conjured up. The sooner she got him patched up, the sooner he could be on his way!

"But he could be a prince exiled from his country and running from those who want to kill him!" Louanne insisted, getting herself all worked up, her voice growing louder with each word.

"I promise that I'm not a prince," their rider chimed in from the back of the wagon.

Mortified, Tessa sent her daughter a glare. "Please excuse my daughter, Mr. Larabee. She's got quite an imagination."

"Don't you worry, Mrs. Wise. I find your daughter charming," James Larabee told her, his lazy Southern drawl drawing out the sentence. Tessa thought his accent was quite nice. Different from the country accents of North Louisiana, there was something else in his voice. She couldn't quite pin it down.

When she glanced back, she noticed his eyes were squeezed shut in obvious pain and he clutched the make-shift bandage wrapped around his leg.

She quickly looked forward and snapped the reins. She was going to have to get that bullet out before infection set in.

❧

It took them more than a few minutes and a whole lot of effort, but they finally got Mr. Larabee into the house and situated in the spare bedroom. One of her brothers-in-law, J. T. Wise, was a doctor, and Tessa sent Louanne after him. Tessa, having served as a temporary nurse during the war, was well acquainted with digging bullets out of men, but she still hoped that J. T. could be found, just in case.

She mixed some laudanum in a glass of water and took it to him. "Here you go, Mr. Larabee. Just drink this, and it should help you not to hurt so bad."

As he took the glass from her, his fingers brushed against hers and their eyes met. Tessa quickly looked away and tried to hide the blush that she knew must be burning her cheeks. What was wrong with her? Why did this man affect her so strangely?

Tessa was carefully removing the shirt-bandage from around his leg when he spoke. "Uh, have you ever done this before?" There was more than a slight trace of worry in his voice.

Tessa lifted an eyebrow as she looked over at him. "Scared, Mr. Larabee?"

"Cautious, Mrs. Wise," he countered. Suddenly they both started to chuckle. It went a long way to ease some of the strain in the room.

She flashed him a smile and started cutting the fabric away from the wound. "As a matter of fact, I have done this before, so you don't have to worry. I patched up quite a few men in the war, both Confederate and Yankee. But if you're still uneasy, I sent for my brother-in-law, who is a doctor."

James shook his head. "I'm sure you'll do just fine."

Tessa gave him a smile that she hoped contained more assurance than she felt. As she examined the wound, she realized that the bullet was lodged pretty deep. She could see part of it, but she wasn't sure that she could get it out without causing him to start bleeding again.

She looked at her patient to ask him if he could feel the laudanum taking effect yet, but his eyes were closed. She gazed back at the wound, took a deep breath, then grabbed the large tweezers and went to work.

James couldn't remember when he'd ever felt worse. Though his head was swimming with the medicine she'd given him, he could still feel the pain as the doctor dug out the bullet. He had to wonder: If it hurt this bad with the doctor doing the surgery, what would it have felt like with an amateur like Tessa Wise doing the job? He was just glad the good doctor had arrived in time!

But, it was all over with now. Doc had sewed him up and wrapped a bandage around his leg and told him that he wasn't to move for two weeks.

Two weeks! He didn't know who took the news worse, Tessa or himself. She had pulled the doctor out of the room in a big hurry, and he could still hear them whispering in the next room. Well, he wasn't happy about it either. Two weeks was going to put him off schedule, mess up his plans! He had a life to get on with and this setback was fouling everything up.

Frustrated, he looked up to the ceiling and railed aloud, "Why me, God!"

"Why are you blaming God?" Louanne said from the doorway, surprising James. He hadn't even heard the door open.

"Why are you eavesdropping?" he countered with a smile.

Louanne, who was now dressed in a pretty green dress with a matching bow in her hair, skipped into the room and sat at the edge of his bed. "How else is a kid supposed to find out things?" she asked with a shrug. She then leaned over and put a hand to his head. "Are you feeling better?"

James squelched a laugh at her motherly action. *She must be imitating Tessa.* "Yes, ma'am," he drawled, playing along. "Doc Wise fixed me up."

"It was such a tragic thing that happened to you out there. I could just imagine that it was me who was injured on the cold, cold ground. . . waiting to die. . .all hope lost," she exclaimed dramatically, clasping her hands together at her chest. "Then, off in the distance a rider approaches upon a pure white steed and rescues me. He would be a prince and he would ask me to marry him!"

This time James did chuckle. "I've never heard anyone take an accident and turn it into a fairy tale. You're something else, Little Lulu!"

Louanne looked at him as though he had just offered her a giant piece of candy. "You called me Lulu! You know, my dad used to call me that," she said in an awed whisper. "It's a sign!"

James opened his mouth to comment then froze. "Used to?" he asked carefully.

"Yeah, my dad was killed in the war."

"I'm sorry," he told her, but his mind was whirling. Why had Tessa led him to believe her husband was still around? An elation he couldn't even begin to understand washed over him, but just as quickly, he squelched it.

Then he thought about what Louanne had said before that. "What did you mean when you said that it's a sign?"

"I can't tell you, right now, because it's a secret! But I can tell you that I was only kidding when I said that I thought you were a prince, earlier in the wagon. I know you're just a regular man." She got closer, as if she wanted to share a secret. "Princes have countries to run and damsels to rescue. They wouldn't be riding through our woods. Besides, I have another reason for knowing that you're not a prince, but I can't tell you that either. I can tell you it has something to do with God, though."

James sighed inwardly. God sure didn't make it easy for people to ignore Him. James wanted nothing more than to get on with his life and never think about God, and instead he was saddled for two weeks with what, apparently, was a deeply religious family.

"You sure do have a lot of secrets for such a little girl!" he commented absently, his attention shifting to his throbbing leg. The medication was wearing off and the pain was returning.

Louanne huffed and lifted her chin in the air. "I'm nine years old, Mr. Larabee. I'm hardly little." He grimaced, and she laid her hand on top of his. "You're looking ill again, Mr. Larabee. Is it hurting?"

He nodded, and she scooted off the bed. "I'll run in there and get Uncle J. T."

Louanne ran into the living room, but not two seconds later, she was back. She sighed a longsuffering breath and informed him, "Mama told me she'd talk to me later then sent me back in here."

She came around the bed and resumed her place beside him, taking his hand into her own. "I know what will help! I'll pray for you. Uncle Donald says that Jesus can heal the sick and afflicted, and since you were shot you're not really sick. I guess we can call you 'afflicted' so this should work," she told him matter-of-factly.

"Lulu, what does your Uncle Donald do?" he asked, though he was afraid that he already knew the answer.

"He's a preacher!"

With a resigned sigh, he nodded his head and let her pray for him.

No, God surely didn't make it easy.

"J. T., just what were you thinking telling that. . .that. . . stranger that he should stay off his leg. . .at my house! I can't have a man stay here! What will people think?" Tessa charged at her brother-in-law. She was upset, not only at J. T. but at herself for the happiness that ran through her at the thought of getting to know James Larabee a little better. That didn't make any sense! She wasn't interested in any man, much less a stranger.

Dr. J. T. Wise just grinned at Tessa, a smile so reminiscent of her late husband that Tessa felt suddenly guilty. "Tess, everyone will think you're doing a poor unfortunate man a favor and doing your Christian duty by nursing him back to health. Besides, he really does need to be watched closely. Infection could easily set into that wound." He picked up his black bag and withdrew a couple of packets. "Give him this if he suffers any pain."

Tessa took the packets but still glared at J. T. "I don't like this, J. T."

"What do you want me to do, Tess? Take him home with me? I already have five kids that I don't hardly have room for! And with Carolyn heavy with the sixth, she wouldn't be too happy if I brought an injured patient for her to care for," he informed her with a pleading expression.

There were seven Wise brothers and every one of them could talk a flea into jumping off a dog. But she knew that he was right. Carolyn was in no condition to care for the stranger. Neither was the rest of the family. It looked like, whether she liked it or not, she was stuck with the man for two weeks.

And despite the butterflies in her stomach, she refused to be excited about it!

"Oh, alright! But it's up to you to explain this to Donald. I don't want him upset at me for having a man in my house!"

J. T. grinned. "You know, Tess, I haven't seen a ring on the man's finger. . . ."

"Don't say it!" she screeched at him then, realizing her volume, lowered her voice. "Don't you dare try to play matchmaker, Jonathon Tyler Wise! We don't know this man from Adam!"

"That's no problem, Tess," he told her as he put on his hat. "You've got two weeks to get to know him better!"

With a growl, she grabbed his arm and marched him toward the door, grabbing his coat off the hook and stuffing it in his arms as she went. "Leave while you still can. Just don't forget to talk to Donald!"

He shrugged his coat on, and just before she shut the door, he added, "I'll tell him he needs to start polishing up on his wedding ser—"

The rest of his sentence was just a mere muffled sound behind Tessa's door. She chuckled and shook her head. That J. T. was something else! She didn't know how his wife put up with him.

Her smile faded as she focused on the door that led to the guest bedroom. She didn't understand why she found it so hard to speak with the man. He was injured and harmless, she reminded herself, but it didn't seem to help the butterflies that churned in her stomach. She knew that James Larabee was a gentleman—she could hear it in his voice and see it in his mannerisms. He was probably a very rich gentleman.

So what is he doing here?

With a determined tilt of her chin and a fortified breath, she started toward the room.

She was about to find out.

Chapter 3

They were praying. Or, at least, Louanne was praying while James Larabee stared down at his covers. Tessa smiled as her daughter's earnest words went on and on. A talent she, no doubt, inherited from her uncle Donald, who was famous for his lengthy prayers.

Since she hadn't been noticed, Tessa took the opportunity to study James Larabee. Despite the pain etched across his features, he certainly was nice to look at. And those eyes of his. . .they were a mesmerizing moss-green color. Surely he'd had many a lady vying for his attentions back in Alabama. Had he ever married? Did he have children?

"And we ask all this in Your name, Amen!" Louanne finished off. James looked up about that time and caught Tessa staring at him with what she knew must be a dreamy expression on her face. Tessa quickly looked away.

It seemed she was destined to be embarrassed around this man every time they were together!

Pulling together her remaining shreds of composure, Tessa folded her arms and addressed her daughter. "Louanne, why don't you finish gathering those eggs I'd started earlier. And don't forget to put on your coat!"

Louanne passed Mr. Larabee a look that said she was not happy with the request then stood up. "A daughter's work is never done!" she wailed as she left the room.

Tessa watched the door close then turned back to her guest. "Well," she said nervously, "how are you feeling?"

Mr. Larabee waved a hand at his leg. "It was hurting pretty bad, but it seems to have calmed down a bit." The last part of the sentence was spoken with a touch of bewilderment, Tessa thought.

She nodded and wiped her palms on her skirts. "Mr. Larabee, I...uh... I hope that you didn't take my getting upset earlier...personal, it's just that it took me by surprise and..."

"It's alright, Mrs. Wise. You and your daughter live here alone, with your husband dead and all, and I am a stranger. Worse than that, a male stranger. If you can just tell me where I can find a room to rent, I'll get out of here first thing."

She felt herself blush again. Louanne must have told him that her father was dead. Now, Tessa not only felt like a bad hostess, she was a liar, too. "No, I'm just trying to apologize, Mr. Larabee. Of course, you must stay here. We have plenty of room and you're going to need someone to look after you."

She'd avoided making eye contact with him, until she spoke those last words. Then she looked up at him, and there it was again. That connection that said so much, yet made so little sense. She quickly glanced down.

He looked away, too. "Well, I surely do appreciate the offer, Mrs. Wise." He paused then spoke again. "Why don't you pull up a chair and let me tell you about myself. It might make you feel more comfortable if you know who I am."

She looked back at him and smiled shyly. "I think that's a good idea. I have to admit that I've been curious about why you were riding through our woods," she replied as she walked over to the corner of the room and pulled the wooden straight-back chair to the side of his bed.

He grinned sheepishly as he watched her get comfortable. "Well, as far as traveling through your woods is concerned, a fellow in Mississippi told me about this trail. Told me it was the best way to get to Oklahoma where I'm supposed to meet up with a wagon train headed out to California."

Tessa shook her head in bemusement. "And now you're going to be late because someone shot you in my woods. You know I still don't know who would have shot you and run away."

James's face grew grim. "I don't know either, but I would like to report it to the sheriff...that is, if Wiseville has one."

"Yes, actually. . ."

James groaned and held out a hand. "Don't tell me it's another Wise brother!"

Tessa laughed, feeling more and more at ease with the gentleman. "I'm afraid so. And I'm sure he'll be over here along with the rest of the clan when they find out that you are staying here." None of them would be able to resist it. They'd been trying to fix Tessa up with every available man in the area and she'd had nothing to do with them. And now having a man living under her roof would definitely get their attention. Wanted or not!

The Wises were good people, but they just didn't understand why she wasn't interested in any of the men they'd introduced her to. It wasn't that she didn't want to marry again, because she did. In fact, she dreamed of having a husband again and being in the same kind of loving relationship she'd enjoyed with her late husband, Will. She wanted more children, too. But she had yet to meet a man she felt a connection to, someone she wanted to know better.

Until now. . .

"I hope that it won't cause you trouble, Mrs. Wise. I know how folks can gossip."

She waved off his concern. "You don't understand Wiseville, Mr. Larabee. They are like overprotective mama bears to those they consider kin. They will be concerned about my safety, not my reputation. They know that I'm a good Christian woman and would never put my relationship with God in jeopardy by doing anything. . .foolish," she told him, hoping that he understood her double meaning. She didn't want him getting any ideas, either!

"But you were going to tell me about yourself," she prompted, changing the subject.

"I am the eldest son of Andrew and Virginia Larabee of Dothan, Alabama. But I didn't know my mother very well, only from what my father told me about her. She died giving birth to my brother, Joseph. So it was just the three of us. We lived in a big plantation house." He smiled reminiscently. "Grew up living the pampered gentleman's life, I suppose, although Daddy kept his promise to Mama and made sure we were in church every Sunday. But that didn't keep us from being a little spoiled. The cotton was plentiful, and we had everything money could buy."

"And you feel guilty about that," she guessed, when he paused.

He stared at her for a moment as if trying to read her thoughts. "Yes, I guess I do," he relented. "That and the fact that we owned slaves. I grew up thinking that it was normal to own other people, but I now know that it's wrong. The system wouldn't have lasted, with or without the war."

He sighed and stared forward as if he were seeing something other than the wall. "When the war began, I immediately enlisted just like all the other men who lived around us. My brother followed. We were patriots, full of enthusiasm to do our part, but reality quickly invaded our zeal. We saw and did things that we never thought we'd have to do. It became a quest for survival and longing for the war to be over and done with.

"Then, I got news that my brother had been killed, and then my father. . . I hadn't even known that he'd enlisted! I just wanted to go home. It didn't matter that I'd been promoted to captain or that I'd managed to come through unscathed. The war had suddenly gotten too close, become too personal. It had taken away my family," he finished gruffly. He closed his eyes for a second then looked at her apologetically.

"Mrs. Wise, I'm sorry. I didn't mean to go on like this. I don't know. . ."

Tessa reached out and laid her hand on top of his. "It's alright, Mr. Larabee. I understand."

He shook his head and turned his hand palm up and grasped her fingers. "Of course you do. I'm not the only one who lost loved ones in that war. I didn't mean to drag up memories for you."

Tessa knew she should pull her hand away, but she found that she didn't want to. There was such comfort sitting there holding his hand and sharing his pain. A kindred bond pulled them together, one that she was unable to understand.

"Mr. Larabee, Will has been gone for three years, and I've made my peace with God about it." She noticed that he dropped his gaze when she mentioned God's name, just as she'd seen him do with Louanne, and she wondered about it. But she didn't pry. Perhaps she'd have the opportunity to bring up the subject later in the week.

The mood that had enveloped them earlier, however, had diminished, and she became self-conscious about holding his hand. Slowly she withdrew her hand and laid it on her lap.

"What happened to the plantation? Did you return to it?" she questioned.

His face grew grim. "It was burned to the ground, along with the cotton crops. My father had buried some money in the graveyard, just in case something like that happened. I decided to take it and start a new life."

Tessa studied his face as she felt the pain laced in his words. "By going to California?"

He nodded. "I'm going to buy a saloon out there."

"You're going to do what!" Tessa screeched as she stood to her feet. "I'm housing a...a...bar owner?" She was so taken aback that she wasn't aware that she was screaming at him.

His eyes widened and he held out a hand toward her. "Now, Mrs. Wise, I don't own one, yet. I..."

"It's the same thing! You gave me the impression that you were raised in a Christian home! How can you even think about living such a lifestyle? Were you not raised to believe in God?"

Her question hung in the air as they stared at each other. "Yes," he answered, after a moment. "I was raised to believe in God. But I prayed every day for God to protect my little brother. That He'd return me safely to my father and our home. But it was all destroyed. It was as though God hadn't cared about me or heard a word that I'd prayed. Why should I keep believing in Him, then, Mrs. Wise?" he asked, his bitterness burning through his words.

Tessa slowly sat back down and stared at her hands. "I don't know why God chooses to answer some prayers the way He does or why He takes some folks and leaves others. I know that He has a plan that we can't even begin to understand and it's not for us to question. But we can also see the blessings that He does give us and be thankful for what we have."

James stared up at the ceiling. "And what do I have to be thankful for, Tessa Wise? You have family left. I don't."

Tessa stood up again, and this time she planted her hands on her hips and glared at him. "I could name a half dozen things right off the top of my head, James Larabee, but I'm not gonna! You are bound and determined to feel sorry for yourself and blame God. But when you are tired of doing that—tired of being bitter—then you need to look around and let yourself see what God has blessed you with and how He can bless you if you'd only let Him."

And before he could say anything to that, she scooted the chair out of her way and marched out of the room.

Well, I've certainly lost the art of knowing how to talk to a lady, James thought sarcastically to himself after the door closed behind Tessa with a snap.

Where did that suave, witty man go who used to know how to charm women of any age? Had his manners died along with his faith in God? Or was he intentionally driving her away because he felt she was getting too close?

Being here with Tessa Wise was just too comfortable, too easy. It was enough to make a man forget his plans, his goals. It could make a man start thinking of things he had no business thinking of, such as a family. A home.

No. He had to stay strong. He had to keep reminding himself of his original reasons for heading to California. He had to ignore the voice inside of his head that told him his mother and father would be disappointed in his saloon plans—that they'd want a better, moral life for him.

And he had to ignore the incredulous eyes of Tessa Wise.

❦

Outside, Louanne crouched down below the spare bedroom window, where she'd been eavesdropping on the grown-ups' conversation.

She propped her elbows on her knees and cupped her face in her hands. This was all so terrible! How were her mama and Mr. Larabee ever going to get married if they were already fussing?

She was going to have to do something about this! They weren't going to come together on their own, it seemed, so she was just going to have to help them.

But how? Suddenly she had an idea. In her fairy tales, everyone always lived happily ever after. Maybe she could get some ideas from her books!

Quickly she ran to the coop to gather the rest of the eggs so she could get back to her room. She had a lot of reading to do before sundown!

Chapter 4

About forty-five minutes after the doctor left, his brother Donald—the preacher—came over with his son, Earl. James held back a sigh as he shook the preacher's hand.

"It's nice to meet you, Mr. Larabee. We just wanted to come over and see how you were doing. J. T. told us about the accident," Donald told him.

James gave the man a shrewd look. "And to check me out," he guessed.

Donald grinned unrepentantly. "That, too. We all feel responsible to look after Tessa."

James nodded thoughtfully. "I don't blame you, Reverend. I hate putting her out, but it doesn't look like I have much choice," he said grimly, indicating his leg.

Donald frowned. "J. T. said somebody accidentally shot you."

"I wouldn't call it an accident, Reverend. For all I know the man had a clear view of me when he took me down. At best, I would call it carelessness and cowardliness. Whoever did this deserves to be punished. To leave a man to bleed to death is just as bad as deliberately shooting to kill. If Louanne hadn't found me, I could have died out there."

A quick intake of breath came from beside Donald. James turned his attention on Earl who was sweating profusely. "What's wrong, son?" Donald asked.

"I...uh...need to ask Aunt Tessa something," he muttered and quickly left the room.

Donald shook his head and looked back at James. "That boy's been acting so strange lately. Well, you remember how it is being seventeen. You don't know whether to act like a child or a man!"

James glanced at Donald then back to the door and smiled absently. "Yeah, I remember," he commented, but his mind was racing. Did Earl know something about who shot him? Acting strange was one thing. Nervous strange was quite another.

"Well, I'll let you rest, but before I leave, why don't I pray for you!"

James thought about declining, but Donald was already laying hands on him and bowing his head before James could get the words out.

James sighed and gave in to the inevitable. There was just no running from God.

Over the next four days, James got a visit from every one of Tessa's in-laws.

Sitting around visiting with the Wises' was about as comfortable as getting teeth pulled. James had the odd feeling that he had been put on trial and the verdict wasn't favorable.

The toughest came from the mother of all the Wise boys, Irene Wise. She sat in James's room and asked him about everything from his childhood to how many girls he'd courted. She specifically wanted to know why he was going to California. He hemmed and hawed and drummed up a passel of vague answers to satisfy her curiosity, but he doubted that she'd been fooled.

He'd gotten to know Tessa better, too. She'd overcome her shyness around him, and she seemed to want to talk to him as much as he wanted to talk to her. She was unlike any woman he'd ever met. It wasn't just that she was beautiful, there was something else about her, something fine—a real quality that made her special.

But now they were all gone—he hoped—and he could rest a little easier. Especially since J. T. had brought in a chair with wheels so that he could get out of that tiny little room.

It was late in the evening, and he watched from his chair as Tessa ran around the kitchen, getting supper ready. She laid out potatoes and peas to be shelled on the table then scurried around and started battering the chicken, preparing it to fry. She was doing everything so efficiently that he didn't want to break her rhythmic dance. But he was so tired of sitting and doing nothing that he spoke up.

"Can I help you do something?"

She looked up in surprise. "What do you mean?"

"I can peel potatoes. That used to be my brother's and my punishment when we were kids. We got to be pretty good at it," he said with a grin.

She looked at him with a raised eyebrow. "I don't doubt it!" she said teasingly. "Well, I never turn down help. I was just about to call Louanne in here to shell those peas. I'm sure she'll enjoy having her work cut in half."

She pulled out a chair from the table then helped him wheel his chair under where the potatoes were. As she let go of the chair he reached up and caught her hand.

"I'm sorry that you're having to cook extra and work harder just because I'm here. You need to know that I fully intend to reimburse you for everything, including room and board," James told her, enjoying the soft touch of her hand. He couldn't resist rubbing his thumb over the satiny skin. He was surprised when she didn't pull her hand away.

She did clear her throat in what James was sure was a nervous gesture. "Don't be silly, Mr. Larabee. It's no more work than usual and I always make too much food anyway," she told him.

"Has it been hard, you know, being left to raise your daughter alone?" he asked, knowing it was none of his business but feeling a desire to know.

She looked at him, surprised that he'd asked such a question. Staring at him, she opened her mouth to say, "Don't be silly," then she stopped. She looked thoughtful then told him truthfully, "Yes, it has been hard. At times, I didn't think that I could make it. But the Wises have helped me along the way."

He stared at her probingly. "But they couldn't fill that void, could they?" he guessed.

She smiled sadly and gripped his hand harder. "No, they couldn't. But God did." She saw him turn his head and sigh, so she emphasized, "I know you don't like to hear that, but it's the truth. And He can do the same for you."

She let go of his hand and threw both of her arms in the air. "That's all I'm going to say!"

He laughed, despite the fact that he was uncomfortable with the conversation. Even though she constantly nagged him about his relationship with God, it didn't lessen his fascination with the lovely woman. "Nothing you can say is going to offend me, Mrs. Wise. I don't want you to be afraid to say anything to me."

She gave him a bemused look. "Strangely enough, I'm not. I feel real comfortable talking with you, Mr. Larabee. You've been great company for Louanne and me."

He watched her talk, how her lips moved and smiled, how her eyes twinkled, how the curls fell about her face, having fallen from their topknot. He felt a quaking in his chest. It was the oddest feeling, and he wondered what was the matter with him. Was he getting sick? Or was he just becoming enamored with Tessa Wise?

It had been so long since he'd been attracted to a woman; he'd almost forgotten what it felt like. But had it ever felt like this before? He couldn't recall any relationship before that matched the intensity he felt for Tessa.

"I feel at ease with you, too. I can't tell you how much I appreciate your letting me stay here, Mrs. Wise. And it's not just because you're taking care of my wounds, but because you've made me feel a part of your family."

They stared at each other for a full thirty seconds before she cleared her throat again and backed up a step or two. "Well!" she said as she blinked a couple of times. "This family is never going to get to eat if we don't get busy!"

He smiled at her knowingly, pleased that she was so rattled. "Sounds good to me. Where do I start?"

She showed him what to do then called for Louanne, and soon they were all chatting while they worked.

James enjoyed watching Tessa talk to her daughter, the easy camaraderie that they shared. He really missed not growing up with a mother. His father had filled his head with stories of how beautiful and gracious his mother had been, but James now wondered if she'd have talked to him and played with him or if she would have been too busy being the grand lady of the plantation to do such things with him. He'd had a nanny, a large black woman who watched after him and kept him in line, but it wasn't the same.

Then his mind wandered to Tessa, the woman. What kind of wife had she been to Will? Had she enjoyed being married? Had she loved her husband too much to love someone else now that he was gone? It would be nice coming home to her, James decided. She absolutely fascinated him—she could tease and be quick-witted, then she could be gentle and nurturing. She wasn't the type to let people take advantage of her, but he had the impression that she would never hurt anyone's feelings, either.

Ah, but what did he know? He'd only known her four days! Maybe tomorrow she'd wake up and the sweetness and kindness would be gone. But he didn't think so.

What was it about her that captivated him so?

"Mr. Larabee, have you ever read *Cinderella?*" Louanne asked him as he picked up his third potato.

It took him a second to focus on what she was asking him. *"Cinderella?"* He thought a minute, then his brow cleared. "Oh, that silly little story about the prince and the shoe?"

Louanne looked at him with pursed lips. "I like that story."

"Uh. . ." He looked at Tessa for help, but she just smiled and shrugged her shoulders, putting the pressure all on him. "Well, what I meant was that I've always figured that story was more for. . .you know. . .girls."

Louanne sighed and rolled her eyes. "Okay, but let's think about what the prince did in the story. He runs after this pretty girl that he's never seen before, and all he finds is a shoe. Then he scours the whole countryside trying on the shoe to find the right owner, because he feels that this woman is his only true love. Don't you find that incredibly romantic?" she asked, wearing that dreamy look on her face that she wore every time she got dramatic.

He looked at Louanne then up at Tessa, who was eyeing him with interest waiting to hear his answer. She was enjoying this, the little minx! "Actually, I always thought that was a really dumb way of looking for her. Why couldn't he just look at their faces? If I'd found my only true love,

I would think that I'd remember what she looks like."

Louanne narrowed her eyes at him, while tapping a pea pod on the table. "Let me put this another way. Let's say it's. . .oh. . .my mama!" she said as if she'd just thought of it. "And she was dressed up in a really fine dress of white silk and her hair was down and curly with roses pinned in it. She wouldn't look anything like she does now, so how would you know it was her?"

James looked at Tessa while Louanne talked and imagined her with that white dress on and flowers framing her lovely face. She would look just like a bride. Then again—no, he couldn't think about that.

Tessa looked up then and caught him staring, but she didn't look away. They stayed like that for mere seconds, but it seemed like an eternity.

"Louanne," he said, still looking at Tessa, "I can't imagine not recognizing your mama, even if she was wearing an old toe sack."

Louanne's laugh broke their connection, and James noticed that Tessa seemed flustered as she hurriedly turned back to her frying pan.

"That's not a very romantic thing to say, Mr. Larabee! You can't write a sonnet using the words 'toe sack!' " Louanne said.

James grinned. "Oh, I don't know about that. Let's see. . . Cardinals are red, but some birds are black, I think you're quite lovely in that old toe sack!"

Both Tessa and Louanne groaned in chorus at the terrible poem, and acting offended, James looked at them both. "If you don't like that one, I have lots more"

"No!" they quickly answered, then they all dissolved into giggles.

James savored the evening, watching Tessa and Louanne, enjoying the delicious meal. He knew with the life he'd chosen for himself it would probably not come again.

⁂

Two days later, Louanne was still trying to come up with a way to get Mr. Larabee to ask her mama to marry him. They were talking, she'd give them that, but it was all too polite. Unless they got on the subject of California and Mr. Larabee's "plans," then they seemed to get all tense and they'd stop talking.

Louanne was baffled. What were his "plans"? Whatever they were, they must be something that her mama didn't approve of. And from the sound of the conversation going on around her at that very moment, she had a feeling it was about to get unpleasant once again.

"James," her mother began. Mr. Larabee had asked her to please call him that instead of being so formal. Likewise, her mama had asked him to call her Tessa. Louanne saw this as progress. "Do you still own the family land in Alabama?"

Louanne's eyes darted from Mama to Mr. Larabee, and from the look on his face, she had a feeling that he didn't like the question.

"Yes." That was all he said. Louanne looked at her mother—a storm was definitely about to brew.

"And. . .?" Tessa prompted.

Mr. Larabee just shrugged his shoulders. "And what?"

"Do you plan to sell it?"

"No."

Mama's fingers were tapping on the table. Not a good sign. "What do you plan to do with it?"

"Nothing. Tessa, can we talk about something else?"

"I just don't understand why you didn't stay there and try to rebuild. That is your heritage, you know."

"Tessa, you cannot change my mind. I know you don't approve, but I have to do what is best for me, right now." Mr. Larabee's eyes were staring intently at Louanne's mama.

"I don't think it is best. I know God doesn't want that for you, James."

Mr. Larabee didn't say anything, and to Louanne's disappointment, the conversation came to a halt, just like it always did when they got on this subject or when Mama mentioned God. It seemed as if Mr. Larabee was mad at God about something, and her mama was trying to help him with it. Only Mr. Larabee didn't seem to want help.

Well, Louanne knew she had to do something or the rest of the meal was going to be miserable!

"Mr. Larabee, have you ever heard of the story of the Beauty and the Beast?"

Mr. Larabee looked at her with narrowed eyes. "We're going to discuss fairy tales again?" he asked warily.

"Louanne, this makes the fourth one that we've discussed. I think you need to start reading something else," her mother admonished.

"But don't you just love the part when Beauty rushes back to the castle and finds the beast dying. And just when she thinks she's lost him, she cries out in a pitiful voice that she loves him. Then, suddenly he starts changing into a handsome prince." Louanne looked at both adults. "I think we can learn something from this."

Mr. Larabee nodded in agreement. "Yes, we should keep our word. If Beauty had kept her word and come right back to his castle, he wouldn't have almost died in the first place!"

Louanne shook her head. "Okay, that is a good point. But I was talking about the main lesson about love."

"I'm not sure Beauty loved him as a man, you know. I think she just loved him like a friend or a. . .pet." Tessa chimed in.

"Oh, Mama! I was talking about the fact that love changed everything!" Louanne stressed, growing agitated.

"Especially for the beast. All that hair had to be itchy!" Mr. Larabee had apparently already forgotten his tiff with Louanne's mother.

Louanne sighed and pushed a piece of potato around on her plate.

Tessa looked at Louanne with a mother's compassion and stroked a hand down her curly hair. "For you to see that in a fairy tale is very insightful of you. It shows that you are a very good reader!"

"It sure does," James piped in. "Not every child likes to read at your age. I can see that you are a very smart and clever girl."

She smiled at James. "Do you really think so?" Louanna asked, her face lit up with expectation.

"I sure do!" he answered with a wink.

The little girl was beaming with pride and happiness as she stared at James. "You know, I think I'll go and read right now! Uncle Donald bought me a new book just the other day!" She jumped up from the table and carried her plate to the sink.

"Good night!" she called as she ran to her room.

Tessa stared after her daughter for a moment then looked back at

James. "You are quite good with children, James. I've not seen her that excited in weeks!"

He shrugged. "I like her. She's a sweet kid."

Tessa grinned at him. "And you're a good man, James Larabee."

His face reddened briefly, but he came back with, "You thought I was an outlaw when you first saw me!"

She giggled. "What else was I to think? I soon realized that you weren't," she defended with teasing eyes. "But I am worried about this saloon business, and I'm not going to quit nagging you about it until you realize that you aren't cut out for that kind of life!"

James groaned as he leaned back in his chair, but Tessa ignored him. She told herself that it was for his own good! But deep inside, she knew it was also for her own.

Chapter 5

Tessa handed James the last dish and watched as he carefully dried it and laid it on the counter. It was night time and Louanne had already gone to bed. The two of them worked side by side as they had for the past four nights, since he'd gotten the wheelchair.

"You don't have to help me with these every night, you know. You are supposed to be resting," Tessa told him as she folded the dishtowel and laid it on the edge of the sink.

"It's just not in me to sit around and be useless. Besides, I've had more rest than any man could possibly need." He wheeled himself around the table and toward the door. "I think I'm going to get some fresh air. Want to join me?"

Tessa hesitated at the thought of just the two of them sitting in the moonlight. It was too intimate—something that a couple would do if they were courting. She should just say no and go on to bed!

"Okay. Let me just pour us some coffee and I'll bring it on out," she answered despite herself.

He smiled at her as he reached up to grab his coat from the hook beside the door. "Sounds good."

Berating herself for being so weak where James Larabee was concerned, she reached under the cupboard and grabbed a couple of cups. She slipped on her own coat and went out onto the front porch while holding the cups of hot coffee carefully in her hands. She handed him one then took a seat in the rocking chair beside his.

"It's getting colder," she commented. "If I didn't know better, I'd say it felt like snow weather."

He nodded and took a sip of his coffee. "Tessa, I. . . ," he began then paused and tried again. "Tonight at supper, I didn't mean to be rude. I know you're just trying to help, but I—"

"Don't need my help," she finished for him. She cradled the warm cup between her palms as she stared down at it. "James, can you just tell me what made you decide to move to California? And why a saloon?"

He glanced over at her, then turned to look out at the moonlit trees before him. Crickets were singing and he could hear a couple of owls that seemed as though they were competing for who could hoot the loudest. And as he sat there on the small front porch, enjoying the crisp wind as it brushed his hair and chilled his face, a feeling of peace invaded his heart—a peace that he hadn't felt since before the war. Before he knew it, he was telling Tessa Wise things that he hadn't even admitted to himself.

"I don't want to have to think about home," he said quietly. "I don't want to look at things that remind me of my father or see people that knew my brother. I don't even want to do things that they would have done, so I don't have to think about them."

"Is it working?" she asked, compassion laced in her soft voice.

James thought about that as he gripped his cup. "No," he answered finally, truthfully.

"I thought about moving, too. When my husband's body was brought home, I couldn't even sleep in our room. Everything I touched had been made by him—the house, the furniture, Louanne's toys. . ." She drifted off and looked at him. "But I didn't have a buried treasure like you did, James. My parents have been dead since I was fifteen and my aunt whom I'd lived with had died that winter. I couldn't pack up and move off to a new place because I didn't have the money. And I'm glad I didn't."

She reached out and covered his hand. "I would have been running away from my pain instead of dealing with it. I wouldn't have known the strength and comfort that God has given me that has made me a stronger and better person. He can do it for you, James. Just ask Him!"

James held onto her hand and looked steadily at her. Part of him wanted to believe what she was saying. Wanted to obtain what she had been given, but he just couldn't seem to take that step. There was too much bitterness, too much pain. *Would he ever be a whole person again?* he wondered. It seemed too easy to simply ask for God's help and believe it would all be better, when he still blamed God for it happening in the first place.

"I can't. Not yet. Maybe someday."

"Then, I'll just keep praying that someday comes sooner than later."

He grinned at her, admiring her spirit. "You don't give up, do you!"

She smiled back at him. "Never!" she declared, letting his hand go and taking another sip of coffee.

He sipped while studying her over the rim of his cup. "What about you, Tessa? You ever going to marry again? It's been three years, hasn't it?"

Tessa threw him a dry look. "Now you're beginning to sound like J. T.! And the answer is yes. I do want to marry again, but as bad as I want more children, I'm not going to be in a hurry. God gave me a good man the first time, and I feel lucky that I was able to spend eight years with him. I know that He'll bless me a second time."

"Louanne says that you've had four offers of marriage in the last year," he couldn't help but mention.

He watched as she put a hand to her cheeks as if they were burning, and James had a feeling that they were. "She shouldn't have told you that!"

"You mean it's not true?"

"Well. . .yes. But she still shouldn't have told you!"

James began to chuckle. "Tessa Wise, the only thing that surprises me is that you haven't had more than four ask for your hand."

"Oh, for goodness' sakes!" she exclaimed and took another drink of coffee as if to hide her face.

"I know that if I were living here in Wiseville, I'd be asking for your hand myself!"

Suddenly, the teasing laughter left his voice and face. A stillness descended over them, and James found he could hardly breathe.

"You shouldn't tell me that," she said in a breathless, panic-filled tone. She was staring down, not looking at him.

He mentally kicked himself, wishing he could take his words back, while knowing that they were true. "I know. I'm sorry. It's just that. . ." He stopped and ran an agitated hand through his hair. "I didn't mean to embarrass you, Tessa. Just pretend I didn't say anything, okay?"

She didn't say anything for a moment. Then, when she did, he had to bend near her to hear, for she spoke so softly. "If you lived here in Wiseville and had asked for my hand, James Larabee, I just might have said yes."

James sat there, so stunned at her admission that he couldn't even answer her when she suddenly brushed past him and said good night.

As he listened to the screen door slam behind her, he wondered if going to California was so important after all.

❧

The next morning Tessa watched from the corner of her eye as James wheeled himself into the kitchen. She noticed that he'd made good use of the tub of hot water she'd set in his room for him. She couldn't help but notice that his hair was curlier when it was wet, although it looked as if he'd tried to comb it down.

Goodness, she was nervous this morning. Especially after her little "confession" the night before. What had possessed her to say something like that? It must have been the moonlight and the romantic atmosphere. She was normally a prudent, levelheaded person. She never said things without thinking, never blurted things out that might embarrass her or anyone else.

Where was that levelheaded person last night? Certainly not sitting in the moonlight with James Larabee!

"Good morning, Tessa," he greeted, his voice low and husky.

She took a deep breath. *Just act normal!* she willed herself before turning from the sink with a fixed smile on her face. "Good morning! Did you sleep well?"

He looked straight at her with a frank expression. "To tell you the truth, no. I didn't sleep well—I tossed and turned all night thinking about what you said to me."

Okay. So much for acting as if nothing happened. She quickly turned back around, biting her lip and clenching her eyes tight. He wanted to talk about it? Couldn't he just leave well enough alone?

"Why don't you call Louanne to the table. Breakfast is almost ready," she said in a calm voice, deciding to ignore his comment.

"Come on, Tessa. Talk to me. What is going through your mind?" he pleaded, wheeling closer to her.

She fiddled with a stack of plates. "Why discuss it, James? What's it going to accomplish?"

He tugged at her skirt. "Tessa, I. . ."

She whirled around and confronted him. "You are going to California and I'm staying here. You have plans that I cannot agree with or condone. I serve God and you don't. Are you saying that any of that is going to change?"

Minutes seemed to tick by as they stared at each other. Tessa's heart was beating so hard she wondered if James could hear it. A silly irrational hope sprang up in her heart, a hope that he would say yes. Yes, things were going to change. Yes, he would give up his plans. Yes, he would give God a chance.

But, of course he didn't say that, though he didn't exactly say no.

"I don't know what I'm saying, Tessa. All I know is that something happened between us last night. Something changed, and I don't want us to go back to the way we were before."

He reached up and took her hand. It felt so warm and safe enclosed in his rough palm. "Oh, James," she cried softly, "I just don't think—"

"Is breakfast ready yet?" Louanne asked as she skipped into the room. She skidded to a halt when she saw them quickly release their hands. Her eyes grew large as her gaze darted between them. "Y'all were holding hands!"

"Yes."

"No."

Louanne frowned. "Well, which is it? Yes or no?"

James intervened. "Lulu, why don't you set the table while I finish talking to your mama."

Louanne rolled her eyes and threw up her hands. "Nobody tells me anything!" she cried as she stomped to the china cabinet. "And my name is not Lulu today, it's Pocahontas!" This morning she had her curly hair in a pair of quirky-looking braids and was wearing a tan, fringed Indian dress over a pair of long johns.

James chuckled at the wild costume then looked back at Tessa. "We're not through discussing this."

She looked at him sternly. "Yes, James, we are."

He just smiled and winked at her as he wheeled himself toward the table.

Tessa's legs were shaking as she brought the dish of eggs and bacon to the table. What did this all mean? She just didn't understand the feelings that she had for James. They were too fast. Too strong. With her husband, Will, she'd fallen in love slowly. She'd known him all her life, yet she had to warm to him as more than just a friend when he began to court her.

But what she was feeling for James was instantaneous—something had happened the moment she'd laid eyes on him. It didn't make sense. He was a stranger. He would be leaving in just a week.

As she put the eggs on the table, she caught him staring at her and her legs became even shakier. What was she going to do once he left? Why did she feel as though she was going to lose something precious. . .something wonderful?

She shook off her thoughts, willing herself to quit fretting over something she had no control over.

She was taking the seat across from him when Louanne called out to her. "No, Mama. I've fixed this place for you." She motioned toward a seat next to James.

She narrowed her eyes at James, who shrugged his shoulders. "I didn't have anything to do with it!" he defended himself with an innocent look.

"Louanne, I always sit here," she explained, trying to figure out what her daughter was up to.

"Please, Mama!" she begged. "I went to all the trouble. . ." She let her voice drift off, sending her pleading look to her mother.

Tessa looked at James then back to her daughter. "Okay," she sighed and sat down in the chair Louanne indicated.

James nudged her with an elbow. "I think she's matchmaking," he whispered in her ear.

Tessa froze. Was that what her daughter was doing? Was that what all the silliness with the fairy tales had been about? She looked at Louanne and found her smiling at them, obviously reading something into their close position.

"It's a sign...," Louanne said with an excitement in her voice, although it seemed as if she were saying it more to herself.

"You know, that's the second time I've heard you say that, Lulu...I mean Poca. What do you mean by it?" James asked curiously.

Louanne looked from James to Tessa, her expression hesitant. "I'm not sure I should say..."

Tessa had had enough. "Spit it out, Louanne. You've been acting strange...well, stranger than usual...and I want to know what's going on in that little brain of yours."

Louanne fiddled with her crooked braid. "Well, I guess I can tell this much," she said slowly. "I think that God meant for Mr. Larabee to stay in Wiseville. That's why he ended up in our woods."

Tessa stared at her daughter, worried. "Oh, Louanne," she said gently. "I know that you are enjoying Mr. Larabee's company, but that doesn't mean that God sent him to stay here."

"But there have been signs!" her daughter insisted. "I think that he was sent here for us, Mama! I mean Mr. Larabee's always looking at you, Mama, when he thinks you're not looking, and the same goes with you! I can tell you're in love with him!"

Now, Tessa was not only alarmed, she was embarrassed. She had been staring at James. Her face was burning so hot that Tessa doubted that it'd ever be normal again.

But then...James had been staring at her, too?

She wouldn't think about that now. She couldn't. Her hopes would run high, this attraction that she felt for James would grow deeper, and then she'd be left with a broken heart. Or had it already grown deeper? Had she already begun to fall in love with him?

And what about Louanne? She didn't want her daughter's heart to be broken when James left them. What was she to do?

"Louanne, honey. We need to talk about this!" she told her daughter.

But Louanne shook her head.

"I know what you're going to say. You don't want me to get my hopes up, and I don't. I just have faith is all."

Tessa felt James take her chin into his hand and turn it toward him. She averted her eyes down, unable to face him.

"Is that true?" he asked softly. "Are you in love with me?"

"Uh. . .you know, I think I'll just take my breakfast in my room and let y'all talk about this," Louanne said with a smile on her face and excitement brimming in her eyes.

"No! Louanne. . . ," Tessa called out in a panic.

"Yes, thank you, Lulu. We'd appreciate that." He stared at Tessa as he spoke.

She was looking at him now, unable to look away.

"Are you going to answer my question?" he prompted.

"No."

"What if I told you that I'm falling in love with you, too?"

Tessa felt her heart skip a beat, and for a moment she couldn't seem to breathe. "It's too soon! We don't really know each other," she cried, trying to come up with excuses.

His hand left her chin and cupped her cheek, his thumb rubbing softly under her eye. "I don't understand it either, Tessa. And I don't want Louanne to get hurt. All I know is that I don't want to leave anymore." He paused a minute, thinking. "Why don't we do this: why don't we use this next week as a time to really get to know each other. It'll give us both time to make sure that what we're feeling is for real."

All the reasons why this suggestion was not a good idea drifted through Tessa's mind. But she knew that she would take his offer. Not only would she have time to get to know him better, she would have time to pray. That was the only way she would know for sure.

She smiled shyly at him. "Okay, I think that would be wonderful."

He grinned at her, his eyes shining with emotion. Then he leaned closer to her, and Tessa knew that she was about to be kissed. Part of her wanted to run, the other part of her wanted to lean closer.

The latter won. She met him halfway and touched her lips softly to his.

He made a sound from his throat and pressed more firmly, moving his lips in a caressing motion over hers. It felt so wonderful. It had been so long since she'd been kissed.

As he gently broke away, he pressed a quick kiss on her cheek and looked at her. "You know you never answered my question, Tessa. Are you falling in love with me?"

She lovingly ran her gaze over his handsome features then smiled. "Yes, I think I am."

Chapter 6

Saturday evening, J. T. had brought by a couple of crutches and told James that he thought it'd be okay for him to get up and exercise a little. It felt so good to be able to move around, so James took the opportunity after the doctor had left to explore outside around the little white house.

The last four days since they had decided to examine their relationship had been truly life changing, James thought as he looked around the small clearing surrounded by tall pines. Tessa and he had made good use of their time together and had really gotten to know each other. He told her things that he'd never told anyone about himself. He hadn't meant to, of course, but Tessa just seemed to pull it out of him.

And he learned important things about her. He knew that she longed for a husband and more children. Since she'd been an only child, she had vowed that she would have a house full of children when she married. She had truly loved her first husband, but somehow, that didn't bother James. It just proved that she was the type of person who made good choices for herself.

He saw how she cared for Louanne, even teaching her at home, since they'd lost the town's schoolteacher in the last year. She was a caring and nurturing woman.

She was also a devout Christian, and she never stopped trying to get him to talk about his anger toward God. And it was working. There had to be something great about God for Tessa—who was such an intelligent, levelheaded person—to be so faithful to Him.

As he shuffled around trying to get used to the crutches, he took in his surroundings. The small barn was clean but badly in need of paint. The fences had been mended but were still sagging in places. He saw her garden, now dormant, and he wondered how hard she had to work to keep food on their table. He knew that the Wise brothers helped her, but they had families of their own. All that he saw around him had been tirelessly worked by Tessa.

He wanted to make life easier for her, somehow. She deserved better than this existence. *Are you planning on taking her away from all this, Larabee?* A voice in his head taunted him. *And what do you have to give her? A burnt-out piece of land that you are too cowardly to rebuild?* He didn't know what he could offer. He just knew that he wanted to be a part of her life, somehow, some way.

But was it possible?

"*Pssst!* Mr. Larabee!" A whispery voice called out to him from behind a tree. "Over here!"

James squinted in the darkness and made his way over to Louanne who was hidden in the shadows. "What are you doing out here? I thought you'd gone to bed!"

She stepped out into the moonlight where they could see each other better. "When I heard you go out of the house, I knew I had to talk to you. It was a sign!"

James sighed. "I thought we were all through with this 'sign' business, Lulu."

Louanne rolled her eyes. "I know, but this was one I couldn't ignore." She then shook her head. "I've been reading *Romeo and Juliet*, you see, and when I saw that you were standing outside, I knew it would be perfect!"

"What would be perfect?" he asked guardedly.

"For you to present a soliloquy under Mama's window!"

"A soli. . . How do you know such a big word?"

"I read a lot," she told him with her usual panache. Then when he gave her a questioning look, she admitted, "Okay, so it was a vocabulary word from last month.

"But anyway, in *Romeo and Juliet,* Romeo goes beneath Juliet's window and. . .well, you remember, don't you? He tells her. . .well. . .I really didn't understand what he told her because it was something about the light breaking through the window over yonder and then something about being sick and green and eyes being in her head. . .But that doesn't matter! What matters is that Juliet really liked it when he did that! I think you need to do something like that under Mama's window!"

James bit his lip and tried not to give in to laughter. "You think she'd like that? Because you know that I love to make up poetry," he teased.

She looked appalled at that statement. "Oh no! You better not make up any of your silly poems. Why don't you just tell her how pretty she is and that you really like her!"

James pretended to think it over. "I don't know. What if she doesn't come to the window? Then I'd look pretty dumb standing there talking to the side of the house!"

Louanne gave him a patient look. "She'll come, I promise." She pointed toward the house. "Look. There is her window over there. I'll go with you and sit underneath it where she can't see me. I'll tell you what to say, okay?"

"Well, alright. If you think that this will work!" he said as they made their way over to the window.

"Say, didn't Juliet have a balcony? I don't think it's going to have the same effect with her room being on the ground floor," he whispered.

"Shh!" she admonished. "It'll work. Now, just call out her name."

"Tessa," he whispered.

"You're going to have to say it louder than that!"

"Hey, Tessa!" he yelled, enjoying himself immensely.

"Oh, that was romantic!" she groaned, covering her head with her hands.

The window sash was suddenly thrown up and Tessa's tousled head poked out. "James, for goodness' sake! What are you doing out there in the cold?"

"I'm supposed to be reciting a soliloquy."

"A what?"

Louanne groaned aloud. "Tell her that she's beautiful!"

49

"Tessa, you look so beautiful, even though your hair is a mess!"

Another groan came from under the window, and Tessa stuck her head farther out. "Louanne? Are you out here, too?"

Louanne reluctantly got up. "I was trying to help Mr. Larabee court you, but it's proving to be just too difficult."

James laughed. "I tried, Lulu."

Tessa stared back and forth at the two of them as if they were crazy. "What does standing outside freezing to death have to do with courting?"

"She has a point, Lulu. I don't think it was near this cold when Romeo was yelling up at Juliet's window."

"I give up!" Louanne declared. "You two can just work this out on your own." With that she turned and made her way to the door.

James looked back at Tessa and her rumpled state. "You know, I wasn't kidding when I said you looked beautiful." He stepped closer and put a quick kiss on her lips. "Good night, Juliet!" he said with a wink, and before she could reply he was hobbling back inside the house.

James knew that he'd changed. It was evident the next morning when he decided to attend the Sunday church service with Tessa and Louanne. She'd already missed one Sunday because of him. He didn't want her to have to miss another.

"Are you sure about this?" Tessa asked then bit her lip the way she always did when she was worried.

He stood up, balancing himself with the crutches. "I want to go with you. I just hope I'm not too casual in these duds. I had planned to buy nicer clothes when I reached San Francisco," he explained, looking down at his chambray shirt and dark blue pants.

"You look fine. This is Wiseville, not New Orleans!" She reached up and brushed a lock of hair back from his forehead. It was such a "wifely" thing to do that James couldn't help but wish he could be the recipient of her touches all the time. "Wife" was a word that was sounding mighty good to him.

"That's just what Sleeping Beauty would have done," Louanne said, "when the prince awakened her from her deep sleep. A lock of his hair would be hanging from his forehead, and as he drew back from his tender kiss, she would reach out and gently smooth it back. . . ." Louanne drifted off in a dramatic sigh, and she stood in the doorway of the living room, watching them.

"Oh no. Not the fairy tales again! I thought you'd given up on us!" Tessa groaned.

James grinned. "I need to buy you some good westerns to read."

Louanne looked appalled. "Those kind of books aren't romantic!"

"There's romance in them!" he defended with mock indignation.

" 'Hop on the back of my horse, Darlin', and help me round up the herd,' is real romantic! I read that once in one of J. T.'s western novels," Louanne told him dryly.

James just shrugged while throwing Tessa a conspiring wink. "He could have left her at home!"

Louanne groaned and headed toward the door. "I really am going to give up this time!"

"Promises, promises!" Tessa called after her.

Chuckling, James and Tessa looked at each other and then followed her out of the house.

The church service was just as James expected it would be. They sang songs and listened to Reverend Donald Wise preach his lengthy but interesting sermon. He also knew that it would stab him with guilt about his anger toward God. He still couldn't yet make that step—that little, yet huge step that would bring him to a right relationship with the Almighty.

To her credit, Tessa never looked at him or asked him whether he was enjoying the service. She wasn't the kind to pressure. But he knew she was thinking about it.

James had the awful feeling that if he didn't make his peace with God—there would be no relationship between him and Tessa. But he couldn't do it for her, no matter how much he wanted to.

No. He had to do it for himself.

But he couldn't. Not yet.

When the service was over, the three of them made their way out of the sanctuary. James could feel his leg start to really ache and he groaned.

"Are you okay?" she asked, obviously worried.

He gave her a brave smile. "Sure, it's just a little twinge."

"It's probably more than just a twinge!" J. T. said from behind them in a stern voice. "I said that you could get up every once in awhile. I didn't mean that you could gallivant all around town!"

"Aw, it's not bad," James said. "Besides, I didn't want Tessa to miss another Sunday."

Suddenly J. T. swung in front of them, stopping them from going out the door. He looked at both of them with shrewd eyes for a moment, then his mouth spread in a knowing smile. "Ahhh. . .I see."

Louanne glared at him. "Now, J. T. . . ."

"Hey! What's going on with you two?" Donald chimed in from the doorway where he'd stood to shake hands with his parishioners.

"They're courting!" Louanne blurted out.

James and Tessa looked at the little girl in surprise. "She's only teasing," Tessa told her in-laws quickly.

"Oh no, I'm not! James asked Mama if she was falling in love with him, and Mama said that she was!"

"Louanne!" Tessa scolded.

"Now, Louanne. Don't go upsetting your mother," James admonished.

J. T. raised an eyebrow. "Are you saying that it's not true, James?"

"Well, no. I'm not saying that."

"Oh, good gracious!" Tessa wailed, covering her red face with her hands.

Then Louanne told her uncles, "You see, God sent Mr. Larabee to be my daddy."

Chapter 7

J. T. and Donald Wise stared at the couple as if they'd just heard the best piece of news they'd heard in a long time. "Daddy, huh?" J. T. probed.

James tried to ignore them. And while he patted Tessa on the shoulders in a comforting gesture, he scolded Louanne. "Now, Lulu, I think you've said quite. . ."

"No, this is getting interesting," Donald interrupted.

"James, could we please go," Tessa pleaded.

"Uh, I think my leg is hurting, after all," James muttered, trying to get out of the sticky conversation. "Maybe we'd better head home."

He let Tessa go ahead of him, then he, too, brushed past the brothers, nodding at them politely.

"Yes, we want you to get well so you can walk without any pain," J. T. called out. "It's not very seemly when a groom limps out to meet his bride."

They ignored that particular comment! "Tessa, your face is red," James whispered in her ear as he hobbled down the steps of the church.

"I just never know what those brothers are going to come up with next!" she muttered, embarrassed. "I should be used to them by now. They are both such big teases."

"Tessa, we really haven't talked about what Louanne said, about me being an answer to her prayer. Now she's told her uncles the same thing. Does it upset you?" James ventured to ask.

Tessa bit her lip. "I was wondering if it bothered you."

James stopped and motioned Tessa off to the side away from the stream of churchgoers. "At first it scared me, but I don't think I'm scared about it anymore," he told her honestly.

"You don't?" she asked breathlessly.

James smiled a secret smile as he reached out to brush a dark lock of hair that had blown across her lip. Her skin was so soft to touch, and he ached to kiss her and hold her in his arms. He probably would have if they hadn't been standing in the churchyard in full view of the townsfolk of Wiseville.

"It's sounding better and better all the time," he told her as his hand trailed down her cheek.

"Is that faith I hear in your voice, Doubting Thomas?" she teased.

"Among other things, Miss Smarty! Don't get too smug, now!"

"I won't. I'm too happy to be anything but grateful."

"Yeah, me, too." They gazed at each other for a moment, not caring who was looking at them.

Could I really believe? James wondered. Could he let go of the past and all his bitterness and learn to trust in God again? Tessa made it all seem possible.

"Good afternoon, Tessa," a young woman said as she passed them on the sidewalk. She had a child on one arm and was running toward a fellow who was sitting in a wagon with another child a little older than the first.

"Hi, Mary!" she returned and James saw her grin.

"Who's she?"

"That is Mary, and the man she's getting into the buggy with is her husband, Frank. She became a Baptist while he was at war, and since he's a staunch Methodist he was none too thrilled about it." She shook her head with amusement. "But they seem to have come to a happy compromise. He brings her to church every Sunday, then goes to his church down the street."

James laughed with her as he watched the young couple embrace and smile at each other. "It looks like it didn't cause too much trouble, though. They seem happy."

Tessa sighed a womanly sigh. "They are. He loves her very much."

"Do I look at you like that?"

She glanced at him with a saucy smile. "All the time."

He nodded. "I thought so," he said quietly.

She turned as if to steal a look at him, but he just kept on walking, smiling to himself and enjoying the feelings that were blossoming within him.

Then suddenly James came to a quick stop. Across the churchyard he saw a flash of blue and black. It triggered a memory. A memory of someone wearing that same jacket, running away from him.

His happiness evaporated into oblivion and old, comfortable feelings quickly replaced it. Feelings of anger and bitterness.

It was the man who shot him. It had to be!

Forgetting the pain in his leg, he started toward the group of boys standing outside of the churchyard.

"James! Where are you going?" he heard Tessa calling out to him, but he ignored her. Anger was beginning to boil in him as he drew closer. Here he was, the man who left him to die.

"Hey, you!" he called out in a harsh yell. All seven of the young men looked up curiously at him, limping toward them. "You in the blue-and-black coat!" he said specifically.

The man, a boy really, answered, "What's the problem, Mr. Larabee?"

James came to a halt. It was Earl Wise, the Reverend Donald Wise's son. Rage spread through his whole body like a raging river. His limbs shook as he glared at the innocent-looking young man. This boy had been in the same room with him and had spoken to him when he'd first been shot. He had stood there as James had told Donald of what happened. And he'd never said a word.

"You are the one who shot me and left me for dead," he charged. "I saw this jacket when you ran away from me. What kind of man are you to let someone bleed to death?"

Earl stood there in shock, unable to speak at first. "M. . .Mr. Larabee, I. . .I didn't shoot you—"

"Don't lie to me!"

"James, what are you doing?" Tessa cried, running up beside him.

"It was Earl. He's the one who shot me."

Earl looked pleadingly at Tessa. "Aunt Tess, I promise I didn't—"

"James, you have to be mistaken. . . ," Tessa told him, laying a hand on his arm.

He shook it off, feeling betrayed that she wouldn't believe him. "Where's the sheriff! I want this boy arrested!"

"I'm right here, Mr. Larabee," Daniel said in a calm voice as he walked up to the group. James barely noticed that the friends who were standing by Earl were all backing away from them.

"Sheriff, this is the man who shot me. I recognize the coat; it was what he was wearing when he ran away from me."

"Uncle Daniel, I promise that I didn't shoot him," Earl defended. He looked scared but was reluctant to speak, as if he were hiding something.

"Do you know who did?" Daniel asked shrewdly.

Earl looked down at the ground and kicked at a pebble with the point of his boot. "I lent someone my coat, Uncle Daniel. I had a feeling he had done something that he wasn't telling me, but I don't know for sure."

James let out a frustrated breath. "Quit lying! Why don't you just take responsibility for what you did!"

Tessa came around to stand in front of James. "James, please. Earl wouldn't lie. He's a good Christian boy who's been studying to be a minister like his daddy. He would have never left you there to die."

James looked at her, her eyes shining with tears and her cheeks flushed. He almost gave in. But old wounds had been opened and were urging him on. He couldn't think rationally. All he knew was that he'd been taken advantage of for the last time. This time someone was going to pay for his misfortune. And why wasn't Tessa standing by him? Why wasn't she demanding that something be done? Didn't she love him? Where was her loyalty?

"Just because someone claims to want to be a clergyman doesn't make him a saint." He looked away from her, his face hard. "You know my feelings about God anyway. Stay out of this, Tessa!"

Tessa backed away from him. He could hear her sniffle and knew that she was crying, but he wouldn't look. "I thought you'd changed your mind. I thought you were a different man," she told him, then she ran to her wagon to where Louanne sat, trying to see what was going on. He heard the sound of the wagon's wheels as she pulled away, obviously too upset with him to even wait.

He hardened his heart against her words and looked back at the sheriff. "Are you going to arrest him? Or am I going to have to find someone other than 'family' to do it?" he growled.

Sheriff Daniel glanced at him with his knowing eyes, and James got the strange feeling that the man could see right through him. James looked away. Then the sheriff addressed Earl. "Who's the boy, Earl? The one you lent your coat to?"

Earl looked at his uncle then looked away, clearly torn. "I don't even know for sure, if it's him, Uncle. How can I rat on a friend?"

"Someone broke the law, son," his father, Donald, spoke up as he, too, joined the group. "Tell us who the friend is so Daniel can ask him some questions."

James's leg grew steadily weaker as he stood there watching them talk back and forth and getting nowhere with the boy. James shifted on his crutches, trying to relieve some of the pressure, but it did nothing to ease the pain.

He moved again but lost his balance, causing the crutches to slip out from under his arms.

The last thing he remembered was falling and hitting his head on something really hard.

⚘

"I just thought I'd tell you that James is at J. T.'s office. He fell and knocked himself out cold," Daniel told Tessa, as he stood in her living room with his hat in hand.

Tessa's heart dropped, and she felt a panic rise up within her. "Is he alright?"

"Yeah, I reckon," Daniel said lazily. Tessa knew that he was playing this for all it was worth. She was going to have to drag the information out of him, it seemed.

"Come on, Daniel. Please tell me how he is," she pleaded.

He twirled his hat around a time or two. "Hmmm. You seem pretty upset about this. It appeared to me, out there by the church, that you'd washed your hands of that Alabama man. I wouldn't figure you'd care one way or another."

Tessa folded her arms around her waist and glared at her brother-in-law. "You are really starting to get on my nerves, Danny boy, so spit it out." He hated to be called that name, so his brothers and occasionally Tessa called him Danny boy just to rile him.

He sighed. "He'll live, if that's what you're worried about. But when he came to, he started going on and on about having Earl arrested. It took awhile for us to explain that the boy who'd borrowed Earl's coat confessed that he'd been the one to shoot him." Daniel shook his head. "It was Clevis Packard's son Ned. He's only thirteen, and he got scared when his gun went off and he hit James. He didn't know what to do, so in typical 'kid' fashion, he ran away and tried to pretend it didn't happen."

"Is James going to have him arrested?" Tessa asked.

"No. When he calmed down, he was able to talk to Clevis about the boy. Clevis agreed not to let Ned handle a gun until he's had proper lessons on how to handle one, and then only in the presence of an adult." Daniel looked down a moment then glanced back up at her. "But, you know, Larabee's still pretty mad at you, though."

Tessa eyes flew open in disbelief. "What are you saying? Why would he be mad at me? I should be mad at him for the way he spoke to me!"

Daniel shook his head sympathetically, as if he knew something that she didn't. "He's mad 'cause you didn't stand by him. I know that you were just defending Earl, but it came off to James like you were against him. When a man doesn't have any family to call his own anymore, and he thinks he's finally found someone to make a new family, he expects that person to be loyal just like family."

"Oh, for goodness' sakes, Daniel! I am loyal! But I couldn't let him accuse Earl when I knew that he was wrong!"

"You should have told him that when you didn't have a crowd to overhear you."

Tessa gazed at Daniel and then shook her head, looking away. "This is the craziest thing I've ever heard!"

Daniel just shrugged and flipped his hat back on his head. "Well, I'd best be on my way. I'm supposed to be setting up shooting lessons for Clevis's son so he won't be maiming anybody else in the future." He winked at her before walking out of the door. "You have a good day, now."

Tessa rolled her eyes and pushed him the rest of the way outside. "Good-bye, Daniel."

She then leaned on the door and looked up at the ceiling, lost in her thoughts. How could James be mad at her? It just didn't make any sense! She hadn't gone nuts in front of the whole church.

Chapter 8

As soon as Louanne heard her Uncle Daniel leave through the front door, she ran out the back. She'd eavesdropped on the whole conversation and now things were beginning to make sense.

James Larabee, her promised daddy, wasn't coming back. He wasn't going to be her daddy, and he wasn't going to stay in Wiseville. She had to do something and quick!

Like a rabbit, she darted through the woods as fast as she could, heading in the direction of Uncle J. T.'s house.

She would talk to James. Maybe she could make him not be mad at her mother.

After about ten minutes, she barged into her uncle's office on the front side of his house, slamming the door behind her.

"Whoa there, young'un!" J. T. scolded with eyebrows furrowed. "This may be a tiny little place, but it's still a doctor's office!"

Louanne, breathing hard from her run, brushed the stray hair from her face and looked determinedly at her uncle. "Uncle, I've got to see Mr. Larabee. It's a matter of life and death!"

J. T. just raised a lazy eyebrow. Apparently he didn't see the urgency that his niece did. "Life and death?"

Louanne rolled her eyes and stomped her foot. "You know what I mean! If I don't get in there and talk to him, I ain't never going to get another daddy!"

"You're never going to have—" J. T. corrected.

"Isn't that what I just said?" she huffed then pleaded, "Please, Uncle J. T.!"

J. T. nodded toward the door that led to the small room adjoining his office. "Go on in."

Louanne let herself into the room, and she went to where James was sitting on the edge of the bed rubbing the back of his head.

"Mr. Larabee?" she called out softly.

James looked up and winced at the sudden movement. "Huh? Oh, hi, Lulu. What are you doing here?"

Louanne took a deep breath and sat in the chair in front of him. "I came to talk you into staying in Wiseville."

James looked at her with compassion. "Louanne, there is nothing for me here. I need to move on. . . ."

"But what about you and Mama! I know that you love her!"

James grew very still, then after a long pause he looked away. "That is really none of your business, Lulu."

Louanne let out an annoyed breath. "I've got two eyes to see with, Mr. Larabee! You going to deny it?"

James looked at her then and grinned. "No, I'm not. But it doesn't make any difference. Your mama and me just ain't suited. And besides, I've got plans in California."

Louanne nodded. "You're going to open up a house of ill repute."

James scowled. "That's not what I'm doing! I'm opening a saloon! Not... not that!"

"Uncle Donald thinks it amounts to about the same thing," she told him with innocent eyes.

James picked at a string on his pants. "Well, it ain't."

They sat there silent for a moment, then Louanne reached out to grab James's hand. He looked at her with confusion.

"Well, since you're going to go away from us and leave us here all alone," she began with a dramatic tremor in her voice, "I'd better say a prayer for you, so that you'll be safe on your journey."

Prayers. James sighed and nodded, figuring, *What could it hurt?*

Louanne squeezed his hand gently as she closed her eyes tightly and began to pray. "Dear Lord, please be with my friend Mr. Larabee as he leaves on his journey. Keep him real safe and watch after him so that no Indians will scalp him along the way."

James bit his lip to keep from laughing at that comment, but her next words quickly squelched all humor.

"And, Lord, You know that Mr. Larabee is upset at You, and I pray that You will bless him so much that he'll not be mad at You any more. He's such a good man, and I thought for sure that You had sent him to our woods because You wanted him to be my new daddy. But I guess it was just wishful thinking and not an answer to prayer like I'd thought."

She sighed as she said this, and James felt a lump the size of a boulder rising in his throat. She'd thought that James was an answer to her prayer. He didn't know what to do. How could a child have so much faith, when he as an adult had so little?

"I know that You love Mr. Larabee, Lord, just like Mama and me do. You see, I know this because I've been listening at the door," she added as if she felt the need to explain and confess.

"I'll close now, because I know that Uncle Donald already takes up a lot of Your time with his long prayers, but I thank You for letting me get to know Mr. Larabee, and I ask You again to please take care of him. In Jesus' name, amen."

James could do nothing but sit there and stare at the little girl for a few moments. Never in his life had he felt so loved, yet so despicable at the same time.

He'd spent so much time shaking his fist at God and blaming Him that he'd allowed bitterness to cloud his good thinking. And all that time, God had faithfully watched over him and brought him to a place that he could receive his heart's desire—a family.

Yet, he almost missed it.

But every man wised up sooner or later, and James was glad it was still sooner, at least he hoped it was where Tessa was concerned.

"Louanne," he said softly, raising her chin with his fingers. "Do you still want me for a daddy after all the ruckus I've caused with your cousin and all?"

Louanne nodded but then puckered her brow. "Yes, except I really didn't understand what all went on this afternoon," she explained.

James smiled. "That's alright. It's water under the bridge. Now, all that's left is to try to make things right with your mama."

"Well, now's your chance so you better make it good," a voice from the doorway said.

James looked up in surprise as Tessa stood there leaning on the doorframe with arms folded. "Tess!" He got up and limped over to her. "Will you please forgive me, Tessa? I didn't mean to cause all this trouble or to talk to you the way I did this afternoon."

Tessa reached out to take the hand that he held out to her. "If you can forgive me for not taking your side. I didn't mean to seem disloyal."

"It's a deal," he said, bringing her hand up to kiss it.

He then drew Tessa farther into the room and reached down to draw Louanne from her chair. "Now that the apologies are out of the way, I think we need to start talking about the future."

"Are you going to ask us to marry you?" Louanne asked with excitement, her smile beaming at them both.

James lifted an eyebrow. "Well, I don't know. Do you think that your mother will say yes?" he asked Louanne while looking into Tessa's shining eyes.

"Of course she will!" Louanne blurted out confidently then added as an afterthought, "Won't you, Mama?"

Tessa looked intently at James. "I can only marry a man who loves God as well as myself. Can you do that, James?"

"I realize that I've been blaming God wrongly, Tessa. Louanne was the one who opened my eyes to it. I've been complaining and railing at Him for years now and all this time He's been leading me to a place of healing. He loved me despite my hatred. I can do no less than to love Him and put Him first in my life." James paused, then added, "And never ever doubt my love for you, Tessa. I loved you from the beginning."

Tessa smiled as her eyes shone bright with tears. "Then I can do no less than to answer your question. Yes, James. I love you and would be honored to become your wife!"

James leaned over and kissed her then. Brushing her soft lips with his own, he felt the love and passion for this beautiful woman rise up within him. Had he ever felt this way? Had he ever felt so much warmth and contentment? Everything he'd ever wanted or ever needed was surrounding him in this room.

⁂

Tessa savored his kiss as she slid her arms around his neck and cuddled against him. Her heart thundered within her chest, and she could hardly breathe, but it didn't matter. She had been so worried just a moment ago, and now she was being given the wondrous gift of love for the second time in her life.

It was different this time around, greater somehow. Maybe it was because she was older and had been through tragedy and hardship. Whatever the reason, she knew that this man, this sweet, handsome man, was a gift from God, and she was going to spend the rest of her life thanking Him for it.

"I'm feeling a little left out here," Louanne said.

Their kiss ended abruptly as Louanne's words startled them both. They looked down at Louanne's knowing look and her tapping foot and started to laugh.

James put his arm around the pretty girl and tugged her into their family circle. "I don't want you to feel left out, Lulu. In fact, now that we're all here and talking about the future," he started to tell them as he threw a wink at Tessa, whose cheeks were still red from their kiss, "I had an idea that just came to me, or maybe God gave it to me."

Tessa hugged them both. "What is it, James?"

He thought a moment, then told them, "It's about the money that I was going to take to California with me."

Tessa looked dismayed. "Please don't tell me you still want to go to California because, honestly, James, I really don't..."

"Shh...," he hushed her, giving her a quick kiss on the lips. "I wasn't going to suggest that. But I wondered how you would feel about moving to Alabama," he mentioned hesitantly.

Tessa looked at him wide-eyed, then her face broke into a brilliant smile. "Oh, James! Are you thinking about going back to the plantation?"

He returned her smile. "I would like to, but only if you don't mind leaving Wiseville. I know that you have family here and—"

This time it was she who kissed him to make him quit talking. "I want to go. James, I think it would be the greatest thing in the world, to return to your heritage!"

He let out a breath. "But you know that there isn't a house left; just a few of the old slave cottages are standing. It'll be hard for a while."

"I don't care, James. As long as I have you and Louanne there, we can rebuild the Larabee Plantation together."

"Does this mean there's going to be a wedding?" another voice came from the door.

They turned around to see all the Wise brothers crowded into J. T.'s little office and all trying to see into the room. "Oh, for goodness' sake J. T.! Don't you boys have anything else to do besides meddle in my love life?" Tessa asked, exasperated.

J. T. frowned and glanced at Daniel and Donald standing on either side of him. "No, actually we don't! James, there, is my only patient and he seems to be righter than rain!"

Tessa giggled. "Well, if it'll make you all go on and leave us alone, I'll tell you! Yes! We are getting married. Now, go away!"

"Ha! I knew it!" J. T. yelled. They all were talking at once, but at least they moved away from the doorway.

James gave Tessa another kiss and then looked down at his soon-to-be-daughter. "Is this like they do it in the fairy tales, Lulu?"

Louanne smiled with a dreamy look on her face that was familiar to them all. "Oh no! This was soooo much more romantic!"

James gave the girl a quick squeeze, then reached back for his crutch that was leaning on the bed. "Now, let's go catch up with Brother Donald so that he can marry us and we can be on our way!"

Suddenly horrified, Tessa looked at him as she followed him out the door. "Oh, James! You don't mean that we're going to get married now! Today!"

"The sooner the better!" he yelled over his shoulder as he made his way toward Donald.

Tessa threw her arms in the air. "But there is so much to do! I mean, I have to make a dress, get my house all packed. . ." Her voice faded as she ran to join her husband-to-be.

"This is the way *Romeo and Juliet* should have ended!" Louanne declared with much flamboyance and flair as she ran after them.

THE TIE THAT BINDS

by Susan K. Downs

Preface

Between 1854 and 1930 over 200,000 orphaned or abandoned children traveled via orphan trains from the east coast of the United States to points west in hopes of finding new homes. Through this industrious "placing-out" program, as it was referred to in those days, trains carried a company of children to rural communities where people would gather and choose a child. Typically, prior to the train's arrival, a local committee evaluated applicants to determine whether they could provide a good home for a child. However, few committees bothered asking whether those interested in adopting were married or single or why they wanted a child. Despite this loosely structured plan, many children found loving and caring families—thanks to the orphan trains.

Chapter 1

Well, Miz Watson, I see you still haven't forgiven me for my proposal of marriage," Frank Nance rasped in a futile attempt at a whisper.

Emma swept past Mr. Nance's imposing figure as he held the door open for her. Stepping out of the bright sunlight into the dimly lit interior of Shady Grove's Mercantile and Dry Goods Store, Emma found herself momentarily blinded. The stale, musty air tickled her nose, nearly making her sneeze.

The wind blowing off the prairie was unseasonably hot. But Emma couldn't blame the wind or the afternoon sun for the perspiration now prickling her forehead along her bonnet's brim. The presence of Frank Nance always caused her internal temperature to rise and her stomach to clench in irritation.

"Shush!" Emma responded curtly. "I've not told a soul about your proposal, and the last person I'd want to overhear is Katy Greene!" She scanned the store for a glimpse of the clerk who always made it her business to know everyone else's business. Emma's panic eased just a bit when she caught sight of the town's busybody assisting other customers at the far end of the store.

"Have it your way, ma'am. But the offer I made a year ago still stands. It's a cryin' shame for a pretty lady like yourself to be widowed—alone and childless—at the tender age of twenty-eight. Everyone in the county says we'd make a great lookin' couple. And you could close up that little seamstress shop of yours and be taken care of at home, where a woman belongs. Besides, I could sure use someone like you to help me out on the farm."

Emma gaped in disgust. "How dare you mention my age! Just how on earth did you know it anyway?" Without waiting for a response, Emma rushed, "You certainly have gall to even suggest that my seamstress shop is an inappropriate occupation for a lady!

"And, furthermore..." Widow Watson's corset under her starched white shirtwaist dug into her ribs, and she gasped sharply before continuing her tirade. The smirk of amusement on Frank Nance's face only added to her fury. "And furthermore, wheat farming must not be the easy job you boasted it would be when you gave up cattle-driving. Otherwise, you wouldn't be so determined to find a wife to take care of the homestead. And you think I should jump at your offer because I need someone to take care of me? Contrary to your obvious opinion, Mr. Nance, I am quite capable of taking care of myself. I do not need you—or any other man in my life, for that matter."

Emma punctuated her speech by turning abruptly and stepping to a glass display case, which held an assortment of scissors and knives. Surely, her curt rebuff would end this uncomfortable interchange. But even as she feigned an interest in the nickel-plated pinking shears, she could feel Frank's intense scrutiny. Did he suspect that her words had not been totally honest?

If the truth were known, she had often entertained the idea of re-marrying. She didn't look forward to an entire lifetime of widowed loneliness. In fact, since Frank Nance broached the subject a year ago, she found herself imagining what life might be like married to this rugged outdoorsman. He obviously possessed the same adventuresome spirit she had loved in her departed husband, Stanley.

Stanley Watson had always been on the lookout for the next thrill. His death three years ago occurred when he tried to break the bronco dubbed "untamable" by every horse-tamer in the county. Stanley took their edict as a challenge to conquer the beast. But the bucking steed threw Stanley within seconds of his mount. Emma could never erase the image of her husband's lifeless body inside the corral fence. His neck snapped as he hit the ground, and her beloved, impulsive husband had died instantly. Still, it would have been the kind of death Stanley would have chosen had he been allowed such a choice.

Oh, but Stanley. Why did you have to go and die so young? Why did you have to leave me alone in this world? Emma struck up this one-sided conversation with her deceased husband as naturally as though he were standing next to her.

Why didn't the good Lord grant us children? I prayed for a child. Your child. If I had borne your child, my grief and incredible longing for you might be just a bit more bearable. How I wish I had more than just my memories of you. If we had been blessed with a child, I wouldn't even listen to the likes of Frank Nance. But it's so lonely without you.

Her thoughts of Stanley caused her to shiver in revulsion at Frank's blatant offer for a loveless marriage. A marriage of convenience. She had known the man only briefly before he proposed. There hadn't been the slightest opportunity for love to grow between them.

Well, Stanley Watson and Frank Nance might have been kindred spirits, but Emma knew, without a doubt, that Stanley had been desperately in love with her—as she had been with him. Frank Nance, with all his good looks and lofty promises of comfort and security, couldn't give her the one thing she longed for most, someone to love, who loved her in return. Besides, unlike Stanley, Frank was a quiet, inexpressive man. Every time she pondered the possibilities of marrying Frank, she remembered the disastrous outcome of her own mother's second marriage to the stone-faced, stern Josiah Trumbull. What if Frank's silent disposition hid a personality as cruel as that hateful man's? Mr. Trumbull had ruined her mother's hopes for a happy life. He had driven Emma away from her mother and her home. Emma would remain single for eternity before she'd enter into the risky union Frank offered. His proposition was simply too full of unknowns.

Still, the persistent Mr. Nance wasn't quite ready to accept Emma's no as a final answer to his long-standing proposal. He sidled up to the counter, wedging his way between Emma and the scissors display. His voice slowly increased in volume as he continued in his attempts to weaken her fierce independence. "It isn't as though you have a passel of eligible men to pick from in these parts." Frank's nervous fidgeting with the suede fringe on his leather vest belied the cockiness of his banter. " 'Less'n you consider the undertaker McHenry. He's buried three wives already and has one foot in the grave himself—"

"Mr. Nance, please keep your voice down! And please pay me the courtesy of never addressing this matter again. A marriage for convenience's sake, whether it be your convenience or mine, doesn't interest me in the least. My answer of last year remains my answer today. NO!"

Emma's final word echoed through the store and the attentions of Katy Greene and her customers immediately turned to the pair. The rotund store clerk's eyebrows rose in obvious question, but she swallowed her curiosity for the time being and simply said, "Mr. Nance, Miz Watson, I'll be with you directly."

"I imagine Katy Greene is havin' a field day with this orphan train business," Frank said, looking in the shopkeeper's direction. "It's created quite a buzz around town."

Despite her firm rejection of Frank's repeated proposal, Emma was slightly taken aback by his abrupt change in the course of their conversation. Was he, at last, abandoning his idea of marriage? Or did he have a new strategy in mind?

"Excuse me, but I'm afraid that I don't know what you're referring to," she snapped, wishing he would simply do his business and leave.

"No offense, ma'am, but a person would have to be as blind as a post hole not to notice that somethin's goin' on here in Shady Grove. Didn't you see the crowd in front of the *Gazette* office when you walked by?"

Emma glanced out the storefront window to see a dozen or more of the town folk clustered around the newspaper office. Apparently, her inability to focus on more than one task at a time had left her, once again, oblivious to her surroundings. Emma's thoughts and energies for the past three days had been consumed with the completion of Lizzy Baxter's wedding gown. Sometimes, especially on days like today, she found it rather surprising that she could even walk and think at the same time.

Attempting to disguise her deficient observation skills, she turned to

Frank and calmly replied, "The citizens of Shady Grove are in a constant state of ruckus. What has them stirred up now?"

Stepping up behind Emma, Katy Greene interrupted with her own answer. "Of course, it wouldn't concern you, Miz Watson—what with being a widow and all—but a rail car full of orphans is headed for our little village, straight from New York City. They're looking for folks who will adopt 'em and give 'em a good home. My husband Orville is on the screening committee. He says that several folks have already inquired about adopting these children and the *Gazette* only posted the notice in Monday's paper. He's hopeful that all fifteen of the orphans will wind up right here in Shady Grove. Why, we might even take one ourselves."

Frank, unobserved by the rambling Mrs. Greene, rolled his eyes at Emma in a look that could only be interpreted as an expressive. "Oh, brother!"

Despite his irritating ideas, he still possesses a certain boyish charm. The unwelcome thought caught Emma off guard. However, the feelings quickly passed as Frank, eyes twinkling, dashed aside any admiration Emma might have been developing for him.

"Perhaps I'll look into taking one of the boys, too. I've heard tell those orphans make good workers."

Even though his words seemed to be spoken in jest, Emma wondered if his teasing tone was a cover for his ultimate motive. Could this man truly be so cold-hearted as to adopt a child for the sake of gaining a helping hand? Emma's ears heated with anger at the very thought. It's bad enough that he would propose a marriage of convenience to a grown woman...but only an ogre would adopt an innocent child just for the work he could get out of him. Did Mr. Nance think that adoption was something akin to the purchase of a new pack mule?

She studied his classically handsome features, searching for some answers to her question, but she received none. His mahogany eyes simply reflected his own speculations and appraisals back at her. Under ordinary circumstances, Emma might very well find herself agreeably inclined to Mr. Nance's overtures. Fleetingly, she wondered if she might react differently were the man to at least show some sign of affection for her, some predisposition of falling in love. The thought left her stomach in a disgusting flutter.

An overwhelming urge to run back to the cocoon of her seamstress shop flooded Emma. She didn't want to think about Frank Nance any more today. He flustered her beyond reason, and she refused to stay another moment in this infuriating man's presence.

Emma turned to the shopkeeper and announced, "Mrs. Greene, I really must return to my shop. If you would do me the favor of gathering together the muslin I ordered, along with two dozen shirt buttons and thirty cents worth of seed pearls, I'll be back at four-thirty to pick them up." Then she whirled on her heels and clamored out the door, murmuring a perfunctory "good day, sir" as she passed Frank.

Politely picking her way through the townsfolk still clustered in front of the *Gazette* office, Emma managed to position herself in front of the posted news board. The bold "WANTED" headline seemed more appropriate for a bank robber than adoptive families, but the article that followed tugged at Emma's heartstrings:

WANTED!
Homes for 15 orphan children

A company of orphan children under the auspices of the Children's Aid Society of New York will arrive in Shady Grove Thursday afternoon, June 24.

These children are bright, intelligent, and well disciplined, both boys and girls of various ages. A local committee of five prominent Shady Grove citizens has been selected to assist the agents in placing the children. Applications must be made to and endorsed by the local committee, which will convene at the town hall on Thursday, June 24 beginning at 9 A.M. Distribution of the children will take place at the opera house on Friday, June 25, at 10 A.M.

Come and see the children and hear the address of the child-placing agent.

The engine of Emma's one-track mind began building up steam. As she turned from the signboard and made her way down the street toward her shop and home, her thoughts quickly traveled into uncharted territory.

Why not a widow like me? Emma mentally shot back a response to Katy Greene's earlier statement. Then, as naturally as she drew breath, Emma's thoughts turned into a silent prayer. *Lord, why not a widow like me? One parent would certainly be better than no parent whatsoever. And I would make a great mother! I have a lot of love to give. I could definitely provide a more suitable home for a child than the stonehearted Mr. Nance.* A spark of self-righteous indignation burst into flame, sending Emma's unspoken prayer to the far recesses of her mind.

The very idea that Frank Nance might even tease about adopting a boy as an extra farm hand. . . Emma's temples began to pound in anger as her thoughts turned, once again, to the infuriating farmer. *Why, if this committee might approve the likes of Frank Nance to adopt a child, surely I can convince them to recommend ME!*

Chapter 2

Emma stepped from her spacious porch and across the threshold of her white frame home. Swiftly she rushed through the tastefully decorated parlor and into her workroom, where a worn rolltop desk held her Bible. Emma picked up the Bible and settled into the straight-backed chair that complemented the desk. The room was filled with the necessities of the trade: stacks of fabric in rainbow hues, dressmaker frames, two full-length mirrors, a privacy screen for the customer's convenience, and a trundle sewing machine—Stanley's wedding gift.

With the smells of new fabric surrounding her, she mentally pushed aside thoughts of work and fervently asked God for wisdom. In her typical daily routine of prayer and meditation, she studied her Bible in a systematic fashion. But today, with her thoughts flitting in all different directions like the evening fireflies, she found it impossible to concentrate on one particular Scripture passage. Instead, she thumbed through the yellowed pages of her father's aging Bible, asking God to give her some sort of promise or sign. Did this newborn idea of adoption stem from selfish motivation? Was she simply acting on a desire to prove something to Frank Nance? Or could taking an orphaned child as her own be a part of God's perfect plan?

Instinctively, Emma turned to Psalms—the book of the Bible where she had most often sought and found comfort following Stanley's death. As she skimmed the well-worn pages, her attention rested on a verse just above her right hand. Her index finger pointed to the sixty-eighth Psalm and she started reading verses 5 and 6. She must have read this very chapter, these same verses, numerous times: "A father of the fatherless, and a judge of the widows, is God in his holy habitation." Yes. She distinctly remembered pondering the fact that God proved Himself a merciful and loving judge to widows such as herself. But never had the words of Psalm 68:6 leapt out at her like they did now. "God setteth the solitary in families."

Was the Lord showing her a sign? Could it be that a solitary little girl now rode on a train bound for Shady Grove, hoping and praying for someone to love and care for her? Emma knew full well the meaning of the word "solitary." These past three years since Stanley's death she had wallowed in loneliness and solitude. Now, her heart ached to think of a mere child facing life without the comfort and security of a home or family.

God setteth the solitary in families. Throughout the remainder of the afternoon the words rang repeatedly through her thoughts until they became a chant. Over the course of the evening, the melodious words turned into song as Emma bathed, washed her hair, and prepared for the next day. *God setteth the solitary in families. God setteth the solitary in families.* Like a soothing lullaby, the psalm soothed Emma to sleep.

When the summer sun's first rays at last broke over the horizon, Emma threw back her bedcovers and sat on the side of her bed. As she glanced across her small, tidy quarters, the psalm still rang through her head. *God setteth the solitary in families.* Once the idea of adopting a little girl had taken root in Emma's mind, her thoughts refused to dwell on anything else. Miss Baxter's wedding dress remained unhemmed. She had even forgotten to return to the mercantile yesterday afternoon to retrieve her order from Katy Greene.

The early morning minutes moved slower than February molasses as Emma waited for the appointed hour that the committee would consider adoption applications. With each loud tick of the mantle clock, her conviction and determination grew. Adopting a child was the right thing to do. Emma pulled up her wavy chestnut hair. Then she stood in her undergarments before the open doors of her wardrobe and riffled through an assortment of dresses. As a seamstress, she didn't lack for clothes. But what would be considered appropriate attire for a widow hoping to adopt a child?

Finally, Emma settled on a dark green taffeta with a white lace collar and black velvet trim. If she were to err, Emma preferred to err on the side of overdressing. Besides, the green cloth brought out the emerald flecks of her otherwise gray eyes. She smiled with smug satisfaction at her mirrored reflection as she buttoned up the bodice to her dress. *They won't turn me down for lack of good looks.* The thought only briefly skittered through her mind, but it was swiftly followed by a rebuff for such self-admiration, lest it border on conceit.

Emma felt like a hostage to time, just waiting for the mantle clock to chime nine o'clock. By the time the clock rang once, announcing 8:15, she was already fumbling with her front door key as she prepared to leave. She couldn't wait one minute more. She really wanted to be among the first in line. Thoughts of tiny arms around her neck, night-night kisses, and playing peekaboo swirled through her mind as her black leather high-top boots clipped a staccato beat on the boardwalk. With certain determination, Emma headed down Main Street toward the town hall.

The swinging doors leading into the meeting room announced her arrival in grating squeaks as she stepped over the threshold. As she had hoped, Emma was apparently the first applicant to arrive. Seated in an intimidating row behind a long table were the two women and three men who composed the recommendation committee. In unison, this team of prominent Shady Grove citizens stopped their busy pursuit of shuffling papers and consulting one another to turn and stare at Emma. The sun's bright rays, spilling in from the high windows, seemed to create a dream-like chasm between Emma and the prospect of adopting a child. Her heart pounding with anticipation, she plunged into the sphere of light as if she were embracing the prospect of adoption all over again. With each of the twenty steps it took her to cross the room, the floorboards creaked in protest, but the noise sounded like nothing less than a sweet melody to Emma. Nothing. . .nothing could dampen her joyful anticipation. . .nothing. . .not even when she suspected the committee's silent scolding, *you're a widow. You're wasting our time.*

Twisting her handkerchief between perspiring palms, Emma cleared her throat and began, "I–I want to adopt a child. A ch–child from the orphan train."

The silver conchos that decorated the outer legs of his tanned leather chaps clinked softly together as Frank Nance hung the protective britches on a peg just inside the kitchen door. Typically, he reserved his chaps for rides out on the range, but today he had worn them as an apron, of sorts, to protect his best wool trousers from getting soiled during his early morning chores. He had no Sunday-go-to-meetin' clothes, so his newest britches would have to suffice. The washtub, which he had pulled into the middle of the kitchen floor last evening, still held the soapy remains of his bath, the clouded water long turned cold.

Crossing from the kitchen to the parlor, Frank stood in front of the room's single adornment, a garishly gilded mirror that hung on the south wall. Only traces of the reflective mercury remained behind the glass, and Frank had to tip his head at just the right angle to catch a glimpse of his reflection. Frank licked his fingers and twirled the ends of his freshly trimmed moustache. Then, he ran his hand down his clean-shaven chin and gave his parted and bear-greased hair a final smoothing pat.

"There you are—all citified and sissified," Frank said to his reflection. "But if gettin' gussied-up helps me adopt a boy, then gussied-up I'll get." However, he hoped and prayed he didn't run into Emma Watson today, looking like he did. She'd for sure think he had gone soft. Or would she? Frank never knew just how that woman would respond. Where the doe-eyed Widow Watson was concerned, or any ladies for that matter, Frank didn't have a notion about what to do.

When he had made a proposal of marriage to the young widow, he thought sure she would find his offer hard to resist. He'd been told on more than one occasion that he was a handsome man. He was strong and young and could provide security and stability to a wife.

Frank had never been one to drink or carouse, thanks to his saintly mother, who had raised him to practice good Christian morals and ethics. She had seen to it that he learned right from wrong. Surely those traits held the marks of a good husband. Even though he had not been a particularly religious man of late, he still tried his best to avoid any big sins.

His bachelorhood didn't stem from any odd deficiency or personality quirk. Only his previous profession as a drover along the Chisholm Trail had kept him single and unattached. He knew from watching the married cow-hands that life as a cowboy and the duties of a husband don't mix.

After the death of his mother, which left him orphaned at age fourteen, Frank had ridden the range, driving cattle along the Chisholm Trail from Texas through Indian Territory and on into the Kansas plains. Frank learned quickly what it took to survive in the Wild West. Alongside his gun and a good horse, a cowboy needed a gruff exterior and a callused heart. Frank was an expert at keeping his emotions and opinions to himself.

But the need for cowboys to push longhorns along the trail had grown mighty slim, thanks to the ever-expanding railroad and the fencing in of the plains. Frank had traded his adventurous life as a cowboy for the comparatively mundane existence of a Kansas wheat farmer. Since this drastic change, he found the old familiar loneliness much more difficult to bear. But he found admitting his need for companionship a difficult prospect—even with Widow Watson.

He had hoped beyond hope that Emma would have at least given his marriage proposal last year a glimmer of consideration. The two of them would be a good match. But the Widow Watson made it perfectly clear that she was not interested in even entertaining the idea. Maybe he should have courted her awhile before stating his intentions. He hadn't known her all that well when he first proposed, but Frank was a man who made up his mind quickly and he didn't see any sense in wasting time. Unfortunately, Emma seemed to think he was much too practical with his straightforward approach.

Despite what the prim and proper widow thought, no other woman interested him. Frank was not just seeking a marriage of convenience. In truth, most of the "conveniences" of his life were cared for by Pedro and Maria Ramirez, the husband and wife team whom Frank had hired to assist him on the farm. He wanted a life partner. He wanted Emma for his wife. Frank dreaded the thought of facing any more years alone.

When Emma snubbed him again yesterday, Frank determined then and there that he wouldn't wait forever for Emma to change her mind. Ideas of proposing to another woman certainly crossed his mind. Frank had been exposed to more than one coy smile from the collection of young maidens in Shady Grove. However, he had soon dashed aside any notion of marrying another. Thoughts of marrying someone besides Emma Watson simply held no fascination for him—not that he was by any means in love with her. She simply held the maturity and grace that appealed to Frank. Yes, that was it—maturity and grace, nothing more.

So, if he couldn't have the companionship of Widow Watson, he would turn his attentions to other things. The idea of adopting a boy rather appealed to him. While a boy could in no way meet his longing to have Emma for his wife, Frank's desire to be a father would be fulfilled in an adopted son. He and such a boy would be good friends. Best friends.

When Frank had told Emma he might take a boy from the orphan train, he had spoken the words in jest. But the longer he entertained the whim, the more he liked it. After all, he had been orphaned as a child himself. Certainly, he could relate to a boy who felt all alone in the world. As a father, Frank would have a lot to offer a son.

Slamming the back door behind him, Frank tromped across the well-worn path that led from the kitchen to the barn. The strong, earthy smell of hay mixed with manure assailed Frank's nostrils as he slid open the barn door. Shadow, the mustang that Frank had lassoed and tamed as a colt, nuzzled up to his arm as he slid the bridle into place. Within seconds after lifting his saddle from the top rail of the horse's stall, Frank had cinched the straps securely and mounted the steed for the short trip to town.

Emma's impassioned appeal ultimately convinced the panel members to grant her the coveted and necessary commendation to adopt. The two women on the panel had actually been brought to tears as Emma expressed her deep loneliness since the death of her husband and her desire to relieve the desolation of an orphaned child. The Reverend Barnhart agreed that Emma was faithful in church attendance and would provide well for the spiritual nurture of a young soul. Even the committee's businessmen, mercantile owner Orville Greene and *Gazette* publisher Ben McGowan, nodded their heads in approval when Emma addressed the fact that she could teach her child the art and trade of dressmaking and thus assist the girl in becoming a useful and productive citizen of society. But their approval came with a condition: Emma would be allowed to choose a daughter only if no married couples stepped forward first to claim the child. Clutching the recommendation letter securely in her gloved hand, Emma backed out of the room, nodding her head in appreciation to the committee all the way to the door.

God setteth the solitary in families, her heart sang with joy as Emma stepped from the meeting chambers into the hallway that extended the length of the town hall. She found the passageway clogged with several applicants nervously queued in pairs. The first couple in line pushed their way past her through the open door, and Emma received little more than a curious glance or two as she zig-zagged her way through the small group and into the dust-filled street.

A cacophony of horses, wagons, carriages, and pedestrians met Emma as she closed the door.

"Are my eyes deceivin' me, or did I just catch you coming out of the town hall?" a familiar voice softly spoke in her ear.

Jumping, she turned to stare straight into the right shoulder of the towering man. Lifting her gaze to meet his, her breath caught at the sight of Frank's freshly scrubbed and strikingly handsome face so close to hers. The aroma of strong lye soap still clung to his whiskerless chin. The crow's feet that framed his dark mahogany eyes crinkled as he responded with a grin to her startled response.

"W—why, y—yes. I—I—I. . ." Mad at herself for stammering, Emma's shoulders tensed and her toes curled inside her boots. Why on earth was she reacting to this man like a schoolgirl in the throes of her first crush? Surely the noise and excitement of the morning were wearing on her, for she had never been so challenged in maintaining her composure with Frank. *Or perhaps you simply want to believe you have never been so affected by him*, a rebellious voice taunted. Emma clamped her teeth in aggravation. *Frank Nance holds no place—absolutely no place whatsoever—in my heart! Period! The very idea is nothing short of lunacy!*

"You didn't by any chance seek a recommendation from the orphan train committee, did you?" The mischief dancing in his dark eyes told

Emma that he already knew her answer. But the sparkle quickly disappeared behind a veil of seriousness as he followed the unanswered question with another, more urgent inquiry. "Were your efforts met with success?"

Emma studied the face of this mystifying man. From her previous dealings with Mr. Nance, she had long ago concluded that, despite his dashing good looks, the man was incapable of feeling any deep emotion. Yet, as he stood before her now, his voice took on an almost pleading tone. Why were her adoption plans important to Frank?

Doggedly determined to regain her cool demeanor, Emma raised the coveted recommendation letter for him to see. "Fortunately for me, the committee didn't feel that a widow adopting a child was as absurd an idea as Katy Greene believed it to be. I shall be allowed the opportunity to adopt any young girl that is not claimed by a married couple first." Before Frank could examine the paper further, Emma slid it into her beaded caba.

"Now, Miz Watson, that's powerful good news," he enthusiastically replied, undaunted by her curt reaction. "After I left the mercantile yesterday, I felt sorry for funnin' around about this orphan train business. Truth be known, I gave the matter considerable ponderin' last night. I'm on my way to meet with the committee myself and see if I can't convince 'em to let me take a boy."

"No, Fran–er–Mr. Nance. You mustn't. . . You can't. . . Why, the very idea of you. . ." An all-too-familiar irritation surfaced as flashes of yesterday's conversation flitted through Emma's mind. Would Frank Nance really adopt a boy just for farm labor?

"And why not, Miz Watson? Why shouldn't I adopt a son? You've made it perfectly clear that you are unwilling to consider my proposal of marriage. Would you have me forever condemned to live a life of loneliness and solitude?"

His sincere words dashed aside all her previous negative thoughts. Never before had the man spoken so openly with Emma. His soul-revealing speech made her squirm uncomfortably against the snug taffeta gown. As she studied his features in hopes of confirming or denying his sincerity, the psalm that had replayed through her thoughts all morning now took on new meaning. *God setteth the solitary in families.* Could this scripture possibly contain a promise for someone like Frank Nance? The idea of his actually needing human companionship had seemed almost preposterous to Emma. Could she have somehow misunderstood this man? If so, was his proposal based on more than he had admitted? Her stomach produced a betraying flutter. *Stop it!* She wanted to scream.

"You're preachin' a double-standard, Miz Watson. One that's tipped in your favor, if you ask me." A note of irritation crept into Frank's voice as he continued, waving an arm in front of his face to shoo away a pesky horsefly. "Evidently, you believe adoption to be quite fine and dandy for a widow woman such as yourself but somethin' strange and suspicious for a bachelor like me.

"Don't get me wrong, here, Ma'am." Frank fixed his gaze on Emma's face, still whisking at the air to deflect the buzzing bug. "I admire your wantin' a child, and your gumption to see this business through. From what I can tell, you have the makin's of a wonderful mama. Just because you aren't inclined to marry again doesn't mean you shouldn't grab at the chance to raise a young'un, if such a chance comes along. But I reckon you shouldn't begrudge me the same opportunity."

With the force of a slammed door, a steely glaze hid the soft vulnerability that Emma had glimpsed, ever so briefly, in Frank's eyes. "I'd like to stay and visit with you all day," he said, glancing over his shoulder at the town hall, "but there's important business to tend to."

Tipping his broad-brimmed, gray felt hat, Frank excused himself with an exasperating smirk. "Oh and Miz Watson," he said, turning to face her once more, "may I say 'thanks' for plowin' the ground ahead of me and plantin' the idea that it's all right for an unmarried person to adopt. If all goes well with me and that committee, I'll see you at the opera house tomorrow."

Chapter 3

T he ever-present prairie wind blew down Main Street on Friday morning, swirling the dust into miniature cyclones and whipping at Emma's skirts. She instinctively held a rose-scented handkerchief over her nose to keep from choking on the dry air, heavy with the pungent smell of livestock and working men. She paused before crossing the road and surveyed the collection of people now congregating outside the opera house doors.

Katy Greene's squeaky voice carried above the crowd, prickling Emma's nerves like straight pins jabbing an unthimbled thumb. "Well, Orville wants a boy. But I insist on a girl so I can dress her up like a little doll. There's just not much you can do to fix up a boy, don't you know. . ."

The mousy woman whom Katy Greene had cornered continued to bob her head in tacit agreement as the vociferous Mrs. Greene droned on. Ignoring the storekeeper's rambling babble, Emma anxiously fingered the blue satin ribbon on the gingham-wrapped parcel she cradled in her right arm. The package contained a china-faced doll with real hair the same chestnut color as her own. A gift for her daughter-to-be. Emma had spent several hours yesterday evening making the doll's frock out of this powder-blue gingham. On her sewing table back home lay another piece of the fabric. She planned to sew her new daughter a dress to match the one the doll now wore. But as she scanned the gathering assembly, doubts now punctured the confident assurance of impending motherhood she had felt just moments before. How many of these couples wanted girls? And exactly how many girls had the orphan train carried into town?

Emma forced these negative contemplations to the back of her mind and, once again, inspected the amassing band of townsfolk. Half a dozen farmers in bib overalls and their plump, plainly dressed wives composed the majority of the prospective parents waiting to enter the opera house. Were they all hoping only to find a new farm hand from among the orphan train riders? Or did they truly want to provide a good home to a child?

Emma had witnessed the area farmers' gab sessions, which took place on the boardwalk in front of the Shady Grove feed store. She knew that a good many ill-conceived ideas came from these weekly meetings. If they discussed adopting for free labor, had Frank been among them?

Until her most recent encounter with him, she would have strongly suspected his being the mastermind behind any self-serving plot, despite the teasing tone he used when he mentioned adopting a boy to help out on the farm. Now she hesitated to charge Frank with certain villainy. For a few unguarded moments Frank Nance had revealed a different side, a vulnerable side to Emma. Just those few seconds, when she saw softness and emotion in his eyes, caused her to question her previous conviction that he was totally callused and cold. Nonetheless, a few doubts still lingered.

But where was he? Just yesterday Frank seemed doggedly determined to follow through on his adoption plan. It was unlikely that he had changed his mind. Emma craned her neck to see if she could spot the one farmer she knew would stand head and shoulders above the rest. Still, he was nowhere to be found. Could it be that his request for a child had been denied?

A whistle sounded from the train station down the road, indicating that the appointed hour had come. Vaguely hoping to catch sight of Frank, Emma crossed the street and nudged her way to the opera house doors. No sooner had the whistle fallen silent than the garishly ornate double doors of the opera house swung open.

"On behalf of the Orphan Train Committee, I welcome you all," Reverend Barnhart exclaimed. "Please come in. Those of you who are here in hopes of being matched with a child, we ask that you find a seat among the first few rows of the auditorium. If you are here to simply observe the occasion, please take your seats toward the rear." The dignified and refined minister, bedecked in his black preaching suit, shook the hands of the men and nodded respectfully at the women as they filed past him, instilling an aura of solemnity among the people.

The freshly lit kerosene lanterns that lined the far aisles and front of the stage filled the air with a heavy, sooty smell. The lights' flickering shadows set a mysterious scene for this true-life drama, in which the audience would soon play the lead parts.

Emma discreetly found a seat in the third center row, next to the aisle. But once all the couples had taken their seats, an empty place remained beside Emma. Absently, she wondered if some of the couples assumed her spouse would soon arrive. The rest of the seats in the auditorium quickly filled with more than fifty onlookers from Shady Grove's curious citizenry. Seemingly, no one wanted to miss out on the biggest show to ever come to town.

Up on the stage, the rotund publisher of the *Gazette*, Ben McGowan, cleared his throat and shifted from one foot to another as he waited for everyone to find a seat. "Ladies and gentlemen," he began in his deepest bass voice. "We are gathered here today to witness a truly newsworthy and momentous event. For, within a matter of minutes, the young ones who arrived via the orphan train yesterday evening shall be escorted from the Imperial Hotel. Accompanying this band of orphans is the child-placing agent, Mr. E. E. Hill, who shall address this body before the matching of children to parents commences.

"But prior to turning our attentions to the business of the day, may I take just a moment to express my appreciation to the citizens of Shady Grove for the privilege and honor of serving on this select committee. . . ." The verbose newsman continued his pontification, blatantly stalling for time until a chorus of giggles and shushes filtered through the rear doors.

As one body, the crowd's attention turned away from the stage and toward the commotion. Emma shifted in her seat just in time to see none other than Frank Nance, grinning from ear-to-ear, jauntily striding down the aisle. On Frank's shoulders rode a toddler whose face was hidden under the brim of the ex-cowboy's weathered Stetson. Behind him children of various ages, shapes, sizes, and gender followed in a single line.

Just like the Pied Piper, Emma couldn't help but think, suddenly irritated by Frank's uncharacteristically childish antics. Did she owe her perturbed attitude to a twinge of jealousy? For not once—not even when he had proposed marriage—had Frank shown to her the kind of emotion he so freely displayed with the children. Then again, why should she care? The man meant nothing to her. *Nothing,* she insisted. Wasn't it she who had rejected him? Emma reminded herself that she was not the least bit interested in Frank Nance. However, her mind betrayed her as it insisted on meandering to another question. Was Frank capable of showing that kind of affection for a wife?

Immediately, she squelched any notions she might be developing for the man. *He is not a dedicated Christian,* she firmly told herself. *Even if he is handsome, even if he declares his undying love and devotion, he never darkens the church door!* Emma simply could not involve herself with a man who did not share her passion for the Lord.

When the "orphan parade" reached the stage steps, Frank lifted the tot from atop his shoulders and uncovered the cherub's face as he retrieved his hat. A gentle pat on the young boy's backside sent him scurrying onto the stage to find a seat. Relieved of his charge, Frank turned to search the audience until his gaze rested on Emma and the vacant seat to her left.

Scrunching down in her seat, Emma dug her fingernails into the red velvet armrests, hoping and praying that Frank would find another place to sit. But a quick scan of the lantern-lit room told her there were no other seats as close to the front as the one next to her. Would she ever shake this man?

Bringing up the rear of the orphan processional, a gentleman with an infant in his arms walked to the center of the stage and said, "As he's taking his seat, I'd like to extend my sincere thanks to Mr. Frank Nance for coming to my aid today." Seemingly nonplused by the hubbub around him, the man intercepted the baby's reach for his glasses while introducing himself as E. E. Hill, the child-placing agent from New York City. While he spoke, he pushed his spectacles back up the bridge of his nose with one thumb before securely clutching the infant's curious fingers in his grasp. His crumpled suit looked as though he had slept in it for several nights.

"Unfortunately, one of the young orphans amongst our party fell ill," Mr. Hill continued. "And my assistant, Mrs. Ima Jean Findlay, found it necessary to remain behind at the Imperial to care for the ailing child. Mr. Nance happened to be eating breakfast at the hotel and observed my single-handed struggles with the children. He graciously volunteered to assist."

Frank, who had already left the stage and was heading for the empty seat next to Emma, paused to respond. Although he spoke softly, the acoustics of the room caused his voice to reverberate throughout the audience. "No need to say 'thanks,' Mr. Hill. I was happy to help out.

"But I don't mind tellin' you. . ." Frank pointed with his hat in the direction of the squirming children. "Herdin' cows is a heap easier than corralin' them kids!" A ripple of lighthearted laughter filtered through the crowd as he came to a stop beside Emma.

"Is it all right with you if I sit there, ma'am?" Frank whispered as he nodded toward the empty seat. Emma sensed, without even lifting her gaze from the package on her lap, that every eye in the building was watching this exchange. Her face heated and the tops of her ears stung with embarrassment over the attention now focused toward her.

Unlike yesterday, when she wanted to wear her best to impress the committee, today Emma had purposefully tried to shrink into the shadows and remain inconspicuous. As the only widow woman seeking to adopt, she didn't want to endure a morning full of stares. She had even chosen a nondescript brown muslin dress, rather than one made of a finer material or brighter color, for the express purpose of blending in with the crowd. But the boisterous Mr. Nance seemed intent on including her in his spectacle.

What had gotten into him, anyway? Never before had Frank behaved in such a frivolous fashion. Without verbally responding to his request, Emma shifted her skirts to allow him to squeeze past her and occupy the vacant seat. Then, with a flick of her wrist, she opened her whalebone and lace fan and began waving it furiously in front of her face. Despite the early hour, the room already felt uncomfortably stuffy and warm. But then, Frank's presence seemed to always elicit a heated reaction in Emma. In the past she experienced the heat of irritation. But this morning something else was certainly mixed with the irritation, which exasperated her all the more.

"Good mornin', Miz Watson. I reckon you were wonderin' if I was gonna show. Well, here I be. And you'll be happy to know that the committee also approved the likes of me." He waved his approval letter tauntingly in front of her.

A flurry of smart retorts flew through Emma's thoughts. However, when she raised her head to respond, she was struck by the gleam of excitement in Frank's eyes and she held her tongue. The vexation that typically accompanied her every encounter with this man now softened. She didn't want a sour mood to spoil this special day for either of them.

Emma, blinking rapidly, tried to hide the smile of anticipation that bubbled up from within. Frank wasn't the only one excited. The ambiance of the day so swept over Emma that she found herself actually complimenting Mr. Nance.

"You seem to have a real gift for dealing with children. I must confess, I am impressed." The words startled Emma, but not half as much as the spark of admiration that sprang into Frank's eyes. Flustered, she fanned herself all the more fiercely and nodded toward the stage. "We'd best turn our attentions to the platform, or we may miss something."

Forcing herself to stare forward, Emma wondered whatever possessed her to offer such a coquettish response. Now, she was nothing short of awkward and uncertain of her every move.

Up on the stage, Mr. Hill handed the baby boy he had been jostling to one of the four older orphan girls seated behind him. He smoothed his coat lapels and cleared his throat before turning to address the crowd. "I realize that many of you are anxiously waiting to be matched with a child, but first we must outline the procedures we will follow and establish a few ground rules. . . ."

Mr. Hill continued with his remarks, but Emma's attentions were compellingly drawn to the children seated behind him. As she focused on the children, Frank's imposing presence seemed to blur. Each of the boys wore new knickers, suit coats, starched white shirts, and neckties. The four girls were outfitted in identical navy blue cotton dresses and stiff white pinafores.

Only four girls, Emma noted with a twinge of disappointment. *O Lord, is one of them to be mine?* She eagerly studied each of their faces as she prayed. They were all a bit older than she had expected them to be—at least nine or ten years old. None shared any obvious physical characteristics with Emma. None reminded Emma of her deceased husband, Stanley. Yet, as they doted and fawned quietly over the baby boy placed temporarily in their care, Emma was favorably impressed with their tenderness and affection toward the child. They appeared polite and well behaved. Certainly Emma could welcome any one of these four girls into her home.

Out of the corner of her eye, Emma caught a glimpse of Frank discreetly waving at the toddler boy whom he had carried "horsy-back" style into the opera house. The youngster scrunched his shoulders and returned Frank's greeting by waving with both hands. Emma simply shook her head in bewilderment at this mystifying man. What had happened to the always logical, practical, emotionless Mr. Nance? If the truth were told, Emma liked the new Frank much better than the old. Still, only time would tell whether the changes were lasting and sincere or just another self-serving scheme.

"In conclusion. . ." Mr. Hill's closing remarks jarred Emma from her daydreams, and she forced herself to focus on his words. "Before we call the first couple to come and select their child, let me emphasize two key points. These boys and girls understand that they are here in hopes of finding a new home. Unfortunately for several of them, their search for a family will not end here—for we have fifteen children among our group, including the one that is ill, and only a dozen homes which have met the standards for committee approval. Despite the unfavorable odds, we will not force any child over age eight to go with a family. The ultimate decision rests with the orphan. If they do not feel comfortable with any of the couples here today, they will board the train with us and travel on to the next town. Our journey west will continue until all of the children have been placed in suitable homes."

Without turning his back on the crowd, the speaker took three steps back and stood between two young boys who were poking at each other. Mr. Hill's close proximity to the youngsters immediately caused them to cease their banter and sit up straight in their chairs.

"Secondly," Mr. Hill continued, "there is a one-year waiting period between child-placement and legal adoption. If, during that period, a family is grievously dissatisfied with the child placed in their care, as has happened on a very rare occasion with our placements, the family should contact us immediately and the child will be removed from the home."

Mr. Hill paused just long enough to pull a large white handkerchief from his back pocket and wipe the perspiration from his brow. "I believe that concludes my remarks. Approved couples will be called in random order as their names are drawn from this hat." He held a black top hat high into the air. "As I call your name, bring your letter of recommendation and join me on the stage. We will meet with our two single candidates for child placement following the matching of all married couples with a child. All right, shall we begin?"

Emma nervously licked her lips and scrutinized the four girls. Would one of them remain for her? She relived that seemingly supernatural assurance which had swept over her when she was approved to adopt. As she looked at the limited number of girls, new doubts assailed her.

The children were instructed to stand and line up across the front of the platform. As soon as the girls stood, they huddled around the oldest one, who held the baby in her arms. The younger boys eagerly jumped from their seats, each trying to shove his way to the front of the line. The older ones took a military stance, their faces solemn and stony. But Emma couldn't help but notice one boy, about ten, who lagged behind, his chin drooping to his chest. His frail body and pale complexion added to the aura of gloom on his face and he stood a full step behind the others. *Why, what a sad little boy,* Emma fleetingly thought. However, her concentration quickly shifted to Katy and Orville Greene, whose names Mr. Hill had just called.

Without a moment's deliberation, Katy walked straight toward the four girls. Emma nervously chewed on her fingernails as she tried to guess which girl the annoying Mrs. Greene would chose. To her amazement, Katy reached out and took the dozing baby boy from the arms of his young caregiver. "Oh, Mr. Hill, Orville and I have always wanted a baby boy," Katy gushed. "This is simply a dream come true."

Emma's jaw dropped in amazement. Turning to Frank, she nearly choked on her surprised exclamation. "Why, I distinctly heard Katy say that she had to have a girl!"

Frank rolled his eyes. "That woman's more perplexin' than a two-headed cow!"

Shaking her head, Emma chuckled as Katy carried her new son down the aisle and out the back door while Orville stayed to complete the necessary paperwork.

The next couple called to the platform were strangers to Emma. They appeared shy and withdrawn, obviously the type of folks that preferred to keep to themselves. Straightaway, they walked toward the wan and fragile boy who trailed behind the others. The husband and wife bent to talk with the child, their words inaudible to everyone but him.

"No!" the boy protested, his determined voice ringing out in sharp contrast to his meek demeanor. "I won't go with you. I don't want no new family." Emma leaned forward in her seat, straining to catch the snatches of the ensuing discussion between the boy and Mr. Hill. But she started when Frank nudged her forearm.

"You watch, that boy's gonna be mine," he whispered, beaming like a man who had seen his destiny.

Chapter 4

W hat on earth are you talking about?" Emma sputtered. "That boy obviously has more problems than two parents could hope to handle, let alone one. Besides, I thought you wanted an able-bodied worker to help out on the farm." As the sharp words left her mouth, Emma wondered if she should have voiced them. "I mean, he certainly looks too feeble and peaked to assist anyone in that regard. Why would you want to take on such a child? Really, you are full of more surprises than Katy Greene!"

"I know this sounds strange, comin' from the likes of me," he said with a tinge of mockery lacing his words. "But there is no logic or reason behind my hunches. There's just a certain feelin' deep down inside of me. I believe I could really help that boy. And as for being full of surprises, well, I suppose that's true. There's plenty about me you don't know." Frank tugged at the end of his moustache as he continued. "I am not the heartless monster you insist on making me out to be. This isn't the time or the place to discuss the matter, but I believe that a little hard work ain't goin' to hurt a boy. Fact is, a hard-work ethic might be one of the most valuable things a father could pass on to a son."

Her thoughts a mass of confusion, Emma looked at Frank and then back up to the pasty-faced boy. Although Frank's words were spoken almost tenderly, they echoed the stern sentiment she, as a young girl, had heard her harsh and despised stepfather express many times before.

Emma's own father died in battle during the Civil War, and her mother, left nearly destitute, had remarried Josiah Trumbull when Emma was eight-years-old. From that infamous day until the cold March morning when she finally screwed up the courage to run away, Emma had been forced to work like a slave girl in her own home. Although sympathetic, her fearful mother could only cower in submission and resignation to this tyrannical man. Mr. Trumbull's unwieldy insistence that a child be taught the value of a hard day's work robbed Emma of childhood's simple pleasures, and she grew old long before her time.

Would Frank treat this young boy with the same oppression that she had suffered under Mr. Trumbull's authority? Or was he speaking the truth when he pronounced that he was not the heartless monster that she had surmised him to be? Could Frank show true affection for a child? Emma longed to believe that the latter would be true. The poor boy cowering on the stage didn't appear able to withstand much more trauma in his young life. If any child needed a loving, stable home, it was this pathetic specimen of a child.

Emma found herself hoping that Mr. Hill could convince the boy to go with the reserved couple now looking to take him home. Then Frank would be forced to turn his attentions to one of the other orphan boys. But the melodrama now unfolding on the opera house stage continued as Mr. Hill turned his back on the pathetic waif and addressed the mild-mannered pair loud enough for the first few rows of the audience to hear. "If you don't mind my interference, I believe I know the ideal child for you. First, however, I need to ask. Would you consider a girl, or did you have your hearts set on a boy?"

The wife, twisting a handkerchief nervously, looked up to her husband and shrugged her shoulders in submissive deference to his wishes. "We're open to either, Mr. Hill," the balding man replied, running a hand over his smooth head. "Which child did you have in mind?" At this, Mr. Hill led the couple toward the cluster of twittering girls.

"She seems to be the perfect match for them," Frank whispered when the oldest of the orphan girls meekly nodded her assent to Mr. Hill. She stepped between her new parents and waved a timid good-bye to her friends as they walked off the platform.

That leaves only three girls, Emma figured fretfully. *O Lord. Is one of them going to be mine?* Her crumbling assurance that she was going to become a mother on this day dwindled as Mr. Hill proceeded through the list of married couples, for soon there were two girls remaining on stage. Then only one.

Despite her vested interest, Emma couldn't hold back her tears of joy at the sight of Ty and Rebecca Brownstone walking up to the platform and warmly embracing the last orphan girl. The Brownstones' only daughter, Sarah, had drowned two winters ago, after skating onto thin ice. Ty and Rebecca's acceptance of this orphan girl, who strikingly resembled their Sarah, signified their readiness to recover from their grief and lovingly parent once more.

However, hot tears of disappointment supplanted Emma's tears of joy when the Brownstones escorted their new daughter down the aisle. Emma's final hope for a child exited along with the departure of this last orphan girl. She could not begrudge the Brownstones a fresh start. Nor did she resent any of the other couples who had chosen the other three girls. But how could she have so totally misread the will of God? Emma had felt such a peace in her decision to adopt. Hadn't God given her Psalm 68:6 as her own special promise or sign? Had her secret wishes and desires superseded God's plan for her life? Hadn't her motives been pure?

As her mind filled with more unanswered questions and doubts, Emma whisked away any evidence of tears with the back of her gloved hand. Why would God deny her a child? Why? Hadn't she faithfully served Him and sought His will? Emma ground her teeth and forcefully swallowed the knots of anger nearly choking her. Anger toward God for rejecting her request to be a mother. And, however illogical, anger toward Frank Nance, for his earlier premonition about his child appeared likely to come true.

The auditorium began to quickly empty as the final adoptive couple approached the stage. Standing next to Mr. Hill, the pair faced the five remaining orphan boys. After several long moments of contemplation, they moved closer to the anemic, sour-faced boy who had so vehemently refused to go with the first couple. Perhaps the child's clear need for love and attention was tugging at many hearts. With his arms folded across his chest, the pathetic little urchin once again shook his head back and forth in refusal when Mr. Hill asked him if he wanted to go with the nice gentleman and lady to their home.

"Mr. and Mrs. Fletcher," Mr. Hill's voice echoed through the emptying auditorium, "I sincerely regret the obstinate nature of this boy. Rest assured, I shall have a stern word with him about his behavior today. However, you would surely be happier with one of these other fine and well-mannered young men." The placing agent cast a quick scowl in the direction of the offending youngster as he steered the Fletchers toward another boy.

Seemingly content with their newly matched son, this final couple made their way off the stage. As they left the hall, Mr. Hill stood at the edge of the platform and watched them depart. "Andrew Clymer, I'd like to speak with you over here," he said, motioning with his index finger for the skinny, sad-faced boy to join him. The youth stepped away from the other three boys, who seemed resigned that they had not been chosen this round.

As if he were ensnared in the plot of a classic play, Frank leaned forward, his every attention on the child he had declared would be his.

"Andrew, I don't mind telling you—you try my patience!" His stern but gentle voice floated from the stage, despite his attempts to speak confidentially. Placing his arm around the orphan's shoulder, Mr. Hill tenderly chided the child. "Don't you know, you are only hurting yourself and postponing the inevitable? You should have jumped at the chance to have a new family like the Fletchers. Nice folks like them don't come around at every train stop."

The chastised boy clutched the rim of his new hat as he calculated his response. "I ain't goin' nowhere without my sister, Mr. Hill. Not as long as I have any say."

"Er–um." Clearing his throat, Frank gently touched the top of Emma's hand. The brief pressure of his fingers against hers sent an unexpected tremor of tingles racing up her arm. Since Stanley's death, occasions for even the most casual of physical contact with a man were few and far between. But had she reacted so because a man touched her or because Frank touched her? Blinking in confusion, Emma tried to concentrate on his words.

"Excuse me, ma'am, but could you let me by?" Obviously, Frank had no inkling of Emma's response to his touch, for he focused solely on the boy. "I'd like a chance to speak to that boy and Mr. Hill."

"Certainly." Emma's knees began to tremble uncontrollably and fresh tears welled in her eyes as she shifted in her seat, allowing the preoccupied Frank to pass. "I suppose I should be going now, anyway," she muttered, a wave of loneliness washing over her. Not since the months immediately preceding Stanley's death had Emma felt so bereft. And her growing reaction to Frank Nance only heightened her despair and frustration.

She looked around the large hall to see that only a handful of spectators remained. Emma pulled her caba and the package containing the doll close to her chest in preparation to leave, but the peaks and valleys of emotion she had traversed over the past few days now sapped her strength. Suddenly, she didn't trust her trembling limbs enough to stand. She closed her eyes and drew a deep breath as she waited for her strength to return.

In this reflective moment, Emma's mind replayed a sentence just spoken by the boy being chastised on the stage. *I ain't goin' nowhere without my sister. . .not as long as I have any say.* At once, a strong dose of curiosity dashed aside thoughts of leaving. Her eyes popped open in time to watch Frank approach Andrew and Mr. Hill. What did the boy mean when he said he'd go nowhere without his sister? There were no girls left on the stage. Immediately, Emma recalled something she had dismissed earlier. Mr. Hill said an orphan was sick at the hotel. Was the sick child this boy's sister—a girl? A spark of hope ignited in her soul.

Frank knelt on one knee in front of the child. "Listen, I really think you need to come home with me," he said in the usual straightforward manner, which left Emma wincing in memory of his proposal to her.

"Yes, why don't you try and talk some sense into him," Mr. Hill interjected. "I've talked to him 'til I'm blue in the face, but my words seem to fall on deaf ears."

Rising to his full height, Frank towered over Mr. Hill. The child-placing agent took Frank by the arm and ushered him aside.

Emma leaned forward, straining to hear Mr. Hill's words as a new flood of possibilities caused her palms to moisten with anticipation. Once again, the psalm of promise began a slow etching on her mind. *He setteth the solitary in families.*

"The situation is this," Mr. Hill said, his whisper once again audible from Emma's close vantage point. "Andrew's four-year-old sister, Anna, is the one I mentioned earlier as being so sick. She contracted a nasty case of whooping cough, and we couldn't possibly bring her out in public until her health improves."

The words seemed a command for Emma to rise. Still clutching the box containing the doll, she tiptoed toward the stage in hopes of catching his every word. Evidently there was another orphan. A girl. And her name was Anna. *He setteth the solitary in families.* Her heart pounded ferociously as fresh tears stung her eyes.

Anna. My grandmother's name. Emma mouthed the name again silently. *Anna. O Lord. Is this the girl meant for me?* The prayer wove in and out of Emma's soul as Mr. Hill continued.

"Fact of the matter is, we can't proceed with our journey until she gets better. She might not survive another day on the train. You see how thin young Andrew, here, is?" Emma's gaze followed Frank's and Mr. Hill's as they surveyed the boy. "Well, he's plump as a melon compared to little Anna."

Mr. Hill released Frank's arm and approached Andrew, laying a gentle hand on his shoulder again as he spoke. "We don't like to separate family members if we can help it, but so often we must. Certainly, splitting up siblings and placing them in good homes is preferable to the street urchin's life they would lead in New York City.

"I see no other way but to wait 'til Anna's better and then place her with a family farther on down the line." Mr. Hill slowly shook his head from side to side. "But Andrew's luck is going to run out soon. He's passed up several gracious offers from folks willing to give him a good home. There aren't many couples looking to take on a ten-year-old boy as puny as he is. It sure isn't likely that we can find a family to take both him and Anna into their home."

He setteth the solitary in families. He setteth the solitary in families.

"Might I have a word with you, Mr. Hill?" Emma called out, unable to remain silent a moment longer. What had begun as a prayer and a hunch now blossomed into certainty. Little Anna surely was the child God had meant for Emma all along. Her skirts swished beneath her as she scampered up the stairs onto the stage. "I believe I can recommend a reasonable plan."

Emma's boots tapped loudly against the wooden platform as she hurried forward. Due to the quick traverse onto the stage and her nervousness over this hastily conceived plan, she was short of breath. She put her hand to her heart and gasped as she addressed Mr. Hill. "Why not . . .let–let me. . . take Andrew's sister?" She was finally able to fill her lungs sufficiently to finish the sentence without halting. "And place Andrew with Mr. Nance?"

Emma cast a sideways glance at Frank. From his puzzled look, her atypical behavior had left him mystified for a second time within a morning's span. His bewilderment was understandable. Rarely did she act so impulsively.

In all honesty, she should have discussed the matter with Frank first. For, if they each took a sibling, they would surely be forced to face one another with frequency. In light of their current situation, such regular encounters might prove uncomfortable at best. The varying questions flitting across Frank's face reflected Emma's own thoughts.

Have I given this matter sufficient thought? She had been so confident that this was God's plan that she hadn't even paused long enough to breathe a prayer. Well, she couldn't stop now. Emma would smooth things over with Frank later, if need be.

Nervously grinding her boots into the grit on the stage floor, Emma continued pleading her case with Mr. Hill, not daring to look at Frank. "You see, sir, the two of us are acquaintances, and I'm sure we could come up with a suitable visitation arrangement for the children. We've each been approved to take one child."

Emma rummaged through her purse and pulled out her prized paper, hoping that her sweaty palms didn't cause the ink to run. "See, here's my letter from the committee."

"I think you've come up with a satisfactory plan," Mr. Hill said, giving the proffered document a perfunctory skimming. "No doubt Anna's recovery would be hastened under a mother's care. And if you could manage to take her home today, the rest of us could catch tomorrow morning's train for Dodge City. Still, I'm not the one who needs convincing." He tucked his thumbs under his suspender straps as he turned to face Andrew. "What do you think of this nice lady's idea?"

Before Andrew could object, Frank crouched down and looked the young fellow square in the eyes. "The plan seems perfectly logical to me. Don't you agree? It wouldn't bother you none just havin' me as your paw— and no maw, now would it?"

Andrew shook his head slowly from side to side. "No, sir. I wouldn't mind. I'm used to not havin' no womenfolk around, less'n you count Anna." He threw a sheepish glance in Emma's direction as he explained. "You see, my mama died when little Anna was borned. Then, two years ago, our granny that watched after us joined Mama in heaven, too. That left our papa to take care of us kids the best he could.

"Not havin' a mama don't bother me one bit. Truth is, I kinda take to the idea." Emma caught Andrew warily looking at her once again. "B–b–but. . ." The boy hesitated before speaking his mind. "But, my papa always tol' me that if anything ever happen' to him, I was to watch after my little sister and take good care of her. I always promised him I would. Last March, our papa died whilst savin' me and Anna when our apartment buildin' burnt. So, as long as I'm still breathin', the promise I made my papa is a promise I aim to keep.

"Please don't take no offense," Andrew said, bowing his head submissively before the trio of adults. "I'm not meanin' any disrespect. But I don't see how I can watch after li'l Anna if you split us up."

"Take your time and think things through, young man." Emma sandwiched his right hand between her gloved palms. "You and your sister would live close to one another. Mr. Nance's farm, where you would live, is on the outskirts of town. I live right here in Shady Grove—just a block or so down the street.

"I promise you, little Anna would have a loving home and she'd be a real comfort and companion to me. You see, my husband died a few years back and I've been awfully lonely ever since.

"If you go to live with Mr. Nance on his farm, as he's asking you to do,

I'm sure he'd allow you to visit Anna frequently. Now, wouldn't you, Frank?"

At the casual use of his given name, Emma shot a glance at Frank to see if he'd noticed her slip. His dancing gaze met hers, obviously enjoying this first crossing of verbal propriety. He briskly nodded as a smile tugged at the corner of his lips. "Certainly, Emma," he replied, seeming to take great pleasure in emphasizing her given name. "You know I'd do anything I could to help the boy keep a solemn vow."

Emma turned her attention quickly back to Andrew before Frank could see the color rising in her warming cheeks. If only the man were more. . .were more affectionate and. . .and dedicated to the Lord. . . .

"I'd love your sister, Andrew, and I'd take good care of her," Emma rushed, intent on sweeping those disturbing thoughts about Frank from her mind. "What do you say? Can we at least give it a try?"

Chapter 5

Frank rose from his kneeling position to tower over the boy. He jumped brusquely back into the conversation before Andrew could respond.

"The idea makes good sense to me. Remember, your sister's sick. You don't want her to have to get back on that train again if you can help it, now, do you? And you've no guarantees that a better situation will come along. Might pay you to be reasonable about this. What do you say?"

Frank looked down at his pant legs and began slapping at the dust his knees had gathered while kneeling on the well-traversed stage. "I could sure use a young man such as yourself to help me out on my farm."

Oh, Frank. Hush, will you? Emma wanted to scold him aloud. *Let the boy think things through for himself. Don't you realize that you always push too hard?*

Fresh fears gripped Emma as she watched him talking to the boy. Before her eyes, Frank was rapidly returning to his forever logical and emotionless ways. Perhaps she had acted too hastily in proposing this placing-out plan. For despite the fact that she was gaining a daughter, it also meant that this poor little boy would be going to live with Frank.

In her eagerness to parent his sister, had she sentenced Andrew to a fate worse than orphanage life—a future with a duplicate of her stepfather, Mr. Trumbull? Whatever it took, Emma would not allow such a tragedy to occur. Andrew Clymer didn't know it yet, but if the need arose, he had a formidable ally in her. Then she remembered Frank with that toddler.

Sighing in resignation, Emma hoped Mr. Nance would disprove her concerns.

The boy's ashen face appeared paler still as he bit his lower lip and contemplated the situation. He stared at the floor for several long moments while the adults waited for his reply. With the toe of a new black leather shoe, he kicked at a loose slat in the wood floor and haltingly began. "W–w–well. . .I suppose we might give it a try. Mrs. Watson seems like a nice lady, and bein' as how she's a widow and lonely and all, I know Anna would keep her in good company." Andrew tossed Emma a weak smile before throwing his head back to look up at Frank.

"Mr. Nance, sounds like you could use a hand on your farm. But you'll have to teach me, sir. I ain't had no experience working in the out-a-doors."

"Now, Andrew," Mr. Hill said, "I believe you have made a wise and mature choice. I'm confident you will be very happy with Mr. Nance. But let me remind you, this agreement works two ways. Mr. Nance may decide to return you to our care if you do not behave yourself in a manner befitting a proper young man. Is that understood? You are not to cause this kind man any trouble. Rather, you are to be a help to him."

Mr. Hill turned to Frank and Emma. "An agent from the state will come by Shady Grove to check on all our orphans in a few weeks. After that, we expect to receive a report concerning the children at least twice a year. If there are problems, you may certainly contact us at any time."

"So, the matter's settled then," Frank stated, reaching for the agent's hand and enthusiastically pumping it up and down. "Where's that contract I'm supposed to sign?"

Mr. Hill turned to retrieve the necessary paperwork from a table set up just off the stage, but Andrew called after him, a fresh note of panic in his voice. "Wait. I can't go with Mr. Nance yet. I've got to tell Anna good-bye."

Instinctively, Emma reached out to offer motherly comfort and assurance to the boy, but she stopped and hastily pulled her arm back to her side. The three remaining boys slumped in wooden folding chairs, awaiting instruction from Mr. Hill. Emma understood the nature of young boys well enough. If she were to hug Andrew in front of his friends, the act would thoroughly embarrass him. Instead, she affirmed him with an assuring wink and turned to Frank.

"Mr. Nance, I know you're itching to get back to your farm. Undoubtedly you've got work to do and I hate to impose. . . ." Her voice trailing, she worried that Frank would think she was overstepping her boundaries by meddling once again. But his nod gave her the courage to go on.

"You'd be doing me a real kindness if you'd allow Andrew to be the one to tell Anna of their separate placements before you leave town. Such news would be better coming from him than from a stranger like me—and he'd have a chance to say his proper farewells."

Andrew nodded his appreciation to Emma for interceding on his behalf. And when both Frank and Mr. Hill agreed to her request, she watched the boy's fretful countenance relax.

As soon as all of Frank's and Emma's child-placement legalities had been tended to, Mr. Hill shoved the official documents into an already bulging leather case and prepared to go. Then the rag-tag parade of orphans and adults marched, by twos and threes, down the stage stairs and out the opera house door.

After breathing the fumes of burning kerosene all morning, Emma eagerly filled her lungs with the dry June air as she led the processional toward the Imperial Hotel. Mr. Hill fell into step beside her, followed by Frank and Andrew. The three older orphan boys brought up the rear.

Emma attempted to appear attentive when Mr. Hill launched into a verbose anecdote about a recent adventure on the orphan train. But in actuality, she was straining to catch the conversation between Frank and Andrew as they walked behind her.

Above the squeaks and clatter of passing buggies, Emma could hear Frank answering his new son's rapid volley of questions about life on the farm. By the sound of the boy's interested voice, a transformation was beginning in the sullen child. A smile played at the corners of Emma's lips while she eavesdropped on their amiable conversation. She prayed that all her worries about Frank's coldheartedness were invalid.

This unmarried farmer might very well be the perfect father for the boy after all. Andrew needed someone like Frank—someone to devote undivided attention to him. Emma's smile of pleasure became an inner chuckle as she thought that, perhaps, Andrew might soften Frank's rough edges a bit as well. Surely a ten-year-old could chisel into that granite heart. Teach him how to love. Get him ready for a wife. . . Frank had a long way to go before Emma would reconsider his proposal of marriage, but she'd seen a glimmer of hope in his reaction to Andrew today.

The swinging signboard of the Imperial Hotel came into view, and Emma's pulse pounded in her temples. A marriage of a different sort replaced all thoughts of Frank. For today she and Anna would enter into the union of mother and child. Refusing to succumb to cold feet, Emma had already committed "to have and to hold" Anna as her daughter from this day forward. She had accepted and assumed responsibility for the child—sight unseen.

The anticipated moment of first meeting drew nearer with each clipped step she took down the boardwalk. Soon Emma's dream of a daughter would take on flesh and bone. The group followed Mr. Hill through the Imperial's frosted glass doors, across the lobby, and into the hotel's ornate sitting room. The lavish furnishings and gilded fixtures created an air of opulence that seemed out of place in the prairie town of Shady Grove.

"Miz Watson. . ." Mr. Hill removed his top hat and picked at invisible lint on its brim. "I'd appreciate it if you'd just have a seat for a few minutes and allow me to situate these boys in their rooms. Then, I'll accompany Andrew to his sister's bedside as he shares the news of their placement with her. Someone will come to fetch you soon, ma'am, so you can meet little Anna."

Pushing his bent wire-rimmed spectacles up his nose, the agent's sagging shoulders testified to his fatigue as he turned to address Frank. "I appreciate your patience, sir. I know you're anxious to get your boy home. I don't expect this to take long. Please excuse us." Mr. Hill offered a courteous bow to Emma, then led Andrew and the other boy out of the room.

From across the lobby, Andrew glanced over his shoulder and waved at Frank. The beaming new father returned the gesture as the boy disappeared up the stairs. "Well," Frank said, turning to face Emma, "there's no use in standin' if we can sit. After you." He motioned to two empty chairs beside the grand piano.

Emma perched on the edge of the overstuffed chair and settled her package and purse on the lamp stand as Frank plopped into the seat next to hers. "I'm glad to see that you aren't upset with me for suggesting that I take Andrew's sister. I wasn't sure just how you would respond."

"I thought your idea was a grand one. Why would I have been upset? Fact is, I'm still hopin' you'll reconsider my proposal of marriage. The way I figure, this new connection we share with Andrew and Anna will increase my chances at changin' your mind." He produced an audacious wink that left Emma with no choice but to reach for her lace and whale bone fan and wave it furiously in front of her face.

"Mr. Nance," she said firmly, "there is no reason for you to continue—"

"No reason, Emma?" he teased.

"Really! Would you please—"

"The facts are, ma'am, either you're warmin' up to me or my name's not Frank Nance."

"My feelings for you in no way—"

"So! You do have feelin's for me?"

"I never said that," she insisted, glancing across the lobby at the distracted hotel clerk.

"Well, regardless of what you care to 'fess up to, my offer does still stand."

"So does my rejection! You need to know, Mr. Nance, I am a woman of deep faith. I could never—absolutely never—marry a man who—"

"Hey! I've got faith!"

"But you never darken a church door!"

"I'll go to church if that'll make you happy." He smiled hopefully.

"I'm terribly sorry, but we seem to be miscommunicating in the most severe manner. I'm talking about– about—what I'm tryin to say is–is. . ." She snapped the fan closed.

"Well, go on."

"I would never marry a man who isn't dedicated to the Lord—with his whole heart. I'm talkin' about more than just a shallow acknowledgment that there is a God."

"I'm not a heathen, by no means, Emma," he drawled. "I've been a

Christian since my maw led me to the Lord when I was about Andrew's age."

"But is Christ Lord of your life. . .or are you?" The question settled between them, creating a chasm that she knew would never be removed unless Frank could answer in the affirmative.

With the question left unanswered, Emma walked toward the white marble fireplace. Before turning her back to Frank, she caught him watching her with an esteem she had not previously seen on his countenance. Strangely, she sensed that, for the first time, she had somehow gained Mr. Nance's complete respect. How odd that the very issue that separated them would also deepen his regard. Firmly pivoting away from him, she awaited until Mr. Hill returned.

Regard? Did Frank Nance perhaps care for Emma more than he had admitted?

"Are you ready?" A renewed burst of energy seemed to enthuse the agent as he appeared in the arched doorway. "If so, come on with me. Andrew did a fine job of preparing Anna to go with you. She seems excited about meeting her new mother."

Emma skittered lightly across the lush oriental area rug to grab her beaded handbag and the gingham-wrapped baby doll. Frank rose from his chair while she gathered her things. His dark eyes reflected the sincerity of his apology as he spoke. "I'm sorry about forever bringin' up my proposal. There wasn't any call for my bein' so selfish while you were waitin' to meet your little girl. I hope all goes well for you upstairs. That's the gospel truth."

"Thanks." She glanced up to see those dark eyes spilling forth with words unspoken. And for the first time, Emma admitted to herself what she had desperately wanted to deny. Despite her attempts to voice her dislike of him, Frank Nance had stirred her pulse for many months.

Nervously excusing herself, she joined Mr. Hill in the hotel lobby and forced all thoughts of Frank's proposal from her mind. A lightning bolt of anticipation seemed to shoot through her, and she shivered with giddy energy. She would have taken the stairs two at a time had no one else been watching.

Mr. Hill led the way down the carpeted hall to the door marked 2-D. Without bothering to knock, he turned the brass doorknob and swung the door open wide, then waited for Emma to enter ahead of him. She stepped past him into the austere room to see a thin woman, dressed in black, sitting in a straight-backed chair next to the room's lone window. The weary woman gave Emma a cursory nod in greeting, making no effort to stand.

At the head of the brass bed, holding onto a post, Andrew stood as though guarding royalty. But the sad-faced child Emma had observed at the opera house was gone, replaced by a grinning ten-year-old. "Here she is, Anna," Andrew bent over the bed and exclaimed. "Your new mama. See, I told you she was pretty."

Nothing could have prepared Emma for the breath-catching moment that followed. A knot of emotion clogged her throat. Goose flesh erupted down her arms. Tears blurred her eyes and spilled onto her cheeks. For eyes the color of roasted chestnuts, big and round as coat buttons, now peeked timidly over the top of crisp white sheets. The flush of fever painted rouge-red circles of color on the child's cheeks. A mass of flaxen ringlets framed her china-doll face.

She's the most beautiful little girl I've ever seen, Emma thought as she approached the bed. *And she's my daughter. My child.* Anna reached out to Emma with twig-thin arms and, in that simple act, erased any of the new mother's misgivings about adoption. Emma rooted her maternal bonds the instant she scooped the child into her arms and held her close. As she buried her hands in Anna's curls, she knew she held the miraculous fulfillment of God's promise. The Lord had answered her prayers.

God setteth the solitary in families. The psalm that had become Emma's constant prayer was now her song of celebration. But another scripture verse joined her chorus of praise. Echoing Hannah of Old Testament days, Emma's heart sang, "For this child I prayed; and the LORD hath given me my petition which I asked of him."

Yes, the Lord had surely heard and answered Emma's prayers.

❧

Thirty minutes later, Emma stepped over the threshold of her daughter's bedroom with Frank and Andrew close behind. "This is your very own room, sweetheart," Emma announced to the flushed, fevered child Frank carried in his arms. "I fixed it up just for you."

Anna's dark eyes grew round with wonderment as she surveyed the room. White Irish lace curtains adorned the windows. A cushioned rocker stood in one corner, ready to soothe both mother and child. On the dressing table sat a lace-trimmed basket, brimming with hand-sewn hair ribbons of every hue. The pearl-handled mirror with matching brush and comb looked too pretty to use.

"I'll just pull back these blankets and we'll tuck you right in." Emma turned back the bedding and vigorously plumped a down-filled pillow before motioning to Frank to lay down the child. She wanted to open the bedroom window and circulate the stifling air, but she feared that a breeze, perhaps filled with dust from the road, would aggravate Anna's croup. As they had prepared to leave the hotel, Anna had suffered a severe coughing spell. Emma wanted to avoid a repeat of that painful episode, at all costs. The window remained shut.

Under the watchful eyes of Andrew, Frank gingerly settled the four-year-old between the starched white bed linens. From the end of the bed, Emma shook out a lightweight summer quilt and spread it on top of the sheets. Then, smoothing the covers as she worked her way around the side of the bed, Emma wrapped them snugly around the wisp of a girl so that only her little head poked out.

Beneath the layers of bedclothes, Anna cradled her new doll baby, refusing to relinquish her treasure even momentarily. Emma couldn't resist the urge to brush back the tangled mass of blond curls from Anna's forehead and deposit a feather-light kiss.

Straightening to ease the crick in her back, Emma noticed Andrew standing in the middle of the room, still holding the small parcel of Anna's things. She walked to the boy and extended her hands to accept the twine-tied package.

The curious boy, relieved of his burden, craned his neck to inspect every inch of Anna's new quarters. "She ain't never had no room of her own before," Andrew said as Emma shook out Anna's new dress and hung it in the cedar wardrobe. "Until we went to the orphanage, she always slept with me."

Emma detected a twinge of jealousy over his little sister's good fortune as Andrew posed a question to Frank. "Uh, Mr. Nance, do I get my own room at your place, too?"

In response, Frank reached over and ruffled Andrew's mousy brown hair. "You can take your pick from several rooms on the second floor of the farmhouse. The folks I bought the farm from had a passel of kids, so they built the place real big.

"But, boy, if you keep on referrin' to me as Mr. Nance, you'll be sleepin' in the barn. Why don't you just call me 'Paw'?"

Andrew scratched his head and studied his new shoes. " 'Pahw,' huh?" he said, attempting to mimic Frank's southern twang. "If that's what you want, sir, I'll try."

"Well. . ." Frank hesitated. "You might have to ease into this 'Paw' business. I understand your feelin' awkward and all. Take your time. I won't push you none. And I was just funnin' with you about makin' you sleep in the barn." The laugh lines extending from Frank's eyes creased deeply as he smiled at Andrew.

Watching this bonding interaction between father and son, Emma felt a familiar fire rising in her cheeks and causing her palms to perspire. But the frustration and anger she had once felt in Frank's presence didn't cause this flood of warmth. This heat stemmed from her happy surprise in seeing again—as she had on several occasions throughout the day—a pleasantly different side of Frank. Emma longed for Frank to understand what she was trying to tell him in the hotel lobby.

"All this talk about home reminds me that there's plenty of work waiting for us at the farm," Frank stated, ushering Andrew toward the door. "The cows will be beggin' for milkin' soon. You'd best be tellin' your sister good-bye.

"Emma. . .er. . .Miz Watson. . ." He paused to expose her to humorous scrutiny.

Her cheeks warming, Emma needlessly fussed with Anna's covers.

"Unless there's somethin' else you're needin' from us, we'll see ourselves out."

She glanced up just in time to see Andrew instantly tense at the

113

pronouncement of his imminent separation from Anna. "Wait!" Emma blurted, desperate to ease the boy's fears. "None of us have had a chance to eat lunch yet, and I left a pot of beef stew warming on the stove this morning. I can throw a meal together in a matter of minutes. It's the least I could do since you've been so kind to carry Anna home from the hotel and all."

Frank lifted his head and sniffed at the air. "I've been smellin' your cookin' since I walked in the door. I was hopin' you'd ask us to stay. Andrew, why don't you look after your sister for just a bit while I help Miz Watson set the table for dinner."

"I've got an even better idea," Emma interjected. "Let's prepare meal trays for us all. We can eat right here in Anna's room, so she won't need to be left alone."

"Lead the way, ma'am." Frank waved his arm in grandiose fashion, pointing to the open door. "Or would you rather I just follow my nose?"

Preceding Frank into the kitchen, Emma walked straight to the cupboard and began pulling soup bowls from the shelf. As she placed them on the counter next to the potbellied stove, Frank stepped beside her and lifted the lid from the iron soup kettle. A cloud of fragrant steam escaped into the air. Inhaling deeply, he leaned over to Emma and asked, "What can I do to help?"

When he spoke, her hands traitorously quivered as she spooned stew into the bowls. Emma had not been alone in a room with a man these past three years. She was far from prepared for the rush of growing excitement Frank's presence evoked. In the hotel lobby, he expressed his suspicion of her reaction to him, and just knowing that he suspected made her quiver all the more. Emma reminded herself that just two days ago she had stormed out of his presence, hoping never to see him again. But had she really desired to rid her life of Frank?

She handed him the soup ladle, resisting the urge to look into his eyes, lest her renewed resolve disintegrate. "You can take over this chore, if you don't mind. I need to slice up some bread."

In the moments that followed, Emma scurried about the kitchen collecting the makings of an impromptu feast. On one tray, she placed the soup bowls and a crockery pitcher of buttermilk. On another, she precariously piled plates of thick slices of cheese, sourdough bread spread with strawberry jam, and a molasses pie. While she worked, she chattered incessantly, reliving the day's Christmas-like excitement, leaving no opportunity for Frank to comment. At all costs, she couldn't allow him to suspect her vulnerability.

Within half an hour, Frank and Andrew sat on the homemade rag rug in the middle of Anna's room and crisscrossed their legs in preparation for their indoor picnic as Emma arranged the trays next to them. When she announced that she would offer grace, the ten-year-old sheepishly dropped the cheese he held halfway between the plate and his mouth. And although she had a lengthy list of blessings for which she wanted to give thanks to the Lord, she kept her prayer brief. She didn't want to torture the young boy.

Emma watched in amazement as the scrawny Andrew inhaled his meal. Judging by the way he attacked his food, he hadn't eaten his fill in quite a while. Frank protested when the boy grabbed the last piece of bread, but he consoled himself with a generous slice of pie.

"Save some appetite, son," Frank teased the boy. "I'm roastin' you an elephant for supper and I'll be expectin' you to eat it all." Andrew, whose face was buried behind his bread, stopped eating just long enough to confirm that Frank's words were spoken in jest.

"You keep eating like that and I'll stay busy making you bigger clothes." Emma chuckled.

"You're a good cook, ma'am." Andrew wiped the jam from his mouth with the sleeve of his shirt. "I ain't eaten this good since our granny died."

Unfortunately, Emma's efforts to feed Anna were not met with Andrew's same measure of success. The infirmed child allowed her new mother to spoon-feed her only three bites of stew before she pursed her lips together and refused to eat more.

When the meal had been consumed and Andrew had all but licked the plates dry, Frank stood to his feet. "Andrew and I will carry these trays back to the kitchen for you, then we'd better be gettin' home. The boy's right, though, Emma. You are a great cook."

Despite the pleasure his praise evoked, Emma refused to look directly at Frank, for fear of repeating her earlier heart-fluttering reaction. She rose from Anna's bedside and stacked the bowl of barely-touched stew on top of the other dirty dishes. "Perhaps you and Andrew could come for dinner after church a week from Sunday? Lord willing, Anna should be better by then." *And I'll have my emotions back under control,* she added silently.

"Yeah, I be better then." Anna's hoarse whisper floated from the feather bed, soliciting smiles from all the others in the room. But even this brief attempt to contribute to the conversation brought on a fit of barking coughs. Emma hurried to her side and, scooping the child into her arms, began rocking Anna back and forth.

After several long seconds of violent crouping, Anna began gasping for air. Emma looked at Frank for assurance, but instead saw genuine concern in his face.

"I'd best be gettin' Doc Gilbert, don't you think?" The rhetorical question needed no answer, for he and Andrew were already headed for the door.

Chapter 6

P oor little thing is weaker than a kitten, Mrs. Watson. She's so worn out from coughin' that she fell fast asleep in the middle of my examination." Dr. Gilbert softly closed the door to Anna's bedroom and joined the anxious trio of Emma, Frank, and Andrew in the hallway.

"That croup of hers does sound mighty bad. I expect you're gonna fret over every coughin' spell, seein' as you're a new mama and all." Shady Grove's aged physician stroked his bushy gray beard as he spoke. "But listen to me and believe me when I say, I'm sure the child is goin' to pull through, what with your good nursin' and attention.

"There are several things you can do to help her." The doctor's soothing voice took on a serious tone as he rattled off his list of instructions. "First off, soon as I leave I want you to hang a wet sheet near her bed to put moisture into the room. That should help control her cough. And, don't let her lie flat. Keep her propped up so her airways are clear. One good way to do this is to hold her and rock her. You probably wouldn't mind that, now would you?"

The doctor set his black leather bag on the hall runner and stooped to fumble through its contents. "Now, she will likely fight you over it, but you must persist. I want you to give the young'un a teaspoon of this elixir every time she starts a coughin' spell." He pulled the cork stopper and passed the bottle under Emma's nose. "I want you to smell it 'fore I leave it with you, because most folks think it's ruined when they get their first whiff."

117

She jerked her head back instantly, her eyes watering at the pungent stench.

"Hey, let me smell," Andrew said, boyish curiosity oozing from him. The doctor obliged his request and all the adults laughed aloud at his sour face. "Cowboy howdy!" he exclaimed. "I hope I don't never get sick."

The doctor resealed the dark glass container and handed it to Emma. "I know it smells powerful bad. Made it myself from onions, garlic, paregoric, and spirits of camphor mixed in with honey, and I know the potion works. Other than this, the only other medicine I can recommend is time. The cough should run its course in a few days."

Emma stuffed the amber bottle of cough syrup into her apron pocket as the physician picked up his bag and prepared to leave.

"We'll follow you out, Doc," Frank said. "I need to get the boy settled and tend to my chores.

Pinching the crown of his felt hat between his finger and thumb, he politely tipped the headpiece toward Emma before donning it. "Andrew and I will see you a week from Sunday for lunch, if your offer still stands."

"Certainly," she replied. "I'll save you two a place on our pew at church as well. Service begins at ten-thirty."

"Well. . ." His lips formed into a stubborn line. "I'll make certain the boy is there."

So that's it. That's your answer, Emma thought, while gritting her teeth. He had not fully answered her questions about his relationship with the Lord in the Imperial Hotel's lobby. Until now. And the obstinate tilt of his square chin suggested that Frank Nance wouldn't bow at an altar in prayer for any woman.

That's all fine by me, Emma thought as Frank and his son stepped onto her massive porch. *If and when you do decide to give your all to the good Lord, it needs to be something for yourself, not for me.* Nonetheless, the dull ache in Emma's spirit attested to her keen disappointment.

But no sooner had she shut the door on her three visitors than a sole, painful cough rang through the house, dispelling all thoughts of Frank's infuriating ways. She paused briefly, her back against the door, and took a deep cleansing breath. Emma's prayers had been answered. She was a

118

mother now. But did she have the skills necessary to nurse such a sickly, frail child? Pinpricks of fear stabbed ever so lightly at Emma's euphoria.

Holding her breath against the hope that there would be no new coughs, she peeked around the door into Anna's bedroom. The wisp of a child had awakened and was sitting up in her bed, stroking her doll's hair. Her daughter. This precious little girl with big brown eyes—her daughter. Anna's soft voice would soon call her "Mama." The two of them would share the same family name.

Had only a few hours lapsed since Emma first laid eyes on her? The thought seemed odd as she surveyed this heartwarming scene. Anyone would think, to look at Anna now, that the little princess had always ruled from this quilted throne.

One week later, Frank leaned against the front porch railing and finished his morning cup of coffee as Andrew crossed the barnyard to begin his morning chores. In just a week's time, he had seen tremendous changes in the boy. Thanks to Maria's starchy Mexican dinners and the hours they'd spent together outdoors doing chores, Andrew no longer looked sickly-pale and starvation-thin. Emma was sure to be surprised when they showed up for lunch the day after tomorrow. The imagined scene left Frank smiling in amusement. He derived certain pleasure at the prospect of proving to Emma that a few days' work did any boy a good service.

Frank looked forward to Sunday afternoon for other reasons as well. He wanted Andrew to see for himself that Anna was all right. Despite the growing camaraderie he and Andrew shared, Frank knew the boy worried about his sister constantly. Several times throughout the course of a day, Andrew would turn to him and ask how he thought Anna was getting along. Seldom had he witnessed such fierce loyalty in grown men, much less a child. His devotion to his sister constituted more than a deathbed promise made to his father that he was honor-bound to fulfill. Andrew obviously cared deeply for Anna. Yes, for the boy's sake, he was anxious for Sunday to come around.

But Frank wouldn't be honest if he didn't admit that he was anxious for Sunday to arrive for his own sake as well. Over the past week, when he'd lain down to sleep, a pleasant memory replayed over and over in his mind. Miz Emma Watson had been nothing short of flustered in his presence since that meeting in the general store. And Frank was beginning to look back on their yearlong acquaintance and suspect that she might have been trying to hide her true feelings for quite some time.

However, a new problem now surfaced with the fair lady. She said she wanted a man who was more committed to the Lord. At first, her comments had amused him. Then, they had angered him. How dare she be his spiritual judge? But now, her words had grown into a recurring mantra in his mind and left him less than comfortable. The truth of the matter was, he knew he could do better by the Lord. Much better. And now that Andrew had come along, the boy deserved the same kind of religious upbringing Frank had been given. But he just wasn't certain he was ready to turn the whole thing over to the Lord. He was nice and comfortable keeping the Lord at arm's length.

Tossing the cold dregs of his coffee into the cracked dry ground next to the porch, he stood and dismissed the disturbing thoughts. *We could sure use some rain*, Frank said to himself as he studied the morning sky. The wispy, streaked clouds didn't hold much promise of breaking this insufferable hot and dry spell. Scanning the horizon, Frank was seized by a strong sense of foreboding for a peculiar gray haze enveloped the western wheat fields. At once, Frank noticed the faint, unpleasant acrid smell that always accompanied a distant fire. His gut twisted in dread. He had heard that a plague of grasshoppers had turned the skies black over Colorado, leaving devastated crops in their wake. But grasshoppers did not produce such a smell. Frank decided to investigate.

Just then, Andrew emerged from the chicken coop and began scattering feed. Frank paused a few moments more to watch his son. The boy's shoes quickly disappeared beneath the brood of bantam chickens as the birds pecked frantically at the seed, their red combs bobbing feverishly. "You've been cornered by chickens, son." Frank laughed with a father's pleasure, and Andrew waved happily to his pa.

Feeding the chickens had become one of Andrew's favorite chores, for when he was done he could hold the cheeping chicks that filled a warming tray just inside the hen house door. Frank had long ago forgotten how much fun such simple pleasures could bring a boy. He had caught himself laughing and smiling more in the past few days than he had in many years. A boy was good for a man's soul.

Suddenly, the gravelly bark of a coonhound in the barnyard shattered the early morning quiet to announce the arrival of a visitor. Frank stepped off the front porch and waved in greeting to a worried-looking man mounted on a sweating, stamping horse. After a brief exchange of words that confirmed Frank's former suspicions, the rider turned his horse, spurring the animal into a full gallop as he rode toward the rising sun.

"Andrew, come here, boy. I need to talk with you." Frank, his stomach clutching ever tighter, didn't wait for the puzzled child to catch up with him. Instead, he hurried into the barn and set about the task of saddling Shadow. Andrew was panting by the time he reached the busy stall.

"Listen, there's a grass fire threatenin' to destroy the Taylor farm, and they're roundin' up as many neighbors as they can to help fight the blaze. I've got to go and see what I can do to help. What with this confounded drought and all, if the Good Lord doesn't help us, them hungry flames will soon spread onto our own land.

"Oh, and Andrew, I realize you don't speak Spanish, and Señor and Señorita Ramirez's English ain't too good. But when they get here, do your best to explain things to them. Draw pictures if you have to, but the smoke should speak for itself. I expect Pedro will come and help us as soon as he gets the word. I don't have time to gab about it. I'll be home just as soon as I can. Maria will watch after you when she arrives. Until then, you are to stay here and tend to your chores, do you hear? I don't need to be worryin' about you on top of everything else."

"Yes, sir. I understand. Don't you fret about me. I'll be just fine."

Andrew watched until Frank rode Shadow over the horizon, then he turned and walked slowly back toward the chicken coop to complete the first of his unfinished chores. The warm prairie wind blew the smell of smoke into the barnyard. A rush of painful memories seized him as, in his mind's eye, he saw his father rushing back into the burning apartment to rescue Anna. Was he to lose another father to the flames? Did some kind of curse follow him?

And what of the fire? Would it spread into town and perhaps burn the Widow Watson's seamstress shop? His father's dying words now haunted him: *Watch after your little sister. Take good care of her.* Yet his new pa's words seemed a direct contradiction to his duty: *You are to stay here and tend to your chores, do you hear? I don't need to be worryin' about you on top of everything else.*

But if he stayed at the farm, Anna might die in the fire. What had he done, allowing a stranger lady to take on his responsibility while he'd headed off to play on the farm? He must check on Anna. Now. When last he'd seen her, Anna had been frightfully sick.

Chapter 7

The fidgeting Anna danced in front of the full-length mirror as Emma attempted to pin a straight hem into her swaying full skirt. "Honey child, please!" she begged, licking a bead of blood from her pinpricked finger. "Hold still for just a minute more."

"But, Mama, I'm pretendin' to be a princess. I can't wait for Andrew to see my new dress." When Emma sat back on the floor, the pinning job sufficiently complete, Anna began twirling around the seamstress shop until the stiff taffeta floated on air.

Anna had surprised them all with her strong will to recover from whooping cough. Each day, she spent more and more time out of bed, and the doctor was calling it nothing short of a miracle. Today, only an occasional cough remained. So for the past day, Emma and Anna had been excitedly making plans for Sunday and the child's first public appearance. Their initial item of business had been to make Anna new clothes for the occasion. A remnant piece from Emma's emerald green taffeta dress proved large enough to piece together a matching "coming out" frock for Anna's first time at church.

No doubt, Katy Greene would twitter that such an outfit for a child was frivolous. And, no doubt, Katy's words would be true. Still, there were times that called for more than a little frivolity.

"Hallo, Anna? You in there?" a voice warily called through the opened window.

Emma and Anna paused to exchange a nonplused stare. "Andrew, is that you?" Emma asked, hurrying toward the window.

"Yes'm," Andrew said, shuffling his feet. His dark eyes brimming with concern, he stuffed his hands into the pockets of his work britches. "I was worried 'bout Anna—"

"Andrew!" Anna squealed from behind.

"Come to the front door," Emma said.

As she opened the door and the boy hesitantly stepped into the parlor, Emma wondered where Frank might be. She scanned the street, bustling with the usual early morning activity, but saw no sign of the boy's father. At once, her heart twisted with a twinge of concern and perhaps a touch of regret at his absence.

Before Emma could interrogate Andrew, Anna ran from across the room and threw her arms around his neck. "Andrew, I'm all better now. And my mama made me a new dress." A slight cough followed her words, and Emma patted the child's back, hoping the excitement over seeing her brother wouldn't instigate a coughing spell.

"That's good news, young'un," Andrew said, tousling her hair. "I was worried about you. That's why I came around." He cast a shamefaced look toward Emma before bowing his head. "I hope you aren't too mad at me, ma'am. I didn't mean to startle you none."

"Where's your pa?" Emma glanced out the door once more to verify Frank's absence as new thoughts whirled through her mind. Had the boy run away because Frank worked him too hard?

"He don't know I'm here. The neighbor's fields were afire and he took off on Shadow to offer his help. That smell of smoke made me want to see Anna somethin' fierce." He drew his sister close to his side. And, despite the boy's attempt at bravado, Emma noticed his bottom lip quivering while he spoke. "I snuck off 'fore Pedro and Maria arrived for work, and if I don't make it back home before Pa gets there, I reckon there'll be grief to pay."

"You're probably right about that, but I'm not about to let you out of my sight. You can't just go traipsing around the countryside—not without your pa knowing your whereabouts and especially if there's a fire. I don't care if you are all of ten years old." As she looked the boy up and down, she inwardly praised Frank for the healthy changes: the glow of his cheeks, the noticeable weight gain, and his fresh-scrubbed cleanliness. Perhaps Frank Nance was a better father than Emma ever imagined.

His year-old proposal became an undeniable possibility in Emma's spirit as she fussed over starting breakfast for Anna and Andrew. Certainly, if Frank were such a good father, he might easily be a good husband. Her heart palpitated at such a rate that Emma could barely stir the hotcake batter. Her previous concerns that Frank might be like her stepfather began to melt like wax before the fires of respect. Andrew showed no signs of being overworked and under-loved—something Emma had readily sensed in a child on more than one occasion. On the contrary, Andrew seemed to be blossoming under the care of his new father.

With all the discretion she could muster, Emma tried to pry more information from the boy as she worked at the stove. She desperately wanted to verify her assumptions as fact. She asked about their daily routine and the chores that he'd been assigned, looking for the slightest hint of Josiah Trumbull tyranny. But young Andrew was full of nothing but praise for his new father. He held Frank Nance in highest esteem. And Emma was certainly beginning to think Frank deserved his son's admiration. Wistfully, she envisioned the four of them as a family.

O Lord, she prayed. *Is there anything I might say to make Frank realize his need of a deeper walk with You?*

All morning, Emma prayed that prayer. And by the noon hour, she had certainly begun to pray for other concerns as well. Frank still had not come after Andrew. While she understood that Frank didn't actually know Andrew's location, Emma also figured he would start looking for the boy at her house. Even though the task of fighting a fire was certainly time-consuming, she was beginning to worry about Frank. Andrew had lost one father in a blazing inferno; surely God wouldn't allow him to lose another. Her soul trembled in dread as she tried to stay yet another of Andrew's questions about his father's absence. Instead, she directed the children back to the spacious kitchen to sit at the sturdy oak dining table.

She had no sooner set the plates of beans and cornbread in front of the children than pounding resounded from the front door. She caught her breath, wondering if Frank were the visitor.

"That's probably Pa," Andrew said, his eyes bright with expectation.

"Probably," she said, her heart singing with hope. After removing her apron, she tucked stray strands of hair back into her chignon. The more she encountered Frank, the more Emma fretted with her appearance. Just before opening the door, she pressed her lips together, hoping she wasn't unusually pale after her long days and nights of nursing Anna while trying to keep abreast of her sewing schedule.

But when she opened the door, all concern for her appearance vanished. A gasp slipped from her lips at the sight of the soot-covered man who stood on her spacious porch. If Emma hadn't expected him, she would not have recognized Frank. All the hair had been singed from his face. The lack of eyebrows and lashes added to his wild-eyed look of terror. He held his hands cautiously in front of him, exposing several blistered burns.

"Andrew's missing," he blurted, forgoing salutations as he stepped inside. "He's nowhere to be found at the farm, and Pedro said he's not seen hide nor hair of him. Is he here by chance?" Frank craned his neck to look past Emma. He seemed oblivious to his serious injuries. His only concerns were for his son.

"Yes, he's here. And he's fine," she replied, touching his forearm in concern. "But you don't look as if you are. We must send for Doc Gilbert to care for your burns."

"I'll see the doctor in good time," he said, stepping past her. "I've got more important matters to tend to first. I'd like to take a gander at Andrew, just to set my mind at ease. Then, if you don't mind, I need a private word with you."

Turning, he paused long enough to expose her to a pleading gaze. She caught her breath, wondering exactly what Frank had in mind. She had made her conditions clear in the parlor of the Imperial Hotel. Could it be that Frank had at last understood his need of a total surrender to the Lord? Emma had prayed for exactly that all morning!

Her mind whirling with the implications of the moment, Emma led the way back to the kitchen and watched as Frank crouched slowly and painfully on one knee next to Andrew's chair. For several long moments, he stared intently at the gaping boy. "You had me scared spitless!" Overcome with emotion, Frank closed his eyes tight.

Andrew's lips shook. "I'm sorry, Pa." He flung his arms around Frank's neck. "I know you tol' me not to go, but. . ."

Although Frank winced painfully, he did not discourage the boy's affection. Instead, he gingerly rested his burned hands against Andrew's back.

"The fire!" Andrew continued. "I was worried ta death it was gonna spread to town and kill Anna. And now you. . .you. . .you've been burned up, just like our papa!" Andrew choked on a sob. "Please don't die. . .don't die! I promise. . .I promise, I won't never run off again."

Emma pressed her fingers against her trembling lips and rushed toward Anna, now fretting because of her brother's outburst. She scooped Anna from one of the sturdy oak chairs and held her close. "Don't worry, little one," she crooned. "Everything is fine."

"Andrew's cryin'," she whined. "His pa is all burned up."

"Yes, but he's okay. Everything is fine."

The budding love expressed by father and son dashed aside any remaining doubts that Frank Nance was indeed a wonderful father. . .that he would indeed be an exceptional husband. The man had at last begun to allow Emma to see his true emotions. *O Lord, if only he would let down the barriers with You.* Certainly, Emma realized that these boundaries Frank had erected between himself and others were the very boundaries that were keeping him at a distance with God.

At last, Frank assured Andrew that all would be well and he was indeed fine. After a quarter hour of Frank's calm and assuring words, Andrew finally turned his attention back to the beans and cornbread. Frank grimaced as he rose to face Emma. "Do you think Andrew can look after Anna here in the kitchen for a short spell so you and I can visit in the parlor? There's somethin' I'm needin' to get off my chest."

"Don't you think we should at least put some salve on those burns first?" she asked, settling Anna in front of her noon meal. "I keep a jar right here next to my stove." Chattering nervously, she riffled through the cabinet next to the potbellied stove in search of the illusive ointment. "Seems like I'm constantly splattering grease on myself," she said, barely able to concentrate on the words tumbling from her lips. For all she could think of was Frank, standing so close to her. Despite herself, she began to wonder what it would feel like to have his arms around her. Was he about to restate his proposal? And if he did not profess a renewed love for the Lord, did she have the spiritual strength to refuse him?

As Emma continued in search of the elusive salve, a tense silence settled between them, and she began an internal, heavenward plea. *O Lord, give me the courage to stay with my decision, despite the fact that I. . .that I think I am fall–falling in love with him.*

"The salve can wait a few more minutes," Frank insisted from close behind.

Emma stilled. Her heart pounded. Her palms moistened.

"This is important, and I don't reckon it will take too long."

Swallowing, Emma silently turned from her task and moved toward the parlor, not daring to look into his eyes. A quick glance over her shoulder proved Anna and Andrew still sufficiently distracted by their meal. All the while she walked toward the parlor, Emma prayed for courage and strength and wisdom. She paused beside the French doors and watched as Frank walked toward the front window, complemented by lace curtains. A tense silence followed, and Emma knew that Frank Nance was deeply troubled.

"Old Man Taylor lost his life today," he said. "And I came close to losin' mine." Frank pivoted to face her. "We had formed a bucket brigade and were attempting to douse the flames of his burning barn when a support beam gave way, sending a portion of the barn roof down on top of us and buryin' Mr. Taylor in flame. I had the wind knocked out of me for a time. As quick as I could, I tried to rescue the old man, but to no avail."

Wearily, he rubbed at his blackened forehead with the back of his wrist. "During those moments everythin' you said to me at the Imperial Hotel started to make a heap of sense. All I could think was that I was really livin' my life for me and. . ." He paused to swallow. "And how far from the Lord I had strayed. . .and just how much I. . .I love you, Emma." His words came out on a broken whisper.

Her eyes filling with tears, Emma laid a trembling hand against her chest.

"And if you want the gospel truth, I think I've been in love with you for a good deal longer than I ever wanted myself to know it." He closed the distance between them and reached to touch her cheek, only to wince with renewed pain.

"We need the doctor—"

"No. Not until I've had my say. I prayed all the way from the farm for two things: that Andrew would be here and that you'd...you'd reconsider my proposal. This time, I can promise you, I don't have a single convenience in mind, Miz Watson." His pain-filled eyes produced a mischievous twinkle. "And I can also promise you that the Lord has grabbed my attention and I've done my business with Him." He paused to hold her gaze, his eyes revealing a sincere man. "This isn't any religion of convenience either. The Lord has taken hold of me like He never has before."

Tears trickling from the corners of her eyes, Emma nodded in understanding.

"If only you could find it in your heart to try to love me—"

"Oh, Frank. . ." Emma choked on a sob. "I think I've been on the verge of falling in love with you for months. And all morning I've prayed you'd say just what you've said. I—"

Emma's words were cut off by Frank's whoop of joy and his lips pressed firmly against hers. And in that moment Emma once again understood what it felt like to be madly in love with a man. . .and to have a man madly in love with her.

❧

In the hallway, Andrew, holding his sister's hand, peeked into the parlor to see his pa and Anna's ma kissing. "Yuck!" he whispered. Turning to Anna, he wrinkled his nose.

A soft giggle escaped Anna. "I like your pa."

Dashing aside his aversion to the grown-ups' kiss, Andrew picked up his sister and twirled her around. "Good! 'Cause it looks like he's gonna be your pa, too!"

Epilogue

C risp autumn air swept off the Kansas prairie and down Church Street as Andrew and Anna clambered up the wooden steps leading into the white frame church. "Whoa. Wait up, you two," Frank called after them. "Give your ol' paw and mama a chance to catch up."

"Anna, did you say hello to the reverend?" At her father's prompting, the just-turned-five-year-old curtsied politely to the pastor, then wiggled her first loose tooth for him to see. In the meantime, Andrew had already escaped inside.

"Mornin', Reverend Barnhart." Frank removed his hat and extended his right hand, still pink and scarred from the June fire. "We've got us a beautiful day to worship!"

"I do believe you'd say the same in the midst of a cyclone, Frank. I hope you never lose your enthusiasm for serving the Lord!"

"Seein' as how He's blessed me, I'd be a lowdown skunk if I didn't give Him praise." Before he could expound any further, Anna reappeared from a brief sojourn into the inner recesses of the sanctuary and grabbed both Frank and Emma by a sleeve.

"Come on, Mama, Pa. Church is gettin' ready to start and Andrew's savin' us a seat right down front." Frank's eyes crinkled in quiet laughter, and he exchanged a look of parental pride with Emma while Anna dragged them down the center aisle.

When the Nance family had situated themselves on the second pew, Emma gently nudged Frank and nodded for him to look at the children.

He turned his head toward Andrew just in time to see the boy playfully stick his tongue out at his little sister. Before Frank could interfere with this sibling squabble, Emma leaned over and whispered into his ear. "Seeing him act like a kid does my heart good; how about you?"

Emma secretly intertwined her fingers in Frank's as he offered to share a hymnal during the opening song. Then, Andrew and Anna, Emma and Frank joined their voices in heavenly harmony while the congregation sang,

"Blest be the tie that binds
Our hearts in Christian love;
The fellowship of kindred minds
Is like to that above."

Amen.

A HOMESTEADER, A BRIDE, AND A BABY

by JoAnn A. Grote

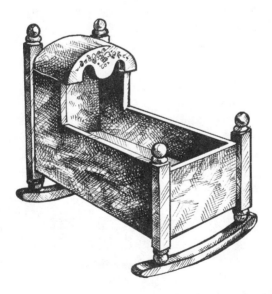

Dedication

To my grandniece and grandnephew,
Alexis Olsen
and
Brett Olsen
who are descended from Minnesota pioneers

Chapter 1

Minnesota prairie, 1878

I didn't even have a chance to say good-bye."

The prairie wind snatched away the whispered words as soon as they left Lorette Taber's lips. The ever-present breeze swept through the tall prairie grasses that surrounded the four fresh graves, as though asking, "Why are their deaths more important than those of the thousands of other creatures I've seen die in this land?"

The wind whipped waving strands of prairie grass around the simple wooden crosses that stood at the heads of the graves. *Already reclaiming Bess and Tom and swallowing up their dreams for this place,* Lorette thought.

The earthy smell of freshly turned graves and wild grasses, the rough untamed land beneath her feet, the forlorn whistle of unceasing wind, all joined in concert to punctuate nature's power and man's helplessness in attempting to conquer these lands.

Viney stems of tiny pale pink wild roses were wrapped about each cross. The meaning of their presence came through the fog of Lorette's loss and pain. Someone else missed her sister and family.

The child in her arms stirred, rubbing his eyes against the shoulder of her once-crisp blue traveling suit. He uttered tentative cries, pausing briefly between each, waiting to see whether the comforting presence of the parents for whom he longed would be given before he began crying in earnest.

Lorette's heart crimped. She rubbed one hand lightly over the nine-month-old baby's back, pressed her cheek gently against his soft, short baby hair, and murmured, "Poor Samuel. Your mommy and daddy still love you. They'll always love you. You'll never be alone, I promise. I'll always be with you."

Her eyes blurred. Could Samuel comprehend that he'd never see his parents and older brother and sister in this world again? Of course he was too young to understand their deaths in terms of logic and words, but did his infant spirit sense his loss in some mysterious way known only to God? Over the last twenty-four hours, had he felt abandoned by the four people who had cared for him all of his short life?

"Miss Taber?"

At the sound of a man's deep voice, she swung around, pulling Samuel protectively closer. She didn't answer, only stared at the blond man whose steady gray gaze met hers.

The wind didn't blow away the powerful odor of dirt, sweat, and kerosene emanating from him. He wore the flour sack shirt and heavy denim trousers of a farmer. A wide soft-brimmed hat, a sweat ring about the crown, hung from one hand.

"I'm Chase Lankford, your sister's neighbor. I helped out on their farm some."

A bit of tension left her muscles at his gentlemanly manner and the knowledge of his name. "Bess mentioned you in her letters. She said you were a good friend to her and her husband."

He nodded once, briskly. "Yes, Miss. They were good people. I'm sorry for your loss."

Samuel pushed himself away from Lorette with his tiny fists, then with pudgy arms outstretched leaned toward Chase. "Uh. Uh."

His sudden, unexpected movement threw Lorette out of balance. She leaned with him, attempting to adjust her hold.

Chase grabbed him. "Careful there, big boy."

Lorette caught her breath as she watched him swing the baby to his side. She started to reach for Samuel, hesitated, then let her hands drop to her sides. Chase looked comfortable with the child, she realized, as though he'd held Samuel many times.

Watching them, Lorette pushed from her blue eyes a strand of black hair, which the wind had tugged from the thick figure eight at the back of her head. She thought it a wonder the wind hadn't blown off her dainty traveling hat.

Chase lifted Samuel until their eyes were on the same level and grinned. Samuel grinned back. Giggling, he touched his round little fingers to Chase's unshaven cheeks.

Lorette smiled. Obviously Samuel and Chase were friends, the boy happy with someone he knew. Her heart ached with the thought that Chase might be the only person left whom Samuel truly knew.

She turned back to the graves, blinking away tears. "It's so hard to believe they are gone. I got off the train expecting them to meet me. Instead I was met by a woman I didn't know who told me they were dead and handed over Samuel." She spoke painfully around the lump that had formed in her throat. "Diphtheria, she said."

Lorette was aware he stepped up beside her, that he swallowed as though he had a lump in his own throat. "Yes, diphtheria."

"It was so sudden. How could it happen so fast?"

"At first they thought they only had sore throats. When Bess and Tom realized that their sickness was more serious, Tom went after the doctor. Doc was miles out in the country on the other side of town on a call. By the time Tom found him, Tom was so weak himself from the diphtheria that Doc insisted he stay where he was while Doc came here. He was too late. Aaron and Liza, Bess and Tom's oldest children, were already dead. Bess died within hours. Tom never made it home again. He died at the farmhouse where he found Doc."

"Samuel never took the disease?"

"Hasn't shown any signs of it. Doc thinks the others caught it through contaminated milk, and Sam wouldn't have had any, him being. . ." Chase's tan took on a dusky tint.

Him being still at his mother's breast, Lorette completed silently, feeling her own cheeks heat.

"Bess had her hands full taking care of herself and the sick children,"

Chase continued, "so Kari Bresven offered to care for Sam until they were better."

"She was the one who met me at the railway station."

"Yes."

"Why couldn't the funeral have waited until I arrived? They only died yesterday."

"The bodies had to be buried right away to keep others from getting sick."

"I didn't even get to say good-bye." Her voice broke. Sobs welled up inside her, forcing their way through her chest and throat. She pressed a hand to her mouth, desperate to hold back what she feared would be a flood. A shaky gasp escaped.

A curious frown drew Samuel's blond eyebrows together. The fingers that had been playing with the top button of Chase's shirt stopped, and Samuel stared at her. She turned away, not wanting the boy to see her break down. "P–please, may I have a few minutes alone?" The strangled sobs mixed with her words, and she wasn't sure Chase could understand her.

She was relieved when he said, "Sure. Sam and I will be waiting in the yard."

Soft swishing sounds told her Chase was walking away through the tall grass. Lorette sank to the ground beside the black dirt covering her sister's grave. "Oooh, Bess!" Realization of her loss cramped her stomach. She wrapped her arms about her middle, bent into the pain, and let her sobs flow onto the prairie winds.

❦

Lorette hesitated at the yard's edge and surveyed the house. The two-story white frame building was simple in design. It looked like many others she'd seen in the nearby town and passed in the country on the way here. A porch ran across half the front of the house. The paint looked new, glistening merrily in the sunlight. Lilac bushes, past their blossoming season, waved near the corner of the porch. What Chase had referred to as a yard was swept dirt and poorly cropped prairie grass.

Chase and Samuel sat beside the well. It was topped by a twirling windmill that made Lorette think of a misshapen steeple. She could hear

Samuel's baby laugh as a black and brown dog with a waggling tail poked its nose into Samuel's face. Chase grinned down at the two. Lorette smiled at the sweet picture they made. Then her eyes misted. No one looking at this cheerful home and the man, baby, and dog would suspect the life-and-death struggle that had so recently transpired here.

She took a deep, shaky breath and started toward Chase and Samuel. A strong odor caused her to wrinkle her nose. What was it? Nothing that smelled like any farm she'd ever been on.

Chase looked up as she neared. The gray eyes set in a spray of wrinkles were laughing. She assumed the wrinkles came from years of squinting against the sun. He nodded at the dog. "Meet Curly. He and Sam are great friends."

She smiled in return. "I can see that."

Samuel buried his head in Curly's fur and rubbed his face back and forth, a funny little baby growl in his throat. Curly just wiggled. Chase and Lorette laughed together at the sight.

Chase stood. Without his support, Samuel tipped from his sitting position to his side in the grass. Curly stuck his nose in Samuel's stomach, instigating a delighted giggle.

Chase reached for a dipper tied to the well, dipped it into the wooden bucket, and handed it to Lorette.

"Thank you," she murmured. The cool water felt good. It tasted more metallic than the water back in Philadelphia. She handed the emptied dipper back to him. "I'd like to see the inside of the house."

"That's not possible."

His quick response startled her. She drew herself up, squaring her shoulders beneath her wilted traveling jacket. "You might recall that I am Bess's sister." She whirled about and started toward the house.

"Lorette! Miss Taber!"

She ignored him. A moment later she felt his large hand on her shoulder. She kept walking, and the hand slid away. Chase fell into place beside her, with Samuel caught securely about the middle in one strong arm.

"I apologize, Miss Taber. I'm not trying to order you about, but the house is being disinfected."

She stopped short. "What?"

"Doc said it had to be disinfected with sulfur smudges. After everything was washed down, that is. You'll barely be able to breathe if you go inside now. It needs to be aired out."

"Oh." So that was the strange odor she'd smelled, sulfur. She felt ashamed for her hasty conclusion that he considered himself in a position to tell her what she could and could not do. Lorette tipped her head to one side, studying Chase's earnest face. "Are you saying you did this yourself, disinfecting the house?"

"Well, yes." He shifted Samuel's position. "I hope you don't feel I was invading your family's privacy. I didn't think you should have to clean up after. . .everything. . . ." His usually strong voice tapered off.

Lorette could think of nothing to say. This stranger had taken upon himself the task of cleaning up after the death of his good friends in order to spare someone he didn't know the unpleasant experience. Surely such a chore had been difficult for him. "Thank you." Her gratitude hoarsened her voice on the inadequate words. "The crosses. . .did you make them, too?"

"Yes. You'll want to replace them, I'm sure, but it didn't seem right, nothing marking the graves."

No wonder there were deep gray circles beneath his eyes. He must have been up all night taking care of things that would normally have fallen upon her shoulders. "And the wild roses on the graves?"

"Mrs. Bresven brought them. They grow wild on the prairie. Neighboring farmers dug the graves, and their families came for the service, those who weren't sick themselves. Bess and Tom were special people. Everyone liked them."

A cloud of helplessness enveloped Lorette. The house with its sulfur fumes was not available to her. There was nothing more she could do at the graves.

Chase cleared his throat. "What are you planning to do now?"

She tried to focus her thoughts. "Bess arranged a position for me as a governess with a family in town."

"The Henrys. She told me."

"I suppose I should speak with them next. I'm not certain they will welcome another child in their home." Her gaze shifted to Samuel, who was beginning to struggle in Chase's arms, impatient for release and new experiences.

"I'm sure the Henrys will understand if you take a day or two to get your bearings first, all things considered. The Bresvens would welcome you at their place for a few days, until you get things straight in your mind."

She remembered Kari Bresven, the plump, middle-aged Scandinavian woman who had met her at the station, had extended that offer when she drove them out to the farm in the Bresvens' buckboard, but Lorette had been too much in shock to register her need at that time. "I couldn't impose on strangers. Isn't there a hotel or boardinghouse in town?"

"Yes, miss, but I think you and the boy would be more comfortable at the Bresvens', if you don't mind my saying so. No one's a stranger to Mrs. Bresven. She likes having children around. She must. She has a passel of her own."

Lorette brushed the back of her hand across her forehead, noting with mild surprise that her skin was not only sweaty but also gritty from the dust blown about by the wind. She felt weary to her bones. She shouldn't accept a neighbor's hospitality when there was a hotel in town, but the town suddenly seemed a continent away. "If you're certain Mrs. Bresven won't mind—"

Bouncing on the hard seat of a buckboard beside Chase Lankford on the short ride to the Bresven farm, Lorette ran quickly through possibilities for her immediate future. They appeared dismally few in number. If the Henrys would not take her on because of Samuel, what would she do? She no longer had a position to return to in Philadelphia. The family for whom she'd worked there had already hired a new governess. Finding another position anywhere would be difficult. Parents who hired a governess usually wanted all the governess's attention given to their own children.

Lorette drew the boy in her lap into a quick hug. Abandoning him to strangers wasn't to be considered. He was the only family she had now, and she was his only family. They needed to stick together.

Standing beside the rough driveway on the Bresven farm, Lorette

THE FARMER'S BRIDE COLLECTION

watched Chase drive away on the clattering buckboard, dust rising in small clouds from beneath the wooden and metal wheels. Samuel whimpered in her arms, already missing Chase.

"It's all right, Samuel," she whispered in his ear. "I'm not going anywhere. It's you and me now."

The Lord always makes a way.

The words she'd heard her mother repeat hundreds of times spoke softly in her mind. Lorette's gaze swept the prairie. In the distance she could see Bess and Tom's house. A couple other farmhouses stood on the horizon. There were no trees, only fields, and a seemingly endless ocean of undulating prairie grass, amongst which Chase and the buckboard and the dust clouds were already lost to her view.

Could the Lord make a way for her and Samuel even in such a place as this?

The wagon jolted along over the road that was barely more than two deep ruts in a prairie that had been unbroken and untamed ten years ago. Chase felt as jolted emotionally as he did physically, bouncing along on the leather cushioned seat.

He'd been working without sleep since he'd discovered the deaths of his friends. He closed his mind now as he had again and again to the horror of discovering Bess and the children and hearing the story of Tom's desperate and futile search for the doctor before Tom succumbed to the disease himself. Helping with the graves, putting together the makeshift crosses with shaking hands, disinfecting the home—he'd worked through it all grateful to have someplace to put his energy, grateful for the reprieve from the depths of grief he knew were to come.

He was teetering on the edge of grief's abyss now, he knew. He recognized the place and dreaded it.

It was the realization that Sam, the last living part of Tom and Bess, might soon also leave his life that brought him to the edge. The hardest thing ever required of him was to ride away leaving that little boy in a stranger's arms, even though that stranger was Bess's sister. Even though he knew from everything Bess had told him of Lorette that Bess would completely trust Sam to her sister's care.

Chase didn't trust anyone but himself to care for that boy. Lorette hadn't even laid eyes on Sam until a couple hours ago. How could she possibly care for the boy as much as Chase cared?

He wished it were possible to keep the boy from missing his parents. He wished he could bring him up with laughter and love and a respect for the land and hard work and faith in God, the way Tom and Bess would have raised him. He wished. . . .

"I just want to protect him," he whispered fiercely.

There was no reply to the words, which had been a prayer. Only the insects that dwelt in the prairie grass and cornfields spoke, creating the incessant music of the homesteaders' rolling land.

He hadn't been able to protect Tom and Bess and the kids from diphtheria. Now he couldn't protect their son from grief or from anything else. He had no right. It was Lorette who would decide Sam's future.

The pain that had been building inside him burst. The tears he hadn't had time to shed flowed down his cheeks.

Chase flicked the reins, urging the horses into a canter. He longed to escape the pain that engulfed him. He wanted to run. But he knew that there was no hiding place from this sorrow.

Chapter 2

L orette sat beside Mrs. Henry in church, the service going by in a daze. She sang the hymns and responded with the rest of the congregation to the readings without comprehending the words. Her only communication with God was the constant cry in her heart and mind, *What now, Lord? Help us!*

Mrs. Henry had drawn her aside right before they left for church. The scene replayed through her mind. It had started with a compliment. "You are wonderful with our children," Mrs. Henry had said. "The two weeks you've been with us have proven that. There's no question of your ability or dedication, but we hired a governess because we want our children to have that person's undivided attention. You must admit that with Samuel here, you are unable to give my children your first duty. Mr. Henry and I would like you to stay on as governess, but it will only be possible if you find another home for Samuel."

Lorette's fear for her and Samuel's futures swirled through her. On her meager salary, could she possibly afford to pay someone to care for Samuel while she was at work each day? Not likely.

When the service was over she followed the rest of the congregation outside into the early summer sunshine. All around her people chatted in friendly groups, but she knew only the Henrys.

"Good morning, Miss Taber."

She blinked in surprise at the masculine voice and looked up at the tall man beside her. He looked familiar, but she couldn't place him. Samuel, who had been watching the crowd from the safety of her arms, lunged for the man. Lorette gasped and leaned with the boy.

"Whoa, there, fella." The man grinned as he effortlessly lifted Samuel from Lorette's arms.

"Why, Mr. Lankford, I didn't recognize you." Lorette pressed gloved fingers to her lace-covered throat, realizing too late that he might take her comment for an insult. The man wasn't covered with sweat and dust today. He was dressed in a simple brown suit and was as clean and close-shaven as any of the other men in church.

"There's a number of churches out near the farm site, but their services are in Norwegian or Swedish or German due to the immigrant settlers. I try make it into town for services whenever I can."

Lorette relaxed slightly. She rather liked it that this young man would make the uncomfortable trip to church without prodding from a mother or sister or wife.

Samuel bent forward and put his lips about the brim of Lankford's hat. "Samuel, don't." She tried to pry the brim from Samuel's busy mouth and tight grip.

"That's all right, miss. It's an old hat."

Lorette tried not to cringe, realizing it was the same sweat-stained hat the man had worn the day they met, though it looked as though the worst of the dust had been knocked from it. She gave Mr. Lankford a wavering smile and continued with her attempts to release the hat. "Just the same, it's best he not try to eat it."

Lankford cleared his throat. "I was wondering if you'd like to see your sister's house. I've been airing it out and the sulfur smell's gone now. Well, mostly gone. I thought perhaps you'd have the afternoon free, since it's Sunday and all." He nodded toward the dirt road where a couple dozen buggies, carriages, and wagons were lined up behind tethered horses. "I brought the wagon and would be glad to drive you out to the farm."

The fog of confusion that had hung about her since Mrs. Henry's announcement lifted momentarily. What a welcome break it would be to have a couple hours away from the Henry home and the talk she must eventually have with Mrs. Henry. "Thank you, Mr. Lankford. That would be lovely."

The smell of sulfur still lingered strong in the home when Lorette stepped over the threshold in spite of Mr. Lankford's assurances. Her nose wrinkled in reaction to the spoiled-egg odor. Samuel squeezed his eyes shut and screwed up his face in distaste. Lorette and Chase burst into laughter, and the protective shell of fear and grief that had encased Lorette's heart began to crack.

Sunshine poured through white curtains with blue and yellow embroidered flowers, cheering the large, high-ceilinged kitchen. Blue and white dishes brightened an open cupboard along one wall. The nickel plating on the combination cooking and heating stove glistened as if polished yesterday. A cast-iron teakettle sat atop the stove ready for use.

Lorette ran a gloved fingertip lightly across the top of the rectangular wooden table where the family had shared meals. Except for a kerosene lamp, which needed cleaning, the table stood empty. It was as if the room waited for Bess to enter again and bustle about caring for her family. "Bess was so excited about this house."

"So was Tom."

Chase's words startled her. She hadn't realized she'd spoken aloud.

"Bess and Tom spent a winter planning this house," Chase continued. "When the snow is covering the ground for months, a farmer has time to make repairs and plan for spring. Every time I'd stop over that winter Tom and Bess were seated at this very table in their soddy pouring over their sketches of this house, arguing good-naturedly over the size of rooms and where to try and save money."

Lorette shook her head. "I could never imagine my sister living in a sod house."

"She never complained." Chase swung a hand casually toward a window through which Lorette could see the barn. "They turned the house into a barn after they moved in here."

Lorette felt her cheeks blanch, not only appalled that her sister had lived in a dirt home but one that had become a home for farm animals. Yet Bess's letters had always been filled with plans and hopes and dreams and the excitement of her life with Tom in this land.

A Homesteader, a Bride, and a Baby

Chase indicated a doorway with his hat. "Sitting room's this way."

Lorette moved to the doorway and stopped, surveying the second of the two first-floor rooms. Just as Bess's kitchen took the place of both kitchen and dining room, the "sitting room," as Chase called it, combined both parlor and family room. She knew Bess had hoped to eventually add on a parlor and dining room.

Blushing tan roses on a rich brown background papered the walls. Maroon velvet draperies framed the tall windows. In the center of the room stood a large round table of dark wood, a kerosene lamp with a painted glass shade in the exact middle of the table's marble top. A gentlemen's chair, an armless ladies' chair and camel-back sofa, all framed in intricate carving and upholstered in plush fabric which matched the draperies, were set about the room with small marble-topped tables beside them. Dainty, snowy white crocheted pieces protected the furniture from hair oils.

"I remember how proud Bess was when she wrote of buying this furniture," Lorette said.

A bittersweet sadness twisted inside her. Everything in the room shouted its newness. To Lorette, the room seemed a pitiful attempt to capture the beauty of a parlor from back East, an impossible task in a four-room house on the prairie.

Samuel was poking with a pudgy finger at the watch which hung from a silver breast pin on Lorette's green swirled gingham dress. After a moment of observation, he flopped his head forward and tried to put the watch in his mouth.

"No, Samuel." Lorette pried the strong little wet fingers from his mouth and the watch from his fingers, then set the boy down on the floor. He immediately crawled toward the sofa.

The most comfortable looking piece of furniture was a rocking chair that didn't match the fancier pieces. Before it was a low footstool, just high enough to keep a woman's feet above the drafts that run along floors. She wondered whether Bess had made the embroidered footstool cover and the matching sewing bag that hung beside the chair.

Chase must have seen her looking at the rocking chair. "Tom surprised her with that chair right before their oldest, Aaron, was born. Nearest railroad station was at Benson back then, thirty miles from here, so that's the closest he could have the chair shipped. Tom and me took a buckboard to pick up a load of wood and came back with the wood and the chair both. There was no road between our settlement and Benson back then. Just ruts across the prairie." A grin split his wide face. "That chair rocked so hard it had twice as many miles as the buckboard by the time we reached here. Tom nearly burst with anticipation. All he could talk about was what Bess would say. Wish you could have seen Bess's face when we pulled up in front of the soddy with that chair."

Lorette tried to will away the knot that caught high in her chest. Chase's grin had gentled into a shadowy smile, and his eyes had the faraway look that eyes take on when one is watching memories. Lorette wished desperately that those memories were hers. She forced herself to smile. "I expect Tom wasn't disappointed in Bess's reaction?"

Chase chuckled, and she found her smile widening at the sound. "No. He surely was not. I can see her now, standing in front of that soddy with her apron and hair blowing in the wind. She took one look at the chair and her eyes grew as large as buggy wheels. Then she came across the yard as fast as her delicate condition allowed. Tom's boots had barely touched ground when her arms went around his neck. She like to squeezed the living daylights out of him."

Lorette studied his face, curious at the way his voice had softened at the end.

A large picture in an oval tortoise-shell frame caught her eye. She walked toward it slowly. It hung above a sideboard, another reminder that the little house did not have a proper dining room.

She hugged herself tightly as she stared at the family photograph. Bess's face, her beautiful, thick brown hair pulled severely back into a bun, stared back at her. Tom stood behind Bess with one hand on her shoulder, a proud young family man. Samuel's older brother and sister stood one on each side of Bess, leaning against their mother's lap. Bess held Samuel, his long embroidered gown cascading like a beautiful waterfall over Bess's dark tailored skirt. The children all had blond hair like their father. Lorette shivered and hugged herself even tighter.

"That was taken a couple months ago." Chase spoke from behind her in a low voice.

"I know." Her voice came out in a hoarse whisper. "She sent me a small copy of it."

Between Chase and Lorette hung a heavy, awkward silence, so common when one has lost a loved one and there is nothing anyone can say or do to bring them back or prevent the grief of their loss. Lorette stared at the picture, trying to absorb everything she could about her older sister. Bess had looked so different when she left Boston years ago as a young bride.

"She was happy." Chase's voice was gentle in its masculinity. "She loved being a mother and she loved Tom. She even loved this impossible-to-tame prairie."

"Her letters were filled with her joy."

Crash!

Lorette whirled about. Samuel was proudly surveying the sewing basket he'd tipped over. He reached eagerly for a ball of pale blue yarn stuck through with knitting needles that had tumbled from the basket. Lorette darted forward, but Chase reached the boy first.

"That's not a toy, fella." Chase righted the basket and began replacing the spilled objects. "I'll keep him entertained if you want to look around a bit more."

A dainty ladies' desk stood beside a window. Curiosity stirred within Lorette. What reminders of herself had her sister left in that desk? Lorette crossed to it.

"Bess wrote her letters to you seated there."

Lorette took a bundle of envelopes from a cubbyhole, recognized her own handwriting on the top envelope, and quickly returned them to their keeping place. She pulled out a drawer. She didn't know what she expected to see there, but what she found was a book bound in rich brown leather. Curious, she removed and opened it.

This will be our first night sleeping in our new home. It's been a long day and my eyes are closing in exhaustion as I write, but I could not go to bed without recording the great joy Tom and I are feeling this day.

Tears blurred the script. Lorette returned the journal to the drawer. She knew that later she would read and cherish this record of Bess's thoughts. Yet Lorette's pain was still too new to read it now. She closed the drawer and turned her back to the desk.

Chase was on the floor beside Samuel. Four wooden blocks sat in a row on the thick brown rug. Chase slowly balanced a block on top of the others. "See, Sam? It's easy." He placed another block.

Samuel stared, his brown eyes wide below lifted blond brows, his little bow mouth open slightly.

"Going to help me, Sam?" Chase placed one of Samuel's hands on a block. Together they lifted and placed it.

Chase's tanned hand seemed to swallow up Samuel's tiny white one. Lorette smiled at the sweetness of the moment. With a pleasant start she realized that for the first time in days she was genuinely smiling inside, too. The smile loosened somewhat the painful knot that had existed in her chest since hearing of Bess's death.

Lorette wasn't accustomed to seeing men play with their children. The fathers of the children for whom she had cared in Philadelphia had been reserved with their offspring. Had Tom played with Samuel, Aaron, and Liza as Chase was playing now? If so, the children had indeed been blessed.

"We did it, Sam," Chase congratulated.

Samuel stared at the blocks a moment longer. Bending forward suddenly he pushed the block they had so carefully balanced in place with the palm of his hand. The block went tumbling. Samuel giggled and slapped his hands on his chubby knees, his face filled with glee.

"Hey!" Chase's face registered disbelief.

Lorette burst into laughter at his chagrin. Chase looked up in surprise. Meeting her gaze, he joined in her laughter.

He stood to his feet, bending over to swoop Samuel into one arm. "Guess the fellow isn't into building yet." He disentangled a hunk of his hair from one of Samuel's fists. "How are things going at the Henrys'?"

"They are no longer 'going' at all." She held out her arms for Samuel.

Blond brows met above troubled eyes. "Haven't they treated you well? Mr. Henry has a fine reputation—"

"Oh, yes," she hurried to assure him. "They simply wish for a governess who can give all her attention to their children." She touched her lips lightly to Samuel's temple. "I can't do that." She glanced into the boy's bright eyes and smiled. "Thank God, I cannot do that," she whispered.

Chase stuffed his hands into his trouser pockets. "Will you be taking Sam back to Philadelphia?"

He stood in an easy manner, but she sensed a tension about him. Was he afraid she would take the only remaining member of his friends' family away?

"Maybe," Lorette responded. "But parents back East don't care for governesses who come with nephews any more than parents here. I'll need to find another way to support us."

"So. . .what are you planning?"

"The attorney read the will to me yesterday. He said Samuel inherits this house and farm."

"And?"

Lorette shrugged. "My first thought was to sell the farm. The money from the sale would be Samuel's, of course. It would all go for his support."

He nodded, his gaze on hers.

"If I can't find another position where I can keep him with me, I can use the money to pay someone else to care for him properly while I work. Or perhaps the money would allow me to stay with him until he is old enough to begin school before I accept another position as a governess."

She waited, hoping for a response from him. He'd been Tom's best friend. Wouldn't he know what Tom and Bess would have wanted her to do?

"I'm afraid the farm wouldn't bring as much money as you think." Chase sounded as though he spoke with reluctance.

Unease quickened her heartbeat. "Why not?"

"Tom made a good start developing this place, but it took a heap of money to do it. Sam must have inherited Tom's debts. Selling the farm would barely pay them off."

"How can that be? They homesteaded the land. It barely cost them anything." Lorette spread her free hand to indicate the home within which they stood. "They had enough money to buy and furnish this new house."

"He used the land and future crops to borrow the money to pay for the house, and for farm machinery to run this place, and to buy another section of land."

His words sent goose bumps running along her arms, and she shivered. "What about the crops? Won't they help pay the debts?"

"It's not as simple as it sounds. Farmers live on credit all year. It's not only the house and machinery they pay for after harvest. If the crops are poor, prices will be good—that is, if you're one of the fortunate farmers with crops to sell. If the crops are good, prices will be low because everyone has a lot to sell. Either way, there won't be enough to pay off normal living debts and the loans, too. 'Course if you're thrifty, there may be enough to pay off this year's loan payments."

The hope in Lorette's chest was rapidly sinking. "I suppose I could rent the farm out. It wouldn't support Samuel and me, but it would help pay the debts and let us keep the farm for Samuel."

"Sure. 'Course, if the renter doesn't pay up or the crops aren't good in the future, you'll need to find another way to make the loan payments or lose the property."

Lorette closed her hands into fists in frustration. "How do farmers manage to live at all?"

He grinned. "Tom always said the only way was by depending on God and using a man's brains and brawn. I'd say he's right."

"But what am I going to do?"

"If you don't mind a suggestion—"

"Mind? I'm pleading for one."

"You don't need to decide this minute. You can stay here while you figure things out. You and Sam would have a roof over your heads and a garden and chickens and a cow for your meals."

"I don't know anything about running a farm. I wouldn't have one idea of what to do with the crops."

"I do."

She stared at him a moment, not comprehending his quiet reply. Understanding dawned rapidly. "Oh. *Oh.* The chickens. . .the cow. . .the other animals. . .*you* have been caring for them the last couple weeks."

Chase shifted his feet and glanced at the floor. "Yes."

"And the crops?"

Chase nodded.

"Oh, my." Lorette moved to the dainty rocking chair and sank onto the tapestry covering. "My thoughts have been only on my grief and Samuel's, and on how I am going to care for Samuel. I've been incredibly selfish, leaving the care of this place on your shoulders. I'll pay you for your trouble. I have a little money coming from the two weeks I spent with the Henrys."

He shook his head vigorously. "I couldn't take the money. I've done what I've done for Tom. He was a good friend. If you decide to move in here for a while I'll be more than glad to continue helping you out."

Everything in Lorette's nature went against accepting such a huge gift, but she knew she must accept it out of concern for Samuel's future. If what Chase said about the crops and debt were true, she'd need her meager funds.

"Thank you. I accept your kind offer." She forced a smile. "I'm afraid you've no idea how much your advice will be needed. I know nothing of life on a farm. In Philadelphia my food came from merchants, not from the land just outside my door."

"You'll catch on."

He sounded as though he had no doubt at all. She wished she were as sure of her capabilities.

At least for the moment, she and Samuel had a roof over their heads and food for only the price of her labor. She needn't worry immediately about finding a position, nor must she rely on Kari Bresven's or the Henrys' charity to meet her own and Samuel's needs. Some of her trepidation at staying on the farm melted away. Depending on Chase Lankford to help her with the farm, she felt as secure as Samuel obviously felt when in Chase's arms.

❧

Chase rolled over, grunting when his shoulder hit a raised nail. He shifted. The wooden floor he'd put in his sod house was a pleasure to walk on, but there was no way to make it comfortable for sleeping. Still, he didn't regret giving the feather mattress from his bed to Lorette. He smiled into the night, playing her name over in his mind. Manners might demand that he refer to her as Miss Taber, but in the privacy of his thoughts he loved the sound of her name.

He hadn't told Lorette that the mattress was his. She'd assumed Mrs. Bresven had lent it, along with the Swedish woman's pillow, sheets, and quilts. He hadn't informed her otherwise. The bedding had been necessary to replace that which the doctor had ordered him to burn.

Chase rolled over again and groaned. He'd order another mattress next time he was in town. At least he still had a pillow.

He let the events of the afternoon roll through his mind. Since their deaths, it had been difficult to be in the home of Tom and Bess. He still missed them sorely. He supposed he would feel that way for a long time.

Still, the sound of Lorette's laughter rang in his memory, and he pictured her face when he'd looked up from playing with Sam. It had been a perfect moment.

The picture was replaced by the sadness he'd caught in her blue eyes. Seeing that pain, his instinct had been to try to protect her, the same way he wanted to protect Sam. It was then that the thought of marriage first crossed his mind.

Foolish thought. Pity was no foundation for marriage. Besides, he couldn't protect her. Not by marriage or any other way. Not only hadn't he the right, the same as he hadn't the right to protect Sam, but grief wasn't a pain from which anyone could be protected by another human being.

When Lorette said she might take Sam back East to raise, he'd felt a pain in his stomach worse than the worst sickness he'd ever known. He'd had to all but bite his tongue to keep from asking her to marry him right then.

He snorted and drew his quilt up to his chin. Didn't make any sense to ask a woman he barely knew to marry him, even if Bess had been telling him about Lorette for years. He might not have known Lorette long, but he'd seen enough to admire her pluck. He was glad she wasn't the kind of woman who'd consider Sam's inheritance something to feather her own nest. And she sure wasn't sore on the eyes.

The only other woman he'd ever thought of marrying was Anna, and he'd known her for years before he asked. She had turned him down flat. A life of a farmer's wife was too hard, she'd said.

So he'd taken up his homestead claim and closed his heart.

Until now. Until Lorette.

He snorted again. No reason in the world to believe she'd have said yes to his proposal even if he'd been rash enough to make it.

He dug his head deeper into the pillow and muttered, "Must be lonelier than I realized to even invent such a thought."

While the vision of Lorette's eyes played in his thoughts, Chase drifted into sleep.

Chapter 3

The dawn streamed through the lace-covered windows as Lorette arose early the next morning. The sweet music of Samuel's baby jabberings drifted from his cradle beside her bed, providing a pleasant start to her day. She talked with him while she dressed, glad he never seemed hungry until he'd been up for a while.

"You're such a good-natured little boy." She ran a hand over the cradle's hooded bonnet with its carving of roses. The wood was butter smooth. Tom must have sanded it for hours and hours. "Your mother wrote me about this cradle, how your father made it and gave it to your mother the Christmas they were expecting Aaron."

Samuel grinned and kicked his feet.

Lorette wondered whether Samuel could feel his father's love surrounding him when he was in the cradle. Her eyes misted over, and she brushed at them with the back of her hand.

Putting behind her fanciful thoughts, she picked up Samuel and started downstairs. The two rooms behind closed doors across the hall were hard to ignore. She had peaked into them last night. They felt forlorn with mattressless bedsteads and deserted toys: one of Liza's dolls, a slingshot of Aaron's, and a pile of pebbles and arrowheads Aaron had collected. More than anything else, those rooms told the extent to which death had filled this house.

Lorette found Bess's aprons hanging on pegs on the pantry door. She reached for a crisp white apron, then selected a tan plaid which wouldn't show the inevitable results of a day's work as easily. Besides, it complemented her brown-checkered gingham dress, the simplest she owned.

While Samuel played with spoons on the floor, Lorette searched the pantry, discovering what she did and did not have available to prepare meals. She looked in wooden boxes, colorful tins, glass containers, cupboards, and drawers.

Finally she settled her hands on her hips. "Well, Samuel, the only loaf of bread is moldy. Chase must not have thought to clean out the pantry when he disinfected the house. I find flour, but no yeast. We'll have to do without bread this morning. Rather, I will. Milk will satisfy you for a while."

She grunted as she lifted Samuel. "My, you're a big boy."

He grinned as though he appreciated her comment, then leaned forward and gave a harmless bite to her shoulder.

"You must be hungry. Or your new little teeth are bothering you." She picked up a small tin pail and he transferred his attention to it. "It's a good thing Chase showed me last night where the milk was kept or you'd miss breakfast, too," she continued, carrying him out to the well. "I'd never have guessed to look in the well. In Philadelphia, a delivery man brought milk to the house each day."

She set Samuel down in order to free both hands to raise the covered tin bucket of milk from the well. She poured enough milk for Samuel and to make pancakes for herself, then lowered the bucket back into the well. "I hope Chase. . .Mr. Lankford stops by this morning. This milk won't last you the day, Samuel."

She swung the boy up to her hip and groaned. His navy blue dress was covered with dirt. She'd been so intent on getting the milk she'd forgotten to pay attention. "At least it's not mud," she muttered, brushing him off.

Her stomach was growling by the time he'd had his fill of breakfast milk and she'd laid him in the crib in the corner of the kitchen for a nap. In the pen were a tin rattle and a rag doll which had seen better days, likely because it was well-loved.

Ready to make her own breakfast, she sighed. She couldn't make buckwheat cakes without eggs, and the eggs were in the sod barn beneath chickens. Lorette straightened her shoulders. "Trying to avoid the task, aren't you? What is so scary? Hundreds of women collect eggs every day. Thousands, maybe. Children, too." She picked up a basket from the counter and groaned. "Why doesn't that make me feel any braver?"

Lorette started across the yard, swinging the basket, deliberately putting a bounce in her step, and began singing "Oh, Susannah." Her spirits actually lifted until she opened the door to the sod barn.

"Oh! No! No! Oh!" Chickens and a rooster rushed at her, their cackles and feathered bodies filling the air. She threw her arms up, dropping the basket.

Strong arms drew her back. "Don't be afraid, Lorette. They only want to get outside and have their breakfast."

She clasped her palms over her racing heart. "Chase. . .Mr. Lankford, I'm so glad you're here. I. . .I don't know anything about chickens and. . .and eggs and. . . Can you show me what to do?"

She hated her breathlessness, but considering that a feathered army had just attacked her, she felt she was doing quite well.

Then she realized one of his large, strong hands was against her back, steadying her. A flush seemed to rise from the soles of her feet and spread upward to her hairline. She felt herself stiffen as though she were a statue.

He didn't appear to notice. With one easy movement, he leaned down, picked up her forgotten basket, and handed it to her.

"You'll be an old hand at egg hunting in no time."

Strong barnyard smells that she knew must be from the chickens, cow, two oxen, horse, straw, and things she didn't want to think about hung about them as they entered the building.

Even with his help, she definitely did *not* feel like an old hand at egg-gathering after they had collected eight brown eggs. "I feel like I've spent a week trying to keep a room full of eleven-year-old boys still and teach them arithmetic." It was the most tiring experience she could recall.

His laugh rang out clearly in the morning air.

Cheered, she tucked back a strand of hair loosened by the battle with the chickens and started toward the house.

"Uh. . .the chickens need feeding, Miss Taber."

She stopped short. "Oh. Of course."

"I'll show you where the feed is kept. You'll be giving them table scraps, too, naturally." He led her to a large wooden covered box, which stood along one wall.

"Naturally." Her ignorance was beginning to overwhelm her.

"Not everything, of course, but things like potato skins."

"Of course." Behind his back she rolled her eyes. She assumed he meant no meat scraps.

"Moo-oo-oo."

He turned to the cow. "Pansy." His face had the strangest expression.

"Is something wrong?"

He avoided her gaze and kept his own on the cow in the nearby stall. "Have you given Sam any milk yet today?"

"Yes. I'm glad you reminded me. I've used almost all the milk from the bucket in the well."

"There's more where that came from." His voice tangled with laughter, and his mouth twisted in a vain effort to avoid grinning.

Embarrassment flooded her. She felt so inadequate for the demands of farm living. "I know." She straightened her shoulders, attempting to retain a little dignity. "The trouble is, I don't know how to. . .to get at it."

Chase shouted with laughter. Within moments he was doubled-over in his mirth.

Lorette's embarrassment multiplied one hundred fold, but Chase's laughter was contagious, and soon she was laughing along with him. By the time their laughter had dissolved into chuckles, her sides hurt and she was wiping tears from her lashes.

"Let's feed the chickens," Chase said when they were both able to speak again. "Then I'll show you how to milk Pansy. She needs to be milked twice a day, every day. Each morning after milking let her out to pasture. You'll bring her in every evening and milk her again."

❧

She recalled his milking lesson two weeks later while leaning against Pansy's side, feeling the occasional swat of Pansy's sharp, scratchy tail against her cheek and listening to the satisfying sound of milk entering the pail. Deep satisfaction filled her upon mastering this task, which people had been performing for thousands of years. She'd been surprised at the strength it took. Her wrists had been swollen at the end of that first day.

The milking done, she stood stiffly, put her hands on her lower back, and stretched. The gardening, house-work, and care of the animals were all taking their toll on her body. Her work as a governess seemed idle by comparison.

She pulled the heavy pail to safety. "We did well this morning, Pansy." The cow turned her huge head and eyed Lorette.

"Glad to hear it."

Lorette jumped, sloshing milk from the bucket onto her shoes. "Chase Lankford, you shouldn't startle a body so!"

"Sorry about the milk." Chase's grin showed he wasn't too sorry. He jostled Samuel, who was struggling unsuccessfully to get out of the man's arms and into the straw with the cats now winding about Chase's legs. "Stopped by the house. He was a bit perturbed at being there alone. Sounds like you're handling the milking just fine."

"Pansy didn't kick the bucket or step in it this morning. The cats didn't tip it trying to drink. Pansy didn't step on my foot or bump me off the stool. It's been my best milking yet." It was absurd how pleased it made her to tell him so.

"I knew you'd make a great milk maid." He ignored Samuel's continued efforts to get down.

Does he think I'm not caring for Samuel properly? she wondered uneasily. "I hate to leave Samuel in the crib while I do the chores, but it's too dangerous for him in the barn. One of the animals might kick him, or the chickens peck him." She shuddered at the things the straw hid. "I hate to think what he might try to put in his mouth." She poured the milk into the nearby strainer, then set down the empty pail and reached for the boy. "He does love to be close to the animals."

"Maybe I can make a small pen where he can play while you work in here, something smaller than his crib, maybe without legs. For now, if you want to give him breakfast, I'll finish up here for you."

Guilt and thankfulness braided together in an unlikely mix as she crossed the yard in a slow, stumbling gait with Samuel in one arm and a tin pail of milk in the opposite hand. She hated to allow Chase to do any of the chores she could do. He had so much to take care of with Tom's crops, as well as his own. Still, she was glad to be relieved from wiping that fierce-smelling concoction onto the animals. Chase said it helped keep the cow flies from biting them. She did pity Pansy, the oxen, and the horse, Boots, their constant battle with those creatures.

Lorette and Samuel had their share of the bites. She tried keeping herself and Samuel well-covered to prevent the bites, despite the summer heat. She resisted rubbing kerosene on herself and Samuel to keep the flies at bay as Chase and other farmers did. That was more than her Philadelphia-bred genteel self could bear.

At the porch outside the door, she slipped off her shoes. She had learned her first day on the farm what awful, smelly things her shoes accumulated in the barn. Today one of her shoes sloshed with spilled milk, too.

The fragrance of rising bread greeted her as she entered the house. Another lesson from Chase. When she'd told him she needed yeast to bake bread, he'd shown her Bess's supply of sourdough starter and how to make bread with it.

"Seems that man has had to teach me everything but how to change your diapers," she told Samuel, setting him on the kitchen floor.

She hadn't even known Bess had stored canned meats, vegetables, and fruit in the cellar until Chase told her so. She especially appreciated the canned meat. She hadn't been able to bring herself to kill a chicken yet. That was another thing Chase did. So far he had refrained from insisting she learn to do that herself.

She started a fire in the stove, then let it burn down to cooking and baking temperature while she fed Samuel. He was still fussy while he fed. He hadn't liked being weaned suddenly after his mother died. As she usually did, Lorette kept up a steady conversation with him while he drank the warm, fresh milk.

Samuel fell asleep with his blanket on the kitchen floor while she was putting the bread in the oven to bake. It was an overcast morning, and the baking wouldn't heat the house as unbearably as it did some days. Ready to begin breakfast for herself and Chase, she looked around for her eggs.

"I know I collected them. Where are they?" she muttered, glancing about the large kitchen. Then she remembered. Her hands full with Samuel and the milk, she hadn't had enough hands to carry the eggs from the barn to the house. She hated to leave Samuel, even when he was sleeping. But it would only take a moment to run to the barn.

She saw Chase turn about at the sound of her entering the sod barn. "I forgot the eggs." She headed quickly to where the basket sat on the straw-covered floor. She reached for the handle and saw something move quickly beneath the straw.

With a screech she leaped back. "A snake! It's a snake!"

Fear tore up through her like a living thing. She couldn't seem to move fast enough. Her feet felt as though they were in buckets. She couldn't take her gaze from the yellow form gliding through, blending in the straw. Her screams filled the barn and her ears and she couldn't stop them.

They continued while Chase grabbed a pitchfork, stabbed the wriggling form, and rushed outside with it. To Lorette it appeared he was moving at a snail's pace.

Lorette's screams turned into shaky gasps. She stumbled to the door, watching the floor the entire way, certain other snakes must be hiding in the innocent-looking straw covering. From outside she could hear Curly the dog barking excitedly.

She'd barely crossed the threshold when Chase's arms surrounded her, drawing her quivering body close. "It's all right," he whispered into her hair. "I killed the creature. It can't hurt you now."

Her fingers clutched at his shirt. "I've n—never seen a s—snake before. I didn't know there were s—snakes in the b—barn."

"It's just a corn snake."

Lorette thought it absurd to refer to any snake as "just" a snake.

One of Chase's large hands rubbed her back firmly but gently, and her shaking began to lessen. "Corn snakes are common in the fields, but they seldom come into the barn. The cats keep them away."

Even so, Lorette wondered how she would dare set foot in the barn again. . .or take the animals to pasture. . .or bring Chase his lunch in the fields. She didn't know how to tell him the extent of her fear. Bess and other women had lived with the reality of snakes in their world. Somehow she would have to find the strength to do so, too.

Chase's arms were so comforting. She had only experienced a man's arms about her a couple of times before. Never had they felt this strong, this gentle. Held close, her cheek against his shoulder, she could hide her embarrassment at the way she'd reacted, but she could not stay there. Reluctantly, she pushed herself away.

He released his hold immediately.

She wished he hadn't. *Don't be a silly goose,* she reprimanded herself. "Thank you for killing the snake. I'm afraid I'm rather timid when it comes to them. I never saw a snake in Philadelphia."

"Everyone jumps when they see a snake. It's human nature. Corn snakes aren't poisonous. There aren't any poisonous snakes hereabouts."

She appreciated his attempts to reassure her, but they weren't working. She glanced back at the sod barn door. Apprehension sent shivers through her. "Would you mind? The egg basket is still in there."

He retrieved it for her.

Her knees felt as pliant as corn silk as she walked to the house. Her hands shook when she slipped her shoes off on the porch.

Once inside, her hair stood on end. "Samuel! No!"

Chapter 4

Samuel was crawling across the kitchen floor, headed for the hot stove. Lorette dropped the basket and rushed for him, grabbing him up in a bear hug just as he reached out for the silver filigree on the oven door.

Samuel let out a squeal.

She only hugged him tighter. She took two steps back from the dangerous stove and dropped to her knees. Samuel squirmed. She didn't let go. "That's hot. Samuel must never touch the stove. Hot!" The words trembled, but no more than her heart. If she had been a moment later returning from the barn—

She couldn't let herself think of the "what-ifs." Thank God she'd returned in time. Her heart went out to all the mothers who hadn't.

Tears rolled over her cheeks. She rocked herself and Samuel back and forth, trying to comfort herself. *I can't do this,* she thought. *I can't live like this. It's too much. It's too hard, too dangerous.*

Eventually her sobs stopped, her breathing became normal, and her thoughts less wild. Hot stoves were in every house, not just prairie farmhouses, she reminded herself. There was no place she could take Samuel where there would not be dangers. Besides, she should not have left him alone on the floor, even though she had been certain he was sound asleep.

When her legs would hold her again, she put Samuel in his crib in the corner of the kitchen. He howled in protest until she brought him a pan lid and spoons to pound together.

A Homesteader, a Bride, and a Baby

Lorette rinsed her face with cold water, trying to wash away the vestiges of her crying jag, and straightened her hair, which had been mussed from rubbing against Chase's shirt. She felt her face burn at the memory.

Only then did she remember the egg basket. Most of the eggs were broken. A sticky yellow mess covered the bottom of the basket. She picked up the three eggs that remained whole, lifted her chin in determination, and began breakfast for herself and Chase.

She'd insisted Chase take his meals with them and that she would do his laundry in partial payment for all the work he did on the farm. She'd learned quickly that he liked a big breakfast after he'd done chores and before he left for the fields. Today she made fried potatoes, bacon, and the three eggs. Fresh warm bread and her own butter would round out the meal.

Truth be told, she enjoyed the time that she and Chase shared at meals. His companionship kept some of the loneliness of farm living from overwhelming her. She was accustomed to spending most of her days with children, but not to the exclusion of adult companionship.

Determined to put the morning's frightful memories behind her, she forced herself to sing. "What a friend we have in Jesus," she started, her voice quavering, "all our sins and griefs to bear." Before long, the quavering ceased. Samuel kept up a beat on a pan lid that was like no accompaniment Lorette had sung to in the past. By the time Chase came to the house for breakfast, Lorette had herself well in hand.

"It's nice to hear singing in this house again," Chase said when they sat down to eat. "Your sister sang while she worked, too."

Lorette's smile was genuine. His memories of Bess were different than Lorette's, but she was glad they shared memories of her. "Tell me more about her, the way you knew her."

He did. The things he remembered might have seemed insignificant to others, but to Lorette they spoke loudly of Bess's love for Tom and the children and her joy in the life she lived.

Lorette wondered silently whether a corn snake had ever surprised Bess, and if so, how she'd reacted. Lorette doubted her older sister had fallen apart and ended up in the arms of a man to whom she wasn't married for comfort.

The thought brought back the wonderful sense of rightness and security she'd felt in Chase's arms, the strength in the arms hidden beneath the brown cotton shirtsleeves. She had to lower her gaze to her plate to keep her eyes from revealing her thoughts to the man across the small table.

He didn't appear to notice anything unusual in the atmosphere between them. His mind was apparently on more practical things.

"Looks like it might rain later today. Might take advantage of the weather to drive into town and take care of some business. You're welcome to join me, if you'd like."

Lorette looked up in surprise. "In the rain?"

He shrugged. "If it's raining more than a drizzle, I can't be in the fields. If you'd rather not ride in the rain, you can give me a list of things you need and I'll pick them up."

"Oh, no, I don't mind the rain." She wasn't about to pass up a trip to town, regardless of the weather.

After the breakfast dishes were cleared, she examined the items in the pantry and made a list, just in case the trip became reality. Her mood lifted by the minute. She'd taken to wearing Bess's housedresses, as they were more suitable than most of the clothes she'd brought from Philadelphia. Now she changed from Bess's worn housedress to one of her own simple gowns, one that wouldn't be ruined by a little rain. Even Samuel had a change of dress.

Her spirits continued to lighten as the sky grew darker and sprinkles pattered against the windows. She stood in the kitchen doorway and watched the clouds tumble over each other across the sky, glorying in the vast distance she could see above the rolling prairie lands. The smell of rain and wet earth and grasses was refreshing.

In an effort to still her impatience and to keep Samuel entertained and clean until they left, she settled herself and Samuel in Bess's rocking chair with Bess's journal. Lorette had begun the practice of reading aloud to Samuel from the journal the first full day she'd spent in the house.

A small crocheted white cross marked the place she'd left off at the last reading. She started the chair in its gentle rocking motion while she opened the book.

A Homesteader, a Bride, and a Baby

Mr. Lankford had dinner with us today following church services.
Afterward, while I cleaned up the kitchen, he and Tom rolled about
the floor with Aaron and Liza for all the world as though they were
children themselves. Aaron and Liz love Mr. Lankford as though he
were one of us. He is a hard-working, responsible man, a church-going
man, gentle yet strong in his ways.

Lorette was glad for the journal's glimpses into Bess's view of Chase. Her mind drifted to the man who had become such a large part of her life in such a short time. She might as well admit that she not only relied upon him, but she was beginning to care deeply for him—and as more than just a friend.

"Don't fool yourself into thinking he helps out for you," she admonished herself. "He does it for Samuel and because Tom was his friend."

She started as the kitchen door slammed. "Miss Taber? Are you ready to leave for town?" Chase called as he entered the house.

When she and Samuel joined Chase, she was surprised to see a buggy drawn up to the porch. "I didn't know Tom and Bess had a buggy."

"I borrowed it from the Bresvens. Figured you and Sam would get soaked riding in the wagon."

Even with the covered buggy, their ride was a damp one. She was glad for the oilcloth Chase provided to cover their legs and laps.

Bess's journal entry and the minutes Lorette spent in Chase's arms that morning made Lorette all the more conscious of every bounce of the wagon that jostled her shoulder into his. Her heart kept an erratic pace during the journey. She couldn't help but wonder whether the simple, innocent contact reminded him of the time they'd spent in each other's arms, too.

The muddy roads made the journey longer than usual, and Lorette thought they made the ride bumpier than usual, also. Conversation with Chase was somewhat limited. It took all of Chase's concentration to drive as the road grew worse.

The simple general store with its narrow aisles and one room of goods piled upon goods from floor to ceiling looked as wonderful to Lorette as a large emporium in downtown Philadelphia. Chase introduced her to the owner, a middle-aged Swedish man named Larson. Chase explained that she was Tom's sister-in-law, and Larson agreed to extend her credit against harvest.

Lorette and Chase went about the store gathering items from their separate lists. Chase completed his within minutes. "I'm having a leather harness repaired at a shop down the street. I'll run down and pick it up while you finish here."

She agreed and went happily back to examining the bolts of fabric piled on a table in one corner of the store. Samuel was growing fast. He would need new clothes soon.

"How nice to see you, Miss Taber."

Lorette turned to the woman at her elbow. "Mrs. Henry, what a pleasant surprise."

Mrs. Henry leaned forward and tickled Samuel's cheek with a gloved index finger. "Hello there, Samuel. My, aren't you the big boy." She straightened and smiled her formal smile at Lorette. "I hope things are going well for you on the farm, my dear."

"Yes, everything is fine." *Mrs. Henry's words are always right,* Lorette thought, *but somehow her manner makes them sound all wrong.* "How are the children?"

"Fine, fine." Mrs. Henry waved her hand in a dismissing manner. A frown marred her features. "There's something I must tell you." Her voice had dropped a degree.

At her tone, Lorette's stomach turned queasy. She tried to ignore it. What could the woman possibly say that could justify such a feeling? Lorette barely knew the woman. "What is that, Mrs. Henry?"

Mrs. Henry laid a hand on Lorette's forearm. "My dear, I hardly know how to say this."

Lorette wished her former employer would stop calling her "my dear." "Say what?"

"I understand Mr. Lankford spends a great deal of time at your farm."

"Yes. He's been a marvelous help. As you know, I know nothing of running a farm."

"He was a friend of your brother-in-law's, of course."

"Yes. They helped each other with their fields, so Mr. Lankford knows all about Tom's crops."

Mrs. Henry bit her bottom lip for a moment. "People say Mr. Lankford spends a *great* deal of time at your farm." She hesitated, staring directly into Lorette's eyes. "An inordinate amount of time."

The woman's meaning began to sink in. Lorette could hear a roaring sound in her ears. "What are you saying?" Her lips felt numb, but she knew she had asked the question. If Mrs. Henry was saying what Lorette thought, she needed to hear it in plain English.

"People are saying he is living at the farm with you, that you are living together. . .inappropriately."

Chapter 5

T he ride back to the farm was the longest Chase could ever remember. The man at the saddle shop had told him of the ugly
rumor going about town. Chase knew there were men who found
such tales amusing, but he could hardly believe the townspeople he knew
and respected thought him capable of such gross conduct.

Worse, they thought sweet Lorette would descend to such an
arrangement.

The entire situation made him sick.

He'd told the leather worker, in no uncertain terms, that the rumors
were not true. Chase had no illusions that he would be able to squelch
the rumors or convince everyone of their untruth. He knew enough about
human nature to know he could not work such miracles.

Anger at what the rumors would mean to Lorette's reputation made
him drive Boots harder than he normally would under such poor road
conditions. His thoughts swirled in a vicious circle. What was he going to
do? What could he do? Did Lorette know? Had she, too, heard the rumors
in town? She seemed agitated, avoiding his glance, barely speaking, but
perhaps she was only responding to his temperament, which he admitted
to himself was anything but friendly and easy-going.

Lorette was glad when they finally arrived back at the farm and Chase
headed to the Bresvens's with the buggy. The ride had seemed unendurable.
The rumor had shouted through her mind the entire time.

Had Chase heard the awful accusations?

"Oh, no." She stopped short. Did he think she had staged her fright at the snake that morning, had purposely found a reason to throw herself into his arms? The possibility was too horrible to consider.

"How can people be so terrible, making up stories like this about people?" she asked the Lord, unpacking the goods from the wooden box Chase had carried into the house for her.

It was awful enough for her and for Chase, but it almost broke her heart to think what the rumors would mean for Samuel. The sins of the fathers did follow the children. The untrue rumors would follow Samuel if he grew up here. What would Bess think if she knew the disgrace Lorette and Chase had inadvertently brought upon her youngest son? The thought twisted Lorette's heart like a cloth being wrung.

"I thought You would make a way for Samuel and me, Lord. Is this hurtful rumor Your way of telling me that Samuel and I are to move back to Philadelphia? Please, make our path clear, so I do not make any more missteps."

&

The next morning Chase arrived as Lorette was headed to the barn to care for the animals. Did she only imagine that his face looked grim and gray circles underscored his normally smiling eyes?

"I'll take care of the animals this morning." His tone sounded curt.

She longed to take him up on his offer but knew she didn't dare. "If I don't find the courage to go back in the barn today, I might never find it."

For a moment she didn't think he was going to accept her decision. Then he nodded. "We'll work together. You collect the eggs and milk Pansy while I rub the animals down with the fly ointment."

Gratitude flooded her. In spite of her brave words, she was terrified to step into the straw that hid snakes and other creatures so well. "Thank you."

He glanced at Samuel, who was seated on her hip, and raised his eyebrows.

Lorette explained about the stove incident from the day before. "I don't dare leave him alone in the house anymore. He's not satisfied with crawling any longer. He pulls himself up on everything. Any day now he'll be walking."

When they were done with the chores Chase carried the milk to the house while Lorette carried Samuel and the eggs. "I won't be needing any breakfast this morning," he said without meeting her gaze. "Fields are too wet to get into today. I'll be using the time to mend some things about my own place."

He turned abruptly, leaving before she could say good-bye.

The day wore on drearily long. Lunch and dinner seemed too much work to prepare for only herself. She settled for bread with butter and sugar and didn't bother to cook. She was glad when it was time to bring the animals back from pasture, even though it also meant entering the barn again, and this time without Chase's comforting presence.

She was inordinately pleased to find Chase's wagon in the yard and Chase in the barn when she returned. He was raking an area clear of straw. With a wave of his hand he indicated a legless wooden pen similar to the crib in the kitchen. "Thought we'd better set up a safe place for Sam in here right away."

"Thank you. I know how difficult it must have been for you to find time for this."

"Needed doing."

She set Samuel in the pen and went to get a pail of water from the well. The animals' legs and undersides were mud-caked from being in the pasture after yesterday's rain. Pansy's udders needed washing before milking.

Once she started milking, Lorette was so busy watching the floor for snakes that the milk bucket was missed as often as it was hit. She gritted her teeth and forced her attention on her work.

She and Chase worked in silence, at least in as much silence as one could find in a barn with a cow, oxen, a horse, chickens, insects, a woman milking, a man raking and tossing straw, and a ten-month-old boy trying to get anyone's and anything's attention. Lorette wondered how one small earthen building could hold so much tension. Then she wondered how her much smaller body could contain that much tension.

Still in silence, Chase accompanied her and Samuel to the house. He set the milk down on the porch. "We need to talk."

His demanding tone surprised her. "All right. Let me get a shawl to protect Samuel from the gnats."

He was pacing the porch when she returned. He stopped a foot from her. In the twilight the lines in his face looked set in stone. "I don't know if you heard the rumors in town yesterday—"

She nodded, too embarrassed to answer.

His shoulders lowered slightly, and she knew he was relieved not to have to put the rumor into words for her. "I haven't been able to think of anything else since I heard them."

"It's been the same for me," she admitted.

"I think I have a solution."

Immediately her spirits brightened. "Yes?" She should have known he would come up with something. Hadn't he had an answer for all her problems from the very beginning?

He took a deep breath. His hands formed into fists at his sides. "Marriage. I mean, I think we should marry. That is, will you marry me? Please, Miss Taber?"

Shock rolled through her. Her mouth dropped open. She couldn't make her throat work. Her first thought was to blurt out that of course she could not marry him, but something within her checked the words. It couldn't have been easy for him to offer this proposal. Her answer should be as kind as she could make it.

Lorette had to swallow twice before she could speak. She lifted her chin and straightened her shoulders in an attempt to gather as much dignity as possible about her. "It's kind of you to try to save my reputation from the rumors, Mr. Lankford. However, I assure you—your generous sacrifice is not necessary."

"I'm not asking because of your reputation. Well, not entirely, though I've seen how easy it is for a woman's reputation to be ruined. I'm thinking mostly of young Sam. His life might be affected by these rumors, too."

Lorette turned and stared out over the farmyard to keep him from seeing that she recognized the truth of his words. "I can take him back East."

She felt his hand firm and gentle on her shoulder and caught her breath sharply.

"Miss Taber." His voice was as gentle as his touch. "Together we can make good parents for Sam, and if we're married, I can stick around to help you run Sam's farm."

Unexpected pain ripped through her. His arguments were true, but they weren't what her heart wanted to hear. She had always dreamed of her future husband expressing undying love for her when he proposed marriage. This man only wanted a ready-made family, and a housekeeper, and maybe Samuel's farm.

No, that's not true, her heart forced her to admit, *not the part about Samuel's farm.*

Lorette wished Chase would remove his hand from her shoulder. His touch made it more difficult to think clearly. But what was there to think about? There could only be one answer.

She pulled her shawl more tightly about her and Samuel. The boy nestled against her chest, his eyelashes resting against his fat cheeks as he drifted off to sleep. If only she were as restful.

"I know you love Samuel, Mr. Lankford, and it's a fine thing you are willing to raise him as your own." She did love the way he loved the boy. "Even so, my answer to your proposal is. . .no." It was harder to say than she'd anticipated.

He took a deep breath. "I understand your reluctance, Miss Taber, but my proposal stands, should you change your mind."

His boots clumped against the porch's wooden planks as he left. She watched him, barely more than a dark shadow against the twilight skies, as he walked down the rutted dirt road toward his neighboring farm. Finally, as he crossed a cornfield a bend hid him from sight.

She lowered herself slowly onto the top step. Her thoughts reeled. The same questions and the same problems and the same possibilities replayed over and over while the twilight faded into night and the nighttime insects' songs grew loud. Samuel's breathing grew slower and more even, his tiny chest rising and falling rhythmically against her own. Curly laid down beside her, resting his head against her thigh with a melodramatic sigh.

Like most unmarried women her age, Lorette had dreamed for years of marrying. Even in a large city like Philadelphia, a governess had few

174

opportunities to meet marriageable men. Properly chaperoning and teaching children did not include becoming overly friendly with vendors and clerks. The few men who had asked to escort her she had met at church. Most were widowers looking for someone to care for their homes and raise their children. She'd wanted more in a marriage. She'd wanted a man who wanted her for herself. "Is that so much to ask, Lord? Is it terribly selfish to want to be loved for me?" she whispered into the night.

Curly stirred, looking up at her with a soft whine. She smiled down at him. "It's all right," she assured him quietly. "I'm only indulging in a little self-pity."

The night was clear and the stars sparkled with more brilliance than a Philadelphia jeweler's window. She loved the prairie sky. She couldn't remember it ever looking so large back East. It reminded her of the entry she'd read in Bess's diary that day.

> *Each day as I look out over this vast land, I am amazed anew at what Tom and I and others like us are accomplishing, the homes and communities we are building on this prairie. The sky, the fields, the prairie grasses seem to go on forever. When our children are grown, will there be any wild land left to tame? I hope the children will still be able to feel the wonder of this place. Today when Tom came in from the fields, Aaron ran to greet him and asked when he can be a farmer. I thought Tom would burst from pride that his son at even such a young age wants to work alongside him. Will our boys still want to work beside Tom in the fields when they are grown? At least in this fine land they will have the opportunity to do so if they choose.*

Lorette had told Chase she could take Samuel back East to protect him from the rumors about her and Chase. If she did, would Samuel have the opportunity to choose the life of his father, as Bess and Tom wished for the boy? Could she deny him the opportunity to claim the heritage for which they'd fought so hard for him?

If her refusal to marry Chase was the right thing, why didn't she feel at peace? Instead she felt restless inside.

Lorette pressed a soft kiss to Samuel's head. She loved the way he rested against her with complete abandon, with complete trust. She couldn't imagine a better man than Chase to raise him. She hadn't a doubt Tom and Bess would approve. Chase would make an honorable and faithful husband. "But, Lord, I don't know if I can give up the dream of marrying a man who loves me."

Even for Samuel? The words whispered through her mind.

She'd asked the Lord yesterday to make clear the best path for her and Samuel. Was marriage to Chase His answer?

Chapter 6

C hase risked a glance at Lorette over the breakfast table. She didn't
meet his glance. Her gaze was on her plate, where she idly pushed
a piece of sausage about with her fork.

Gray circles shaded the area beneath her eyes. She looked like she
hadn't slept any better than he had last night. Could she have reconsidered
his proposal? He didn't have the courage to ask, and she didn't mention it.

They barely spoke two words to each other all morning, not during
the barn chores and not since. The silence between them was thicker than
cream, and not nearly so pleasant.

He glanced down at his own plate and realized he hadn't eaten any
more than Lorette. He took a bite of fried egg. Cold fried egg.

Misery slithered through his chest. He'd enjoyed Lorette's company
almost from the beginning. Had he ruined all chance of friendship
between them by his proposal last night? He had convinced himself it was
the sensible thing to do.

Lying in bed last night he finally admitted the truth to himself. He
was falling in love with Lorette. He admired that she hadn't for a moment
considered the possibility of not raising Sam, that she was willing to do
anything necessary to care for him properly. He liked the courage with
which she took to farm life. He enjoyed her cheerful companionship at
meals each day.

And he couldn't bear the thought that not only Sam but Lorette might
move East, out of his life forever. That fear had been behind his proposal.

Had he been a fool to broach the subject of marriage?

Lorette cleared her throat.

His gaze darted to her.

She was still staring at her plate. "About last night. . ."

He waited.

She took a deep breath, not lifting her gaze. "I've been thinking. If I take Samuel back East, I'll likely have to sell the farm." Her words began to come in a rush. "I know from Bess's journal and letters that it was important to her and Tom that the children grow up out here. The farm is Samuel's heritage. I want him to have the choice of living here when he's grown. I know Tom and Bess would want that for him, too. I can't take that away from Samuel."

She paused again, pressing her lips together so hard they turned white. He could barely breathe for waiting for her to finish.

She took another deep breath. "So, if your offer still stands, for Samuel's sake, my answer is yes."

"Yes?"

Lorette nodded, lifting her lashes but not her head to peer at him, as if to judge his reaction.

"Yes." Joy relieved the pressure in his chest. "You said yes?"

A smile tugged at the edges of her lips. Her gaze darted from one side to the other and back to him in an embarrassed manner that delighted him.

He reminded himself that she wasn't marrying him because she loved him, but for Sam's sake. It surprised him that the knowledge only slightly diminished his joy. "When?"

She shrugged, looking confused.

"It should be soon. To squelch the rumors, I mean."

A shadow passed over her face. He could have kicked himself. How could he be so insensitive? They both knew the rumors were the reason he'd proposed. No need to keep dragging them up. "Is this evening too soon?"

"This evening?" Her voice sounded small and frightened.

Was she frightened to marry him? The thought dampened his spirits. "We can go into town this morning for the license."

"What about the crops?"

"They'll have to do their growing without me this morning. Get yourself and Sam ready. I'll hitch Boots up to the wagon. I want to stop by Bresvens' on the way."

By the time they were ready to leave, Lorette had changed into a slim peach-colored dress with lace trim and a matching bonnet. The dress was much fancier than the calico and gingham dresses covered by aprons she normally wore about the farm. She blushed prettily when he complimented her.

Lorette waited in the wagon while he went to speak with Mrs. Bresven. When he told her of the marriage, the Swedish woman hesitated only a moment before her round face burst into a smile. Her plump hands clasped his arms. "The Bible says it's a good thing when a man finds a wife. You've found yourself a good one in Miss Taber. I'm happy for you both," she congratulated in her singsong accent.

The reserve with which he'd been protecting himself fell away. "Thank you. We want to get married right away. Tonight. I was wondering—could we be married in your parlor? I know it's a lot to ask on such short notice, but I want it to be special for her, and—"

"A wedding in my own parlor!" Her eyes sparkled. "Yah, I should say you can marry here."

She insisted on going out to the wagon to congratulate Lorette. They found the future Mrs. Lankford in the wagon bed finishing up changing Sam's diaper. Chase watched Lorette's face anxiously as Mrs. Bresven eagerly congratulated Lorette and told how honored she was that Chase and Lorette wanted to be married in the Bresvens' home.

Lorette's surprised gaze met Chase's over Mrs. Bresven's head, but she answered with only a slight stammer that it was very kind of Mrs. Bresven to agree to their request.

As they continued their journey Lorette said, "I thought we would be married by the judge in town this morning."

Chase didn't want to tell her that he thought such a marriage would appear clandestine, an admission of guilt to the gossiping townspeople. He looked right into her eyes and said, "A marriage should be a joyful occasion.

179

I want it to be a nice memory for you."

He allowed her to study his eyes, knowing she was searching for the truth. Finally her face lost a little of the tension he'd seen in it all day. Her smile was soft. "Thank you."

Chase smiled back, his chest expanding beneath his clean brown work shirt. He felt like he'd just been handed the world.

Sam, who was the cause of the marriage and was seated on Lorette's lap, giggled for no apparent reason and clapped his baby hands with glee.

That evening Lorette was surprised and humbled when she entered Mrs. Bresven's parlor. The room wasn't fancy. The furniture wasn't as new or as beautiful as Bess's. Yet Lorette's heart was touched by the effort this newfound Swedish friend had gone to on her behalf.

Vines of pale pink wild roses stretched delicately across the tops of the windows and door. They wound among the items on the lace-covered table at one end of the room, in between a huge bowl of punch, plates of angel food cake, and delicate china plates and cups that Lorette knew Mrs. Bresven must count among her treasures.

"Everything is beautiful, Mrs. Bresven. Thank you so much."

Her neighbor beamed. "Please, call me Kari. If you are to be married in my home, we must be good enough friends to call each other by our first names."

"Yes, and I am Lorette."

"Your dress is beautiful."

"Thank you." Lorette looked down at her emerald green silk gown. The dress did not have the trim silhouette that was currently popular. She ran a gloved hand lightly over one hip, feeling the skirt's fullness. The long train caught up on the sides with silk flowers adding an elegance to the gown. "It was Bess's wedding dress."

She had found it in Bess's trunk. It had taken hours this afternoon to iron out the wrinkles.

"You look beautiful in it."

Lorette looked up in surprise at Chase's gravelly voice. She hadn't realized he was so close.

He cleared his throat. "Bess would have been happy that you chose to wear her wedding gown."

Lorette smiled at him, glad he recognized that wearing the dress made her feel closer to her sister.

The Bresven children rushed about alternately helping their mother prepare for company and reluctantly obeying her orders to keep away from the food and to be careful of their Sunday clothes. They all wanted to hold Samuel and play with him. Lorette enjoyed the bustle. The conversation with the children kept her mind off the enormity of the event ahead.

She was surprised when neighbors began stopping. "I thought only the Bresvens would be at the wedding," she said when she and Chase had a rare moment alone.

"I wanted my friends to celebrate with us. Do you mind very much?"

"No."

He touched her cheek softly with the back of one hand. "I wish your friends could be here."

At the gentleness of his touch and his thought for her, sweet pain throbbed in her chest. Her gaze caught in his and she forgot there were other people about them.

"Here comes the minister," someone shouted.

The announcement jolted Lorette back to the parlor.

The ceremony was simple and solemn. Lorette was thankful that Chase had arranged for the minister to perform it, rather than the judge she had at first thought would marry them. She believed deeply that marriage was not only a legal but also a spiritual union.

It was frightening saying the vows, pledging to spend her life with this man she'd known such a short time. But working on the farm together, didn't they know each other better than most couples who courted in the prescribed manner?

She barely noticed the ring when he slipped it on her finger. When the ceremony was over and his friends were toasting them with Kari's punch, Lorette realized she was twisting the ring nervously and looked closer. She gasped at the beautiful jewelry. The stone was a large, rectangular blue sapphire mounted in a delicate, intricate setting. She looked up at Chase and saw he was watching her. He seemed to understand her question.

"The ring was my mother's," he said in low voice for her ears alone. "If you don't like it, we'll buy you another."

"No." She slid her right hand over the ring. "I'll cherish it."

He took her hands between his own and squeezed them lightly. Then he raised an arm and waited for the crowd to quiet. He thanked them all for sharing the special day. He slid an arm around Lorette's shoulders and looked down at her. "And I thank God for bringing the gift of Lorette into my life."

Lorette's heart stumbled. He seemed so sincere. She wanted to believe he thought her a gift, but it felt like trusting in daydreams. Hadn't she given up the dream of marrying a man who loved her?

The ride back to the farm wasn't nearly long enough, Lorette felt. Chase had explained that as a bachelor, he hadn't put time and money into building a 'real' house yet. He lived in a one-room soddy. They had agreed it was best to live in Tom and Bess's home.

She was trembling when he helped her down from the wagon. He kept his hands lightly on her waist. She didn't dare lift her gaze to his but stared into his shoulder.

"If you want, I can spend the night at my soddy."

She shook her head. "No," she whispered. What if the neighbors spotted him heading to Bess and Tom's from his own place in the morning? It would be terribly embarrassing.

He bent his head and touched his lips to hers, quickly and lightly. Slowly his arms slid around her waist, drawing her closer. Her heart tripped over itself. He kissed her again, his lips soft, lingering, questioning, sweeter than she'd imagined a kiss could be.

Lorette wanted to abandon herself to his arms and kisses, but her chest burned. How could she give herself freely when he hadn't said he loved her? She pushed lightly against his shoulders.

He pulled his lips from hers immediately and rested his head against hers. His breath was coming quickly and unevenly. They stood that way for many minutes, until they heard Samuel fussing in his makeshift bed in the back of the wagon.

Lorette felt cold when Chase released her to pick up the boy. He placed Samuel in Lorette's arms. "I'll put Boots away while you put Sam to bed."

She nodded and started up the porch steps. Her heart hammered in her ears. What would happen when Chase came inside? Would he expect. . .

"Lorette."

She couldn't see his features as he stood in the late evening shadows beside Boots.

"It's all right, Lorette." His voice was gentle. "I'll sleep in one of the other rooms."

Lorette wasn't sure whether she felt relief or regret as she carried Samuel up to her bedchamber.

Chapter 7

T he first few days after their marriage, things felt strained to Lorette between herself and Chase. Marriage hadn't changed their daily lives much. Chase had been an integral part of her life and Samuel's before the marriage; now they just lived under the same roof.

That they no longer referred to each other as Mr. Lankford and Miss Taber, but as Chase and Lorette, was only a symbol of the true changes. Her emotions were vulnerable in a new and terrifying way. She was self-conscious about every look between them, every casual touch. Her life and Samuel's were no longer hers alone to control. She was tied to Chase and this land forever.

One rainy evening in late July Chase took a fussy Samuel into the family room while Lorette cleaned up after the meal. She shaved soap into the enamel dishpan and poured in hot water from the steaming teakettle. Setting the kettle back on the stove, she paused at the sound of Chase's deep voice singing a lullaby.

Smiling, she tiptoed to the doorway and peeked in. Chase was seated in Bess's tapestry covered rocker, dwarfing the delicate chair. He didn't notice her. His attention was on Samuel lying on his lap in total trust, his eyes closed. The homeliness of the scene was endearing.

When Chase finished the simple melody for the third time, she cleared her throat to get his attention. He looked up with a silly grin that showed her he was embarrassed.

Not wanting to awaken Samuel, she walked softly until she was close enough to whisper. "My mother sang that to Bess and me when we were little."

"Tell me about your childhood."

She lowered herself to the small crewel-covered footstool and told of growing up in Philadelphia. It had been a happy life until her parents were killed in a train accident. Soon after, she'd found a position as a governess, and Bess married Tom and moved to the Minnesota prairie.

Inclement weather made the room darker than usual for the hour, and Lorette hadn't lit the lamps yet. Perhaps the atmosphere made it easier for them to confide in each other in new ways.

Chase told her about his own life, his early childhood years in the East, coming west to Wisconsin with his parents to farm, then moving here to homestead as a young man. He hadn't as much land under acreage as Tom. He'd begun assisting Tom for money, working his own land at the same time. It was a long, hard road, but Chase didn't mind.

"Tom used to talk about when Sam and Aaron would be old enough to work beside him in the fields. He hoped to eventually buy more land so he could help them get started on their own farms."

"Bess spoke of that, too, in her journals." *I made the right decision, marrying Chase,* Lorette thought. *He understands and shares Bess and Tom's dreams for Samuel. It's obvious he loves the boy.*

"By the time Sam is grown and claims his inheritance, we'll have a real house on our land."

This was the first time either of them had spoken of their distant future together, when it would be just the two of them in a marriage without the boy who had brought them together. She'd been too busy with everyday life to consider that such a time might come. The thought was a disturbing one to Lorette. "I'd best get back to the dishes before the water gets cold."

His words stayed with her. "*We* will have a real house on *our* land."

Always in the back of her mind she'd wondered whether Bess and Tom's land and their new house had been important factors behind Chase's proposal. The way he spoke tonight, it didn't appear so. "*We* will have a real house on *our* land." His words seemed filled with promise, as though he believed one day their marriage would be beautiful and rich in its normalness.

For days his words came back to her at odd times while she played with Samuel, or cared for the animals, or worked about the house. Weeding in the garden two weeks later the picture of Chase rocking Samuel and singing the lullaby filled her mind. "Oh, my!" Her hands stilled the hoe as a surprising and dismaying thought struck.

"This is the life I wished for when I was back in Philadelphia," she told an uncomprehending Samuel, who sat in the dirt happily yanking at a stubborn weed.

Wonder filled her at the realization. She hadn't wished to be a farm wife, she thought, placing a hand on her lower back and stretching stiff muscles. But she'd wished for her own family. Bess's letters, which had bubbled over with love for Tom and the children, had stirred embers of envy in Lorette's heart.

"Now I have my own family—and all because Bess and Tom died." She looked across the land to where the crosses were barely visible through wind-whipped prairie grass. She didn't believe God allowed Bess and Tom to die in order to give Lorette a ready-made family. But living on the prairie, she saw that nature and God waste nothing, even death. In one way or another all death brought new life out here.

Her gaze dropped to Samuel. "No!" She darted to him, bending over and pulling his hand from his mouth. She opened the sticky, dirty fingers and removed a granite colored stone with a sigh of relief. "I have to watch you every minute."

"Uh! Uh!" He made grasping motions with his fingers.

"No."

Samuel struggled to his feet and started down the row, trying out his newfound independence in walking. Three steps along he tumbled into the dirt. Curly, who was never far away when Lorette was outside with Samuel, stuck his nose in Samuel's face to be sure he was okay. Samuel pushed himself up on his forearms and shook his head until his curls shook, too. "No. No, Da."

Lorette laughed. Samuel's vocabulary only included four words: mama, papa, no, and da for dog. Sometimes he called her mama and Chase papa. It was hard to hear. She and Chase agreed Samuel would always know who his parents were, but he wasn't old enough to understand yet.

She took his hand as he struggled to his feet. "Let's go back to the house and get dinner ready."

Contentment filled her as they walked slowly along with his little fingers clutching hers. Every few steps he'd fight for balance, sometimes winning, sometimes losing. "You're getting better at walking every day," she told him.

She and Chase and Samuel were getting better at being a family every day. She knew Chase loved Samuel. She was pretty sure Chase liked her. But liking wasn't loving. *That's the part of my dream that's missing*, she thought, her heart twisting, *a husband who loves me*.

❧

Lorette stole a moment to look out Kari Bresven's kitchen window at the late summer fields bathed in sunshine. The crops were abundant and beautiful, but they wouldn't be standing long. Harvest was going well. Chase, like most of the area farmers, had hired men to help. The neighbors were helping each other out, too. Harvest on Chase and Lorette's crops had been completed yesterday. Today Chase was helping in the Bresvens' fields, and Lorette and other neighbor women were helping Kari in the kitchen as the women had helped Lorette previously. Kari's children watched Samuel and some of the other wives' young ones so the women could work unimpeded.

Throughout the last week Lorette had fried chicken, peeled potatoes, and baked ten loaves of bread and a dozen pies. Now she was peeling potatoes again and wondering whether she would have any skin left on her fingers after harvest.

"Watching for a glimpse of that good-looking husband of yours?" a voice teased behind her.

Lorette turned with a smile but ignored the jest. "Catching a bit of breeze." She liked Susan, a dark-haired young farm wife. Lorette thought Susan seemed much younger and more carefree than herself, though she was only a year younger and had been married five years.

Lorette stepped back to the worktable and glanced in dismay at the pile of unpeeled potatoes on which she and Susan were working. It looked like it had grown in the few seconds she'd spent at the window. Already she missed the breeze. She'd grown accustomed to the prairie winds. They were quieter than usual today, and the house was hot from the oven that had been going since before dawn. The smell of fresh-baked bread and pies didn't make the heat any easier to bear. Her dress stuck to her and her hair itched.

Susan finished peeling another potato and continued her teasing. "A number of young ladies had their bonnets set for your husband when he was single."

Lorette glanced at her in surprise. Unmarried men greatly outnumbered unmarried women in the area. Why hadn't it occurred to her to wonder before why Chase, who loved children and family, hadn't married before she came along?

"Good thing he waited." Kari set a kettle of cold water on the table for the peeled potatoes.

Lorette began to feel uneasy with the turn in conversation. The women were talking as if they didn't remember the rumors that precipitated Chase's proposal. She shifted her worried gaze to Kari.

The practical woman said quietly, "I've known Chase a long time. It's easy to see you make him happy."

Her words warmed Lorette's heart. She knew the hasty wedding hadn't fooled Kari, but the dear woman believed she and Chase could make a happy marriage even with such a beginning.

"He's not as good-looking as my husband of course," Susan continued with a laugh, "but he's a good man."

Lorette smiled. "Yes."

Kari brushed her hands down her apron. "There's nothing wrong with Chase Lankford's looks that I can see."

Susan shrugged good-naturedly. "I guess handsome is in the eye of the beholder."

Lorette shared in the laughter Susan's misquote brought. It was fun to be teased about Chase. She thought him by far the best looking man she'd seen since her arrival from Philadelphia, but it wouldn't have mattered if he was bald and had to bend over to see his boots. It was Chase's heart she loved.

A HOMESTEADER, A BRIDE, AND A BABY

Out in the yard, large pieces of wood were set on sawhorses and barrels to form a long table. At noon when the men came in from the fields Lorette watched eagerly for Chase while carrying food from the house to the table. They only shared quick smiles as they passed. Lorette enjoyed the visiting that went on with harvest time, but she missed the family meals with just her, Chase, and Samuel.

The table almost groaned under the heavy load of food. Lorette walked down one side filling coffee cups while the men loaded their plates. Each of the men had washed up at the pails of water on the back porch before sitting down, but it seemed to Lorette that the washing hadn't decreased the smell of sweat and kerosene one iota.

When she came to Chase he lifted his cup for her. "Things going all right this morning?"

She met his gaze, found him smiling into her eyes, and returned his smile. "Yes, fine. How are things going in the fields?"

He hadn't a chance to answer. Susan's husband, Ben, seated across from Chase, spoke first in a loud voice meant to draw attention. "Can sure tell yer a newlywed, Lankford. Come from a hot morning in the fields and yer more interested in speaking to yer wife than eating."

Ben's eyes sparkled with fun, but Lorette knew her cheeks flamed from his comments. She went on with her work.

Susan didn't ignore him. "Stop your teasing, Ben. Every man should look at his wife the way Chase looks at Lorette."

"Better listen up, Ben." Laughter threaded Chase's words.

Lorette darted a surprised look at Chase. He grinned at her in a manner that was downright flirtatious. Flustered, she murmured something about getting more coffee, though the pot still felt heavy, and retreated to the hot kitchen.

During the afternoon, Chase's looks and words danced through Lorette's mind. Ben's comments hadn't appeared to embarrass Chase at all. Still, she tried to avoid giving cause for further comments at the group supper and was glad when they finally left for home.

Chase brought in the large tin tub from the shed to the kitchen and Lorette heated water for their Saturday night baths while Chase took care of the animals. Samuel was the first to be bathed. Lorette had hoped the long day with the other children would have tired him, but it seemed to have energized him instead. She was glad Chase offered to watch the boy in the sitting room while she bathed.

The change into clean clothes felt good after the long hot day. She towel dried her hair and combed it out, letting it hang loose to dry.

When she entered the sitting room, Chase was holding Samuel and standing in front of Bess and Tom's family picture. Chase glanced at her. "Sam looks more like his father every day."

Lorette compared the boy to the image of the man. "Yes." Even in the lamplight the similarity was noticeable. So were the lines in Chase's face. He looked weary. She was sure he was wishing Tom and his family hadn't died. He would think it no use saying so; his wishing wouldn't bring them back.

Samuel wriggled and pushed at Chase's chest, and Chase set him down. "I'll watch him now," Lorette said.

"He's mighty full of life for so late. He's trying to climb up on everything, when he's not chewing it."

"I'll rock him and read to him. I read to him every day from Bess's journal. I like knowing he is hearing his mother's words, even if he doesn't know they are hers." She shrugged, self-conscious at her revelation, half expecting him to laugh.

Chase touched her cheek, brushing his thumb slowly and gently over it. "When he's older, I'll tell him you did this for him, and he'll read her journals himself."

His sweet intimacy was unexpected. He never touched her in such a personal manner. His understanding made it a moment she knew she would cherish. "Thank you," she whispered.

A frustrated grunt cut the moment off as effectively as a slamming door.

"No!" They hollered at the same time. Both lunged for Samuel. Chase reached the boy first, swinging him up with only an inch to spare before Samuel would have grabbed the fringed table covering that was beneath the fancy lit kerosene lamp.

A Homesteader, a Bride, and a Baby

Lorette was shaking when Chase put the boy into her arms. "Close call." Chase shook his head before heading for the kitchen and his bath.

Lorette had to rock the struggling youngster for a few minutes to calm herself before she could read. She and Samuel had read almost the entire journal; they were up to the last entry. Lorette looked at the date and a sadness welled up in her. The date was the day before Bess died.

> *Aaron and Liza are complaining of sore throats, and mine is feeling a bit scratchy. Such a time to come down with something, with Lorette coming in a couple days. I can barely contain my excitement at seeing her again! I keep thinking of things I must tell her, and must ask her, and memories I want to relive with her. I do hope she will be happy working for the Henrys, though I confess another fantasy has crossed my mind a few times since she agreed to come out west. I like to pretend she and Chase fall in love. . ."*

Lorette's voice stumbled. She glanced at the closed kitchen door. Had Chase heard? She lowered her words to barely a whisper.

> *I like to pretend she and Chase fall in love and marry. Tom tells me to quit being fanciful, but it would be such fun to have my sister and Tom's best friend for neighbors. Our children could grow up together.*

She closed the book. "That's your mother's last entry, Samuel."
He plopped both hands on the leather cover. "Mama."
Tears leaped to her eyes and she hugged him close. "Yes."
The door opened and Chase stuck his wet head into the room. "I'm going out to check on the animals one last time." A moment later she heard the outside door squeak open and close again.

In a shaky voice, she began singing a lullaby. After what seemed a long time, Samuel fell asleep. She placed him in his crib and went to stand on the porch.

The weather was pleasant, having cooled off after the sun went down.

191

An orange harvest moon brightened the landscape. In the pale light she saw Chase walking back from the graves.

"I was thinking," he said when he arrived at the porch, "that we should use some of the money from the crops to buy headstones."

Gratitude flooded her. "I'd like that. You were wonderful to make the crosses, but. . ."

"They aren't permanent like a headstone."

"No."

He came to stand beside her, leaning against the rail and looking out over the land.

"I'm going to miss the crops," she told him. "I liked watching them grow and change. As they grew they changed the landscape. Sometimes the colors changed from hour to hour, depending on the height of the sun, and the movement of the clouds, or the wiles of the winds."

He chuckled. "They'll be back next year."

Lorette looked down at the wooden rail and ran her fingers lightly along it. Her heart beat hard against her chest as she built up her courage to ask the question she'd been wondering about since morning. "Why didn't you marry before you met me?"

He was silent so long that she finally looked at him. His face looked taut in the shadows cast by the moon.

"Never mind. I shouldn't have asked."

He took a deep breath. "You have every right to ask. You're my wife. You can ask me anything."

Lorette tried to drink in the wonder of his words before he continued.

"I'd been courting a girl when I decided to move out here and homestead. Thought I loved her. Thought she loved me, too. When I told her my plans and asked her to marry me, she said she'd never marry a farmer."

Lorette didn't know what to say. She reached out and tentatively laid a hand on his forearm. He covered her hand with his own and went on with his story.

"Gave up on the idea of love and marriage after that. Then I met Tom and Bess. Tom, he sure was crazy in love with your sister. After awhile, seeing them together, I began to have second thoughts about getting

192

married, but I didn't meet anyone I wanted to spend my life with." He squeezed her hand. "Then God brought you into my life."

Her throat tightened. Was he saying he truly cared for her?

"I saw the sacrifices you were making for Samuel, the hard life you took on without a whimper of self-pity. Every day I found myself liking you more, and then it was more than liking."

Lorette could barely breathe. Was he saying he loved her?

He slid his hand from hers, and her fingers felt suddenly cool in the night air. "It was wrong to ask you to marry me the way I did." His voice sounded hard.

"Wh. . .why?"

"You were grieving for Bess and you'd just found out about the rumors. No one could be expected to think clearly about what they want and need at such a time." He shoved both hands through his hair and turned to her. "I was so terrified you might move back East that I was glad for an excuse to press you to marry me. But maybe I've ruined your life. Maybe you would have been happier back East, and now I've tied you to me and to this land."

He'd wanted to marry her for herself, not only for Samuel! Joy flooded her at the realization, but he still hadn't said he loved her. She chose her words carefully.

"I'm beginning to understand Bess's love for this land. When I first came here, I thought the prairie was a threatening place. Living on the farm has made me aware of nature's life, death, life cycle. I'll never stop missing Bess, but I'm able to accept her death better now. I realize the land isn't the enemy. We aren't in battle against it. We're in partnership with it." Lorette could feel his gaze on her.

"We?" His tone was wary.

Lorette met his gaze. "I've no desire to move back East. Every day when you leave for the fields or chores, it seems all Samuel and I do is wait for you to return."

His hands lifted slowly and framed her face. "I love you, Lorette. I've loved you almost since you moved out to the farm, but I didn't think you'd want to hear it."

"I do want to hear it. I want to hear it every day."

He pulled her into his arms and whispered against her hair, "I love you, Lorette. I love you. I love you."

She relaxed against him, drinking in the words she'd waited so long to hear. "I love you, too," she replied shyly, whispering the words she'd been waiting all her life to say.

He chuckled, lifting her in his arms and swinging her around in a circle again and again, his boots thunking against the porch boards. "I want to hear it every day, too," he demanded.

He kissed her soundly on the lips, his arms tight about her waist, then lowered her slowly until she stood on her own feet. His kisses didn't stop. They grew sweeter and lingered longer and longer and longer.

"I should get you inside before it gets too cool out here," Chase finally said.

Lorette nodded against his shoulder. Her last thought as they walked into their home wrapped in each other's arms was that the Lord had indeed made a way for her and Samuel; He'd made a very nice way indeed.

THE
APPLESAUCE WAR

by Ellen Edwards Kennedy

Chapter 1

New York State, September, 1901

Verity McCracken swallowed the bite of pancake she'd been chewing and frowned at her father over the breakfast table. "I don't believe it. You're saying that you and Mr. Delorme aren't speaking? You've been friends all your lives. Why now?"

Jacob McCracken poured more of his homemade maple syrup over the already sodden pancakes and stared intently at the mess. "Druther not talk about it." He dropped his fork and crossed his arms over his chest. "Just please do what I ask." His salt-and-pepper eyebrows dipped ominously over his pale blue eyes.

Verity looked over at the big, black, wood-burning stove where her mother stood. "Are you mad at the Delormes, too?"

Grace McCracken rolled her eyes, then turned toward the stove, and wrapped a dishtowel around the handle of the steaming coffeepot. "Don't bring me into this!" Hefting the pot, she filled the cups around the table, her husband's, her own, Verity's.

"But why? What caused this?"

Grace smiled down at her only chick. "I'm sure I couldn't say," she said, "But if y'ask me, it's all a lot of applesauce," she added with a meaningful glance at her husband.

Jacob didn't meet his wife's eyes. "Now there's another thing 'at gets my goat!" he said, returning to his breakfast with clumsy enthusiasm. "Why are people always sayin' something's 'applesauce,' as if it was of no account?" He pointed at the ever-present bowl of the stuff. "Applesauce is good for you— and dee-licious!" He spooned a large dollop on his plate for emphasis.

"Papa, it's just an expression. It doesn't reflect on your apples." Verity had to smile.

Jacob caught her at it. "This is no laughing matter, Missy. I'm dead serious."

Verity immediately sobered and her heart sank. Papa wasn't joking, as he frequently did. Whatever difference stood between Papa and Gerard Delorme, it would have to be important. Yet Mama seemed to take it in stride. The situation was all very puzzling. Especially the part about Gerard Delorme's youngest son.

"What's Pete done? Why are you mad at him, too?"

Jacob's face remained screwed up tightly. "I never asked much of my only daughter, just this one thing," he told the cream pitcher. He looked over at Verity. "Are you going to mind me, girl?"

"You mean to stay away from Pete? I don't know, Papa; after all, it's not my fight. Besides, Pete's away at college. I haven't laid eyes on him since Christmas and that's—what?—nine months, at least. And we were never really that close."

Verity turned to her mother. "I'm going to the mercantile today. I might see one of the Delormes on the street. You want me to ignore them?"

Grace sat down at the table. "No, siree, we don't!" she said, frowning at Jacob as she stirred her coffee. "You were raised to be a lady and a lady you shall be!" She tapped the drops off her spoon and took a sip. "No matter what anybody says." She took another. The law had been laid down.

"O' course I want you to be polite," said Jacob, slightly chastened. "Just no. . .lollygagging, understand?"

Verity drew herself up straight in her chair. "Papa, I have never 'lollygagged' in my life," she said frostily, "though I never did know what that word meant."

Jacob drained his coffee. "You know perzactly what I mean, though, Missy." He glanced at the old school clock on the kitchen wall. "Six thirty-five already—I'm burnin' daylight! Got chores to do." He bent to kiss his daughter, then his wife. "Don't forget my peppermints," he reminded Verity, then clapped on his hat and was out the back door.

Having already milked six cows before breakfast, Jacob would usually be inspecting the state of his apples in his thousand-tree orchard, or, in the company of his lone hired hand, Fred, chopping the weeds from an autumn crop of cabbages. Time was of the essence this far north in a valley of the old York State's Adirondack region. Cold weather came on fast once the leaves started turning, and it was only a week before the all-important apple harvest. But today, Jacob had more pressing matters to tend to and an appointment to keep.

The newly risen autumn sun caused him to squint as he walked briskly between the rows of low-hanging apple trees to the narrow strip where his land bordered Gerard Delorme's. There was a stone wall there, with a wild raspberry bush nearby and a three-step stile that he climbed over with long-accustomed ease.

There, while watching Delorme's calm Guernseys grazing, he leaned against the stone wall, pulled a crisp apple from his pocket, and thought about his daughter's future as he munched.

A hand slapped his shoulder roughly. "Well met, Jacob McCracken!" Gerard Delorme had come down the path along the fence instead of across the pasture, as expected. " 'In thy face I see the map of honor, truth, and loyalty.' "

Jacob swallowed, then grinned. "What's that, Gerry? More Shakespeare? My pa allus said you'd spoil your eyes with all that readin'."

"*Henry the Sixth*, act 3," admitted Gerard, "but if you don't want to associate with bookworms, you'd best look to your own household. I hear Verity took high honors at Plattsburgh Normal School."

Jacob blushed with pride even as he shrugged away the compliment to his daughter. "It's true, but we don't mention it much. Can't have her gettin' the big head."

Suddenly, Gerard's expression changed. He looked over each shoulder. "Did you do it?" he asked eagerly.

Jacob regarded his apple core thoughtfully, then tossed it into the bushes. "Ayah, but I didn't like it much."

"No more than I. When I told my family this morning, they all thought I had lost my sanity."

Jacob shielded his eyes with his hand and stared out at the Delorme dairy herd. "Nothin' they didn't know already."

"Very funny. What did you give as a reason?"

"Didn't give none. Refused to discuss it."

Gerard threw back his head and laughed heartily. "Well done! That's exactly the tack I took! Two great minds with but a single thought!"

Jacob shrugged. "That's mighty nice talking and all, but I dunno if this thing's gonna work. My wife—"

"You told her?" Gerard's brown button eyes widened.

"O' course. But she's promised to keep mum."

Gerard sighed. "Good." He slapped Jacob's back. "Fear not! It's a masterful plan and can only lead to—"

"Gerry, I don't understand why we just can't tell them we'd like 'em to keep company and get married someday."

"Kiss of death, Jacob, kiss of death! Could anything be less romantic than a match arranged by Mother and Father? Certainly not!"

"I guess I see what you mean. They are pretty bull-headed kids, but maybe nature will just...take its course. They'll be at the barn dance at your place next month and they'll see each other around town...."

"We can't chance it. Your daughter and my son are attractive young people. What if they found somebody else in the meantime? Disaster!"

"But—"

"It'll be the romantic story of the Montagues and Capulets all over again. The Bard's immortal tale. What could be more enticing than forbidden love?" When he smiled, Gerard's plump cheeks resembled the round, red McIntoshes hanging from Jacob's trees.

"But didn't that Romeo and Juliet thing end up kinda sad?"

"That's because the families were really feuding! As soon as we see Cupid's arrow fly, we reconcile, bury the hatchet, smoke the peace pipe, and all's well that ends well!"

Jacob took off his hat and scratched his head. "Well, I guess so. We've already got the ball rolling. So what do we do now?"

"Just watch that ball roll, Jacob! You said your girl will be in town on errands today? Well, so will my son. He begins his legal career reading law with Ted Essex's firm this very morning." He looked at the sky. "When shall we meet again? In thunder, lightning, or in rain?"

Jacob was puzzled. "What's the weather got to do with it?"

Gerard sighed. "Just a quoting from *Macbeth,* act 1, scene 1."

"Well, rain or shine, I'll be here tomorrow at the same time. I hope this thing works out." Jacob replaced his hat on his head.

Gerard grasped his friend's hand firmly. "It will, I assure you. Perhaps before too many more autumns, we'll be calling each other *Grandpere.*"

Jacob chuckled as he shook Gerard's hand. "Hmm, Grandpa. Sounds pretty good. If that happens, it'll be worth every smidgen of this foolishness!"

Chapter 2

In her absentmindedness, Verity overlooked two newly laid eggs during her trip to the henhouse. Then, she scattered far more feed corn than was necessary, to the chickens' frantic delight.

"Verity," Grace asked as her daughter meandered through the kitchen, lost in thought, "what happened to the leftover bacon?"

"What? Oh." Verity looked down at the empty platter sitting by the sink, waiting to be washed. "I guess I put it in the dog's dish with the leftover pancakes."

Grace sighed as she pumped water into the sink. "Well, it's gone now. I was going to add it to the beans." She nodded towards a large pot simmering on the back of the stove.

"I'm sorry, Mama. I was thinking of something else." Verity turned her head, scanning the kitchen. "Where's the dishtowel I just had in my hand?"

Her mother ran a soapy dishrag around the rim of a coffee cup. "Hangin' over your shoulder." She dipped the cup in the steaming rinse water and handed it over. "Punkin, you better get your head on straighter than your hat before you go into town. Can't have you coming home with a big sack of salt instead of flour!" She smiled, wiped one hand on her apron, and pushed a shiny brown curl from Verity's forehead. "And quit frettin' over this thing with the Delormes. It'll all come out in the wash."

" 'Come out in the wash.' What does that mean, exactly?" Verity had learned in college that it was important to define one's terms.

"I can't say any more."

Verity began to feel angry. First, Papa's weird statement at breakfast and now Mama talking in riddles! "But this quarrel or whatever it is—what about forgiveness? Is this falling-out so bad they can't forgive each other? It's not Christian!" Verity waved her hand in the air dramatically. The damp coffee cup in her fingers flew across the kitchen and shattered against a pine cupboard.

"Oh! Oh! Mama! I'm so sorry!" She dashed over, knelt, and began picking up the shards. "Oh, it's ruined! Your cup!"

Her mother patted her shoulder. "Run along. You'll cut yourself; you're that addlepated this morning. It's not my best china." She took the fragments from her daughter's hand. "Go on; get dressed for town. There's a nice shirtwaist in your cabinet, and wear that straw hat with the bow. You looked so pretty in it when you stepped off the train."

Nodding gratefully, Verity fled.

"Poor mite. This thing has got her in such a dither," muttered Grace as she swept the remains of the cup into a dustpan.

Verity's hands shook as she unbraided her long hair. Being a full-grown woman of nineteen required that she wear her hair up, but sometimes the effort was just more trouble than it was worth. "I miss being ten," she told the mirror. "I could wear boy's overalls and braids and climb trees, and Papa and Mama acted like normal parents."

Bending forward, she gave her brown mane several long, downward strokes with the hairbrush. Then, she placed a little rectangular pillow, curiously called a "rat," on the top of her head, lifted her hair over it, and fastened the ends in a coil at the base of her neck with the half-dozen U-shaped hairpins she held between her lips. With satisfaction, Verity surveyed her result in the mirror. The rat gave her silky hair fullness on top, as fashion dictated.

"What to do?" She asked herself as she buttoned up her shirtwaist. "I didn't promise Papa anything, really," she mused as she pulled the shoe buttons through their buttonholes with the long metal hook. "I'll just have to play things by ear," she decided as she fastened her fashionable new hat to her hair with a wicked-looking, six-inch hatpin. Not that she had need for them in Enfield, but her friends at college had reminded her that hatpins could serve as more than decoration on a long train journey or in a big city like Albany.

As she climbed into the wagon, Verity remembered the last sermon she had heard in the college chapel, on the Ten Commandments. " 'Honor thy father and thy mother: that thy days may be long upon the land,' " she quoted aloud over the back of the two old reliable grays, Thunder and Lightning.

Thunder stamped impatiently until Verity clucked at the horses and jiggled the reins. "Giddap."

Papa was right about one thing. He'd been a remarkably indulgent father, asking little of her, only the standard daily chores, and the respect due him as her parent. Never once had he discouraged her dream of going to normal school. He'd even dipped into the family savings for the tuition and had pressed a five-dollar bill into her gloved hand as she boarded the train. "For some silly girl thing or 'nother," he'd whispered and kissed her cheek.

Verity dabbed a tear off that same cheek with the back of her glove. It was the least she could do, respect her father's wishes, and steer clear of the Delormes as much as possible. Given time, the thing, whatever it was, would probably heal itself. Verity sat up, whispered a prayer, and resolutely turned her mind to town and the items on her mother's list.

Pierre Delorme, better known as Pete to the people of Enfield, New York, and the surrounding countryside, was having much the same debate with himself as he sat at a desk in the office of Essex and Westcloth, Esquires, Attorneys at Law.

"Reading law," meant serving as an apprentice in a law firm. Before him lay the daunting task of researching and reviewing a complicated legal precedent for his employers. He had done everything in preparation: gathered a healthy stack of paper, sharpened six pencils into the metal wastebasket with his penknife and even pulled down several relevant volumes from the walls of the firm's copious law library.

Now, all that remained was for him to crack open a book and get busy, but his mind simply wouldn't focus. It didn't bode well for his first day of employment.

Pete picked up a pencil and wrote a heading, *What are the central points at issue?* Then he underlined it three times.

Good question, he thought.

What on earth had gotten into Father this morning? Breakfast had been exceedingly strange: the astonishing little speech, delivered with many long words and trite expressions; Mother, crying quietly into her napkin; David and Anne exchanging shocked looks and even Nancy, the cook, pretending to be deaf as she carried in the tray of sausages.

"But why?" his brother, David, had demanded. "What have the McCrackens done?"

"I have spoken," said Gerard. "There will be no further discussion."

And there wasn't. Although David's wife, Anne, was unable to finish her oatmeal and begged, in a whisper, to be excused from the table long before the meal was over.

Mother had stopped him in the dark front hall as he left for town. "Oh, Pierre, please say a prayer for your father!" she whispered as she dabbed her eye with a delicate lace handkerchief, "I truly think he has lost his mind! He refuses to say another word, only forbids us all—forbids! Did you hear him use that word?—Forbids us to have any truck whatsoever with the McCrackens." She blew her nose and gazed up at him. "Our dear friends! How can he do this?"

Pete looked down fondly into the wide eyes of his dainty blond mother. "I don't know, but Father has always been good to us and I guess we'll just have to trust that this thing is important to him. It'd have to be." He kissed her forehead. "We'll both pray, Mother, and everything will turn out all right. I know it."

Marie Delorme threw her arms around her youngest son, the child most like herself at heart. "Thank you, dear, and now go do your best work for Mr. Essex. We're so proud of you! I know you'll make a splendid lawyer."

Pete jolted from his reverie when his pencil point broke with a loud snap. He had been pressing too hard. He picked up another and tried to return to his task.

. . .the central points at issue. . .

He made a decision. He loved his father and Pete would do as he asked, have little or nothing to do with anyone of the McCracken clan. It was a pity, though. He'd heard that Verity had finished school and was back to stay. Rumor was, she was prettier than ever, and he'd have liked to have seen for himself.

Pete blinked hard and took a deep breath. Better tackle the task at hand before Messrs. Essex and Westcloth decided they had no need of such a lazy law clerk. "Let's see now..." He opened a volume and began to turn the pages.

🙚

Verity completed her shopping far earlier than she expected.

"That's the last of it," said Mr. Bernard, as he hefted a huge sack of flour into the back of the wagon. "You sure you don't want me to pull down those bolts of new gingham my missus ordered? It just come in, and if I say so myself, the colors are pretty as a picture!" The merchant smiled broadly. "You've got enough time to run up a new dress for the barn dance next month!"

Verity hadn't the heart to tell him that gingham was no longer in fashion among college girls. She smiled. "Perhaps another day," she said, surveying the main street for familiar faces. She hadn't spotted a single Delorme so far this morning, and she felt vaguely disappointed.

She was about to accept Mr. Bernard's help in climbing aboard when her eyes fell on the sign for the Carnegie Library across the village park. The lending library had been a favorite spot of hers before she went away to college. A nice book would take her mind off the strange happenings at home.

"If I may," she told the storekeeper, "I'll leave the wagon here for just a bit." It could be done in a small town like Enfield. In a larger city, someone might steal her cargo.

"Verity McCracken!" said Verna Reilly, the librarian. "Back from Plattsburgh Normal School, a full-fledged teacher, I hear!"

"We'll find out when school starts," said Verity modestly as she shook the elderly woman's hand. "In the city, they start much earlier, you know."

"Oh, but the children are needed to help with the harvest, dear," Miss

Reilly reminded her. " 'Happy is the man that hath his quiver full of them,' " she added, quoting Psalms. "Every hand is needed." She took a long look at Verity. "I must say, I really like that hat! Very becoming!"

Verity looked around the dear, familiar little library. The building had been the post office in years past, but when Enfield's fortunes had turned the village into a town, the post office had moved to larger quarters. Volunteers had torn out the old fixtures and replaced them with bookshelves, tables, and chairs; and the Carnegie Foundation had supplied the funds for the purchase of books.

Miss Reilly clapped her hands. "But, of course, you've come for something to read. I remember you liked Dickens. Have you read *A Tale of Two Cities*? It's about the French Revolution, and it's just thrilling." She pointed as she resumed her seat at the reception desk. "You know where everything is. Just make yourself at home, my dear."

Miss Reilly's suggestion appealed to Verity. It was one of the few Dickens' books she had not yet read. The turmoil of the French Revolution might prove a welcome change from the present unnerving situation. She made her way into the stacks—*or stack,* she pointed out to herself as she humorously compared this little one-room establishment to the massive collection of volumes available in the college library. She pulled out the book in question and turned to the first page. "It was the best of times, it was the worst of times—" she read the first line to herself in a whisper.

"Why, Pete Delorme!" she heard Miss Reilly say, "here you are, back from college, big as life!"

Verity stiffened.

"And what a coincidence! I believe we have a friend of yours here," the little lady added merrily.

Chapter 3

Verity hugged *A Tale of Two Cities* to her chest and listened.

"Really?" There was cheerfulness and amusement in Pete's deep, familiar voice. "Who is it?"

Could the feud be all in Papa's head, or a misunderstanding, perhaps? Oh, let it be so!

"Miss Verity McCracken, fresh from normal school," Miss Reilly announced gaily.

Verity held her breath.

Silence.

"Oh, Verity," Miss Reilly sang out, "would you come out here, please? I don't think Mr. Delorme believes me."

Verity sighed deeply and stepped from behind the bookshelf, holding the book to herself like armor. Her fears were confirmed when she saw Pete's face: lips compressed, eyes elusive, hands unconsciously thrust in his pockets.

"Good day, Mr. Delorme," said Verity stiffly, offering her gloved hand.

"Miss McCracken," he responded, looking intently at the hem of her gown. His grip was weak, and he released her hand as quickly as though he held a poisonous snake.

Verity felt a prickle of tears forming in her eyes. Why was she suddenly feeling so desolate?

"Excuse me, please," he said, and stepped around her. After a brief, stricken glance at her face, he disappeared behind a bookshelf.

"Um, well. . ." Miss Reilly, feeling the chill in the air, hastened to smooth things. "Did you wish to check out that book, dear?"

Verity looked down at the volume she held tightly against her chest. "Er, yes, thank you," she said, and was surprised that her voice sounded so weak.

"An excellent choice!" said Miss Reilly as she picked up a pencil, opened the long ledger book, and began the tedious task of recording Verity's choice. Carefully, she recorded Verity's name and the title and author of the book she had chosen. With infuriating slowness, she consulted a wall calendar that bore the picture of a kitten and promoted the virtues of a patent medicine. "Is one week time enough, dear?"

"Of course," Verity said, more sharply than she had intended. She felt dizzy. She needed air.

A book slammed to the floor in the back of the library.

Verity flinched.

"Oops, sorry," said Pete.

Verity remembered Pete saying those words before. Five years ago, at a hayride, when he and another boy had burrowed under the hay and popped up here and there, causing squeals among the girls. He had been a smart-aleck pest back then, with a rebellious yellow cowlick sticking up in the back of his head, full of himself and his newly grown height. The older girls had liked him, of course, but fourteen-year-old Verity was determined not to waste her time with boys. She would get an education first.

And she had, she reminded herself, trying not to think about the long, cozy evenings in the dormitory, where she and her friends had shared their dreams and Verity had verbally sketched her idea of the Perfect Man: tall, strong, pious, articulate, a bibliophile. And a person well-read enough to know the meaning of the word.

"Here you are, my dear," said Miss Reilly, handing the book back to her.

Verity made a courteous good-bye and hurried to the waiting farm wagon.

❧

Pete heard the library door closing and realized he'd been standing stock-still, his fists constricted painfully. The fallen book lay splayed at his feet.

An image of Verity McCracken obscured the wall of books before him: not too tall; a halo of shiny brown hair around a pale, oval face; a delicate pink mouth, clamped into a thin line as she extended her hand—so tiny, that hand—and a silvery line of tears forming along the bottom of wide, pale-blue eyes. She was trembling as she stood there; he had sensed it rather than seen it.

So, it was true. The feud was real, and Verity McCracken, as any loyal daughter should, was observing her father's wishes.

An anathema, Pete thought, *I'm anathema to her.* He was rather proud that the Latin word had occurred to him. *I am cursed, excommunicated, taboo, as far as Verity McCracken is concerned.* He wondered at the pang he felt at the thought.

Verity's just one of the hometown girls, he reminded himself, and she had always been a terrible snob, even as a kid. Never kept company with any of the Enfield boys. Not like the girls who had flocked around him in high school, eager to kiss any fellow who asked them; who thought reading a book was a waste of time.

Pete shook his head and picked up the fallen book. A nice, smart girl. And he was duty-bound to have nothing to do with her.

"Arrrgh!" Verity kicked the huge sack of flour. A hole opened in its side and a little spilled out onto the dirt of the country road. "Oh, no!" She collapsed on top of the huge bag. Things were going from bad to worse.

When the wagon, improperly balanced, began to run into a roadside rut, it had only seemed sensible to stop and rearrange the cargo in the buckboard. With all her strength, she had tugged the sack of flour over to prop it against one side. She intended to balance its weight by rolling the keg of nails to the other, but the heel of her shoe had caught in the hem of her skirt, and both Verity and the flour had tumbled over the side.

She had been fortunate—she could have broken her neck—still, it was difficult to feel thankful. Her twisted ankle was beginning to throb and small white clouds of flour were being carried off in the late summer breeze. She knelt, pulled out her long hatpin, and used it to fasten the edges of the flour bag together. As she sat back to survey her handiwork, her pretty new straw hat, its black velvet ribbon flapping, flew off her head. She crawled after it, only to have a sudden gust roll it a good twenty feet away. She sat back and only just caught herself from giving the flour sack another pounding in her frustration.

"What do I do now?" she asked Thunder, who stood patiently observing over his massive gray flank this strange behavior, while Lightning, as usual, remained oblivious. "Do I leave it?"

Verity knew that horses couldn't shrug, but Thunder's expression carried much the same sentiment as he gazed at her. She stood and leaned against the horse's expansive middle, taking comfort from his strength. She consulted the tiny brooch watch that had been her graduation present from her parents. It was after four o'clock already. Someone should be coming along the road pretty soon. Surely they'd give her a hand with the huge sack. It was simply too wasteful to leave it. Besides, her mother was nearly out of flour.

⁂

Pete Delorme was proud of himself. In spite of many challenging diversions, he'd given his employers a good day's work, and Mr. Essex had been pleased with this progress.

He smiled as his horse, Sandy, cantered gently. There was no hurry. Dinner wouldn't be for another hour and a half. He'd have time for a talk with his father. It was imperative that he get to the bottom of this outrageous situation with the McCrackens. His mind returned to the scene in the library, and he experienced a heavy sadness. It was ridiculous. He had no quarrel with Verity McCracken, and he was eager to reestablish acquaintance with her. Very eager indeed. But what could be done about it?

He spotted the hat first, skittering along the road in a brisk breeze. It looked familiar and in need of rescue, but before he could dismount and retrieve it, the straw skimmer with the charming black velvet bow rolled away among the forlorn stumps of a harvested cornfield to his right.

Where had that come from?

He rounded a curve in the road and saw a wagon and horses ahead. He urged Sandy forward and narrowly missed trampling a gigantic sack of flour.

211

Where was the driver? He looked at the horses, and with a sickening lurch, recognized them.

McCracken horses! Verity had been driving this wagon. Where was she? Hurt? Kidnapped? He dismounted and called frantically, "Miss McCracken! Verity! Are you all right?"

"Here," he heard a faint call from beneath a roadside tree.

Hastily fastening Sandy's reins to the wagon, he jogged over to where Verity was struggling to stand.

"I'm so sorry," she said as she brushed grass from her skirt; "I must have fallen asleep." She looked up at him, froze for a split second, then said breathlessly, "Oh, it's you, Mr. Delorme! I am so...glad to see you." She was hatless and disheveled. Strands of hair had fallen out of her chignon and straggled down her back. There was a smudge of flour across her forehead. "I really am," she added.

It seemed to Pete that a golden glow began to fill the landscape, though the hour was long before sunset. He gave her his arm, which she took without hesitation, and they stepped carefully among the rocks and fallen branches, making their way back to the road where the three horses and the wagon waited.

"How did this happen?" laughed Pete when Verity stopped and stood balefully beside the fallen flour sack.

Laughing at herself, she explained in vivid detail, with a range of gestures and a lively vocabulary that astonished him. Especially touching was the sight of the attempted repair of the hole with a hatpin.

"And that's how you lost your poor hat," he finished for her with a chuckle as he removed his suit jacket and handed it to her. Rolling up his sleeves, he hunched up under the weight of the enormous sack and heaved it aboard the wagon in one groaning motion.

"Oh, my," Verity's eyes were huge. "I could have never done that. I am most obliged to you."

He helped her into the wagon. "It was nothing, honestly," he said, sudden bashfulness sweeping over him. Then, he brightened. "I think I know where your hat is, too!"

"Oh, I couldn't let you—" she began, but he was already dashing down the road and across the uneven cornfield. The deed of capturing the hat took only a minute, but the rush of pleasure he experienced as he finally brandished his trophy amazed him.

Verity clapped her hands in delight and received the prize with solicitous tenderness, sweeping away crumbs of dirt with delicate fingertips. "Oh, Pete—Mr. Delorme—I'm so grateful to you. . ." As she handed his jacket down to him from her perch on the wagon, her blue gaze was all he could see.

He stumbled on the words, but he was determined to get them out. "I—am—just—so—sorry."

No explanation was necessary.

"No—you—I mean—" She shook her head violently and a tear flew out of one eye. "I just wish I knew what it was about."

"So do I!" he said with amazement.

"You mean you don't know, either?"

"No!"

They shared a laughing moment of bewilderment, then, "May I drive you home?" Pete asked shyly.

She gestured to the seat beside her. "Please do." Her lips were drawn up in a gently curved bow.

As they drove, ever so slowly, toward the McCracken farm, they discussed the extraordinary mornings they each had experienced and marveled at the remarkable similarity.

"What's going to happen?" Verity asked as they neared the turnoff to her home.

Pete shook his head. "I don't know. But something's got to be done; that's certain."

"Absolutely."

"Would you—I mean—could we, um, pray about it?"

"Oh, yes," said Verity eagerly. "Please."

Together, they bowed their heads and prayed, in turn, for understanding, for peace, for resolution. When they raised them again, both Pete and Verity sensed a change had taken place.

"It's going to be all right, isn't it?" Verity said breathlessly.

Pete handed her the reins and climbed down off the wagon. "It certainly is. I don't know just how, but. . .yes." He untied Sandy, mounted, and rode around to bid Verity good-bye.

"Thank you," she said, brushing a brown lock from her eyes.

He nodded and smiled. "You're quite welcome."

"Good-bye," she said, and urged Thunder and Lightning forward, down the drive. They didn't need to be asked twice. Their stalls and suppers awaited.

"Au revoir," he corrected under his breath as Verity and the wagon disappeared behind the big McCracken barn in the distance. "We'll meet again."

Chapter 4

That evening during supper, Jacob McCracken asked Verity, "How was your trip to town? Did you remember to get my peppermints?"

"Oh, yes, Papa," his daughter said, nodding at the neat paper packet sitting on the kitchen counter.

Jacob sawed his pork chop. "And flour? You get that flour your mother needed?"

He popped a large portion of meat in his mouth and chewed rapidly, his eyes darting back and forth between the two women in his family.

Grace McCracken nodded and helped herself to applesauce. "That's funny. I could have sworn it was you that unloaded it." She winked at Verity.

"Oh, yeah. Guess I did." Jacob cleared his throat. "See anybody in town?" he asked, shaking the pepper shaker vigorously over his plate.

"Oh, you know," Verity said casually, "the usual people you see. Mr. Bernard at the mercantile, of course, and Miss Reilly at the library."

"See any Delormes?" Jacob said, and sneezed violently.

"God bless you, Papa." Verity filled her voice with concern as she racked her brain for an evasive answer.

"The Del—wha—wha—" Jacob struggled to speak, sneezed again twice, then wiped his face with his napkin. "What about Delormes? You see any of 'em?"

Verity had never lied to her Papa in her life. She dropped her fork. "Oh, dear, just a second." She ducked under the oilcloth table cover. "I

215

think perhaps I saw Pete Delorme in town," she said from beneath the table. When she popped back up in her seat like a duck on a pond, her face was red. Verity lay the fork on the table, picked up her spoon, and began eating her applesauce. "Mmm," she said, and blinked rapidly, "everything's so delicious, Mama."

At least I didn't lie, she told herself.

Jacob opened his mouth to speak.

There was a knock at the door. "I'll answer it." Verity hurried out of the room, relieved to be away from her father's suspicious stare. *Oh, dear Lord, I hate this! Please help our family!* she prayed.

The knocking continued, growing in insistence and ferocity. Verity's hand shook as she turned the big oval brass knob and pulled the door open. "Why, Mr. Delorme, hello!" she said pleasantly.

Gerard had no corresponding greeting. "I'll thank you to fetch your father, young lady!" he snapped, and pushed past her into the dark front parlor.

Verity scurried after him and lit the gas lamp. "Certainly," she assured him, "just a moment. He's at supper."

"I don't care if he's at the county fair! I would speak with him forthwith! Run along!" Gerard paced a circle in the room, jingling change in one of his pants pockets.

Verity left and returned quickly, with her father close behind, napkin still in hand. "What's all this about?" she heard him say as he stepped into the parlor.

With a grunt, Gerard slid the heavy pocket door closed. Just as it slammed into place, Verity heard him whisper gruffly, " 'The course of true love ne'er did run smooth,' my friend—"

True love? My friend?

Verity slipped into her seat at the big kitchen table. "Mama, that's Mr. Delorme in the parlor. Please tell me what's going on!"

Grace McCracken rolled her eyes. "I promised I wouldn't, dear, but please believe me when I tell you that there's nothing to worry—"

A tremendous roar from the parlor interrupted her. "HOWWWW DAAARE YOU, SIR!"

"Jacob?" Grace said in a small voice. She and Verity hurried to the front hallway and stood uncertainly outside the parlor door, listening, as a wild argument raged behind it.

"My goodness, Delorme, you ain't got the manners of a goat, coming into a man's own house like this!" Jacob's voice cracked as he shouted the words.

" 'How sharper than a serpent's tooth it is—' " Gerard intoned, but Jacob interrupted.

"One more word of that Shakespeare guff, Gerry Delorme, and I'll punch you right in the nose!"

The women gasped and clung to each other.

"Oh, that's right, I'd expect violence from a clod like you!"

"Waaal, don't dish it out if ye can't take it!"

"Ignoramus! Savage! Imbecile!" Gerard's voice became higher with each word.

"Don't you go throwin' that high-falutin' lingo at me, you puffed up ol' snob," Jacob growled, "You got your education at that one-room school same as me. Everybody knows that the swill you spout come right out of that Bartlett quote book!"

There was a pause.

Grace and Verity held their breaths.

"I see that I am no longer welcome here," they heard Gerard declare in a clear, even voice. There were fumbling noises and the heavy pocket door opened, sliding back into the wall with a decisive thud. "I will take my leave now. Excuse me, please, ladies." He shouldered his way past Grace and Verity and out the front door with Jacob hard on his heels.

"You are kee-rect, Mr. Delorme, you ain't welcome here and never will be again!" Jacob shouted after the retreating Gerard. "And that goes for your entire family!"

Then he turned on his heel and marched back into the kitchen, stuffing his napkin into his collar as he walked. "Let's eat!"

❧

"Have you forgotten what's supposed to happen next week?" Grace's voice floated up from the kitchen as Verity descended the stairs three hours later.

She cringed at the sharpness in her mother's tone and pulled the cord of her dressing gown tighter. The hall clock struck eleven times. She frowned. Mama and Papa always went up to bed at nine sharp.

Verity had excused herself from the supper table shortly after the evening's painful scene, leaving her pork chop untouched. She had performed her evening chores mechanically, then had gone up to bed early. An empty, grumbling stomach had awakened her and sent her downstairs for a glass of milk.

"Y'ain't listenin'," Jacob was saying wearily. "We got nothin' to worry about."

"We're going to need the Delormes' help with the apple harvest!"

"They'll help, they'll help, you'll see. I already told you a dozen times: We know what we're doing." Verity heard a long yawn. "Grace, we gotta get some sleep. Let's go on up to bed."

Verity slipped into the darkened parlor just before her parents mounted the staircase. "I just hope you're right, Jacob," she heard her mother say, "I surely do."

Verity slipped to her knees and laid her head on the rough horsehair of the old settee. "Dear Lord," she murmured into the worn fabric, "something terrible and strange is happening to my family. And to the Delormes." A tear slid down her cheek and sank rapidly into the seat.

She sniffed and wiped away the others that followed with the back of her hand. "Whatever has gone on between Papa and Mr. Delorme, please send Your Holy Spirit to replace this terrible anger with peace and forgiveness. And please," she whispered as a sob rose in her chest, "show me what I should do. I feel so alone. There's nothing I can do. . ."

You can keep praying.

A still, small voice from somewhere inside her resounded. She had heard the voice before.

And you're not alone.

The image of Pete Delorme's face floated into her mind. Verity sat up. Of course! She wasn't alone. She had a prayer partner in this crisis. A nameless joy rose into her throat.

"Oh, thank You, Lord! In Jesus' name I pray, amen."

She rose and hurried to the kitchen, forming hopeful plans in her mind as she poured herself a glass of milk and sliced off a piece of Mama's good bread. Tomorrow morning, she was to go into town and meet at the school with the other teachers to prepare for the upcoming school year. Somehow, she would manage to see Pete.

Verity sighed happily as she chewed the last of the bread. God was already working this all out.

Chapter 5

The next morning, Jacob McCracken waited for Gerard Delorme at the stile until seven o'clock before giving up and returning home to begin his chores. "Hope he's okay," he mumbled. "I was afraid he'd bust a gasket last night. But it sure was a rip-snorter of a show." Jacob slapped his knee in pleasure and laughed all the way back through the elderly, gnarled trees, festooned with ripening apples.

※

"I'm so sorry to interrupt your work this way, Mr. Delorme," Verity said as she shook hands with Pete in the front room of the offices of Essex and Westcloth, Esquires, Attorneys at Law. "I would never disturb you if it weren't very important. This should only take a few minutes."

"No disturbance at all, Miss McCracken," said Pete gallantly. He turned to his employer, who stood smiling at him from his office door. "I've just finished my work on the Albany brief, sir." He handed the older man a thick manila folder.

Theodore Essex quickly leafed through the pages. "Well done, Pete! If this work is as good as what you did on the last one. . .well, you certainly deserve a few minutes off. Go on, buy Miss McCracken a phosphate." He winked and pulled out a large pocket watch. "It's two now. I won't expect you back till our strategy meeting at three."

Verity's eyes widened and she opened her mouth to speak, but Pete took her quickly by the elbow and steered her to the door. "Thank you, sir. I really appreciate it."

Verity descended the steps to the street in a cold silence, then stopped on the sidewalk, and turned to address Pete. "Mr. Delorme, if you think I came to your office just to. . .to. . ." She groped for a word. "Lollygag. Well, you've got another thing coming!" She spun away and began walking down the sidewalk. "And I'll thank you to inform your employer that I am not thirsty and have no need of a phosphate or anything else!"

Pete hurried after her. "Ver—er, Miss McCracken, I'm terribly sorry. Mr. Essex had no business assuming anything, but he's really a nice man, when you get to know him." He circled around her, halting her progress. "I'll be sure to correct his impression when I get back to the office. But, first, please, tell me why you came. Come on, we can talk over there, in the park." He gestured toward a bench, then held up his right hand. "No phosphates involved, cross my heart."

Verity had been staring at the ground. She lifted her face to look at his and said, as the hint of a dimple played on her cheek, "Promise?"

Pete felt a surge of warmth in his face. "Didn't you see me cross my heart?" he said playfully. "A man doesn't do a d—drastic thing like this unless he m—means it." It was an old bantering line he'd used with many girls back at college, but somehow, the words took on new meaning when he spoke them before Verity's sparkling blue gaze.

Verity sighed. "All right." She proceeded briskly across the street to the park bench and sat down, waiting for him to join her.

Pete eased himself down on the bench, a good arm's length from Verity, and directed his gaze forward. "Please. Tell me," he urged, trying to ignore the gentle scent of the Yardley's lavender soap now floating on the cool autumn breeze. He wondered if Verity was warm enough in that short-fitted jacket. Quickly, he blinked away the idea of putting his arm around her shoulders and pulling her close.

Verity spoke slowly, nodding to indicate her seriousness. "It's about our fathers. . ."

By the time she had finished telling the tale of last night's horrifying scene, Pete had forgotten his reserve and was looking full into her animated face.

When a sheen of tears had formed over those remarkable eyes, he had been quick to pull a clean, monogrammed handkerchief from his pocket. He wanted to dab the moisture from her smooth, pink cheek. Instead, he handed the cloth over wordlessly and the grateful glance she gave him was worth all his forbearance.

He said, "I wondered where Father had gone last night after dinner. He wouldn't speak of it when he returned, but he looked exhausted. This is just so strange. . . ."

"I thought. . .I mean, perhaps, could we pray about this again? You know, 'Where two or three are gathered together in my name,' " she quoted with a faint smile, neatly folding the used handkerchief and depositing it in her reticule, the drawstring bag that hung from her slender wrist. It would be laundered, ironed, and returned, in accordance with etiquette.

"Matthew 18:20," said Pete. He was getting good at citing quotes, thanks to his law training. He bowed his head and began to speak in a low, gentle tone. In simple terms, he stated the problem and humbly asked God's help, then paused.

Verity spoke then, adding her agreement and thanking the Lord in advance for His divine guidance.

"In Jesus' name, amen." They said the final word together.

" 'If two of you shall agree on earth as touching anything that they shall ask, it shall be done for them by my Father which is in heaven,' " Pete said, "That's the promise that comes right before your quote."

"It does, doesn't it?"

All at once, Pete had an idea. It was so amazing, so powerful, so right, he was astounded he hadn't thought of it before. As Verity sat watching in puzzlement, a multitude of expressions rapidly passed across his broad, friendly countenance.

He's a grown-up now, Verity thought with sudden insight. *I've been seeing him as that nice, silly older boy, but he's really a full-grown man. Such a nice man, too.* A flattering blush tinted her face.

"Miss McCracken," Pete began, "Um, may I call you Verity?"

"Pete, we've called each other by our first names all our lives, up until this year," she pointed out. "Funny, isn't it? I guess it just seemed more proper, now that we've grown up." Verity found herself wondering how it would feel if she snuggled into the shelter of Pete's right arm. She would probably feel safe, and it would be nice to bring her face next to his. . .

She stiffened her back. Such thoughts were not proper.

"Verity, I just had an idea. It's a little crazy, but it might help things."

At half-past seven that evening, there was a gentle tapping at the window of Gerard Delorme's first-floor study.

Gerard looked up from a volume of Shakespeare's sonnets. It was clear to anyone with eyes that he hadn't been reading. The reading glasses that had become so essential in the last few years were perched uselessly atop his shiny forehead. Gerard opened the window. "What are you doing here?"

Jacob McCracken poked his head and shoulders through the window and leaned on the sill. "Where was ye this morning? I waited 'til I couldn't wait any more," he said in a hoarse whisper.

"I was told I was no longer welcome," Gerard whispered back coolly. He placed a firm hand on Jacob's shoulder and pushed. "Now get out of here."

Jacob's wiry frame was made up of solid muscle, tempered by hard farmwork, and he wouldn't be budged if he didn't want to be. "What are you talkin' about, Gerry? That was actin', just like you said!" He chuckled. "Boy, oh boy, we sure give 'em an earful, didn't we?"

Gerard pulled his hand back and crossed his arms. "Acting, was it? What about the names you called me? And threatening to punch me in the nose? You actually drew back your fist!"

"I had to make it sound real, didn't I? 'Sides, it seemed to me that you did your share o' name-callin', Gerry. You called me a savage!" Jacob climbed over the sill into the room, "What's wrong with you? You turn up at a fella's house, sayin' things are goin' too slow; we gotta do something dramatic. I was trying to make it good, like you said!" He closed the window carefully.

"Too good! I know the ring of truth when I hear it! You actually meant those things!"

They continued to speak in whispers.

"O' course I didn't. I was makin' it all up, just puttin' in a few details to make it sound like the real thing."

"What about the one-room school?"

"Well, it's true, ain't it? We did get the same schoolin'. You was always better with books, that's all. You know how it is—some of the kids was jealous—they said things—"

"Which you remembered all these years and saw fit to repeat in front of your wife and daughter. I don't appreciate it, Jacob!"

"Well, it warn't my bright idea in the first place, you know. You're the one come up with this Romeo and Juliet nonsense."

"It isn't nonsense; it's eminently feasible. Ingenious—"

"Well, it ain't workin', far as I can see, and I'll be glad to get shed of it."

Gerard stalked to the window and pulled it open again. The heavy curtains blew in the brisk autumn wind. "Then, by all means, take your leave."

Jacob lifted one leg over the sill. "Well, then, I will. All this stuff and nonsense was a waste of time, you ask me." He finished his cumbersome exit and turned for a final word through the window. "If you start something, Gerry Delorme, you should do it right and stick with it through to the finish. I'm shaking the dust of this place off my feet and not lookin' back."

"And I am happy to wash my hands of you, Jake McCracken. Thank goodness I finally learned your true colors. You are on your own from now on. You and your sorry excuse for a farm. Don't count on any more help from the Delorme clan."

He pulled the window closed and drew the drapes over it, leaving Jacob to trudge home, across the fields and over the stile, gradually realizing that, because of a few ill-chosen words, he might just lose the farm that had been in his family for three generations.

Chapter 6

Pete urged his horse, Sandy, forward in the autumn wind. He breathed deeply of the brisk evening air and thought about Verity. How comfortable it had been to sit on that park bench and make plans with her. How natural it seemed now to be riding to Jacob McCracken's house to ask permission to court her.

"Of course, once our fathers have patched things up, there will be no obligation on your part to maintain the charade," he had hastily assured her. "You will simply say you've changed your mind, and I will accede to your wishes."

"Oh, of course," Verity had answered, studiously straightening the cuff of her glove. "That's exactly what I'll do. . .once things are better."

"Right," Pete had said, wondering why her quick compliance gave him a sinking feeling.

"You know why, you idiot," Pete told himself aloud as he posted jauntily along the dark country road, "because she is just about the most adorable girl in the world and you wish this courtship were real. Because you. . .love Verity."

"I. . .love. . .Verity," he repeated, trying out the taste of the words. He found them delicious.

"Come on, Sandy," he said, urging the horse forward again; "we're almost there."

At the same moment, the object of Pete's affection was, herself, pacing the floor of her room and worrying. There had already been a complication in their plan and she had utterly no idea what to do about it.

"I'll prepare Mama and Papa for your arrival," she had told him during that cozy meeting on the park bench. "Right after supper, I'll sit them down and explain that you and I would like to court. There will be some resistance at first, but they'll come around, I know," she said, smiling affectionately at the thought of her fond parents. "You schedule your arrival for around eight o'clock. That should give me plenty of time."

Pete had agreed, nodding, and tilting his head in that way he had of showing he was taking in the speaker's every word. It was so nice to be taken seriously like that; to have one's opinion sought in a matter of importance. Pete's dark brown eyes, so unusual and striking in a person with blond hair, seemed to see and understand everything.

"Well," he'd said as they arose from the bench just before his three o'clock meeting, "might as well get the ball rolling. You know, Miss Reilly over at the library has had her face pressed against the window, watching us, for the last twenty minutes. No, don't look!" he said, quickly taking her elbow and turning her toward him. "Just give me one of those pretty smiles of yours, and I'll escort you back to the buggy."

It had been fun, thought Verity, smiling at her image in the bedroom mirror, to pretend to be falling in love.

And even if it were real, Pete wouldn't be a bad choice at all. He had been so gallant, helping her into the buggy. Another memory floated into her head, that of the adorable, eager way he had retrieved her hat. And strong. The way he had lifted—

The hall clock began to chime and Verity was jerked back to the urgent present.

After supper, Papa hadn't remained seated at the kitchen table, smoking his pipe as he always did. Still chewing his last bite of custard pie, he had taken a gulp of coffee and said, " 'Scuse me. Gotta go check on something. Should be gone for a bit." Then he had disappeared out the back door. Verity's chance for a family conference disappeared with him.

"Where could he be?" she murmured as the last of the eight chimes rang. "Pete will be here any minute!"

The back door slammed and Verity flew down the stairs to the kitchen.

Jacob, looking bedraggled, was back at his place at the empty table. "Got any more coffee?" he asked his wife.

"Papa, you're back," Verity announced.

"I'm back," agreed her father with a sigh. He nodded his thanks to Grace for the steaming cup she placed before him.

"But where did you go?" she blurted. "I needed to talk with you!"

"Never you mind." Jacob stirred sugar into his cup. "Nothing you need worry yourself about." He took a sip. "Where's the cream?" he asked petulantly. "Ain't we got cream in this house?"

Grace calmly placed the pitcher on the table.

Verity looked from one parent to another. Now didn't seem to be a good time to bring up the subject of courtship, but it couldn't be helped. Now or never. She straightened her spine and took a deep breath. "Mama," she began, "and Papa. I have something very important to—"

There was a brisk, cheerful rapping at the front door.

It had been more than an utter disaster, Pete thought morosely as he steered Sandy back down the familiar road to his father's house. It had been a defeat, a checkmate, a debacle. "A mess," Pete added to his mental list.

Things had seemed to be going well when Verity answered the front door, her eyes wide as saucers. But once she silently ushered him into the front hall, things took a steep decline into chaos.

Jacob had marched up to him. "You!" the scowling man said, sharply tapping Pete's chest with his forefinger, "You got a lot of moxie! Are you here with your Pa's apology, lad?"

"Well, no, sir," Pete began, "I'm—"

"Then I'll have no truck with ye," said Jacob. He then spun Pete around and pushed him roughly toward the door.

"But—" Pete protested, his arms flailing.

"Papa! What are you doing?" Verity yelped.

"Jacob!" Grace added to the din, "You musn't—"

But Jacob already had, and Pete staggered down the front stairs and into the yard before he could stop himself.

The front door slammed, hard. Clearly, there was to be no earnest, dignified meeting in the front parlor between Pete and his intended father-in-law, not even a charade of one.

❧

There was a brittle silence in the McCracken kitchen. Verity and her mother were seated at the table, staring into ice-cold cups of coffee, when Jacob entered. He had spent the last half hour in the darkened parlor, pacing and thinking furiously.

The women didn't look up at Jacob when he seated himself before them. He sighed deeply and began to speak. "I better explain what's goin' on," he said.

Grace continued to avoid his gaze, but stirred her cup, tapped the spoon briskly, and placed it with great deliberation on the saucer. *Indeed you should,* her gesture seemed to say.

His wife's clear agitation disturbed him until he caught a glimpse of Verity's melancholy expression, now turned full force on her father.

You'd think she'd already fallen for the Delorme boy, he thought, then dismissed the idea from his mind.

Grace looked at him then. Her eyebrows were high, her mouth tight. *Yes? Go on,* her face said. *We're listening.*

"This problem I've been havin' with the Delormes? Well, it just got worse."

Verity leaned forward. "What do you mean, Papa? How much worse can it get?"

Jacob avoided his wife's eyes. "The Delormes. They're not helping us with the apples this year."

Grace slid back her chair, stood, carried her coffee cup to the sink, and dumped it out. "I knew it," she said softly, still leaning against the sink, her head bowed. "I knew this would happen."

❧

It seemed to Pete that things couldn't get any worse, but he was wrong.

Gerard called him into the study upon his arrival back at the house. "Sit down, son; I want to have a talk with you."

That's what I was hoping Jacob McCracken would say, Pete thought wryly.

It was surprisingly cold in the study. "Have you had the window open, Father?" Pete asked.

228

Gerard shook his head impatiently. "Never mind that. Sit down. Listen, do you remember that firm in Saratoga that offered you a position?"

"Sure, Daugherty and Daugherty. They were my first choice. But we both decided it would better if I were closer to home."

"Well, Pierre, I think you should reconsider. As I recall, they were extremely eager to have you. I'm sure it's not too late to write them and see if the job is still open."

"Father, I've already begun work here. I like it. Mr. Essex says—"

"Ted Essex will understand, once I have a talk with him. There's just so much more opportunity in a city like Saratoga. The people you meet—"

"The people I meet won't be related to Jacob McCracken; is that what you mean? Just what is going on between the two of you, Father? Can't you see what this. . .turmoil is doing to Mother, to our family, to their family? You've been friends all your lives. Can't you find a way to patch this thing up?"

Gerard shook his head sadly. "No, son. It can't be fixed. The man has despised me all these years, and I'm only just learning of it."

"What about forgiveness? Father, can't we pray together about this?"

Gerard squirmed in his chair. "No, not now. I'm just too agitated. Maybe later." He stood and patted his son on his shoulder affectionately. "Run along and be thinking about what we discussed."

At the door, Pete turned and asked, "What about next week? The apple harvest?"

Gerard didn't even look up from his book. "Out of the question," he said firmly, and turned a page.

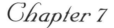

Chapter 7

C an Ben Hayward help us, Mr. McCracken?" asked Jacob's only farmhand, Fred Willard, as he helped his weary employer unhitch Lightning and Thunder from the wagon. Fred's eager expression belied his weariness. It had been a long, hard day with Jacob away in town, looking for men to pick the apples.

Jacob sighed. "Nope. Everybody's tied up with their own harvesting. I even cornered Jack Bacon in the mercantile and asked him. Offered him top dollar."

"But he's one of the Delorme hands!"

"You think I don't know that? I was desperate. I thought mebbe he and a couple of the other fellas there could spare us an hour or two, evenings, or something."

"What'd he say?" There was hope in Fred's lined, homely face as he led the two horses into their stalls.

"Couldn't. Said Delorme'd fire him if he found out—fire him for sure. I don't blame him none; he and Sally got that baby coming and all. But I'll be honest with you, Fred, I just don't know how we're gonna manage."

"Don't forget; I'm here, Papa," said his daughter, walking past, a full milk bucket in each of her hands. "Mama and I can pick apples."

"I hate to admit it, but. . ." Jacob pulled off his hat and scratched his head. "I'm 'fraid I'm gonna need ye."

"Then who'll cook for us?" Fred asked. "The thought of Mrs. McCracken's chicken pie is what keeps me goin', harvesttime."

"Mama and I will be making sandwiches the night before, Fred, so we can be free to help out in the orchard. Maybe when this is all over, Mama can make you some pie."

" 'S'all right," said Fred with a good-natured grin as he ducked down to brush down Lightning's foreleg. "I'll remind you then."

Jacob relieved his daughter of one of her buckets and helped her pour the fresh milk into the tall metal can.

"Why is he doing this, Papa?" Verity rinsed the buckets under the farmyard pump. "It's just so spiteful. Mr. Delorme knows what the apple harvest means to us."

"Hard to say. Wish I knew." Jacob repeated the trite expressions guiltily as he avoided his daughter's eye. "Can't be helped."

Grace held the back door open for them. "Hurry and wash up, Fred," she called. "It's chicken and dumplings tonight, then straight to sleep. We got a long day tomorrow."

❧

The next morning, pink rays of dawn were moving across the sky and the rooster was crowing as Jacob, Grace, and Fred set out for the orchard in the buckboard, loaded with ladders, round bushel baskets, and a stack of rough shoulder bags.

"Wait!" called Verity from the back door. "Don't forget this!" She hefted a heavy hamper, filled with sandwiches and hard-boiled eggs. "And the water!" She pointed to the tall milk can with a curve-handled dipper hanging from it standing on the back stoop.

"Thanks, punkin," said Grace, relieving her daughter of the burden.

"I'll be along just as soon as I can," Verity assured her. "The minute I finish with the milking and the chickens. The dishes are already done."

Fred heaved the water can into the wagon. "You got a good youngun there, Missus McCracken," he said, with a wink at Verity.

The glance that Grace threw at her daughter was filled with love. "You're right, Fred, we do."

Verity stole a moment to watch them ride away. This time last year, seven Delorme hands had surrounded the wagon, full of Mama's good bacon and eggs, joking good-naturedly as they walked alongside. They always had

231

good reason to be cheerful. They would be fully paid for the workday by Gerard Delorme and receive additional pay from Jacob McCracken.

It had been this way since long before Verity was born. The benefits of this arrangement to the Delormes were less apparent than to the McCrackens. Of course, a portion of the apple harvest was always carried directly across the stile, but it represented only a small percentage of the cost of paying the hands. Verity had always assumed that Gerard had helped with the harvest out of the goodness of his heart, but she had reason to doubt that goodness now.

A soft, reproving moo from the barn pulled Verity from her thoughts. She sighed, put on a heavy wool coat, and headed into the yard. "Coming, Matilda," she called.

🍎

Pete, feeling out of uniform in sensible overalls layered under warm wool, leaped over the stile easily and walked briskly between the orchard rows.

In the growing light of dawn, the steadily brightening redness of the apples which hung from the outside branches signaled that the time for picking was now.

After a minute, Pete began to hear the voices of Jacob and his skeleton crew of pickers, clear in the crisp air.

I figured they'd get an early start, he thought. *Good thing I did, too.*

Jacob and the others had already begun picking when Pete walked up to the wagon, pulled a sack over his shoulder, and carried a ladder to a neighboring tree.

"What d'ye think you're doin'?" Jacob snapped, and his ladder wobbled slightly.

"I'm helping pick apples," said Pete, grasping an apple and pulling it from its branch with the gentle, twisting motion that retained the stem. He slid the apple into his shoulder bag and reached for another.

Jacob grabbed a sturdy, low-lying limb, causing half a dozen precious McIntoshes to thud to the ground. "Did your pa send ya? Is he ready to apologize?"

Pete continued to work. "Afraid not, Mr. McCracken. It's just me."

"Then I have no need of your help. Be on your way!" Trembling with

232

rage, he struggled to descend the shaky ladder. "I'll thrash you, boy, so help me!"

Grace, who had been gathering the fallen apples for use in cider, ran quickly to the tree. Looking up at Pete, she implored, "I know you mean well, but please, go now! He'll give himself the apoplexy! Never mind the ladder; just go!"

Pete jumped down and thrust the shoulder bag into Grace's hands. "I'm sorry," he whispered. "I'll find a way to help, I promise!" Then he turned and ran back down between the rows, ducking under the low branches.

❦

Jacob was still grumbling when Verity arrived an hour later. "How is it going?" she asked, dragging a ladder up to a tree.

"It's a-goin'," snapped Jacob.

The four worked steadily, without the cheering banter that had once been part of the fun of harvesttime. The sun made its presence known only briefly, sliding quickly behind a slate-gray curtain of clouds. The thin, filtered light gave little warmth.

Verity's fingers, in their hand-knit woolen gloves, quickly became stiff with cold, and her wrists ached. It was also painful to realize that she was the slowest picker among them. During past harvests, her job had always been to help Mama make the gigantic hot meals that sustained the men, rolling the dough for the chicken pies, chopping the onions for the rich soup, elbow-deep in sudsy water washing the mountains of dirty dishes. It had been hard work, but it had been warm.

I've never seen a colder harvesttime, thought Verity. *In more ways than one.*

She sighed deeply, and the cold air ached as it descended to her lungs. "Dear Lord, won't you help us?" she prayed between coughs.

❦

Pete's whispered prayer echoed Verity's as he left Mr. Wessex's office. He had already apologized for being late and was prepared to throw himself into the research for an important upcoming lawsuit, but his mind still whirled from the morning's events.

Pete shook his head. Going to the orchard had been a silly, impulsive, childish idea. He should have known what was going to happen. And how would he have explained his absence to his kind employer?

As he gathered the documents he would use in his research, Pete prayed again.

Lord, You've put me here for a purpose. Please show me a way to help, not hurt things.

He turned to his work. It was a dispute about land usage. A Mr. Gonyea was suing a Mr. Bentwell, because Bentwell wouldn't let Gonyea's goats cross his land to get to a stream. Water rights are serious business, Mr. Essex had said. This wrangle could keep the two neighbors in the courts for years.

"Don't complain," Pete reminded himself. "Disputes like these are your bread and butter." It seemed a shame, though, that the issue couldn't be resolved quickly and easily between neighbors.

Right. Neighbors like Father and Jacob McCracken? Pete snorted in disgust. Maybe the world needed lawyers, after all.

🌶

To Verity, it seemed like days before Jacob climbed down his ladder and called, "All right, everybody! I reckon it's time for a rest."

Verity swayed slightly and backed slowly down to the ground. Her arms had turned to lead. The shoulder bag was filled with lead. Her whole body was made of lead.

She staggered over and slumped against the warm body of Thunder, who stood calmly as always, his breath coming out in steamy gusts. She laid her cheek against his flank and realized that her whole face was numb.

The little group gathered at the wagon, where Jacob offered up a blessing for the meal. "And if you'd do some kinda miracle and help us get these apples to market on time, we'd really appreciate it," he said. Nobody smiled or chuckled. They had all seen the small number of apples that were picked so far.

Verity chewed gamely at the bacon sandwich her mother had given her. The bacon, once crisp and hot, had gone rubbery in the cold. She rewrapped the sandwich in its cotton napkin and peeled a hard-boiled egg. This was better, especially with the pepper and salt Mama had remembered to pack. She ate two, plus a half of a jam sandwich for dessert.

"What is it, punkin?" Mama asked. "You're shivering." She put her arms

234

around Verity. "Let me warm you up."

Verity laid her head on her mother's shoulder. She could have fallen asleep right here, standing up in the middle of the orchard at noontime. With a supreme act of self-control, she pulled herself away. "I'm all right, Mama. Gotta get back to work."

*

"But what does he hope to gain by not settling this case?" Pete cut into a slab of pot roast, stirred the piece around in the rich, brown gravy, and put the forkful into his mouth.

"Bentwell's strategy is to use every delaying tactic in the book, just to draw this thing out," Mr. Essex said. "He knows Dan Gonyea can't afford to spend a lot of money."

Pete swallowed. "But Bentwell can." He nodded. "I see. Last man standing wins."

"Exactly!" said Mr. Essex, spearing the last chunk of carrot on his plate. He had invited Pete to his home for lunch. "And our job is to keep that from happening."

"Are you ready for dessert, Mr. Delorme? It's hot gingerbread, right out of the oven," Mrs. Essex offered, "with applesauce on top."

"Yes, please."

A guilty thought passed through Pete's mind: *I wonder what kind of lunch Verity is having?*

He turned to Mr. Essex. "Sir, may I propose a hypothetical situation to you? Supposing there are these two old friends, who also happen to be neighbors. . . ?"

*

Verity felt that coming back to the house from the orchard that night seemed a little like entering the gates of Heaven. Everyone sat still at the kitchen table for a while, letting the warmth from the woodstove radiate into them before they spooned out the hot soup Mama had set to simmering that morning.

After draining the last drop from her bowl, Verity laid her head down on the table next to her soupspoon and fell asleep immediately.

"Verity, dear. . ."

She barely heard her mother through the sleepy fog as she was led upstairs to bed.

The next morning, Verity awoke with a sore throat.

"How are you today, Verity girl?" her father asked as she came down to breakfast.

"You're flushed," her mother said, and reached to feel her forehead.

Verity ducked away and hurried to the stove, where she poured herself a cup of coffee. "I'm fine, Mama," she insisted, plastering a smile on her face. "Please don't worry about me."

She had gargled with salt water, added an extra layer of clothing, and pocketed a few of her father's peppermints in preparation for another long day of apple-picking.

And a long day it was. At the end of it, the results were again disappointing, and Verity overheard Jacob tell Grace, "We'll make it, but only if we keep on goin' like we been goin' for the whole two weeks."

Sore throat or no, Verity fully intended to keep going. That same terrible night he had thrown Pete out the door, Jacob had explained what could happen if they didn't get their apples to market. There were payments to be made—for seed, for the new plow, for the mortgage it had been necessary to take out five years ago. Default on these payments, and there would be no more McCracken farm.

"My great-grandfather came here from Scotland," Jacob said, repeating a story Verity had heard all her life, "as an indentured servant. But he worked hard and went on to become the most successful farmer in this county. I'd hate to let it come down to this. . . ."

The despair in her father's eyes had cut Verity to the heart. She would use her last ounce of strength to see that such a thing wouldn't happen.

❧

Pete hadn't slept well. He had lain awake until three in the morning, thinking of the week's perplexing events and his new feelings for Verity. He had no illusion that she returned them with the same intensity. "But if we got to know one another better. . ."

He imagined a future with Verity by his side, and his heart lifted. He imagined a future without her, and sat bolt upright, then slid to his knees and prayed until his eyes would no longer stay open.

"Stop dwelling on this. It's not Mr. Essex's problem," Pete told himself firmly on his way to work the next morning. "I owe him a good day's work."

His employer called him into his office right away. Mr. Essex's eyes danced as he stood over his document-covered desk. "That hypothetical case you told me about yesterday? Well, I've done a little research, and there's something here I'd like to show you."

Verity coughed and pulled another apple from another tree.

If I never see another apple for the rest of my life, I'll be happy, she thought. *If I never again taste cider, apple pie, apple cobbler, apple cake, and especially not applesauce. . .*

Even the name, "apple," sounded funny to her ear now. She repeated the word to herself, all the while reaching, twisting, and dropping, reaching, twisting, and dropping in weary rhythm. "Apple. Aaa-pull. Aaaaaa-pulllllll. Appleappleapple. . ." Verity giggled.

"Apple!" she shouted hoarsely. "Isn't that a funny word?" she called to her mother in the neighboring tree, then was consumed in coughing spasms.

"I guess so, punkin," her mother answered quizzically. "I never thought about it. Hey, I don't like the sound of that cough. Why don't you take a little break?"

"No need," said Verity, struggling not to cough again. "I'm fine." She slipped a peppermint in her mouth and reached for another apple.

"That's it!" Pete said, tapping the deed sharply with his forefinger.

Mr. Essex smiled. "It's here, clear as day. Jacob McCracken owns the strip of land that connects your father's pasture to the stream."

"But we've—I mean, our cows have been crossing over that land for generations."

"There may have been a right established, or there may not. . ." Mr. Essex twirled his pencil and nodded. "Still, Mr. McCracken could take this to court. It would be long and costly, like Gonyea versus Bentwell."

"But that would. . .oh, I see. . .turnabout is fair play, I suppose. This is rough business, isn't it?"

His employer shrugged. "It's why the Bible advises against lawsuits, but people don't always pay attention."

"What I don't understand is why Mr. McCracken hasn't used this against my father."

Mr. Essex shrugged again. "Who knows?"

❧

I wonder, thought Verity, *if I'll be picking apples the rest of my life?* Her arms had slowed considerably in the last hour. Lifting them had become excruciating. Her back had begun to hurt, and she'd gotten shaky. She tried to steady herself by grabbing a thick branch, but she continued to quiver. "Papa," Verity said faintly, between coughs, "this ladder is. . .the ladder. . . it's. . ." She drooped over the branch, then her body began sliding down the ladder.

"Fred!" Jacob barked, "Verity! She's falling!"

Fred, who had been emptying his sack into a basket on the ground, sprang into action and caught Verity's limp form in his strong arms just in time. "Mr. McCracken! She's burning up!"

Immediately, Grace was there, too, feeling Verity's forehead. "She's got a fever. Quick; carry her to the wagon. We've got to get her indoors!"

❧

Fred Willard was pulling the buckboard onto the main road as Pete rode up on Sandy. Before Pete could greet him, Fred called, "Pete—Mr. Delorme— thank Heaven! You can go faster than I can! You gotta ride into town for the doctor. It's Verity. She's very sick! Get 'im back here, quick!"

With a troubled frown, Pete immediately turned Sandy around.

"Tell 'im it's fever—and a bad cough!" Fred called as Pete dug in his heels and slapped the reins.

As he rode, Pete tried to ignore the terrible sick grayness forming inside him. It was the same feeling he had had the night before, when he thought of a life without Verity.

"Fever and a cough," Fred had said. It sounded like. . .Pete closed his eyes, then opened them. No. No use thinking the worst. He would fetch the doctor, who would help Verity get well. Pete would then use the information he had learned this morning to straighten out this mess of a feud, and everything would be all right again.

That is, unless. . .

Dear Lord, he thought, *I'm so desperate. I don't know how to pray about this.* . . .

Sandy stumbled, and Pete slackened the pace slightly. He couldn't risk a fall.

"Careful, fella," Pete said to his horse. "Steady and straight into town."

❧

Verity couldn't understand it. For days, she'd felt nothing but constant cold, but now her skin felt alive with a fiery heat.

"Here, punkin, drink this," her mother said softly as she spooned cool water gently between her lips.

Verity drank thirstily, several spoonfuls, then said, "My head. Hurts." She still hadn't opened her eyes. All at once, violent coughs wracked her body. She writhed as the spasms continued, over and over. It seemed all the air was being squeezed out of her lungs. Would she ever get her breath?

All at once, with a long, squeaky intake of air, the torment was over, at least temporarily.

"My sweet baby," Grace murmured, and Verity heard tears in her mother's voice. "Poor darling." Gentle fingers stroked the hot forehead.

Verity opened her eyes slowly. "The apples," she whispered, taking shallow breaths, because she could feel another round of coughs lurking deep in her lungs.

Grace smiled. "Don't worry about that, punkin. Papa's got it all taken care of."

Verity closed her eyes, relieved. "Taken care of. . ." That meant that the Delormes had come around. Pete must have convinced his father to change his mind. "Pete," she mouthed silently. She smiled at the thought of him. She drew in a sigh and was rewarded with another violent bout of coughing.

❧

"It's whooping cough, all right," said the doctor, frowning. He shook his wet hands and accepted the clean dishcloth Grace handed him. "Pertussis.

239

You can hear it in her chest. That whooping, squeaky sound when she tries to pull in air." He shook his head. "Possibly pneumonia, too. Serious business. Just have to let the disease run its course. Make her as comfortable as possible. Her youth is in her favor."

Everyone knew the doctor was a kindhearted man, despite the great pains he took to conceal his kindness behind a mask of brusque frankness. "We'll know in the next few days if she's strong enough to endure the strain. Hard on the heart." He patted his shirtfront in an unconscious gesture.

"You're going to want to fill the room with steam. Keep filling up a big bowl from a kettle," he instructed, handing Grace a bottle of dark liquid, "and give her a tablespoonful of this every couple of hours, when the coughing is bad. She's not going to have much of an appetite, but try to keep her strength up. Broth, milk toast, that sort of thing."

Pete stopped the doctor on his way out. "How is she?"

"Bad." The doctor shook his head. "She's a sick young lady." He climbed into his buggy and urged his horse down the path to the main road.

Pete stood, lost in despair, watching him go.

"What're you doing here?" a sharp voice broke into the silence.

Pete continued to watch the departing buggy. "I brought the doctor," he said quietly. He turned and looked up at Jacob. "He said it's bad."

Jacob blew his nose, wiped it, and pocketed the handkerchief. "Ayah, it's bad. She's got the whoopin' cough and pneumonia."

"Oh, no."

Jacob sighed.

Pete mounted the first porch step. "May I see her?"

Jacob took a step back. "Look, Pete, I'm obliged to you for bringin' the doctor, 'n' all, but you're gonna have to leave now."

"But I—" Pete was about to say, "I love her," when Jacob interrupted him with a low snarl.

"Ain't you Delormes done enough around here? Why d'ye think my girl's lyin' up there so sick? 'Cause she's been out in the cold, workin' like a dog to help me bring in my apples, that's why! Go home and tell that to your pa! And tell him he won't have to deal with me much longer, 'cause come winter, I'm gonna lose this farm. I just hope he can sleep nights, knowin' that!"

"Mr. McCracken, if you'll just listen. I have some informa—"

Jacob stepped forward and shook his fist at Pete. "Get outa here! I don't want to ever lay eyes on a Delorme again, long as I live!"

Verity had a bad night. When she wasn't coughing, she was lying against a high bank of feather pillows, struggling for breath.

"Can't you let her lie down flat?" Jacob whispered to his wife. "Nobody can sleep that way."

"The doctor says it'll help her breathe better," Grace murmured. She ran her hand along her own collarbone. "He says there's some fluid in the lungs." She cringed and looked over at Verity. They were both remembering: Three Enfield children had died last year of the whooping cough.

Behind her closed eyes, Verity remembered, too. She thought, *I can understand how a child would die of this disease. You cough, over and over, and each time, it squeezes more air out of your lungs, until it seems like you'll never breathe again.*

She'd almost fallen asleep, but felt the ominous contractions begin once more in her chest, and she sat up. Again and again, she coughed: ten, eleven, twelve times, then drew in a long breath of blessed air with a loud wheeze. She fell back on her pillows, exhausted.

A little child would fight, she mused; *he'd struggle to breathe in the middle of the spasm. He'd wear his heart out. I just have to keep remembering, I can get my breath when the coughs die down. And they always do, eventually.*

She smiled faintly. *Pastor O'Neal would say there's a sermon in there somewhere.*

Maybe, *"They that wait upon the* LORD *shall renew their strength"?*

Patience, she thought. *I'm learning patience.* She tried to breathe in the soothing steam, but not too deeply, for fear of starting more coughs.

She wondered where Pete was, what he was doing.

Their efforts at healing the feud had been useless. *Perhaps we should have been more patient ourselves,* she thought. *But he felt as bad about it as I did.*

Dear Pete. She would have sighed, had she dared. *How kind he is. He really listens, too, which is rare. I like the fact that he's tall. And articulate. He uses words so well, but then he'd have to, if he's going to be a lawyer.*

He's strong, too. She remembered the way he had easily lifted the heavy sack of flour. *Just because he works in an office doesn't mean he can't lift. . .well, even lift me,* she thought, and a pleasurable shiver ran down her back.

Best of all, he loves the Lord. That's the most important thing.

Verity settled down more comfortably against her pillows and closed her eyes. She far preferred counting Pete Delorme's good points to counting sheep.

No matter how strong, tall, or articulate a man might be, if he doesn't love the Lord. . .

Her eyes popped open. She had remembered a dreamy conversation with her dormitory friends over hot chocolate one winter evening. "So, to sum up my perfect man," she'd said, "he's tall, strong, pious, articulate, and a bibliophile." The girls had all giggled at that last and her roommate said, "Leave it to Verity to want a bookworm!"

Dear Lord, Verity prayed, *is Pete Delorme my Perfect Man?*

Another cruel round of coughs began.

I mustn't die, she decided, as she waited for her turn to breathe.

I mustn't die, she repeated in her mind, while her chest and ribs ached from the exertion and her weakened heart beat fast against her chest. *Not yet,* she said to herself, while her air-starved lungs cringed in fear of more coughing.

Please, Lord, she prayed, *just let me live long enough to tell Pete—*

Jacob looked at his exhausted wife. "Here, let me sit with her," he said. He took the clean bowl from Grace's hands and draped a clean towel over his shoulder. "You need to get a little sleep."

Grace nodded gratefully and turned to leave. She paused at the door and beckoned him over with a crook of her finger. "I told her the apples are taken care of. What are we going to do about them?" she asked in a low voice.

"Our little girl's more important than all the apples in the world. We'll just let God and the birds take care o' the apples." Jacob kissed his wife's cheek and they exchanged weak, tear-sparkled smiles.

An hour later, as Jacob was pouring fresh steaming water in the bedside bowl, Verity said, "I heard what you said to Mama about the apples."

Jacob set the empty kettle in an enameled pan on the floor. "You what? You weren't supposed to hear that, little lady."

"I know, but Papa, what does it mean?" Verity's concern almost overcame her pain, but she was rewarded for this expenditure of energy by a renewed series of racking coughs. When she had finished and Jacob was wiping her face with a damp towel, he said, "No use lyin' to you, Verity. It doesn't look good for the farm, but once we get you well, we can make some plans. We got plenty o' choices. Uncle Roy'd be glad for my help with his lumberyard over to Elizabethtown, I know, and—"

"Papa, please promise me. . ." Verity waited a moment to summon more strength to finish her sentence. ". . .you'll forgive Mr. Delorme."

Jacob turned and deposited the towel in the enamel bowl. "We don't need to talk about that right now," he said, keeping his back turned.

Weakly, she tugged at her father's sleeve. "But we do. If I'm going to die, I don't want. . ."

Jacob spun around. "Verity!" he said, more sharply than he meant, "Don't say that!" Tears sprang into his eyes.

The smile Verity gave him was filled with love. "Papa, don't be afraid. . . to talk. . .about it." She closed her eyes and opened them again. "I'm not afraid. . . really. . ."

Jacob took her small, chapped hand in his and a sob escaped him.

"I don't want to die. . .knowing. . .you hadn't forgiven him—oh—" she moaned and grasped her chest, and more coughs shook her, over and over.

Oh, dear God! Jacob prayed as he watched the merciless coughing jerk her frame about on the bed. *Have mercy on my little girl!*

"You must," Verity insisted when at last she could rest. "You must forgive him. . .now. Pray," she insisted, pushing the word out with effort.

"I don't know if I can, Verity." Jacob's face was soaked with tears.

Verity smiled weakly. "Just be willing. . .to be willing. . .," she whispered.

"What?"

"God will do the rest." She closed her eyes. She was waiting.

THE FARMER'S BRIDE COLLECTION

So Jacob McCracken bowed his head and prayed a distinct but unlovely prayer. "Dear Lord in Heaven," he began gruffly. "You know what's been goin' on between me and Gerry Delorme. I know it's not Your will that we're on the outs like this, but we can't seem to stop ourselves. I don't much feel like it, but I want to do things Your way, so if You don't mind, would You make it possible for me to forgive that ol'—sorry, Verity—to forgive Gerry? And all the Delormes, I guess. I ask it in Jesus' name, amen. 'Fraid that's the best I can do," he added, speaking to his daughter.

Her faint answer had the ghost of a giggle in it. "It was just. . .perfect, Papa. Perfect."

Jacob bowed his head again. "And while you're at it, Lord, would you heal my girl?" He squeezed her hand gently and Verity responded with a faint, but clear squeeze of her own.

Then, for the first time in twelve hours, Verity drifted briefly off to sleep, holding her father's hand and smiling.

Jacob and Grace established a routine that week, taking turns sitting by Verity's bedside while the other slept. Fred gamely handled the other vital tasks alone, milking the cows, seeing to the chickens, and the hundred other small tasks a farm required. He steered clear of the orchard, though. When Verity got sick, they had all rushed back to the house, leaving baskets, ladders, and sacks scattered about under the trees. No need to fetch them now. The sight of that mess, and all those ripe McIntoshes, surely by now having fallen uselessly to the ground, would have broken his heart.

244

Chapter 8

I was wrong!" announced the doctor on the seventh day of Verity's illness. "Thank heaven, I was wrong!" He put his stethoscope back in his bag and stood up, a triumphant grin on his face. "Miss Verity, I know you don't feel like it right now, but you're getting better. The fever was over days ago and that rattle is completely gone from your chest. I must have been wrong about the pneumonia." He beamed down at her.

"Praise the Lord!" Grace gasped and clapped her hands. "Oh, my! I've gotta go wake Jacob and tell him. 'Scuse me." She scurried out the door.

The doctor continued. "This doesn't mean you can get up and dance a jig right away, though. You'll have this cough for a couple more months. It'll get better gradually, then finally go away entirely. You just need to rest, eat, smile a lot. . ."

Verity complied faintly.

"Good, but weak. You need to give it a little more practice. Now, is there anything else I can do for you?" He bent over the bed for her response.

"Would you tell. . .Mama and Papa. . .to bring me something to read? They think I'm too weak, but I'm getting really bored." She launched into her habitual coughing.

The doctor waited patiently until she was once more settled comfortably and said, "That's an excellent sign. I'll have Miss Reilly over at the library give me some of her newest books to bring you. Good afternoon," he said to Grace at the door. "Good afternoon, Mr. McCracken," he said, addressing Jacob, who was tousle-haired and bathrobe-clad, but beaming back at the doctor.

"I never thought I'd ever say this, but I don't even care about losin' this ol' farm," Jacob told Grace when she returned from escorting the doctor to the door. "Tryin' to save it nearly lost us the most important thing we got." He hugged his wife tightly and smiled down at Verity. "Why, I feel so good right now, I'm almost ready to forgive that polecat, Gerry Delorme!"

Verity dipped her eyebrows in mock disapproval. "Papa."

He patted her blanket-covered foot. "Well, anyway, I can't seem to get up a good mad at him anymore. That's progress, wouldn't you say?"

"I guess so."

There was a loud slam and the sound of heavy boots running on the ground floor.

"What on earth?" Grace backed out of her husband's arms and looked out Verity's door. "What is it, Fred?"

Fred stood in the doorframe, breathing hard. "Sorry to break in on you folks like this—hello, Verity—but it's the Delormes—they're in the orchard—stole nigh unto all them apples!"

"What?" Jacob roared. He began untying his bath-robe. "Let me get dressed. I'll be right down."

"Papa...," Verity called from the bed, "remember your prayer...."

Chapter 9

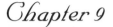

Pete hefted another bushel basket over the stile to a burly Delorme farmhand. "There," he said, as perspiration flowed freely down his face, despite the chilly air. "That's the last of it for now. We'll be back in a few days to pick the rest." McIntosh apples, he knew, ripened from the outside of the tree in, making it necessary for pickers to go over the trees several times.

"You fellows go on back. I'll be along in a minute." He leaned against the fence, pulled out a bandanna, wiped his face, and looked down the even rows of apple trees.

It had been a good week's work. Close to three hundred bushels picked already. The McCracken apples had ripened early and would bring a good price at market.

Slowly, he folded the bandanna in neat squares, remembering the afternoon in the park when Verity had borrowed his handkerchief. How lovely she had been! How long had he loved her? Two weeks? All their lives? It didn't matter. All that did matter was that Verity must get well and be able to hear him tell her so.

"Delorme! Pete Delorme!"

Pete opened his eyes and smiled at the sight of Jacob McCracken as the man came walking swiftly towards him.

What is he doing? Is he going to hug me? Pete stepped forward and opened his arms.

Jacob never hesitated. Pulling back his fist as he walked, he swung and landed a ferocious blow in Pete's middle.

Pete bent double and staggered slightly. "What are—" he managed to say before Jacob landed a sharp uppercut to his jaw. He slumped slightly against a low-hanging branch and looked up in time to see Jacob's fist headed for his face again.

"Mr. McCracken! Stop it!" Fred Willard threw himself between the two men and sustained a painful bruise to his shoulder for his trouble.

"Let me at 'im, Fred!" Jacob barked, bouncing on his feet. "Thief! Rotten sneak thief! My daughter's on her deathbed and you're out here stealin' a man's—"

"Deathbed!" gasped Pete. "Oh, no! Verity!" With his arms clasped around his middle and blood trickling from a split lip, Pete staggered past Jacob and Fred and began running down the rows through the orchard, in the direction of the McCracken house.

"Let me go, Fred!" said Jacob, struggling in the strong grip of the other man's sturdy hands. "I'll teach him to steal my apples!"

None too gently, Fred pushed Jacob against the stone wall and shook his head decisively. "Nope. Not till you calm yourself down. I'm not about to let murder be done, Mr. McCracken, no matter what that boy stole!"

"But—"

"You coulda killed him. He warn't about to fight back, didn't you see that? *Fret not thyself because of evildoers*, the Good Book says. *Vengeance is mine, saith the Lord.* You know what that means, Mr. McCracken?" He shook Jacob's shoulders. "Eh? Do ye?"

"Yes." Jacob took a long, shuddering breath and slid down the side of the low wall until he was seated on the cold ground. "Thank you, Fred Willard," he said, his eyes closed. Then he covered his face with his hands. "Thank you," he repeated.

Half an hour later, Grace met the two men at the back door. "I got coffee made. You two look like you could use it."

"Pete Delorme. He was headed here. Did you see him?"

Grace turned and walked into the kitchen. "Ayah. I did."

Jacob and Fred followed her.

"Where'd he go?" Jacob walked over the kitchen window and pulled back the curtain. Night was falling. It was hard to see out. He seated himself at the table.

Grace put three cups on the table and poured coffee in each one. "He's here."

"You let him in?" Jacob's chair scraped the kitchen floor, but Grace put her hands on her husband's shoulders.

"I most certainly did. You sit yourself down, Jacob Aaron McCracken, and quit bein' a bull in a china shop. Drink your coffee. Here's the cream." She set the pitcher in front of him.

Fred watched her curiously from behind his coffee cup.

Jacob poured the cream, spilling a good deal on the table. "Where is he, then?"

"In Verity's room."

At the top of the stairs, Grace turned and put her fingers to her lips. "Shhhh."

Followed by Jacob and Fred, she tiptoed to the open door of the sickroom and looked fondly on the scene within.

Verity lay quietly against her high pile of pillows, a tender smile on her lips.

Pete was slumped on the floor beside the low bed. He had laid his head and right arm next to her pillows. His eyes were closed and a low, regular snoring emanated from his slackened mouth.

And, as if in time to the rhythmic snoring, Verity's slim fingers stroked his damp, blond head.

Jacob gasped.

Verity looked up. Her eyes widened, then softened. "Papa," she began. Her hand continued its caress. "Pete loves me, did you know that? He loves me, and guess what else—" She reached for a nearby towel as coughs began to shake her body. "He. . .saved. . .our. . .apples!"

Chapter 10

ather felt as bad about the quarrel as you did," Pete explained to Jacob one clear October evening a month later, "but his pride was hurt and the whole thing just seemed to mushroom."

Jacob stirred uncomfortably on the horsehair settee. He was dressed in his best Sunday suit, and the collar was a mite tight. "The important thing is, he did the right thing when it mattered most, and I'll always be grateful to him for that."

"Well...," Pete took a deep breath, "he had a little help...."

"Why, of course he did. All those hands pitched in, and you did, too. By the way, I gotta say again how sorry I am about that ruckus I kicked up—"

Jacob grimaced as Pete stroked his jaw, then replied with a wave of his hand. "It's forgotten, remember? Forgiven and forgotten. But there is something I am obligated to tell you, and since it might prove to the detriment of my father, it's rather difficult..." He pulled papers out of a leather case, spread them on a nearby low table and carefully explained about the access to the water. And how Gerard had changed his mind about the apple harvest as soon as Pete had reminded him of it.

The young Delorme shot a worried glance toward Jacob as he spoke. "Of course you could—and still can— give my father all sorts of legal trouble over this. But it's your right to know about it." He gathered up the papers carefully and replaced them in the case, nervously avoiding Jacob's eye.

"To tell you the truth," Jacob McCracken began, crossing his arms over his chest and twisting his face into a frown. "To tell you the truth, I already knew all about that." Jacob leaned forward. With a stifled grunt, he hauled up one ankle and placed it on his knee.

Pete's jaw dropped and he shook his head slowly from side to side. "You knew? But how long have you known?"

Jacob retied his shoe, then dropped his foot to the floor with a thump. "Pretty much all my life. Delormes been takin' their cows to that stream since back when my grandpa ran this place." He leaned back in the settee, then sat up straight again. It was not a comfortable piece of furniture.

The two men studied each other for a long moment before Pete broke the silence.

"Sir. Mr. McCracken. You are truly a remarkable man. I can understand where Verity gets her strength of character. To think that all the time you and my father were quarreling, you could have used this against us." Pete stood. "Even when faced with certain ruin, you never said a word about what a debt of kindness our family owed yours. What a true Christian gentleman you are." He extended his hand. "Mr. McCracken, may I shake your hand?"

Jacob's eyes twinkled as he returned Pete's firm hand-clasp. He spoke slowly, carefully. "I'm, er, grateful for the kind words, young man. Tell you the truth, in all the excitement, it's hard to say exactly what was goin' on in my mind. I'd like to be able to tell you that I was too noble to do down your pa, but—if I was to swear to it—I believe I'd have to say. . ." He gestured for Pete to resume his seat on the handsome chesterfield chair opposite him. "I'd have to say, I probably plumb forgot all about it." He spoke in an even, almost impassive tone, but his face at once screwed into a cheery grimace. Tiny chuckles began in the back of his throat, slowly at first, then increasing in rapidity until they exploded into contagious guffaws.

Jacob gave himself completely over to the laughter. He slapped his knee repeatedly. He rocked back and forth on the settee. Hot tears squirted from his eyes. His crimson face began to ache from merriment.

"Sir," Pete interjected when the laughter finally died down. "I still prefer the first explanation."

Jacob wiped his eyes with a handkerchief. "So do I, son, so do I." He wadded the handkerchief in his pocket and leaned forward. "But look here. I know you didn't ask for this meetin' just to discuss legal folderol. Mrs. McCracken and me kind of thought you had something else—I mean, someone else—on your mind." He winked and sat back, waiting.

Pete put aside his leather case and straightened his shoulders. "Sir," he said, his expression dignified, earnest, "you were both absolutely right. . ."

Grace had her ear pasted against the closed parlor door and heard the loud explosion of laughter. She smiled. Things were going well. She stepped back and made her way down the hall to the small room at the back of the house where she kept her treadle sewing machine. Time to start an inventory. Pretty soon now, she reckoned, there would be piece goods to buy and a trousseau to run up.

A half hour later, the heavy pocket door slid open and Pete and Jacob emerged, wreathed in smiles and patting one another on the back. "He asked me, Mother," Jacob told his wife, who stood before the mirror on the big hall coat tree, donning her best hat, "and I told him we said, yes."

Grace stepped forward and gently kissed Pete's cheek.

He blushed, then pulled a slim volume from his leather case. "Uh, ma'am, may I go upstairs and speak to Verity? I brought her another book."

Grace stepped back. "No, sir, you may not." She patted his arm to remove the sting from her words. "Verity has arranged a surprise and I will go up now and fetch it for you."

Pete, bewildered, stood waiting in the hall while Jacob shrugged into his coat and grinned at him. "Be patient. They've been working on this all day."

All at once, Pete heard whispering at the top of the staircase. He looked up into the pale, smiling face of Verity as she descended slowly, back straight and step firm. Her tight grip on the banister and the large frilly handkerchief tucked into her waistband were the only concessions to the residue of frailty left behind by her illness.

She reached the hall and held out her hand to Pete. "Another book?" She took it and read the spine. "Oh, good, Browning this time."

"The boy's one o' them—whatchamacallits—book lovers," said Jacob to his wife.

"Bibliophile, Papa," said Verity softly, hugging the book to her. "The word is bibliophile."

Pete said, "The dance tonight. Can you go after all? I mean, are you able to—"

Verity nodded. "I can stay at the dance until I get tired, the doctor says. I'm not quite strong enough to dance myself, so you must let me watch you."

Pete found Verity's coat on the hall tree and brought it to her. "Nosiree! I'm not going to leave your side for a minute!"

"Where'd she get that dress?" Jacob asked as he helped his wife into her coat.

"At college, Papa," said Verity after a discreet cough into her handkerchief. "I wore it to a dance." She looked down at the skirt, pale blue watered silk. "It's a little big now, though. . ."

With a quick glance at Verity's parents, Pete made bold to plant a kiss on her forehead. "It's perfect." Her brow was cool and smooth and soft. She smelled of Yardley's Lavender.

Verity, he thought, *means truth. God has given me a true companion.*

Jauntily, he offered his arm. "Miss McCracken, shall we?"

The tiny dimple in her cheek danced. "Mr. Delorme, let's."

While Jacob McCracken held the door open, the young couple went out into the cold air and climbed into the waiting buggy.

Grace grabbed her husband's sleeve. "You didn't tell them about the announcement. What are they going to think when Gerry Delorme gets up there and tells a whole barnful of people that they're engaged?"

"They're going to think their parents are smart enough to read the signs—oops, that reminds me." Jacob hurried into the kitchen and returned with a gallon jug of amber liquid.

"Cider," he told his wife, "to toast our children and the end of this. . . this. . .applesauce war!"

SUNSHINE HARVEST

by Debby Mayne

Dedication

To my husband, Wally,
and my two daughters, Alison and Lauren

Chapter 1

Florida, Late Autumn, 1892

"Mama, the workers are hungry. Surely we can scrounge together something for them to eat."

"Not now, Anna," Josephine Drake replied from her lookout on the parlor's window seat. "Your father is due home with the supplies any minute. We shall feed them then."

Staring at her mother, Anna knew they shared a striking physical resemblance. She had inherited Josephine's tobacco-brown eyes. And often, when her father approached them from behind, he mistook one for the other—for both women twisted and pinned their wavy, honey-blond hair into an identical style to get it off their necks in the humid heat of Florida. They even wore the same petite size and frequently exchanged dresses. However, Anna's similarities to her mother went no further than these superficial traits. Her personality reflected her father in most regards. In stark contrast to Josephine's perpetual indecisiveness, Anna held a strong opinion about almost everything.

A determined Anna turned and headed for the kitchen. Since their orange groves had reached full production, the harvest required week after week of long, grueling days in order to get the fruit ready for shipment. Now, with the addition of a grapefruit harvest, the days seemed to never end. The men who worked the fields were tired and hungry. She had to feed them something. But what? After three days of feeding entire families of hungry laborers, very little food remained in the kitchen pantry.

Closing her eyes, Anna silently pleaded with God, asking Him to stretch what little food they had left. *Lord, You have been good to us. Please take care of these hardworking people.*

Their family had not attended church in months. Years. Would the Lord bother to listen to Anna's prayers?

No miracles yet, she thought as she opened her eyes to find the pantry's flour bin still nearly empty. And what could have detained her father? He was hours late coming from town with the items her mother had asked him to bring.

She returned to the parlor and, sinking onto the divan, studied her weary mother once more. Josephine's translucent skin and hollow, sunken eyes reflected the laborious tasks their family had undertaken the past few years—adding acre upon acre of new citrus groves, then harvesting their first crop of grapefruit. While other farmers scoffed at the idea of marketing the sour fruit, Anna's father planted the trees anyway, at the advice of his connections in the Orient. The risk paid off. Their entire crop of grapefruit had sold long before harvest. Still, while the business decision proved a good one, Anna suspected they were not quite ready to handle this much produce.

The morning wore on into late afternoon. Anna and her mother deserted their watch at the parlor window and set about tending to household chores. Suddenly, several loud knocks sounded at the Drakes' front door. Josephine flashed a glance of helplessness toward Anna. What if one of the workers had come to demand food? What would she tell them?

Anna wiped her hands on her apron as she headed for the door. Sucking in a deep breath, she then exhaled the air with a whoosh through her clinched teeth. *We mustn't keep putting these people off. They are hungry, and they deserve a decent meal for all their hard work.* Still, she dreaded an encounter with a protesting worker.

She tentatively opened the door just a crack. To her surprise, the person on the stoop was not one of their workers, but rather a tall, slim, dark-haired man in a suit. Someone from town. Obviously a businessman. She remembered seeing him before, but only once or twice; and she wasn't sure of his name.

He took off his hat and nodded, a grim expression on his face. "I have some news, Miss Drake. I need to speak with both you and your mother."

She took a step back and eyed him suspiciously. "I don't believe we've met, sir." She wasn't about to let a stranger into the house without at least knowing his name.

"Daniel Hopkins, ma'am." His solemn expression remained unchanged.

"J—just a minute, Mr. Hopkins," Anna replied, gently closing the door and leaving the man on the stoop. She scurried down the hall to the kitchen to find her mother. "Mama, do you know a Mr. Daniel Hopkins?"

Slowly, Josephine nodded. "He's one of the businessmen who sits on the Orlando city council. Is that who's at the door?"

"Yes. He wants to come in. He has news he wants to share with the both of us."

"Then, by all means, let him in," Josephine said, patting at her humidity-curled hair. "But we can't feed him until your father returns with the goods." Anna's mother rarely let anyone leave their home without feeding them something first.

Anna went back to the door and opened it wide. "Come in, Mr. Hopkins. I'm sorry I didn't know to let you in, but—"

He offered a forced grin as he stepped forward. "That's quite all right, Miss Drake. You can't be too careful these days. I understand."

Anna's mother had made her way back to the parlor and now stood in a prim and proper pose. She offered the best seat in the room to their guest, who took it with hesitation. As Anna drew up a straight-backed chair, she sensed a definite tension in the air. Something was wrong.

"How nice of you to pay us a visit, Mr. Hopkins," Josephine prattled. "I'd love to offer you something to eat, but I'm afraid my husband has yet to return from town with a fresh supply of groceries."

His expression changed to a look of panic. "Yes, I know," he replied, diverting his gaze and shifting in his seat. "That's what I've come to see you about, Mrs. Drake. Your husband."

Instantly, Anna knew something had happened to her father. *Oh, no,* she pleaded in silent, furtive prayer as her heart began to pound. *Please, Lord. Not Daddy.*

"Does this visit have something to do with my father?" Anna asked, a note of apprehension in her voice. "Have you seen him?"

Mr. Hopkins slowly nodded. "Yes, your father. . ." His voice trailed to silence and he looked nervously back and forth between Josephine and Anna, then around the room at the pictures on the wall. When his gaze settled upon Anna once more, he wordlessly reinforced her fears.

Her throat constricted as she rose to stand in front of Mr. Hopkins, urging him to finish his response. "What news do you have concerning my father, sir?"

"After Mr. Drake left my shop, he went to see the mayor. I remembered something I'd forgotten to tell him, so I ran over to city hall. There, I discovered that he'd died unexpectedly while talking with the mayor at city hall." His tragically awkward announcement made, he shifted his eyes to look at the floor in front of his feet.

A creeping blackness threatened to overtake Anna, so she gulped several quick short breaths in an attempt to remain standing. Only the sight of her mother, who had already fainted and collapsed in a limp heap on the floor, kept Anna on her feet.

Without a moment's hesitation, Anna raced to Josephine, scooping her mother into her arms, cradling her like a baby. "Oh, Mama, whatever shall we do?"

Anna's thoughts spun with a thousand different denials. Surely, this Mr. Hopkins had confused her father with someone else. Daddy was much too young, too strong, to die.

Yes, she reasoned with panic. *This is just an unpleasant incident that will amount to nothing more than a tragic case of mistaken identity.*

"You must be mistaken, Mr. Hopkins," Anna said as she straightened to face him. "My father is a very healthy man. I'm sure he'll arrive home any minute."

"I am sorry, Miss Drake," he said. The sympathetic look never left his eyes. Anna stared blankly through the man. Despite the stabbing realization that Mr. Hopkins spoke the truth, Anna's heart clung to a shard of hope. She fell to her knees and, holding her mother once again, Anna's lips moved ever so slightly in muttered prayer.

"Lord, you wouldn't take Daddy when we need him so!" In that brief moment, her faith faltered and in agony she quietly cried, "Lord, how could You do this to us?" She was unable to control the tears, now that she had given in and accepted the reality of her father's death.

Mr. Hopkins stood and crossed the room, pausing beside Anna and Josephine. "Is there any way I can help?"

A quick burst of anger replaced Anna's pain and her gruff response surprised even her. "Here's something you can do to help, Mr. Hopkins. You can go out there and tell those hungry laborers that we have nothing to feed them and that their employer has just died, leaving us without the means to provide for them."

He stared down at Anna. "I'm terribly sorry, Miss Drake. Really. I want to help."

A look of sorrow filled his eyes, and Anna sensed that he truly did care. However, she couldn't concern herself with him now. After all, her father had just died, and her mother lay unconscious on the floor. She now faced, alone, the monumental task of caring for an army of citrus pickers. All the fruit had been sold, yet no money would come in until the goods were harvested, inspected, and delivered. Meanwhile, these people and their families must be fed.

Once Josephine stirred to consciousness again, Anna released her mother and stood. She must feed the workers. But what?

Mr. Hopkins gently touched her arm and repeated his previous question. "Miss Drake, how might I help you?"

She buried her face in her hands and sighed deeply while pondering her response. "Well, sir," Anna said as she lifted her head to meet his gaze, "I appreciate the offer, but I doubt very seriously that you can help. The fact of the matter is, my father went into town to pick up some supplies and food for my mother so we could feed our workers. He was depending on the generosity of the shopkeepers to issue credit until the crops are delivered and paid for. Now we've no food. No money. No credit. Nothing."

Josephine moaned, and Anna knelt down beside her mother. Mr. Hopkins reached down and touched both women with the tips of his fingers. "I'll do what I can," he stated firmly. Then, after a moment's hesitation, he turned and walked out the front door.

Mr. Hopkins had no sooner left the house than Anna began to sob, her body heaving in agonizing wails. Consumed in her mourning, she lost all track of time. When Anna had exhausted her tears at last, she propped herself against the nearby love seat.

"Mama? Can you hear me?"

Josephine, her open eyes appearing unseeing and vacant, still lay crumpled on the floor. "James. James. James," she chanted softly, hypnotized by grief.

The sight of her bereaved mother filled Anna with renewed pain and fear and she called out again, "Mama?"

Josephine slowly turned and faced her daughter. Her anguished expression tore at Anna's heart. "I don't know what to do, Anna," Josephine said with a shaky voice. "Your father took care of everything. Now, I'm lost."

Anna, hiccuping softly from the aftereffects of her crying spell, leaned over to pat and comfort her frightened mother. She was frightened, too. But she could see that if someone didn't take control very soon, Josephine might wind up flat out on the floor again.

"I'll manage things now, Mama. Don't worry."

Even as the promise left her lips, she wondered just how she would accomplish such a feat. A spiraling sense of despair settled on Anna's spirit and, as naturally as breathing, her thoughts became silent prayers. *Oh, Lord. Help. Please, help. Show me what to do.*

Yet, at the time she needed most to cling to her faith, again pricks of doubt assailed her, and she could no longer contain her swelling ire. With a glance upward, she prayed, *How could You let my Daddy die? How could You do this to us? Are You punishing us?*

Suddenly, a surge of self-reliance pushed Anna to her feet. All this grief and sorrow wouldn't take care of the problems at hand. It was time to act. Something must be done to feed the workers, and she wasn't even certain that the Lord would help her now. Anna marched into the kitchen and dumped the last of the flour from the sack into their largest bowl. Then, she added every feasible pantry ingredient in an effort to make the food stretch. Even so, she produced only two baskets of pitifully small biscuits and some fried lard.

Tomorrow, she would have to go into town herself and see what she could do. Maybe someone there would extend her credit. She had no choice but to somehow convince them.

The screen door slammed behind her as she carried her meager meal offerings toward the cluster of backyard tables. While she placed the baskets on the tables, the sound of horses' hooves caught her attention. Anna turned toward the road to see a half-dozen riders approaching, Mr. Hopkins in the lead. Huge saddlebags draped the neck of each horse.

Mr. Hopkins motioned for the men to dismount as soon as they reached the yard, and they paused just long enough to pull sacks and baskets from their bulging saddlebags before approaching her.

"W–what?" she sputtered, confusion etching her voice. "What's all this?"

Mr. Hopkins set his sacks down on the table first, then turned to face her. "I know this isn't much, Miss Drake, but I told some men from the church about your plight, and they wanted to do something."

Anna watched in amazement as the men continued to pull food from the sacks, her heart pounding harder with each emptied bag. *How did they manage to gather all this food so fast?*

"God is good, Miss Drake. He won't forsake you in time of need."

As her throat clogged with emotion, she half-whispered her raspy response. "Then why did He let my father die?"

Chapter 2

Daniel studied Anna Drake for a long moment. Her eyes were still swollen from crying, yet she had managed to scrape the bottom of the barrel to provide for her workers. She showed stubborn determination. He admired her for that. And he suspected that her caustic comments flowed from her fresh grief and sorrow, not from a hardened heart. At least that's what he hoped.

"Miss Drake," he said softly as he came toward her, "the Lord will take care of you and your people. He doesn't always make His plan obvious to us, so we have to learn to trust Him."

Anna licked her lips and glanced nervously toward the cluster of men who had followed Daniel to her farm. They were already spreading the baskets of food on the tables.

"I'd like for you to accept this offer, Miss Drake," Daniel gently urged. "No strings attached. However, once you get back on your feet, we'd love to have you join us at church."

"What do you care if we set foot in church?" she asked with cynicism etching her voice.

"As a Christian and a part-time lay pastor, it is my hope to be able to minister to more than your physical needs. We are here to help you find the answer to your spiritual needs as well." His gaze remained steady as he spoke. He could tell Anna was confused. Daniel was firm in his conviction, yet he felt tenderness when he looked at her.

"Miss Drake, your father and I often spoke about spiritual matters.

Over the course of our acquaintance, I watched his spirit slowly soften. This morning, when we met at my store, he told me that he had recently recommitted his life to the Lord."

"Why didn't we know anything about this?" Anna asked skeptically.

Daniel shrugged and shook his head. "I'm not sure, but I do know that he did intend to share his newfound faith with you and your mother. He mentioned that he planned to bring you and your mother to church with him on Sunday."

She narrowed her gaze, then laughed in a way that didn't become her. "Now I understand. You're only saying this because my father is now unable to refute your statements. You must desperately want to add to your church roster."

Daniel was flabbergasted. "Our intentions are pure, Miss Drake, and I speak the truth, I can assure you. Regardless of whether or not you ever attend our church, this food is yours."

He watched as she made a decision. Obviously, Anna Drake felt as though she'd been placed between a rock and a hard spot, forced to accept something from someone else.

"Okay, Mr. Hopkins, I'll accept this food, only because the workers are hungry. But tomorrow, I'll go into town first thing. This will be the last time the Drake family will ever need to accept your charity."

"This isn't a case of charity, Miss Drake," he explained as tenderly as he could. "We're Christ's children who choose to follow in His footsteps. Whatever decisions you make about attending our church are completely between you and the Lord." He hesitated for a moment before tipping his hat. "G'day, Miss Drake. We'll pray for you and your mother." Daniel's gaze was fixed on Anna, and he felt a tug at his heart. He had an overwhelming urge to protect her from future harm. "Please drop by my dry goods shop next time you come to town."

❦

Anna stood and watched the men mount their horses. The pain lingered in her chest, but she knew she'd been hard on this fellow who obviously wanted to help. They'd only gone a few yards when she hollered, "Mr. Hopkins!"

He turned and faced her, while motioning for the other men to stop. "Yes, Miss Drake?"

She forced a smile as the tears threatened to flow again. "Thank you for all this food. I apologize for being so harsh."

He smiled back at her in a very compassionate and tender manner. "I understand. I have experienced great loss in my past, and if it weren't for the Lord and His mercy, I don't know where I'd be today." Then, he turned and rode away with his men.

Anna could only stand there and watch him leave. With the news of her father's death fresh on her mind, her mother back in the house lying in bed, and the workers still not aware of her father's death, she wasn't sure what to do next.

There was more food laid out than normal, something that would definitely raise some questions. She knew that it would be a risk to inform the workers of her father's death right now because they would fear not being paid. But Anna was determined to continue conducting business as usual, in spite of her lack of experience. She simply must learn the business—and not waste any time in doing so.

Before long the workers began to move toward the yard, where they would typically find a modest layout of food. Anna watched their eyes widen with amazement as they each drew closer to the tables.

"Go ahead and eat all you want. Whatever is left, take home for your families." As she spoke, Anna waged an internal debate. Should she wait until tomorrow to break the news about her father's death? By then, she should have a better idea of what the bankers would do for her. However, they deserved to know as soon as possible. And the last thing she needed was for them to find out from someone else.

She stood and watched as the people piled their plates high with food. They had worked hard, and they were hungry.

Once they were all seated, Anna stood on one of the empty tables and got their attention by waving her arms. As she told them the news, they all dropped their forks, one by one, and started praying. She overheard one man praying that his family wouldn't starve to death because he couldn't find another job. A husband-wife team of hired hands had their arms around each other, mumbling a prayer of thanks for the food they had to eat today. "And Lord," she heard the wife say very clearly, "please take care of Mrs. Drake and Anna."

Anna's stomach knotted. Why did these people think that prayer would help after what had happened? Obviously, their trust in the Lord hadn't budged. Yet her own faith had been shaken by today's horrible turn of events. Then again, Anna's faith had never been too strong. Not since those long-ago days when her family had come face-to-face with hypocrisy.

When Anna was a young girl, the members of their old church had shunned them after her father lost almost everything he owned in a bad business deal. Soon after, he had learned that land near Orlando was being sold for a song, and he wanted to jump at the opportunity to invest. But the church folks, including those they had considered friends, laughed and sneered, telling them that they were only looking for a pot of gold at the end of the rainbow.

One evening during those dark times, Anna overheard her parents debating what they should do. Should they listen to their mocking advisors, who insisted that they knew the Lord's will in this matter? Or should they follow their instincts and pursue the Orlando deal? Did they really want to heed the counsel of hypocrites?

Anna had lain in her bed unable to sleep as, in the other room, her father and mother bitterly recounted other times that the church folk had acted less than Christian. Their final decision to ignore the advice of these so-called friends came when Josephine Drake reminded her husband of the time that one of their field hands was in dire need of medical care. The town doctor, who just happened to be a member of their church, had turned his back on their pleas for help. No one from the church seemed to want to be bothered with someone they considered beneath them, and the man had died, leaving behind a widow and two small children. As her mother's voice carried through the thin walls, little Anna recalled the looks of anguish on the faces of the deceased man's family. Until that moment, she hadn't known the real reasons behind the worker's death.

On that long-ago night, not only did Anna lose confidence in the people who claimed to be "Christian;" her faith in the God they followed faltered as well.

No. Anna couldn't count on the aid of church folks now. She wasn't even certain she could depend on God. Her bitter memories fueled her resolve to handle this crisis on her own.

Standing back up on that table, she got the workers' attention again, this time by clapping her hands. "All business will continue tomorrow," she said. "This farm will go on, no matter what. I assure you that I will do whatever it takes to grow oranges and grapefruit, and then take them to market, just as my father always has."

A man close to where she was standing stood up and cleared his throat. "Miss Anna, I beg your pardon, but it concerns many of us that you've never run a grove before."

Anna understood their concerns. "Maybe I haven't, but I can certainly learn. If you will keep working for me, I promise to do everything in my power to maintain the same pay as before. If you choose not to, I understand. However, once the workday begins tomorrow, I'll reward those of you who remain with me."

She got down off the table and left the group to discuss among themselves what they were going to do. It frightened her to think that the whole lot of them might walk away and leave her stranded with acres and acres of oranges and grapefruit in need of harvest. But what could she do other than what she'd already done?

❧

Anna brought some food in to her mother, knowing she wouldn't be able to eat. The news was too new, the pain too fresh. But she had to at least try, now that she was in charge.

"What did the workers say when you told them?" Josephine asked as she tipped the cup of tea to her lips.

Anna forced herself to smile, in spite of her worry. No need to concern her mother until she knew something for sure. Tomorrow she'd have a better idea of whether or not they'd even have workers.

"They're very sad, of course," Anna said slowly. "But when I told them that tomorrow there'd be business as usual, they were relieved." She left out her feelings of anger that had taken a turn to fear of the Lord. What would He do to them next?

Josephine narrowed her eyes and studied Anna's face. Anna didn't like that kind of scrutiny, knowing that she wouldn't hold up like this for long. "They said that?"

"Well," Anna replied, unable to lie. "Not in so many words."

"Exactly what did they say?" Josephine asked.

Anna swallowed hard. She didn't want to worry her mother any more than she already was, but she couldn't lie, either. Looking down, she said, "Most of them just started praying for their families. We'll have to wait until tomorrow to know what they're going to do."

"I see," Josephine said as she looked into her cup. "Did you manage to scrape up enough food to feed them?" She glanced over at the plate of food Anna had brought up as if seeing it for the first time. "Oh, my." Her hand went to her mouth, her eyes huge from wonder.

"Mr. Hopkins and some men from his church brought food for the workers," Anna said in a soft voice.

Josephine continued staring at the plate for a moment before looking back over at Anna. "I wonder how long they'll keep this up."

"They won't," Anna replied.

With her eyebrows raised, Josephine tilted her head to one side. "And why not, may I ask?"

Anna squared her shoulders and inhaled through her nostrils, then let it out slowly as she fought hard to keep from lashing out at her mother. Josephine might be willing to accept charity, but she wasn't. When she was certain she could speak without anger in her voice, she said, "Because I told them we will not accept charity from anyone."

"Anna, these people are just doing what the good Lord wants them to." She sniffled, then added, "Or at least what they think the Lord would want them to do."

"You don't really believe that, do you?" Anna said.

"I–I'm not sure," Josephine said as she glanced away. Anna could tell she really didn't. Neither of them did.

Anna was sitting here with a citrus grove to run. She knew she must rely on her own strength rather than someone else's. After all, who did she know that could meet their needs?

"Mama," Anna said after several long moments of silence.

"Yes, Anna?" Josephine whispered. Her face was still pale, and her eyes were sunken above hollowed-out cheeks.

"What will we do about burying Daddy?"

Josephine's face whitened even more. She sank farther beneath the blanket and closed her eyes. "I have no earthly idea."

Anna reached out and smoothed her mother's hair from her forehead. "Don't worry, then, Mama; I'll take care of everything."

She'd said it, and she'd meant it. *From now on,* she thought, *I'll take care of everything—the funeral, the farm, and Mama.*

The sun had barely gone down, and there were still traces of light as Anna headed downstairs to the kitchen. She'd left the plate of food in her mother's room, knowing that it probably wouldn't be touched. Her heart was heavy, but she couldn't give in to the weakness of emotion. She had too much to do.

At first, when she heard the knock, she didn't realize what it was. The wind had been blowing, so she assumed that it was nothing more than the wind blowing a tree branch against the side of the porch. But the second time she heard it, she knew someone was at their door.

Anna paused for a moment, unsure of whether she should answer it. She didn't feel like taking callers now, but it might be important. So, she turned back toward the front of the house.

The instant she opened the front door, she regretted her decision. It was Mr. Hopkins.

"Yes, Mr. Hopkins? Did you forget something from your earlier visit?" she asked as coolly as she could without being rude. After all, he had been kind enough to gather food for her. She'd have to remember to find a way to pay him back for his generosity.

He smiled and removed his hat. "I began to think about your plight, Miss Drake—"

"You don't have to think about my plight, Mr. Hopkins," she interrupted. "We're perfectly fine." Anna had to look away from Daniel's soft, caring gaze. She couldn't allow herself to be concerned with this man who was still in God's good graces.

He stood there and studied her while she felt an unfamiliar fluttering in her abdomen. "I'm sorry, but I beg to differ. No one would be fine after hearing such sad and tragic news. I'm here to listen to you."

"I have nothing to say," she snipped.

"Please, may I come in?"

"Persistent, aren't you?" she asked as she backed away from the door to make room for him.

He chuckled softly. "I suppose that's a nice way of putting it."

"Look, Mr. Hopkins, I appreciate all you've done. I'll even go to your church once or twice to show my appreciation. But please don't feel that you have to take us on as the poor widow and daughter left behind."

"That's not how I feel, Miss Drake," he said. "And please call me Daniel."

"I prefer to address you as Mr. Hopkins." Her voice was beginning to crack. She cleared her throat.

"Suit yourself," he said. "But may I call you Anna?"

She shrugged, not taking her eyes off him for a moment. While she felt that she could trust him to tell her the truth, she still wondered why he kept coming around. She'd absolved him of all responsibility, and just because he'd been the one sent to break the awful news that very day, he didn't have to feel it was his obligation to take care of her.

"You may call me anything you like," she finally said.

"I'd like to help with the funeral preparations if you don't mind." His voice was solid and steady, something she needed just then. "Mr. Fletcher, the undertaker, needs to know what arrangements have been made for the body, and I figured that you probably haven't had time to really consider the matter in detail. We have a small cemetery behind the church, or if you'd prefer we can bury your father on your property."

"I hadn't really thought about it," she said.

"Let me know, and I'll take care of everything."

Slowly, Anna nodded. "I'll do that. Thank you, Mr. Hopkins."

For an instant, he looked hurt, then he smiled and nodded. "The people of the congregation have offered to bring food for your workers for the next several days, until you can make other arrangements for them."

"Other arrangements?" Anna asked.

He nodded. "Surely you don't plan to continue harvesting all this fruit. After all, your father was the businessman. No one expects you—"

Anna stood up and nodded toward the door, cutting him off. "Thank you, Mr. Hopkins, but I will feed my own workers. I plan to do quite a few things that no one expects of me. I will continue harvesting the fruit, and I will take over my father's business. I thought I already made myself clear this afternoon."

He stood up and took a couple of steps toward the door. "I see." He turned around and faced her, catching her off guard, making her heart leap. With his blue-green eyes leveled on her, she felt stiff and frozen in place. "So you're telling me that you'll tackle everything all by yourself, no help from a soul other than the workers you have in place, harvesting the crops."

"That's exactly what I'm saying, Mr. Hopkins. I'm glad we've finally come to this understanding."

Mr. Hopkins tilted his head toward her but continued looking at her from beneath hooded eyes, making her dizzy with an unfamiliar emotion. She wanted to hate him, but she couldn't; his voice was too soft and filled with compassion. "I may leave you alone, but I will not quit praying for you." Then he turned on his heel and walked out the door, never once looking back.

Anna stood there staring after him, wondering what good his prayers would do if she didn't acknowledge them. She'd given up praying this very morning, knowing that if God was willing to take her father at a time like this, she must not be in His favor anyway, so why bother?

As she thought about her loss and all that lay ahead for her, Anna leaned against the wall and slowly slid to the floor. Her body began to shake with sobs, her heart feeling like it had been shattered into a million pieces. She had loved her father, despite his bitter spirit following his financial setbacks. Even after he had recovered financially, his bitterness remained. It was only lately that Anna had begun to see a softer side of her father. Now he was gone.

She must have fallen asleep on the floor in the hallway because a stream of light coming in through the window awakened her. Her eyes fluttered from the brightness of a blazing sun.

Anna stood and looked outside for her father before she shuddered with a jolt of remembrance of yesterday's tragedy. She wanted to think this was all a bad dream, but she knew it was reality. And now she had to face it. There was so much to tend to; she felt as though she was swirling in a whirlwind that would never end.

As tempting as it was, Anna simply would not ask for help from anyone, especially Mr. Hopkins. The last thing she needed was to be indebted to a do-gooder who wanted to pound his Bible in her face.

Anna hadn't been awake more than five minutes before she heard her mother call from upstairs. "Anna, come quickly. I need you."

"Coming, Mama," she called in a weak voice. She had to find the strength to stand up to what she had to face this day and each day after. There was so much to be done; she couldn't allow herself to be weak.

"Anna," Josephine said when Anna arrived at her door. "Please be a dear and fetch me some tea."

"Yes, Mama," Anna said. "But I have to run into town this morning, so I want you to try to get up and move around a little bit. At least get dressed and find a comfortable spot in the parlor, just in case someone comes to the door."

"Who would come here in the middle of the week?" Josephine asked.

"Since Daddy died, folks seem to be appearing at our door with regularity," Anna replied, envisioning the form of Daniel Hopkins as he stood on their porch. She shook her head to dispel the image and her thoughts returned to the matters at hand.

"Mama, you must help me if I am to have any hope of doing what needs to be done today. Let me get your tea, then I'll be right up to help you dress."

Anna rushed around in preparation for her trip to town. There was no time to waste. She wasn't sure if the workers had all arrived, but she knew some had. She'd have to get an accurate count this evening when they all came back to the yard for supper.

Typically, when she went into town, she rode in the carriage. But she didn't have time today to hitch the horses, so she simply saddled a horse. She would somehow manage to fit the day's food for her field hands in the saddlebags.

Fortunately, the weather was nice, so she didn't have to worry about that. The brisk air felt good on her cheeks as the horse trotted to town. Hopefully, she wouldn't be met with too much opposition from the grocer, who'd been extending credit to her father ever since he'd added grapefruit groves. People in town were excited about the new crop, so she'd use that to her advantage.

The grocer was more than happy to offer a week's worth of credit. "But, unfortunately, I can't do more. I have to pay for these items when they arrive, and if I go much longer than a week, I can't stay in business."

She nodded as she sighed. "I understand. I'll have your money to you within a week." She picked up a few items and left, feeling dejected. She had no idea how she'd make good on this promise.

Then, Anna went to the next place on her list, the bank. She was greeted with a warm smile. Maybe, just maybe, she'd get what she needed here. But by the time she left, she knew that there wasn't much hope for her to get what she needed in order to keep the groves. Mr. Blankenship, the banker her father had trusted for years, had told her in so many words that, without her father there, she might want to consider selling the farm and moving herself and her mother into a house in town.

"We have some mighty fine places here that I'm sure will more than accommodate you and Mrs. Drake," he'd said.

"That's not what I plan to do," she'd stubbornly argued. "I want to continue running the business my father started."

Mr. Blankenship had dropped the pretense of the smile and leaned forward to face her, his hands folded on top of his desk. "And exactly how do you plan to carry on, Miss Drake?"

She'd inhaled through her nose and let it out in a whoosh through pursed lips. "Obviously not with your help."

The banker had stood up and walked toward the door. "I'm sorry, Miss Drake, but this is business. I'm sure you'll understand someday."

"I understand now," she'd said in a huff as she breezed past him and didn't turn back.

Nothing had gone right. What was she to do, now that there didn't seem to be an ounce of hope?

"Miss Drake!" a voice said from behind. "Anna, please wait."

She spun around and found herself face-to-face with Daniel Hopkins. In spite of how she'd felt about him the day before, she smiled. For some reason, he didn't seem so bad today. "How do you do, Mr. Hopkins?"

Chapter 3

He looked at her as though he didn't believe his eyes. Anna watched him as he blinked back the disbelief she'd initially seen on his face.

It took him a few seconds to regain his composure. "Miss Drake. Anna," he corrected himself. "How are you today?"

Anna shook her head. "At the moment, I'm not quite sure."

"I understand," he replied. "You had so much to deal with yesterday, I'm surprised to see you out and about today."

"I didn't exactly have a choice, Mr. Hopkins," Anna retorted, her voice dropping. No matter how hard she'd tried, she hadn't managed to convince anyone she could run her father's business.

"Is there anything I can do to help?" he asked with concern.

She started to shake her head, but she stopped. "Well, maybe."

"Would you care to discuss this here or in private?"

Anna thought for a moment. She wasn't up to talking about such matters in the middle of downtown Orlando, not with all the people milling about. Besides, she still needed to pay a call on the undertaker to discuss funeral arrangements. "Would you care to come for dinner this evening, Mr. Hopkins? Perhaps we can discuss it then."

He glanced down at the meager sacks of food in her hands and slowly shook his head. "I wouldn't want to come for dinner. I'm not one to do something so ghastly as eat all the food intended for farmhands."

"Nonsense," Anna said as she shifted the sack to her other hand and put it behind her skirt. "There's plenty."

Mr. Hopkins continued to scrutinize the situation before he finally nodded. "Yes, then, I'll be there."

"Good," she said as she tilted her head back jauntily. "I'll expect you at five-thirty."

The instant he walked away, Anna glanced down in the bag she still held in her hand. He was right. She didn't even have enough food for the farmhands, let alone for someone like him. What would she do?

Pulling her drawstring purse open, she glanced inside to see how much money she still had. Three dollars. That used to seem like quite a bit of money to her, but not now. It wouldn't last long if things didn't change around here very quickly. She was afraid she might have to take Mr. Blankenship's suggestion and sell the groves to the highest bidder.

Moving into town wouldn't be so bad, she thought. At least she wouldn't have to worry about feeding the workers. There were other things she remembered her father fretting over. Drought, for one. There were seasons when he watched the sky and prayed for rain. When it didn't come, he always blamed God. When it did, he spoke of how good of a farmer he was. Another thing he'd had to worry about was frost. She remembered her father saying, "A cool snap is good because it sweetens the fruit, but a deep freeze is bad. One long freeze could put us out of business for good."

Yes, moving into town just might be the answer. But she didn't want to admit defeat. Not yet, anyway. She still had some fight left in her. Anna Drake was born on a farm, and she was determined to keep it as long as she humanly could, despite what all the nay-sayers in town thought. Just because she was a young woman, barely an adult, didn't mean she wasn't smart enough or didn't have what it took to run the groves and have a successful business.

But each person she spoke with, each possible lender who could keep her from losing her battle, brought her closer to being forced to move. Her father wasn't even buried yet, and here she was about to lose everything. Anna and Josephine didn't even have the luxury of mourning his passing.

Actually, her mother didn't seem to care what happened. She'd always been one to drift along, not a care in the world, knowing she'd be taken care of. Why hadn't Anna seen this before? All the time Josephine had appeared to be helping, she had been only doing what didn't seem too difficult. Anna knew it was completely and totally up to her to make things right. And so far, she hadn't been successful.

Anna forced herself to turn down the street where the undertaker's establishment stood. Her hand shook as she turned the doorknob and entered the gloomy parlor. Mr. Fletcher mysteriously appeared from behind a heavy velvet curtain and motioned her to take a seat. Speaking matter-of-factly, as though her father died every day, he launched into a detailed explanation of how he had already laid her father's body in a plain pine coffin.

Another expense we can ill afford, Anna thought as she struggled to stay her tears.

At last the undertaker rose from the seat he had occupied opposite Anna's, signaling an end to his morose speech. Magnanimously, he offered to show Anna her father's body, but she knew that with just one glimpse of her father's lifeless form, she would certainly lose control of her fragile emotions. She could ill afford to break down now. She made a hasty retreat toward the door, announcing that she would send word tomorrow concerning the burial arrangements.

With a heavy heart and a jumbled mind, Anna headed back to the house. The decision she must make concerning her father's final resting place seemed almost insignificant compared to the other crushing crises she faced. She had enough food for the evening meal, but after that, she had no idea what she'd do. The grocer would allow her to return tomorrow for a week's worth of provisions, but how would she pay him at the end of the week? The workers hadn't been paid yet, and the money from the previously harvested fruit still wasn't due for weeks.

When she arrived, Anna was shocked at all the activity around the house and yard. "What is going on?" she demanded when she came upon a woman who was hanging laundry out to dry.

"We're from Good Shepherd Church, and we're here to see to it that you and your mother are well taken care of," the woman said as she continued to hang the freshly washed clothes on the line.

"B–but I never spoke to anyone about this. Who is in charge?" Anna nervously looked around. The only person she knew of who went to that small church was Mr. Hopkins. *Mr. Hopkins! He's the one who organized this.* And, without her permission. *Who does he think he is?*

With her jaw set in determination and her eyes narrowed from anger, Anna set out to find the man who needed to explain what in the world was going on. She wasn't about to continue accepting charity, even when she didn't ask for it. Even though she knew she needed it.

Another group of women stood around the tables on the side lawn. There were deep dishes filled with all sorts of food: meat, vegetables, breads, and desserts. Anna's mouth watered at the aroma that wafted through the cool air. She sure was hungry. Last time she'd eaten was last night, when Mr. Hopkins had come with those men.

After asking someone from every group, Anna learned that Mr. Hopkins had sent these people but hadn't come himself. She also began to suspect that his church wasn't as small as he'd led her to believe. She'd never seen so many do-gooders in her life as were on her property right now.

Josephine came outside and stood on the front porch, watching in fascination as people scurried about. Anna waved, and Josephine lifted her fingers, waving back.

With a heavy sigh, she just shook her head. This was one time she didn't have the energy to stop anyone—not after her unsuccessful day in town. At least, she could save the food she'd bought to cook for tomorrow's dinner.

By the time the workers came in from the groves, they were famished. One look at the spread on the tables, and the prayers started. Anna cringed as she realized she and her mother were the only ones who never said prayers of thanksgiving. But what had God done for them besides take away the head of their household? She wouldn't begrudge the workers their faith, but she wasn't about to give in yet.

The workers had all eaten and taken some food for their families when Mr. Hopkins finally arrived. He came with a smile on his face and more food in his saddlebags. "Was there enough for everyone?" he asked.

"Yes, thank you," Anna said coolly. "You really didn't have to go to such extremes."

"I know that," he said, without letting her dissuade him from his intentions. "But the Lord is pleased when we take care of others."

"Maybe you can convince me of that someday," Anna said as she looked around at the grapefruit-filled trees lining the lawn. "But at the moment, things look pretty bleak."

"They often do before He shows us where He wants us to go."

Anna snorted as she shook her head. "All I know is that my mother and I lost my father yesterday, and we're about to lose everything else today. What more could He possibly want?"

"Perhaps for you to sit still, pray, and listen to what He has to say?" Mr. Hopkins offered gently and with conviction.

"Ha!" Anna picked up a plate and offered it to him. "Fix yourself something to eat. Have all you want. We're especially generous on this glorious day." The sarcasm dripped from her voice, but she couldn't help it. She was hurting inside.

"Sit down, Anna. I think we need to talk."

She numbly did as she was told.

Daniel Hopkins sat across the table from her and leaned forward. "Okay, first of all, I want to get a few things straight, Anna. I am not your enemy. I'm here to help you as a friend. And I must insist that you call me Daniel. 'Mr. Hopkins' is getting old."

In spite of the ache deep in her heart, Anna offered him a bitter smile. She had to admit, Daniel sure would be a whole lot easier to say. "Okay, Daniel. What else would you like from me?"

"Nothing."

"Nothing?" she questioned as she stood back up. "Come on, Mr., er. . . Daniel, everyone wants something."

"Like I said, nothing. Everything the good Christian people from my church are doing is because they love Jesus." After a moment's hesitation and a deep breath exhaled, he continued. "All of us have experienced something in our lives, some tragedy that could have turned us away from the Lord."

"H–have you?" Anna stuttered, so stunned by his bluntness, she wasn't quite sure what to do.

Daniel sniffed and nodded his head. "As a matter of fact, yes. I lost my father to a band of thieves when I was merely a boy of thirteen. They left us with nothing, not even the shirts on our backs. After that, it was up to me to take care of my mother and sister."

"I–I'm sorry," Anna apologized, not knowing what else to say after such an open admission. "I had no idea."

"What's more," he added, his voice gruff, "they left us all with ugly scars and more fear than you can ever imagine. If it weren't for the good Lord guiding people from the church to us, we might have been left to starve, not only for food but for His word."

Anna couldn't take her eyes off the man who'd just exposed his soul to her. He'd endured much more than she ever had. "How did you become a successful businessman?"

"With the Lord's blessing, I worked hard; starting with nothing but the willingness to do whatever I had to do. It took years for me to acquire what I have today. It wasn't easy. I understand your pain, Anna, and I can certainly sympathize. In fact, I went through quite a bit of anger myself when I was old enough to realize what had happened to my family. Fortunately, the Christian leaders were patient with me, and their prayers brought me to the Lord. It wasn't easy for any of us. But, today, I know where everything comes from, thanks to that horrifying experience."

Anna swallowed hard. If what he was telling her was true, he did know what her pain felt like. At least, he was consistent. She'd never seen anyone so adamant about anything in her life. Most people would have backed down by now. And, she had to admit, she didn't know anyone else who'd been through anything nearly as dreadful as what Daniel had just told her.

Maybe it *was* time for her to listen. If Daniel Hopkins had something worthwhile to say, perhaps she would be able to do something to save the homestead. He was, after all, a successful businessman and community leader. "Okay, Daniel, what do you suggest I do to keep from having to sell the farm?"

He studied her for a moment, then motioned for her to sit back down.

Once she did, he sat down beside her. Placing both of his hands over his heart, he said, "Do you know what I'm feeling right now?"

"Your heart?" she asked. Her own heartbeat raced as the question escaped her lips and a strange emotion swept through her, making her feel weak inside.

"Yes."

Anna nodded. "But, why?"

He balled his hands into a fist and gently pounded his chest. "This is a heart filled with the love of Jesus Christ my Savior. He lived and died for me so that I may experience the salvation that I don't deserve."

"What's the point of all this, Daniel?" Anna asked. She could tell that he was trying to prove something, but she preferred the direct approach.

"The point of all this, Anna, is to show you that you can't do it all alone. The way I see it, your father was a very shrewd businessman who didn't mind taking chances. They were calculated risks, that's for certain, and as long as he lived to see them through to the end, everything was all right. But now, he's gone, and you're stuck with one of his risks—stuck right smack dab in the middle."

"All right," Anna agreed, "I'll grant you that. But what is your point?"

"As a Christian, it's my job to show you the love of Someone who was nailed to the cross for you."

Anna shook her head. "I'm not sure if I believe I'm worthy of something so big as all that."

With a huge smile, Daniel jumped up and shouted, "You're right! You're *not* worthy!"

He must be insane, Anna thought. One minute he was telling her that Jesus had died for her, and the next, he was saying she didn't deserve it. "Are you having trouble making up your mind, Daniel?" she asked with a chuckle. "Or is this some kind of game we're playing?"

"No," he said very solemnly. "This is definitely not a game. This is eternity. This has to do with forever and ever."

"But what about tomorrow?" Anna asked.

Again, he nodded. Anna braced herself for another tirade, but it didn't come. This time, he just said, "We'll take care of today's troubles today and tomorrow's troubles tomorrow, Anna. But we have to trust Jesus for anything beyond that."

"I sure do wish it was that easy," she said with a sigh. "All I want is to keep this farm."

"There are no guarantees in this life, Anna," he stated. "I'll do everything I can to help you. I don't know the first thing about harvesting citrus, but I can try."

"You'd do that for me? You'd actually help me, even after all the things I've said to you?" she asked.

"Yes, I would. In fact, I insist on helping you."

"But I can't promise to have the same love for the Lord that you do." She narrowed her gaze and stared at him, willing him to back down.

"I realize that, but I also know what you're going through right now. You're angry with God for taking away someone you love. I'm surprised you're still fighting so hard and not crying your heart out in a room all by yourself."

"Maybe that'll come later," Anna admitted. She felt like hiding and crying at the moment, yet she knew that would only delay what she had to do. "But first, I have to make sure that everything my father lived for doesn't all get sold to the highest bidder."

Chapter 4

Daniel sucked in a deep breath, wondering how he should proceed. She was still so angry; she was lashing out at whatever was convenient at the moment. Now he had a better understanding of why James had wanted to wait to share with his wife and daughter about his recommitment to Christ. Their anger was deep.

After a few seconds of pondering the right thing to do, Daniel decided it was time to gently back away from the spiritual discussion. No sense in giving her another reason to be angry with God. She'd already justified her feelings in her own mind, and he suspected this would only fuel the fire. He wouldn't let up on witnessing about his faith—but right now he needed to let the Lord do His quiet work in Anna's heart.

"Why don't I stop by the house and take a look at your books, Anna? That way I can get an idea of what we're dealing with from a business perspective." He stopped talking and waited for her to reply.

She hesitated. He knew she didn't completely trust him, but what choice did she have? Even if she was a genius at bookkeeping, none of the businessmen she needed to work with would take her seriously, simply because she was a young woman. They would listen to him.

Slowly, Anna nodded. "I don't suppose there would be anything wrong with that, Daniel."

He gently placed his hand on her shoulder and looked into her eyes. "You can trust me, Anna. I have no intention of ever bringing harm to you or your mother." Her softness and vulnerability made him want to pull her to his side and protect her. But he knew such a gesture was inappropriate now.

She licked her lips and blinked a few times. Daniel knew this was perhaps the most difficult thing she'd ever had to do in her life. He watched as she contemplated the alternatives. It didn't take her long to agree. "I know I can trust you, Daniel," she whispered softly. "I don't know how I know, but I do."

Nothing she could have said would have brought more joy to his heart. All he'd asked of her was for her trust, and now she'd given it. Daniel's heart was melting around this woman. He knew that her worldly vulnerability was only temporary. She was strong. But she also needed to recognize her spiritual weakness, which was the only thing standing in the way of her contentment.

Then, there was the issue of coming to terms with her father's death, which was something she hadn't yet allowed herself to face. The grief she would face, after she got past this hurdle of keeping the grove, would overwhelm her. Then she would need him once again. He was convinced of that. He wouldn't let her down then, either. The Lord had never let him down at times like this, so he knew he was armed with what he needed to help her.

"Would you like for me to go over the books tonight, or should I return tomorrow?" he asked.

Anna smiled, her face still somewhat guarded but not as hard as before. "You don't believe in wasting time, do you?"

"No, not at a time like this," he replied. "We have something else we need to deal with, too, Anna. Your father's burial."

She swallowed hard as the tears sprang to her eyes. "I–I'm not sure what to do about that," Anna said. "My mother and I haven't really discussed it."

"Tell you what, Anna," he said. "Talk with your mother about it this evening. Tell her about the church's offer. This will make everything much simpler all the way around."

"Yes, I can see where it would," she said. "I'll speak to her."

Daniel didn't want to overwhelm her. Besides, she needed some time alone with Josephine. "I must leave now, Anna. I'll be back tomorrow morning after I finish my own business in town."

Why Anna felt that she could trust Daniel now was something she didn't understand. But she did trust him. So far, he'd been true to his word. She bid him good-bye, then headed upstairs to speak with her mother.

Josephine was in bed when Anna got to the door of her room. "Mama, we need to talk."

"Come on in," Josephine replied weakly. Her face was still pale. She looked so fragile, Anna was afraid she might break, so she walked softly across the room and stood beside her mother's bed. "What did you need to discuss?"

This was difficult for Anna. She didn't want to always have to bring up distasteful conversations, but they did need to decide what to do about her father.

"Where are we going to bury Daddy?" Anna asked.

Josephine's eyes widened with surprise, and then she looked down at the sheets. "I'm not sure. I thought you had already taken care of the matter."

"How could you think that, Mama? I can't make all these decisions on my own!" Before Anna had a chance to catch herself, she'd blurted out what she'd been thinking. She had to take a step back to keep from falling over backward; she was so weak with the turmoil inside her head and her heart.

Josephine shrugged and looked away. "I just always thought those things kind of took care of themselves."

Anna had always known her mother didn't have a mind for business. She was also rather fragile, which was why Anna was an only child. Now, Anna knew that she was in the position of taking care of her mother. Her own feelings would have to be dealt with later.

"What would you like for me to do, Mama?" Anna asked, knowing it was a moot point.

As her hand brushed the wisps of hair from her face, Josephine replied, "Anna, darling, would you mind taking care of this for me? I have no earthly idea what to do in times like this. I–I've never had to make funeral arrangements before."

"Sure, Mama. I'll take care of everything." Anna backed toward the door before she thought to add, "Mr. Hopkins will be back tomorrow to look over Daddy's books."

Josephine grinned in the beatific way she always had. "He's such a nice boy, Anna. I think he may be sweet on you."

"I don't think so, Mama." Anna stood and looked at her mother for a long second before turning and practically running to her own room. She needed to get away from her mother's watchful eye, for it completely confused her. One minute, Josephine seemed unaware of everything going on around her. The next, she seemed so astute. The very idea of Daniel being sweet on Anna brought a flush to her cheeks.

Anna had to admit, whenever Daniel was in her presence, her heart hammered twice as hard, and she was certain twice as loud. There was a kindness coupled with his masculinity that reached a place inside her—a place she hadn't even known existed before now. She fell asleep wondering what it would feel like to be wrapped in his loving embrace.

The next morning, Anna awoke remembering Daniel's promise to return. She rose, dressed, and rushed around the house to make it presentable. Less than a month ago, her father had dismissed the household servants, saying, "There are only three of us, Anna, so it shouldn't be any problem for you to maintain this place. It's big, but we only live in a few rooms, anyway. You can take care of it, at least until we receive payment for the grapefruit."

Anna had agreed, being the practical sort that she was. And her father was right. It didn't take her long to get the place looking spic-and-span.

Daniel arrived late morning, just like he'd promised he would. She directed him to her father's study, opening his ledger books for him and showing him where everything was. "And he kept all correspondence in this drawer," she added, pointing to the right-hand side of the desk. "The key is in the top drawer."

He smiled up at her. "Why don't you go on about your business, Anna? Unless I have any questions later, I don't think you need to remain in here." His gaze dropped. "Unless, of course, you want to."

Anna did want to, but she knew he'd be able to study the books much more thoroughly without her there. "No, I need to see about the farmhands now. I'll be back this afternoon."

Daniel nodded. Anna looked at him one more time before turning and leaving him alone in her father's study, gently closing the door behind her. Then, she shut her eyes as her memory of last night's thoughts and feelings toward Daniel returned. Suddenly, a lightning bolt of longing charged through her.

She went out to the edge of the field where the bushel baskets were lined, waiting to be filled with the grapefruit her father had planted several years ago. Fortunately, the oranges were almost all harvested, so they only needed to gather the grapefruit. The process had been a long and arduous one, which was risky at best. But, based on the number of orders they'd already received, it would pay off in large sums—if only the businessmen in town had confidence in her ability to run the farm.

One of the workers had just come in from picking. "Miss Drake," he said in his heavy accent, "some of the workers didn't show up today. They are saying that you cannot pay us our wages."

Anna gulped. She had expected this sooner or later, but she had hoped it would be after Daniel offered her some advice. "Please give me a few days, Miguel," she said in as firm and confident a voice as she could, given the circumstances. "I will have your wages for you then."

He tried to smile. Then he looked down at his shoes, with holes large enough for his toes to poke through. "I have a family, Miss Drake. I cannot afford to go too much longer without my pay."

"I understand, Miguel. Please tell the other workers who have remained that I will make sure they receive their wages."

"I will tell them," he said as he turned to go back to his work. "It must be soon, or we will have to look for other work."

The second he was out of sight, Anna's legs threatened to give out beneath her, forcing her to sit. She understood their plight, but she had no idea how she'd cover their wages. The only money they had was in her bag, and it wasn't even enough to feed her workers a complete meal. How would she manage to pay them, unless Mr. Blankenship gave her a short-term loan?

She sat there on the ground, looking out over the groves her father had planted, knowing his hopes had been for a large return on his investment.

The only hope she now had was in the hands of the man sitting in her father's study right now. Was there anything Daniel could do, short of asking God for a miracle?

When Anna's strength returned, she slowly stood up, being careful not to fall back down. She needed to drink something. Her mouth was parched.

As she headed back toward the house, she thought of Daniel Hopkins and how he'd talked so openly about his faith. He had known her father, but she could not for the life of her figure out how.

Evidently, if Daniel's words were true, he had held more than one discussion with her father about spiritual matters. Moreover, Daniel had spoken of her father's decision to recommit his life to Christ. Yet, as far as Anna knew, James Drake wasn't a godly man. If her father had gone back to church, it must have been on one of those Sunday mornings when she'd been allowed to sleep late, which had happened a few times since the grapefruit trees had been planted.

When she went inside, Daniel was standing by the window. She could tell he'd been watching her. Had he been there watching her when her legs had nearly buckled?

Chapter 5

Anna knew the answer to her question as soon as she acknowledged him. "Are you feeling ill, Anna?" he asked, a grave expression on his face. She couldn't tell if it was from concern for her or from something he'd found in her father's books.

"I–I'm not now," she replied. "Ever since Daddy died, I sometimes feel weak at the knees."

His face relaxed and he smiled, so she knew that his tense expression was out of concern for her. "I've read some of the correspondence as well as looked at the figures in the ledgers."

"Yes?" she said, anxious to know what he'd come up with.

"Your father was an excellent businessman. He only left one thing up in the air, and that was what would happen to the business if he were incapacitated."

"Or dead," she added, nodding, her heart still aching. She knew that he wanted to soften the reality of the situation, but she needed to hear the truth.

"Yes," he agreed, nodding, "or dead." He began pacing, rubbing his chin as he walked back and forth across the floor between her and the window, stopping every couple of times to look outside.

"Okay, Daniel," she finally said. She couldn't stand not knowing the verdict. "What did you find?"

"I can only see two choices for you and your mother, Anna, and I'm afraid you won't care for either of them." He looked her in the eye, almost as if he needed to evaluate her reaction before telling her what he knew.

"Tell me. Please." Anna sat down in the chair beside the window. She was afraid that once she heard what he had to say, her knees might grow weak again. Daniel had already seen her collapse too many times.

"All right," he finally said, "here it is. Your father purchased the grapefruit trees with money he had stashed away from last year's orange profits. Naturally, I assumed that he bought them on credit, but he didn't. It actually would have been better if he had because that would have freed up some of the available funds for you to pay your workers."

Anna listened attentively. So far, she understood, so she nodded.

"There are two solutions to your problem." He stopped talking and rubbed his chin again. She surmised he was trying to decide where to begin. "The first one sounds like something you're not interested in pursuing, but I feel like I need to state it. You may sell the groves, with or without the property the house sits on. The only problem with that is that you won't have the means to continue living here. So if you choose this option, it would probably be better to sell the house along with the groves."

Anna squeezed her eyes shut and shook her head. That sounded like the kiss of death to her. She'd never known life outside this farm. This was her home. "And what is the other option?" she asked.

Daniel extracted a letter from a file on the desk. "I never would have thought of this if I hadn't read some of the correspondence in the desk, but I feel that it is an excellent solution to your problem. Your father had been working on plans to deed some of the land to his workers in exchange for their labor on the land he continued to personally hold."

"I–I don't understand," Anna stuttered. "He was thinking of giving our land away? That makes no sense. Daddy wouldn't do that."

Daniel held his hands up. "It's actually pretty simple," he said. "Let me explain a little more. You and your mother currently own more than two hundred acres of citrus groves. You may choose to give ten acres to each of the ten workers' families, and you'll still own one hundred acres. If you do that in exchange for the labor, you may not have to come up with the cash to pay them. They will participate in their share of the profits, based on how much their own trees yield."

Anna sucked in a breath and let it out slowly as she thought about this plan. She didn't really like the thought of letting go of so much land, but what choice did she have? "How about living expenses in the meantime?" she asked, wondering what sort of brilliant solution Daniel would have to this problem.

Daniel cleared his throat before he began talking. "I haven't spoken to the congregation at Good Shepherd Church yet, but I was thinking that we might want to help you and your workers out for a while longer, at least until you receive payment on the firstfruits of your labor."

Anna's eyebrows sprang up in surprise. "You think they'd want to do that?"

He smiled. "I'm sure they'd consider it."

As much as Anna hated the idea of accepting charity, the alternative sounded even worse. Then she thought of something that would make it seem less one-sided. "How about if we provide the people of Good Shepherd all the grapefruit and oranges they can eat?"

The corners of Daniel's eyes crinkled as he tilted his head back and belted out a hearty laugh. "I'm sure they'd love that," he replied when he regained his composure. "You sure know how to sweeten the pot, Anna."

If anyone else had laughed at something she'd said, she probably would have gotten angry. But when Daniel laughed, he had a way of making her feel like he was laughing with her rather than at her. His tenderness and sensitive manner gave her a sense of peace. She smiled. "I don't want to owe anyone anything."

That was when his laughter stopped. His expression became very serious as he said, "We are all debtors, Anna. Christ paid our debt of sin with His sinless life."

Anna gulped. It always came back to this with Daniel, didn't it? It wasn't as if she didn't believe in God. She most definitely did. His presence was obvious as she looked around her. What she had a difficult time understanding was how tragedy could happen to good people and how God could do something like send His only Son to die for her. She was an insignificant creature in the big picture. But Daniel seemed convinced that that wasn't so. So convinced, in fact, that he almost had her believing it, too.

Anna leaned back in her chair and thought for a moment before saying, "I don't want you to think I don't appreciate all you've done for my mother and me, but I do have a question."

"And that is?" he said, tilting his head and giving her his full attention.

"Why are you doing so much?"

"I'm not sure I understand the nature of such a question," he said, appearing to Anna that he was stalling for time.

"I've already told you that I'm angry with God. You're a devoted Christian who goes to church every Sunday. You follow His teachings and seem to desire to hold Him close to your heart. Why would you bother with someone like me?"

He nodded in understanding. "It's very basic, really, Anna. In spite of your anger, you are one of Christ's children. Think of Him as your Father in Heaven. When a man's children disobey, even if it's intentional, does he stop loving them?"

"N–no, I guess not," she replied. Anna remembered all the times she'd disobeyed her father, and although he'd disciplined her, she'd never doubted his love.

"It's essentially the same thing, only more so. Christ loves all people, and He desires our respect and reverence in return. I do it out of love for Him, Anna."

She glanced down at her hands folded in her lap. "I see." It surprised Anna to realize that she'd been hoping for another reason—perhaps that he was interested in pursuing more than a friendship with her. Each time she saw him, her heart skipped a beat.

Daniel paused, then said, "Why don't you come over here and take a look at these books?"

Anna stood up, hesitating for a moment. "I've already looked at them once." Did she dare get close to him?

"Let me show you a few things you may have missed."

She crossed the room and stood beside him, all too aware of his size in contrast to hers. While she stood just a fraction of an inch above five feet tall, he towered over her with at least a six-foot frame. His dark hair also contrasted her honey-blond tresses, which she had twisted into a knot on

293

top of her head. Anna started to reach out to feel his shoulders, but she quickly pulled her hands down to her sides. Now wasn't the time. Maybe later.

Daniel ran his finger along one of the lines in the ledger book. "This is your profit if you keep the entire grove intact." Then, he moved his finger to another line. "And this is your profit if you offer one hundred acres to your workers."

She noticed those two different amounts. "Why isn't that number double this one?" she asked.

"Because we're having to subtract the wages of the workers. Your father apparently intended to pay them partly in land because most of the remainder of this ledger is reflecting the sales from one hundred acres."

Anna sighed. She'd looked at the books, but she hadn't seen what Daniel had seen. Now she felt more inadequate than ever. "I wonder if he spoke to the workers about this," she said.

"You should ask them," he replied. "That is, if you intend to make this offer. Otherwise, you might want to keep it between us."

"I don't know what to do."

"I'm sure there's no hurry," Daniel said as he closed the book. "You might want to sleep on it and ask them tomorrow."

"If I don't do something soon, I'm afraid I may lose more workers. Two families have already left. According to Miguel, the one my father put in charge, they've accepted positions on neighboring farms."

"Would you like for me to talk to them?" Daniel asked.

Anna took a step back and studied his face. His lips were slightly parted, his hair was tousled from raking his fingers through it, and his sleeves were still rolled to his elbows, making him more attractive than she'd remembered him being. Seeing him concerned about her welfare touched her heart in a way it had never been touched before. She sensed that he really did care about her. *Could the Lord possibly have something to do with these feelings?*

"I think I need to talk to them," she finally replied, "but I would appreciate it if you were nearby for moral support."

He grinned, flashing his crooked smile that made her insides churn.

Anna found herself weak at the knees once again.

"I'll be more than happy to be with you, Anna. If you need me to say something, I will. If not, I'll keep my mouth shut."

Anna would have been satisfied with that, so when he cupped his hand around her elbow and led her over to the couch, she looked up at him questioningly. His breath fanned the hair around her face, warming her from the inside out. If he hadn't been supporting her arm, she would have surely fallen to the floor, only this time her weakness resulted from his touch. She wanted to stay close to him, to continue to inhale his masculine scent, to know everything would be fine as she now felt it would be.

"I want you to get some rest. Some members of my church will be by later on with food, so you don't have to worry about that. At least, not now." Daniel leaned down and brushed the stray wisps of hair from her face. His featherlight caress ignited her senses.

Anna nodded and watched him leave; she'd been rendered speechless. Once he was gone, she allowed herself to wonder about her feelings.

What she felt for Daniel still didn't negate the fact that her father had just died. She longed for the man she'd always depended on since birth, but she knew that there wasn't a thing she could do about that longing. She also wondered what her father would have wanted done regarding his burial, but from what she knew, he hadn't made any prior arrangements. Should she take Daniel up on his church's offer of having the funeral at Good Shepherd Church?

When she felt certain that her legs could carry her across the room, she stood up and went over to her father's desk. She opened the drawer that was filled with correspondence. Then, she pulled the letters out, one by one, glancing at the return addresses, wondering what all he had had going on in his life.

She stacked them according to their intended purpose. Each stack seemed to reach into a different part of his life. The largest one was related to business, of course, and she saw how he'd taken one calculated risk after another to achieve a certain level of financial success. It irked her that he was willing to put the house on the line like he had.

The second stack was letters from personal friends. She didn't care to read much in those because they weren't issues that interested her. She included some of the political letters in that stack because it seemed that her father's interest in government was more of a personal issue than business.

It was the third stack that had her baffled. Most of them were from Good Shepherd Church. Several of the letters were from the old pastor, and a couple were from Daniel, proving that her father had known him before he'd died. Was that why Daniel had been the one to break the sad news? Had Daniel and her father been close friends without her knowledge?

Anna's fingers quivered as she pulled the letter from the envelope. As she read, her heart pounded. It spoke of Daniel's joy over her father's decision to return to church and to bring his wife and daughter so that they, too, might hear the Good News of eternal salvation.

The letter fell from her hands to the desk as she pondered what she'd just read. Perhaps Daniel was right. Her father *had* become a Christian, and he just hadn't yet found the chance to tell her. According to Daniel's letter, her father had intended to go back to the church and eventually include his wife and daughter. The words about concern over Anna and Josephine's lack of faith worried her, too. Was that why her father hadn't shared his newfound belief with his family? *It must be,* she thought. There was no other explanation.

Anna was now more confused than ever about what to do. But one thing was certain: This new knowledge made it much easier to speak to Daniel about the church service and burial for her father. At least she wouldn't feel that she was being a hypocrite. If her father had intended to join the church, then why shouldn't he be buried there?

Suddenly, Anna felt a wave of emotion wash over her as the reality of the whole situation came into full view. Anna and Josephine had been left behind by a shrewd businessman with a slew of unfinished business— unfinished business that included his telling them of his recommitment to the Lord. It was up to her to make things right.

Anna had never stopped acknowledging the Lord's presence, although her faith had grown weak. She'd allowed the pain of losing her father to make her angry at God, and this anger had quickly turned to fear of what He might do next.

Daniel had spoken to her with kindness, making her listen with a firm but loving voice. The Lord spoke to her through Daniel, letting her know that He was in control and He'd never let her down. She could see that now.

Her grief welled up in her throat, forcing the tears to flow from her eyes. Anna cried silently at first, her body shaking as the tears formed fresh streams down her cheeks. Then, as the tracks of tears widened, so did the volume of her sobs. Besides her mother, no one else was in the house, so she didn't care.

"Anna." She quickly glanced up to see her mother standing in the doorway. "May I come in?"

Anna nodded. "Yes, Mama."

Josephine crossed over to the desk and sat down in the armchair beside it. "I'm so sorry I haven't been available to listen to you. I'm just so grief-stricken myself, I don't know what good I'd be."

"I understand, Mama," Anna said, sniffling.

"Have you figured out all the business yet?" Josephine asked.

"Some of it." Anna braced her hands on the arms of her chair as she sucked in a breath, turning toward her mother. "I've just been thinking about Daddy's funeral."

Josephine wiped her forehead with her embroidered handkerchief. "I'm so glad you're taking care of that, Anna. I wouldn't even know where to start."

"We're burying him at Good Shepherd Church."

"Will they let us do that?" Josephine asked with a shaky laugh. "After all, we haven't set foot inside their church."

Anna licked her lips and sniffled again, finally regaining composure. "Jesus still loves us, Mama." The instant she said those words, she knew they were true. Daniel had said them with conviction, and now she knew she could, too.

"How can you be so sure of that, Anna?"

Daniel's words came to her mind, and the strength of her new conviction washed over her. "Mr. Hopkins said that God loves us like a father loves a child. Even when we disobey, He loves us and wants us to come back."

Anna could hardly believe that these words were coming out of her own mouth. Still, she had meant what she said. A sense of relief flooded her veins, washing away all the anger she'd held inside for way too long.

"Mama, I'm going to find my Bible and start reading a little bit each day. Would you like to join me?"

After several long moments of silence, Anna stood up and left Josephine sitting in the study alone. Apparently, the idea was too much for her mother to consider right now. But Anna felt an overwhelming desire to delve into the Word. She simply couldn't sit back and wait for her mother to join her in this newfound hope.

Chapter 6

*H*ave mercy upon me, O God, according to thy lovingkindness: according unto the multitude of thy tender mercies blot out my transgressions. Wash me thoroughly from mine iniquity, and cleanse me from my sin." Psalm 51:1–2.

Anna must have read the verse at least ten times in so many minutes. And each time she read it, she gained a deeper understanding of God's love. Only a father could love a child this much.

She squeezed her eyes shut, thinking about all the times she had denounced God. She'd shoved Him to the back of her mind, thinking she didn't need Him. But now she knew better. Although she had never quit acknowledging His presence, she'd called on Him only when she wanted something from Him.

And the only way she'd be able to be close to Him now was through His Son, Jesus Christ. All the Scriptures that had been marked in her Bible by the women in her family before her related to Christ's forgiveness. After reading each verse with a mark beside it, she found more comfort.

"All right, Lord," she said aloud, "I know I have sinned by turning my back on You. Please show me the way back to Your path. Lead me to what's right, Lord." As soon as she said those words, she pressed her face into her pillow and began once more to sob.

The tears fell freely, and for the first time in her adult life, Anna knew what it was like to be forgiven and free from sin. Her father had died only a few days ago, yet he had hope because he'd found the way to everlasting life with Jesus Christ. She and her mother only had each other, which was pitiful, because they weren't able to take on the weight of what lay ahead of them. While she knew it wouldn't be easy to let go of her anger, she now had the Lord to help her through it.

That afternoon, Daniel made good on his offer to stand by her side when she told the workers of what her father had wanted to do. She had no doubt that the Lord had brought Daniel into her life to lead her to Him.

Her fears of the workers turning her down were unfounded. They'd all shouted in excitement that this was what they'd always wanted. Several of them fell to their knees in prayer. Daniel joined them.

Before she realized what was happening, Anna was holding hands, forming a circle with Daniel and all the workers, praying for guidance during this trying time. Daniel closed the prayer, thanking God for His blessings.

When Anna said, "Amen," Daniel squeezed her hand. She felt a rush of energy wash over her.

"Have you decided what to do about your father?" he asked. "He needs to be buried right away. We've waited much too long already."

Anna nodded. "I'd like to lay him to rest in your church cemetery," she said. "That is, if the offer is still open."

"Yes," he said with a sensitive smile, "the offer is still open. I've already spoken with the men of the church about it, and they agree. Your father was in the process of talking to them about joining the flock, so we feel that this is fitting."

"Will there be a good time for me to talk with someone about joining the church myself, Daniel?" she said softly, barely able to hear her own words. "I know I still have quite a bit to learn, but I'm willing."

Daniel turned and looked at Anna with pure, unadulterated joy on his face. "Anytime is good when you make this kind of decision, Anna."

Anna breathed a sigh of relief. Everything was now going quite well. "I don't know how to thank you," Anna said as they strolled back to the house.

"But, Daniel, I have one more problem I need your advice on. . ." She paused as she pondered how to put forth the question. Finally, she let the words tumble freely. "I feel as though I need to tell my mother about Daddy's newfound faith—and mine. However, I'm afraid she'll think I'm preaching at her. Or even worse, judging her. What should I do?"

Anna's mouth suddenly went dry. She licked her lips. "What should I say?"

He shrugged. "Anna, I suggest you share your own personal experience with her to start."

"I don't think she'll understand," Anna said as dread washed over her. "Besides, if I say the wrong thing, I might mess everything up."

"Trust me, Anna. Whenever you speak of the Lord from your heart, He's right there beside you. He makes a promise, I believe it's in 1 Peter, verse fifteen: 'Sanctify the Lord God in your hearts: and be ready always to give an answer to every man that asketh you a reason of the hope that is in you with meekness and fear.' "

Anna slowly nodded. She'd read that verse. In fact, she'd read quite a bit of the New Testament last night. That was why she was so exhausted. She hadn't gotten much sleep.

Later that night, when all was quiet around the house, Anna went to her mother's bedroom door and knocked. "Mama, is it all right if I come in?"

"Of course, Anna," Josephine said softly. "The door isn't locked."

This was perhaps the most difficult thing she'd ever had to do. Witnessing to anyone would be trying, but witnessing to her mother would surely prove the hardest. After all, this was something most parents talked about with their children, rather than the other way around. Josephine was sitting in front of her mirror brushing her hair. She was such a lovely woman, and Anna rarely saw her with her hair down around her shoulders. It made her look years younger.

"Mama, have you considered going back to church?" Anna finally asked, after building up enough nerve.

Josephine held her brush away from her head and turned to face Anna. "Why, no, sweetheart. Your father and I had this very same conversation a few weeks ago. I'll tell you the same thing I told him. I like to sleep in on Sunday mornings. Going to church seems like such a waste of time."

"Daddy wanted you to go to church with him?" Anna asked in disbelief. "Why didn't you tell me?"

Josephine shrugged as she resumed brushing her hair. "I didn't think it all that important. Besides, what good did it do your father? He'd started attending services again, and now he's gone."

"But what if he hadn't renewed his relationship with the Lord?" Anna said, still stunned by this new revelation. "He would have died anyway, and we wouldn't have had a peace about his salvation."

"Is this important to you, Anna?" Josephine asked, still smiling.

"Yes, Mama, it is," Anna replied. "Very important, as a matter of fact."

"Then if you want to attend church services, why don't you go with that nice young man Daniel who keeps coming around the house? I have a feeling he'd like to court you."

"Mama," Anna said as she came closer to her mother. She squatted down beside her and took the brush from her mother's hand. "I really want you to go with me."

"No, Anna," Josephine said, standing up and turning to face her daughter. "I won't go. If you want to, that's fine. But leave me out of it. If God had spared your father, I might have gone with him eventually, but I don't want any part of church if this is the kind of god they worship there."

Anna paused, then stood up, backing toward the door. "Jesus loves you, Mama. He loves you in spite of what you just said. And if it weren't for His love, we might just as well have starved to death." As soon as she'd spoken those words, she turned and fled from her mother's room to her own room at the other end of the hall.

The instant she was inside her bedroom, Anna flung herself across her bed, tears streaming down her face. "Oh, Lord. I don't know how much more I can take."

She fell asleep still dressed. When she awoke, she felt as though she'd been up all night.

Daniel arrived in the early afternoon. "I want to study your father's books a little bit more. Perhaps there's one more thing we can do to bring in some extra cash."

"By all means, please do whatever you can," Anna said in a monotone.

"What's wrong, Anna?" Daniel asked as she turned her back on him. He reached out and turned her back around to face him. His face was so close she could feel his breath. She sucked in some air and held it for what seemed like hours. "Anna?"

Anna wasn't sure if he pulled her to his chest or if she fell against it. All she knew for certain was that she was leaning against his strength, both physically and emotionally, and he didn't back away. He was rock solid, and she was grateful.

"Anna, darling, I'm so sorry."

"What are you sorry about?" she asked. "You did nothing wrong."

"I'm sorry about whatever is troubling you. Would you like to tell me about it?"

He kept his arm around her, most of her weight supported by him, as they made their way over to the couch, where he slowly lowered both of them to a sitting position. Brushing her hair from her face, he cupped her face in his hands. "Please tell me."

Anna began telling him about how, long ago, her father had decided that attending church was a waste of time and that he didn't need God in his life. As she explained how she, her mother, and her father would all be in the same house, yet never even acknowledge the others' presence, she realized, for the first time, how odd this must seem. She finished by telling him what had happened last night.

"The whole encounter was awful, Daniel," Anna said as she lowered her face to his shoulder. "My mother all but denied the deity of the Lord."

"Anna, we can't force your mother to believe. At this point, all we can do is pray."

He gently stroked her head. She pulled away slightly and looked deeply into his eyes. "Anna," he whispered before lowering his face to hers and claiming her lips with his own.

The kiss was sweet and tender, yet it reached all the way to her core. "Oh, Daniel," she muttered, her mind still swirling with the impact of her first kiss.

When they finally broke away from each other's embrace, Daniel rose to leave. His parting words were barely audible as he hurried out the door.

"I'd best be going. We both have work to do."

It wasn't long before the people from the church showed up with food. They had provided meals for Anna, Josephine, and the workers every single day since her father's death. This was a testament of their faith, Anna now realized. She was truly grateful for Daniel, the people of his church, and, most of all, for Christ's love and His never-ending mercy.

The next morning, they buried James Drake in the church cemetery after a simple Christian service. Anna wept, while Josephine allowed only a few tears to trickle down her cheeks. Her chin quivered, but she said nothing. Once the services were over, Josephine asked to be returned home.

Daniel spent the next several weeks between his own business in Orlando and helping Anna run the groves her father had planted. They both learned what they needed to know to keep up with the harvest and shipping, but Anna now realized how much was involved in the business side of the groves.

"I never knew he did all this," Anna exclaimed one day after finishing the last of the invoices to several dozen of their commercial customers.

"I'm sure there were a lot of things you never knew about your father," Daniel said as he kissed her on the forehead. His kisses were coming with regularity now, and each one warmed Anna's heart. She'd never imagined herself feeling this close to any man. Yet in the back of her mind were the nagging thoughts: *There is no future for our relationship. I could never live up to Daniel's expectations for a wife.*

Josephine spent most of her time up in her room, doing little things, like sewing and darning. She rarely offered to help out around the house or with the business, but Anna didn't mind.

"I think it is time for us to speak to your mother again about attending church," Daniel said one day.

"I've tried," Anna replied as she snapped the ledger book shut, "but she's so stubborn."

"So I'm stubborn, now, am I?" The voice came from the other side of the room.

SUNSHINE HARVEST

Anna and Daniel both jerked their heads around to see Josephine standing in the doorway to the study. Her expression was cool and stern, leaving no doubt in their minds how she felt about their discussion of her.

Chapter 7

"O h, Mama," Anna said, wishing she'd been more careful with what she said, "that's not what I meant."

"You wouldn't have said it unless you meant it, Anna," Josephine said, her voice as cold as dripping icicles.

Daniel had been glancing back and forth between Anna and Josephine. He finally walked over to where Josephine still stood. "I'm sure our words sounded much worse than we meant them, Mrs. Drake."

"No," Josephine said, slowly shaking her head. "I do have a stubborn streak sometimes, but that's not always bad, is it?"

Anna had no idea how to answer that. If she agreed with her mother, she'd be admitting guilt, but if she didn't, she'd be lying. Fortunately, Daniel spoke up, saving her from having to respond.

"It all depends on what we're being stubborn about," he replied with a chuckle. "But I do know one thing: Your daughter loves you very much, and she is doing everything in her power to make certain this farm stays in the hands of this family."

Josephine's expression instantly turned from aloofness to shock. "Is there any danger of losing the farm?"

"Well, that's always a possibility," Daniel said, in spite of the daggers Anna shot him with her looks. But he went on. "We're having to shuffle things around here quite a bit to get the crop harvested in time to be shipped. There are several hindrances, like spoilage, train and ship schedules, and the fact that we are operating with less hands than we actually need."

"James always said that he used as few workers as he could get away with to keep cost down. Is this a problem now?" Josephine asked, showing an interest in the family business for the first time since her husband's death.

"Yes, Mrs. Drake," Daniel answered, "it is. It wouldn't be if some of the workers hadn't left when we couldn't pay them their wages."

"What about all the money we made on the oranges last year?" Josephine said. "James told me that we did quite well on that crop."

Nodding, Daniel said, "You did, but he spent all the profit on adding more grapefruit trees—and they won't mature for a few years. He was in town working on raising operating capital when he collapsed and died."

Josephine fell back into a chair, letting out a loud sigh. "What will we do?" She sniffled, then said, "I s'pose we could sell this place and buy a house in town."

Daniel glanced over at Anna, who'd just been standing there, taking it all in. She was shocked at how many questions her mother had, as well as how long she'd stuck around after hearing the answers.

Anna finally felt the urge to speak up. "I don't want to do that."

"What will we do then?" Josephine asked weakly.

"Miguel has told me that he will see to it that all the grapefruit gets harvested, even if it means putting all his children out there working from sunup to sundown. Some of the other workers already have their children working alongside them. Miguel loves this farm."

Josephine nodded. Years ago, Miguel had come to this country from Cuba with his new bride. He'd worked for her husband ever since and was devoted to the Drake family.

"People from the church are willing to help, if needed," Anna added.

With a snicker, Josephine stood and headed toward the door. "Well, I'm certain that you'll figure something out. I'm not the only one in this family known to be stubborn!" She shot a quick glance at Anna then turned abruptly, and left the room.

"We need to pray for my mother, don't we?" Anna stared at the empty doorway where, moments before, her mother had stood.

"That is all we can do."

Together they prayed a prayer for mercy and loving care for Josephine. Then, they asked the Lord to watch over the workers as they harvested the last crop of grapefruit that had to be shipped before they could start receiving payment. Finally, they praised the Lord for all the blessings that continued to flow every day. Anna's own faith was strengthened by prayer. While she still felt as though she had a long way to go, she knew she'd come far already.

"Amen," Daniel said.

He opened his eyes and caught her staring at him, something she'd been doing quite a bit lately. He grinned, leaned over, and kissed her squarely on the lips. Anna grinned back and followed with her own "Amen" before they let go of each other's hands. Her heart was filled with a love for Daniel that was growing every day. In her mind, it was a romantic, Christ-induced sort of love that she had no doubt was right for her. But with all the things she had to take care of and all the worries over the farm, she wasn't at liberty to enjoy the feeling. Besides, she continued to wrestle with the lingering doubt that she could live up to Daniel's expectations. She knew she needed to continue to pray about it, but she couldn't help but worry about their vast differences in spiritual depth and maturity.

Daniel had to go back into town to take care of his own business, which had been practically running itself since he'd been helping her. After he left, Anna went to work on more correspondence that seemed to grow by the day. She'd be glad when this last crop was shipped so she could stop and rest.

Small sums of money had trickled in from the retail customers, but only enough to purchase needed supplies and dole out a paltry sum to the workers. There was barely enough money left over for food, so the members of Good Shepherd Church continued to bring food for the workers. Anna no longer felt that she was imposing since she understood their motives. Besides, she always sent them home with bushels of the fruit that had been harvested that day.

Josephine asked questions on a daily basis now, leading Anna to believe that she might actually have an interest in the business. Anna decided not to press, but she always welcomed any help her mother wanted to give.

One afternoon, right after Daniel had left for Orlando, Miguel rushed into the house without knocking, something he'd never done before. "Miss Drake, come quick! There's been an accident!"

Anna dropped the ledger books she was holding, ran out the door following Miguel, and didn't stop until she reached the edge of the groves, where a small group was standing around an older child of one of the other workers. "What happened?" Anna asked, squatting by the child's side to see a pale face and contorted small frame.

"He fell from one of the trees, Miss Drake," Miguel said, his voice filled with anguish. "It's Maria's son, Pedro."

Maria was Miguel's sister who had come to live with him and his wife after she became pregnant out of wedlock. Back in Cuba, she'd been turned away from their parents, and she had no place else to go.

Anna glanced over her shoulder and motioned for her mother who had followed Anna from the house, to join her. Josephine hesitated for a moment, then began walking slowly toward the small group.

"Mama, I need your help! I have to ride to town to get a doctor, but I don't want to leave Pedro here without someone who can help him. He needs a blanket."

Josephine's face turned a ghastly shade of white, but she nodded and abruptly turned back to do what she could. Anna instructed the others to let her mother take care of the boy once she returned.

Josephine rushed out with a big blanket and gently placed it over Pedro. She turned to look at her daughter and said, "I'll be surprised if the doctor comes. I doubt if the people of Orlando think any more highly of farmworkers than they did in our last town."

"Dr. Murphy is a Christian, Mama. He won't neglect this child."

"We'll see," Josephine said. "From my experience, people call themselves Christians if they think they'll get something in return."

There was nothing Anna could say in response to that bitter statement. She also knew her mother was remembering the doctor from before— the one who'd allowed the migrant worker to die, just because he wasn't in the same social class. So she moved as fast as she could to get help. She sure did hope her mother was mistaken about the doctor, or Anna would never be able to break through her bitterness.

The trip to town was the longest ride she could remember. It seemed to take forever to reach the house where Dr. Murphy lived and practiced medicine. He was sitting in the front office chatting with the mayor.

"A child of one of our workers has just fallen from a tree, and he's in desperate need of medical care," Anna said, not caring that she interrupted their discussion of town politics. "It looks to me like he may have broken some bones."

Dr. Murphy grabbed his bag, nodded toward the mayor, and said, "I'll be back this afternoon, and we can pick up where we left off."

"For heaven's sake, Edward, it's just a farmworker," the mayor said. "We have more important business to discuss."

Dr. Murphy stopped in his tracks, glared at the mayor, and said, "If you want to count on my support in the next election, I suggest you change your uppity attitude. These workers are the backbone of our city, Mayor." Without waiting for a response, he turned and followed Anna.

They rode back to the farm as fast as they could, never once stopping to talk. It was imperative that they hurry as fast as they could.

By the time they arrived at the farm, Pedro had regained consciousness and was moaning. People were still standing around, not having any idea what to do. "Please stand aside," Dr. Murphy said as he made his way through the crowd to get close to the boy. "I need all the room you can give me."

Everyone, including Anna and Josephine, stood and watched as Dr. Murphy knelt on the ground and examined the child. Finally, he stood up and rubbed his whiskers. "We need to get him to town immediately. He's not in good condition. Is your carriage ready to go, Anna?"

She shook her head. "It will take some time to get it ready, Dr. Murphy," she said.

"He's in no shape to put on a horse," he replied. "Go ahead and get the carriage ready. I'll do what I can here."

Suddenly, the sound of horses' hooves could be heard from the distance. They were heading toward the edge of the grove where everyone was still standing. As they drew near, Anna saw that it was Daniel.

He quickly hopped to the ground and offered his help. "The mayor said there had been an accident here, so I thought I might be of service," he said.

The doctor shook his head. "I guess he wants my vote, after all. Well, after this, I s'pose he's got it."

Dr. Murphy and Daniel carefully lifted Pedro to the back of the carriage, and Josephine offered to ride with them, in case she was needed. Anna got her horse and rode beside Miguel to town, following the carriage.

No one had said much yet because they had no idea what they were facing. Pedro had just reached his teenage years, and he was still growing. All the way to town, Anna heard Miguel offering prayers to the Lord for His mercy on the child. She prayed a little bit, too, but she was amazed at how powerful Miguel's faith still was, even after the accident.

They arrived at the small hospital, and the men carried Pedro to the examining room. Josephine remained in the front room with Anna, her face still registering the shock from earlier.

"Mama, he's in good hands now. Dr. Murphy is very good."

"Yes, I know," Josephine replied. "I'm surprised he was willing to come all the way out there, just for a worker."

"He's not just a worker. He's a person. And every person is of value—a child of God." Anna couldn't hold back the tears, now that she had done all she could to help Pedro. "Dr. Murphy understands that, and he's going to use his God-given skills to help Pedro."

"We'll see," Josephine said, this time not quite so sure of her own words.

Dr. Murphy had taken Daniel and Miguel into the examining room with him. Someone had fetched Maria, and she arrived right when the men emerged from the examining room.

"My Pedro," she cried. "Where is he? Is he going to be all right?"

Dr. Murphy swallowed and touched her shoulder. "I'm not sure yet, Maria. He has broken his back, and we won't know the extent of the injuries for a few days."

"Oh, dear God," she cried as her eyes squeezed shut, tears hanging from her eyelashes before they began to form a stream down her cheeks.

Josephine crossed the room and put her arms around Maria's shoulders, steadying the woman so she wouldn't topple over. Maria allowed herself to be guided to a chair, and she sat down.

"Lord, please have mercy on my son," Maria began to pray. She praised God through the entire prayer. Josephine stared at Maria in disbelief. When Maria opened her eyes, she looked at Josephine. "The Lord will look after us."

Josephine narrowed her eyes and said, "Just like that, you think your son will be healed?"

"I'm not sure my son will be healed in his bones," Maria said. "If I have to choose between his faith and his body, I want him to be right with the Lord."

Anna sat there stunned herself, amazed at the quiet strength of this Christ-loving woman. Daniel smiled at Maria and nodded. "You're a good mother, Maria. We'll all pray for Pedro."

Josephine took a few steps back as everyone else began to pray for Pedro. When they were finished, she asked if Anna could take her home now.

Both women were silent all the way to the farm. Anna let Josephine dismount before she took the horse to the barn then returned to the house alone.

When she got inside, her mother had already gone upstairs. Anna felt compelled to speak to her, to find out what was on her mind.

"Mama," Anna said as she knocked on her mother's door.

"What do you want, Anna?"

"I'd like to talk to you."

"There's nothing to talk about." Anna could tell her mother had been crying, so she backed away. They could talk tomorrow.

That evening, some people from the church arrived with food. They had sent someone every day since her father's death, regardless of the weather, to make sure the Drake family and farmworkers ate. This was such an amazing act of human kindness, Anna often found herself without enough words of thanks.

Josephine came down to talk with the men who'd brought the food

312

their wives had cooked. "We may not be needing this food much longer, since it appears we'll be forced to sell our farm."

"What?" Anna said, spinning around in disbelief at what her mother had just said.

"Now that it is becoming apparent that our workers can't possibly bring in all the harvest, I must make a decision soon." Josephine lowered her head and then raised it again with pride. "I will let you know as soon as I've thought things through. Thank you for all you've done." Then, she went back to the house and left Anna standing there with the men, all of them temporarily dumbfounded.

"I–I'm sorry," Anna said when she found her voice again, "but this was the first I heard of this, too. I'm not sure what we'll do, but I have no intention of selling the farm."

The men exchanged glances, then nodded to each other. One of them stepped forward and said, "If it would help, perhaps we can get a group together to help harvest the last of the grapefruit."

Chapter 8

"Oh, I couldn't ask you to do such a thing," Anna said. "You've done so much to help us already."

"If we gathered a dozen men, we could help the workers who remain. I suppose we could finish it in half the time that the job would take if we didn't help," one of the men said.

Anna shook her head. "I can't allow you to spend that much time away from your own families and businesses."

Another man stepped forward and looked her in the eye. "If this had happened to any one of us, we'd hope that you'd do the same. We're all followers of Christ, and we feel strongly that He'd want us to take care of you and your family."

Tears instantly sprang to Anna's eyes. She gulped as they headed back toward their horses. They'd told her that they were going to help, and she knew they'd be true to their word. The people from Daniel's church were standing behind their proclamation of faith. This was what Josephine needed to see.

❧

"Anna, I don't understand why you're being so stubborn about this place. It's just a house and a bunch of trees. We can sell to someone who knows what they're doing and buy ourselves a cute little place in the city."

"I don't want a place in the city, Mama," Anna replied. "I want to stay here."

Josephine put down the plate she was holding and stared at her daughter. "You and I both know we're living here on borrowed time. It won't be long before we're forced to give it all up. Why not go ahead and do it now?"

"Yes, Mama, you got one thing right. We are living on borrowed time. But not because of this house and the groves. We're living on the time that the Lord has loaned us. I think we'll do just fine once we get through this year. The men from the church have offered to help, and Miguel said he'd find some more workers before next year."

With a look of resignation, Josephine shook her head. "Anna, dear, those men from the church were just talking. They have no intention of actually coming here and doing all that labor. It was an offer they were certain you'd refuse."

"You'll see, Mama," Anna said softly. How could her mother be such a naysayer after all the kind people from the church had done?

Josephine smiled back at her. Anna felt as though she had to hold onto the farm with one hand and conduct an orchestra with the other; her mother was being so difficult. Maybe, once they had the harvest behind them, she and Daniel could convince her to at least try going to church again.

The very idea of going to church with Daniel sent a rush of excitement through Anna. She knew she was in love with him, even if she could never make him a good wife. He exuded a strength of faith through his actions and words unlike anyone she'd ever seen. He never seemed to tire of carrying out God's Word. With a sigh, she imagined herself being with Daniel for the rest of her life.

There was only a week left before the harvest had to be completed. What had been dubbed the "Sunshine Harvest" by her father now seemed like the "Harvest in Darkness" because there was so much uncertainty. Anna knew that the only hope she had of holding onto the farm was to accept the offer made by the men from the church.

With a sigh, she told Daniel, "I feel as though I've depended on others far too much since Daddy died."

"Nonsense," he said as he tenderly touched her face, giving her that warm glow of relief that came from his caresses. "You have done more than any other woman I know. This farm has been placed in your care by the Lord, and I think you're doing a marvelous job."

His confidence in her brought a new sense of joy to Anna. She nodded and smiled. "Without His help, all hope would be lost."

They gazed longingly at each other for a few seconds. But the spell was broken by Miguel, who began knocking loudly at the front door. "Miss Drake," he hollered, "you need to see this!" It was an unseasonably warm day, and the windows were open, allowing his voice to drift through the house.

Anna's heart almost stopped as she broke away from the man she loved. "What is it, Miguel?" She pulled open the front door to find Pedro sitting at Miguel's feet. Kneeling down, she took the boy's hand in her own. "Pedro," she said softly, "how are you feeling?"

He beamed back at her. "I can walk again, Miss Drake."

Miguel took over for Pedro, explaining, "The doctor said that we can let him take a few steps at a time. We need to be very careful, but the Lord has been very good to us. I wanted you to see this."

"This is wonderful news, Pedro," Anna said to the boy. Then, she looked at Miguel. "Has Mama seen him?"

"No," Miguel said, the smile fading from his face.

"Let me get her." Anna turned to Daniel. "Stay right here, all three of you. I need to get Mama from her room."

"I'll do whatever you need, Anna," Daniel said. Then he bent down and gently laid a hand on Pedro's shoulder.

She ran all the way upstairs to her mother's room and knocked. "Mama, come quick. There's someone downstairs to see you."

"Who is it, Anna?" her mother said as she opened the door. At least she was dressed.

"You'll see." Anna turned and ran back downstairs, hoping her mother would follow. She did.

"Oh, my!" Josephine exclaimed when they reached the porch. "What in the world are you doing out of bed, Pedro?" she asked the boy, who was beginning to show signs of exhaustion.

"I can walk, Señora," he replied.

Josephine turned to Anna, then Daniel, and said, "Is this all right with the doctor?"

Daniel shrugged. "The doctor told him to try taking a few steps at a time, so I suppose so."

With a sincere smile, Josephine leaned over and hugged Pedro. "I'm so happy for you, Pedro. Just make sure you do what the doctor tells you."

"I will," he said, his eyes huge and round. "We have been praying every day."

Anna watched her mother's lips quiver. This child was a walking, talking testimony, and Anna hoped her mother saw that. But even if the Lord had not chosen to let Pedro walk, Anna knew that He knew what He was doing in a way she might not understand. However, she doubted her mother would see things that way.

Daniel pulled out his pocket watch. "I need to run into town and let the men know their hands will be needed to complete the harvest. They will start first thing in the morning."

"Thank you, Daniel," Anna said, touching his arm tenderly.

Anna knew that her mother saw this exchange, but Anna didn't care. In fact, the whole world could find out how she felt about Daniel, and that would be fine.

Once Daniel, Miguel, and Pedro were gone, Josephine turned to Anna and said, "You must be very careful, dear, to guard your heart. I wouldn't want you to get hurt."

"Mama, I've given my heart to the Lord," Anna said with conviction. "If He chooses to let me fall in love with Daniel, then I'm helpless to stop it."

"How can you forget what happened before?" Josephine asked. "Last time we got involved with Christians, we found out just how unchristian people can be."

"That was a different situation, Mama," Anna said softly. "We can't judge all Christians by the actions of a misguided few."

Josephine issued a cynical cackle. "They certainly did talk about it a lot."

Shaking her head, Anna replied, "Maybe so, but I see a big difference here with Daniel and the others from the church. Yes, he is a part-time preacher, but he doesn't just preach. He lives his faith by doing what Jesus would want him to do."

Josephine clamped her mouth shut. She didn't say a word as she walked away from Anna, leaving many words unsaid between them. *Maybe later,* Anna thought. There was plenty of time for discussion. At least the door had been opened.

True to his word, Daniel arrived before sunrise the next morning with a dozen men, all of them ready to work the land. They deferred to Miguel, who was still in charge of the harvest. He gave them each instructions before they set about plucking the ripe fruit from the trees and filling the crates. Anna had no doubt that the Lord was in control.

Josephine awoke several hours later to the sound of Anna's humming. "What makes you so chipper at such an early hour?" she asked groggily.

Anna smiled, took her mother's hand, and led her to the window that overlooked the groves. "Look, Mama. The men came today to finish the harvest."

"Well, I'll be," Josephine said in amazement. "I never thought this would happen."

Anna turned her mother to face her. "Mama, you need to learn to trust the Lord."

Josephine turned away from her daughter, but not before Anna saw the tears that sprang to her eyes. She'd had so much to deal with; she wasn't able to fully understand what was happening. But there would be time for that.

At the end of a long, grueling day, the men came to the house lawn where Anna had set out the food they'd brought that morning. After a blessing given by Daniel, they ate heartily, sitting at the tables with the workers who'd been in the Drakes' employ for years. It didn't matter that some of the men were businessmen from town and others were common laborers. They were all children of Christ, worshipping the same Lord, feasting on the same food. This brought joy to Anna's heart.

"Anna," Daniel whispered as he pulled her over to the oak tree that stood majestically in the center of the back lawn, the only tree that didn't bear citrus on the whole property, "we need to talk."

"Yes, Daniel?" she said, her heart pounding at his touch.

He pulled her toward him with one hand and stroked the hair from her face with the other. "I know this isn't the most romantic place to do this, but I'd like to ask you something."

Anna tilted her head to one side and said, "What is it?"

"Will you marry me?" He asked his question with a bluntness that startled Anna, causing her to temporarily lose her speech. "You don't have to answer now," he added. "If you need time to think about it, I understand."

She cleared her throat as her senses began to return. "I could never marry you, Daniel." Anna surprised herself at her response. Yes, she loved him with all her heart, but she simply wasn't good enough to marry someone as great as Daniel.

"Why not, Anna? I love you." The tenderness in his eyes forced her to look away. She couldn't say what she needed to say as long as he was looking at her like that.

"I could never measure up to being your wife, Daniel. You're the first true and perfect Christian I've ever met. I'm not sure I could live with all heads turned my way, everyone expecting me to be as good as you."

"Oh, Anna, my love, I'm far from perfect."

"I haven't seen that, Daniel," she said, daring to glance at him once again.

He sucked in a breath and let it out slowly. "I have my flaws and weaknesses. I've had more than my share of frustrations and anguish over the murder of my own father. It took years of thought and prayers for me to lose the bitterness I once harbored in my heart. It wasn't until I allowed Christ to work His way into my heart that I was able to forgive and get on with my life. Everything I do is to the glory of God."

Anna listened with rapt attention. She never saw the angry side of Daniel, but as he spoke, she knew he was telling her the truth. "Please allow me to think about your proposal, Daniel."

He smiled and took her hands in his. "Let's pray about it right now."

Together they bowed their heads and prayed. Daniel asked the Lord to show Anna direction and assurance as she considered his proposal, that she would know her true worth and value, and that she would sense his sincere love. He prayed that she'd be filled with the peace that passes all understanding. Just then, Anna shuddered as an overwhelming sense of peace flowed through her soul.

When they were finished with their prayer, Daniel squeezed her hand. "I'll continue to pray for you, Anna." Then he added, "And us. Let's join the others."

She smiled at him, knowing that she still needed to work through some things, but now with the help of the Lord. Daniel was truly a remarkable man.

"Mrs. Drake," Daniel said as they started dessert, "I'd like for you and Anna to be my guests in church on Sunday."

Anna turned and looked at her mother for a reaction. After all the help they'd received from these generous people, there was no way Josephine could turn him down gracefully.

Slowly, Josephine nodded. "Why, yes, that would be nice, Daniel. What time should we be there?"

Stifling a smile, Daniel replied, "Arrive at nine. Services begin around ten o'clock, but I'd like for you to meet some of the ladies who have been cooking for your workers over the past few months."

Anna respected Daniel for being so gentle with her mother. She appreciated the fact that he held back the smile, which she could tell was threatening to break through his solemn expression upon Josephine's positive response. He showed himself as a true gentleman by allowing Josephine her dignity.

The guests left immediately after they cleaned up. Anna followed Josephine to the house, where they both dropped onto the couch.

"This has been one very trying day," Josephine said with a sigh.

"Yes, it has," Anna replied. Her mother hadn't done half the work she had, but Anna knew that Josephine's tolerance for work was much lower than her own. "I'm looking forward to church on Sunday."

Josephine flinched. She sat there in silence for a few moments, almost as if she didn't know what to say.

"Mama?" Anna finally said. "Are you afraid?"

With a slight nod, Josephine broke into tears, at first with a silent trickle, then with racking sobs. Between sniffles, she said, "I miss James. Why did he have to die?"

"Oh, Mama," Anna said as she hugged her mother, "I'm sad, too, but the Lord will take care of us."

"Yes, I know," Josephine said, still sniffling. "He already has."

Chapter 9

The sanctuary was filling quickly with people from all walks of life. Daniel sat beside Anna with his hands folded in his lap. He'd asked another of the lay leaders to preach this morning so he could sit with the Drake women.

Anna studied the faces of the people who entered the room, wondering where they would sit for the services. Many of them weren't able to find seats at all, due to the crowd. However, they found places to stand in the back. And others sat in windowsills that were barely big enough for small children.

As the preacher spoke of God's grace and mercy, Anna stole quick glances at her mother. Josephine seemed to hang on every word he said.

Anna's heart quickened as they closed in prayer and Daniel gently placed his hand in the small of her back. "Are you ready to join the others for a picnic, or do you need to get back to the farm?" He was touching her but directing the question to her mother. His proposal of marriage seemed to have been forgotten. Anna sighed. She knew it was too good to be true.

Josephine thought for a moment and smiled. "I think I'd like to join the others for a picnic." Then she shyly glanced down at the ground before looking back at Daniel. "B–but I didn't bring anything. Do you think they'd mind, if I promised to bring two dishes next week?"

This time, Daniel didn't hold back his laughter, which rang right along with the church bells, the sound more like music than laughter to Anna's ears. "You are never required to bring anything, Mrs. Drake. No one is keeping score."

This was like a dream come true for Anna. She sat between Daniel and her mother, enjoying a wonderful meal with fellow Christians. Anna watched as her mother laughed aloud for the first time in a long time. She knew that her heart was finally softening toward spiritual things, and she fully expected her to accept Christ as Savior very soon.

When the festivities began to break up, Daniel escorted Anna and Josephine to their carriage. As Anna climbed into her seat, he leaned toward her, winked, and said, "I love you."

Suddenly speechless, Anna opened her mouth but quickly closed it when words wouldn't come. Daniel kissed her, this time not letting her pull away to keep her mother from seeing their affection for each other. Was it possible that he hadn't changed his mind about wanting to marry her?

Anna giggled when she heard her mother say, "Oh, my!"

"I'd like to accompany you back to the farm," Daniel announced with a grin.

"Oh, really, Daniel," Anna said, "you don't have to do that."

"No," he agreed, "but I'd like to. Besides, I have something I'd like to discuss with you."

Josephine smiled as if she knew some deep dark secret. "Tell him to come along, Anna," she said. "It would be nice to have a man escort us home. You never know about the dangers on the roads these days."

Daniel rode his horse alongside Anna's and Josephine's carriage. He glanced over at Anna and winked, bringing a deep heat to her cheeks. Over the past few months, she'd grown more fond of him than she'd ever imagined possible. Ideas of a future with Daniel had invaded her mind, even when she slept.

Once they arrived at the house, Josephine excused herself and went upstairs. Anna was alone with Daniel.

"You said you wanted to talk to me about something?" she asked, turning toward the window with her back to Daniel.

He nodded. "Yes, Anna, I did say that, didn't I?"

She felt his hands reach out and grasp her shoulders, gently turning her to face him. They were standing only a few inches apart, their faces directly in front of each other. She saw something in his eyes she'd never seen before, something that melted her insides, forcing her to look down at the floor.

"Anna, please look at me." She did. "I have a very important question for you, and I want your undivided attention."

"Yes, Daniel?" she said, allowing her gaze to meet his once again. "What would you like to ask?"

"I'd like to ask for your hand in marriage," he whispered. "You've had more time to think about it, and I'm not so sure I can wait much longer to have you as my wife."

Anna felt her eyes widen in wonder. So, he hadn't changed his mind, after all.

Slowly a smile took over her face, and she found herself pulling him toward her.

He chuckled as he leaned over and brushed a feather-soft kiss across her lips. "I want an answer, Anna."

She shuddered. "Yes, Daniel, I would like to marry you."

Their arms went around each other for a longer, more lasting kiss. Anna knew this would be the first of many. The Sunshine Harvest couldn't compare to the brightness now in Anna's heart.

"Daniel?" Anna asked when they at last pulled away from their embrace.

He gazed at her, love written all over his face. "Yes, sweetheart?"

"What should I do with this farm?"

"What would you like to do with the farm?"

She gulped. "Would it be all right with you if we kept it?"

"Absolutely," he replied. "Do you think your mother would like to take my place in town?"

"Oh, Daniel," Anna said as she hugged him again, "you're so good to me."

"I want you to be happy, Anna."

"We'll have to tell our children about the first Sunshine Harvest of grapefruit," Anna said.

"Yes," Daniel agreed, "we'll tell all eight of them the whole story."

Anna gulped. "Eight?"

He chuckled. "That is, unless you want to try for a dozen."

Anna laughed with giddiness. "No, eight will be just fine."

※

Every pew in the small church was filled with church members and field workers' families as Anna and Daniel said their vows before God. While Daniel promised to love and cherish her for the rest of his life, Anna felt a sense of peace she'd never known until now. This was definitely the right thing to do; there was no doubt in her mind.

After the wedding, there was a reception feast on the church lawn. Josephine had help from the other ladies of the church in preparing an overabundance of food and desserts. People laughed, ate, and sang as Anna and Daniel lovingly gazed into each other's eyes.

Epilogue

The Sunshine Harvest yielded the first shipment of grapefruit and a larger crop of oranges than James Drake had ever recorded in his ledgers. Anna felt confident that her father would have been proud of her. Daniel did a wonderful job of running the business, but she insisted on knowing what was going on at all times. She knew he understood her need, and he shared every bit of news, both good and bad, which suited her just fine.

The church had grown to a size sufficient for the membership to call a full-time pastor. Daniel was more than happy to hand over the leadership to someone else, but he promised to do whatever was needed to help. Anna and Josephine offered their assistance as well. Daniel and Anna had already begun a Bible study with the migrant workers and that was going remarkably well.

Josephine welcomed Daniel's offer of his house in town. She'd always wanted to be in the middle of the action, and her home was now the frequent meeting place of her many good friends from church.

Shortly after the second crop of trees were planted, Anna waited for all the workers to go back to their houses. When Daniel came inside, she said, "I have some good news, Daniel."

He grinned and kissed her on the lips, something she never grew tired of. "What's that, sweetheart?"

"We're going to have a child sometime during the next harvest."

Daniel pulled Anna into his arms and kissed her tenderly. When he pulled away, he looked into her eyes and said, "I knew the Lord was good. But I never realized how good until you came into my life."

Anna felt the same way. Yes, God had been good to her; there was no doubt in her mind.

NEW
BEGINNINGS

by DiAnn Mills

Dedication

*This novella is dedicated to Beau and Allison
as they step out in their own new beginnings.*

Chapter 1

Wisconsin, 1899

Betsy Anne Wingert had always believed her wedding day would be filled with happiness, laughter, and the excited anticipation of dreams coming true. Instead she felt trapped and miserable.

But what good did remorse do now? In less than half an hour, standing before the mahogany and brick fireplace in the Malone parlor, she'd pledge her life and devotion to Nicholas Parker Malone. She'd carry the title of his wife until the day she died.

Betsy's eyes flooded with bitter tears. How could she have agreed to this? They'd grown up together, like brother and sister. Everyone expected them to marry—pointed to it when they played house as children. But to Betsy, it had been a game. She should have been honest, voiced her true feelings—and certainly never agreed to be his wife.

A lie.

A sin.

Now she'd pay for it the rest of her life.

Studing her reflection in the full-length mirror of the Malone's guest bedroom, Betsy bit back another well of sorrow. *Dry your eyes!* she ordered. *No one must know, least of all Nicholas.* Peering at herself, she decided giving herself to her husband would be something she could endure. Nicholas's embraces were ardent, but gentle.

She shook her head in an effort to dispel the shame racing through her veins. He loved her so much—she'd seen it in his clear blue eyes.

Dear, sweet Nicholas with hair the color of corn silk and such handsome features. His lively spirit attracted young and old, male and female. She'd long since recognized his caring, devotion. . .pure adoration as God intended for a man to cherish his wife.

Help me, Lord, she prayed. *If this is what You want for me, a marriage bereft of love, then help me to bear it. I want to love Nicholas, truly I do.*

The door creaked open, and Eloise Wingert slipped inside the bedroom. Betsy turned to greet her, feigning happiness for the sake of her beloved mother. Despite her resolve, at the sight of the dark-haired woman, Betsy's eyes moistened.

"Oh, my precious darling," her mother murmured, gathering Betsy into her arms. "I shouldn't have left you alone. This is such a special, joyous time for you." She slowly brought her to arm's length and gazed into Betsy's face. "A bride's joyful tears are drops of gold in the eyes of God."

"Thank you, Mother," she replied, wishing she could have remained forever in the security of that embrace.

She cupped Betsy's chin and smiled adoringly. "You are so beautiful, my little girl all grown up." Her mother hastily whisked away any traces of emotion and smiled. "Let me stand back and take a look at you. I want to see the whole gown."

Obediently, Betsy turned around, catching a glimpse of herself in the mirror. Her mother had sewn the wedding dress from a picture she'd seen in *The Ladies' Standard* and purchased the ivory silk brocade from New York— the very latest in fashion. Little three-leaf clovers embellished the fabric, making it appear to shimmer in the light. The tight-fitting bodice closed in front with many mother-of-pearl buttons, and layers of ecru lace trimmed the collar and sleeves.

She whirled around to see the full view of the back. An ivory sash tied at the waist, and tiny pleats gathered at the bustle, leading to a flowing train.

"Mother, I love my dress. Thank you for making it for me," Betsy said, and she meant it. Her mother had always given so much of herself to her family—completely, unselfishly. "I want to be just like you," she whispered.

Her mother shook her head. "I have so many faults, but I do strive to be what God intended. I guess if I have any last bit of advice, it is exactly that. Let the Lord have His way with you. Follow His leading, no matter if you don't understand why."

She nodded and attempted a faint smile. From the worried frown etched across her mother's forehead, Betsy realized she knew something troubled her. Disconcerted, she avoided her mother's gaze and toyed with the pearl buttons on her bodice.

"You don't really want to marry, do you?" she asked ever so softly.

Betsy's silence echoed around her.

"This must be why you've been so quiet the last few weeks. Darling, you don't have to go through with the wedding."

"I must, Mother. I gave my word."

"It's not too late." Her gray eyes narrowed.

"Yes, it is. I won't hurt him." Betsy sighed and swallowed the lump in her throat. "Nicholas is a good man, and he loves me."

"But what of your happiness?"

She picked up her ivory skirts and bravely faced her mother's loving concern. "Mother, downstairs he's waiting for me, just like he always has since we were children. How could I ever disappoint Nicholas and his family by not marrying him?"

"There's no talking you out of this?" Her mother pressed her lips together in an obvious effort to hold back tears.

She shook her head. "I only wish we weren't leaving in the morning."

"I feel the same way, Betsy, but I've heard him talk. Farming has always been a great love for Nicholas, not like his father and grandfather who loved the lumber mill. I, too, detest the thought of you moving to Ohio."

She touched her ivory gloved hand to her mother's mouth. "No more of this," she whispered. "It will all work out." Turning away to the window, she spoke the words of her heart. "I simply wish his Grandfather Parker hadn't left him that land in Ohio. He never asked me if I wanted to be a farmer's wife."

Betsy viewed the many carriages and wagons parked up and down both sides of the road. So many treasured family and friends had gathered at the Malone home for the wedding. The last remains of March snow had melted, and in its place shoots of green burst forth from the rich earth. Earlier the sky had threatened rain, but now beams of sunlight flickered through the treetops. It raised her spirits, giving her hope. Perhaps God had blessed this day after all.

Nicholas deserved a beautiful wedding. She may even see him and feel something more than the childhood friendship they'd always shared. Maybe living on a farm wouldn't be so bad. . .watching things grow and seeing new life in plants and animals.

Deep inside, though, she doubted it.

"I really understand how you feel, but Nicholas thought you'd be thrilled with his surprise," her mother said gently.

"I acted like it was wonderful," Betsy pointed out, chewing on her lip. "And I vow he will never perceive the difference."

"I know you believe this is for the best, but pretending will not make you happy. He'll eventually learn the truth—about it all." Betsy's mother walked over to the window and stood beside her. "If I can't change your mind about today, then I'll simply pray that working together on a farm will be a blessing to your marriage." She touched her cheek. "You need time alone with Nicholas, without your family or his."

A light knock at the door relieved Betsy from her mother's penetrating questions. "Betsy, Eloise, it's time," Benjamin Wingert's booming voice announced.

"All right, Father," Betsy replied, hugging her mother once more. "Come on in. I'm ready."

Her father spanned the width and height of the doorway. Dressed in a dark brown suit, he stood incredibly handsome. His thick silver hair and muscular shoulders made him look so healthy and alive. Betsy took a deep breath. Oh, how she'd miss her father's robust voice and gentle ways. For a moment he merely stared as though stunned.

"Father, is everything all right?" she asked, unaccustomed to viewing him speechless.

He strode across the room and lightly took her hand into both of his. "I've thought about this day since you were born," he said, his voice heavy with emotion. "And you are lovelier than I could ever have imagined."

Betsy felt her eyes grow liquid again. "Oh, thank you. Mother did a splendid job with my gown."

"Nonsense with the gown. I'm pleased with the young woman wearing it. You remind me so much of your mother." He glanced at his wife endearingly. "It's as though time has drifted back to our wedding day." Expelling a deep breath, he turned his attention back to his daughter. "Nicholas is a fine man, and I'm pleased to call him son. May God bless you both richly."

"Can we pray?" Betsy asked timidly.

His mustache twitched upward in an approving smile. "Yes, of course." The three grasped hands, and Betsy willed her shaking to cease. Slowly he began. "Heavenly Father, we praise You for the gift of love. Thank You for allowing Eloise and me to raise such a fine young woman. She's Yours, Lord, just as she's always been. Today I give her to Nicholas as his wife. Bless their union and be with them as they leave us tomorrow. All these things we ask in Your precious and holy name. Amen." He lifted watery eyes and pressed his lips together for a slight smile.

"Oh, Father," she breathed as he drew her close to him. He held her for several long moments until the sound of the piano downstairs pulled them apart.

Her mother tugged and straightened Betsy's gown until it was arranged to perfection. Meeting her gaze, Betsy saw compassion and concern.

"Hurry now, Mama," she whispered. "You'll want to see me descending the stairs."

The beginning chords of another hymn urged them to part. The wedding of Betsy Anne Wingert and Nicholas Parker Malone would take place as planned.

❧

Standing in his father's library amid the floor-to-ceiling books, Nicholas watched the throng of people mingle through the parlor and hallway. Some took seats in overstuffed and straight-backed chairs, and others stood talking in subtle whispers. Instantly they hushed as the pianist struck the chords of "Come Thou Fount of Every Blessing."

Betsy is my blessing, he thought, feeling nervous and impatient. *And I must tell her that every day of our married life.* He loved her with everything in him. She had her father's blue-green eyes, a pert little nose, and a wide smile that caused her whole face to glow. Nicholas grinned to himself, recalling how he used to tease her about her large mouth. She'd cry and tell her mother, and then he'd be forced to apologize. Odd, how one skinny little girl could grow up to be so lovely. Her musical laughter and sweet voice stayed with him constantly—always had, since they were children. Yes, he would love her forever.

Both families had wanted this marriage, and he happily accepted their wishes, although he would have pursued her with or without their blessings. Suddenly he remembered the two of them as children playing in the apple orchard.

"Now, Nicholas, when we're married, we must have juicy, red apples like these. Don't you agree?" she'd asked with a nod of her walnut-colored curls.

"Of course. And if our house doesn't have an apple tree, then I'll plant one," he replied.

"Oh, would you, Nicholas? Just for me?"

"Anything you want."

"May I have a home near my mother?"

"Yes, I promise."

The reminiscing about childhood days left an empty feeling in the pit of his stomach. *I'm taking her away from her family,* he reflected. *I broke my promise.* But they were not children anymore. He was twenty, and Betsy nearly eighteen. He remembered again her reaction to his surprise of inheriting the farm. She hadn't become upset, but she hadn't been overly excited either. Surely she'd have expressed her disappointment.

Nonsense. I'm worrying about something needlessly. Today, Betsy and I will be married, and tomorrow we'll leave for our new home in Ohio. And with God's help, I'll be the best husband and farmer this country has ever seen.

He felt a tap on his shoulder. "Son, everyone is seated for the ceremony. It's time."

Roused from his musings, Nicholas stared into the blue eyes of his father, Phillip Malone. He took a deep breath. "I'm ready."

"Do you have the ring?" he asked with a teasing grin.

"Yes, sir."

His father placed an arm around his shoulders. "I'm very proud of you—your selection of a wife, your decision to farm, and the godly man you've become."

"Thank you. Sometimes I worry that I'm not doing the right thing, but I feel God's calling to Ohio and my inheritance. You know I'm going to miss you and Mother."

"And we are already wishing you were still here in Wisconsin."

They both hesitated. His father initiated a handshake, but his arm slid up to Nicholas's shoulder and neck, ending in a vigorous hug. Finally the elder Malone broke away. "We best take our place. Betsy surely doesn't want a wedding without a groom."

The two walked side by side from the library into the parlor. At the sight of the small crowd, a siege of nervousness erupted inside Nicholas. He wanted and needed to see Betsy. She and she alone would put to rest the unsettling in his soul. Anxiously, he awaited her.

Then he saw his bride.

More ethereal than he'd ever imagined, Betsy appeared to fairly float down the circular staircase, clinging to her father's arm. Radient in ivory silk and lace, wearing a fragile smile, she trembled.

Nicholas's mind stepped back to a time when he'd thrown a rock into an elm tree only to have a nest with three tiny, blue robin eggs topple to the ground. She'd screamed at him, hit him with her little fists, then fell into his arms sobbing. He'd felt so wretched and then protective.

And he'd protect his angel now.

The Reverend Dale Schmidt lifted his head and silently commanded everyone's attention. "Dearly beloved: Forasmuch as marriage is a holy estate, ordained of God, and to be held in honor by all, it becometh those who enter therein to weigh, with reverent minds, what the Word of God teacheth concerning it.

"The Lord God said, 'It is not good that the man should be alone;

I will make him an help meet for him.'

"Our Lord Jesus Christ said, 'Have ye not read, that He which made them at the beginning made them male and female, and said, For this cause shall a man leave his father and mother, and shall cleave to his wife: and they twain shall be one flesh? Wherefore, they are no more twain, but one flesh. What therefore God hath joined together, let not man put asunder.'"

Nicholas stole a look at his bride. Tears dampened her cheeks. That was his Betsy, so easily moved to sentiment. He loved her kind heart and gentle ways. For a moment he thought he'd explode with the joy filling his soul.

The pastor continued. "Into this holy estate this man and this woman come now to be united. If anyone, therefore, can show just cause why they may not be lawfully joined together, let him now speak, or else forever hold his peace."

Nicholas felt her quiver, and he fought an immense urge to hold her until she calmed.

"Wilt thou have this woman to thy wedded wife, to live together after God's ordinance in the holy estate of matrimony? Wilt thou love her, comfort her, honor and keep her in sickness and in health, and, forsaking all others, keep thee only unto her, so long as ye both shall live?"

"I will," Nicholas said, hearing his voice sound loud and clear.

"Wilt thou have this man to thy wedded husband, to live together after God's ordinance in the holy estate of matrimony? Wilt thou love him, comfort him, honor and keep him in sickness and in health, and, forsaking all others, keep thee only unto him, so long as ye both shall live?"

Betsy hesitated. Silence followed. Nicholas turned to her and smiled. She seemed so frightened. Poor girl, he knew how crowds of people left her speechless.

"I will," she whispered, with a shaky smile.

The ceremony soon ended. "I now pronounce you man and wife. You may kiss your bride," the pastor instructed.

Nicholas gazed deeply into the blue-green eyes of his wife. A twinge of alarm rang through his mind and shattered his senses. He didn't see love in her eyes. He saw fear. . .and distrust.

Long after the Malone home hushed and Betsy heard the even breathing of her husband beside her, she reflected over the afternoon. Feeling certain her secret lay secure, she pondered over the uneasiness settling in the core of her being. Guilt robbed her of sleep, and she desperately needed rest for the journey ahead.

The guests had been most kind, bidding congratulations and encouragement for their future. Some prayed God's blessing on their marriage, and Betsy wondered if she would be struck dead for thanking them. As she'd expressed gratitude to each one for sharing in her and Nicholas's special day, she felt her mother watch and silently comfort her. What would she ever do without her constant presence? She hated thinking about it.

When the last guest had departed, Betsy found herself standing in front of the fireplace where she'd taken her vows. Glancing up into a painting of the very same house, she felt an odd sense of peace. At the time she wondered if it was the replica or God Himself letting her know of His presence.

"You like the picture of Laurelwood?" Deborah Malone had asked softly.

"Yes. I've never seen a painting reflect such serenity. Why is it called Laurelwood when that's not what you call your home?" she asked curiously.

The woman laughed softly. "Oh, it's not this house. The painting is of Leah Malone's girlhood home in Pennsylvania—Nicholas's grandmother."

Betsy glanced at her, quite perplexed.

"Ask Nicholas to tell you about it," she suggested. "That will give you two something else to talk about on your way to Ohio," she sighed dreamily. "It's such a romantic story."

Betsy smiled genuinely. She did love Deborah Malone. Regretfully, she wouldn't get to know her better. "I'll be sure to ask him about it. And, thank you again for this lovely wedding. . . ."

Nicholas stirred in his sleep, and she felt his gaze upon her. "Betsy, are you all right?"

"Yes, I'm fine."

"But you're not sleeping." He sounded concerned, so much like him.

339

"Oh, Nicholas, I was only thinking of today."

"Of course," he murmured, wrapping his arm around her. "I should have known."

I'll be a good wife, she vowed silently to God. *Just watch me make him happy.*

Chapter 2

A slow drizzle dampened Betsy's new determination to make the most of her marriage and chilled her to the bone. It began near dawn when she first heard Nicholas rousing, no doubt anxious for the journey to Ohio. Like the many times she'd seen him excited about adventures and new ideas, he suddenly began talking and sharing his dreams about the farm—their future—as though she lay fully awake and felt the same enthusiasm.

Don't pretend, she scolded herself through the fogginess of faint reality. *Wake up and share his dreams. Tell him all the things he should hear from his wife.*

"And we'll be there in plenty of time before plowing and planting," he said, leaning over to her and gracing her cheek with a kiss.

Betsy opened her eyes and forced a smile.

"Good morning, Mrs. Malone," he whispered. She saw the glowing light of love in his clear blue eyes.

"Good morning." She smiled at his tenderness. "Is it time?"

"Yes, I believe so. Do you mind getting up so early? Well, I mean once we are living on our farm, every day will be like this." His face flushed with confident expectation.

She dared not spoil their first day by revealing her disappointment. The idea of leaving her family and friends left her numb and. . .unforgiving. "Is it raining?" she asked, lifting her head from the pillow.

Nicholas stroked her thick hair and drew her close to his chest. "We can wait a few more minutes. It's not even daylight yet, and Mother would never hear of us leaving before sunrise."

"Thank you, Nicholas," she murmured, slowly drifting off to sleep.

"I love you," he whispered.

And she smiled in response.

It seemed she'd barely gotten to sleep again when he awakened her. Odd, she'd been dreaming that he'd changed his mind and decided to stay in Wisconsin and work with his father at the lumber mill. Such a delightful thought, but nevertheless only a dream.

With heavy eyes, Betsy rose and prepared herself. Last night Nicholas had packed their belongings into a wagon so their departure would be much easier. Some of their wedding gifts she hadn't even seen, but since she secretly felt unworthy of them, it didn't matter. They'd be unpacked and put to use in Ohio.

Still, the rain lingered, and she felt the nagging chill. A cozy day by the fire seemed much more to her liking. At least it wasn't snow.

Then Betsy remembered an envelope her mother had given her the previous evening. She hadn't opened it last night but laid it on the cherry dresser of Nicholas's bedroom. Picking it up, she eased it open:

> *To my darling daughter,*
>
> *As you step out in this new life with Nicholas, I want to share this verse to speed you on your way. My heart aches with the fact you're leaving, but I know it's God will for your life. My love and prayers go with you.*
>
> *"Now unto him that is able to do exceeding abundantly above all that we ask or think, according to the power that worketh in us, Unto him be glory in the church by Christ Jesus throughout all ages, world without end. Amen." Ephesians 3:20–21.*
>
> *With all my love,*
> *Mother*

Betsy blinked back the tears threatening to spill. Mother knew the right verses to give her the strength and courage to face the days ahead. She tucked it into her Bible and carried it downstairs to meet Nicholas.

After a hearty breakfast with Deborah and Phillip Malone, they stepped out into a pink tinted sky to bid farewell. Already she missed her parents, but she'd said good-bye to them after the wedding. Betsy had shed enough tears yesterday to last a long time, but again they threatened to surface when she viewed a pair of fine mares in a dapple color hitched to the heavily laden wagon.

"We have something else for you," Phillip said, with a glint in his blue eyes.

"Father, we have no more room," Nicholas insisted.

The older man ignored his protests. "Excuse me while I get it. We'll find room."

Betsy turned to Deborah, whose eyes contained the familiar merriment she'd often found in Nicholas's gaze. Moments later, Phillip returned with a large, rectangular-shaped object draped in an old quilt.

"What is this?" Betsy asked, without an inkling of what he carried.

"Laurelwood," Deborah whispered. "It will always be a reminder of home and those who love you."

Nicholas objected, shaking his blond head. "But we haven't room."

"It's not for you as much as Betsy," his mother stated firmly. "She needs to see something familiar when her family is so far away."

"Oh, thank you," Betsy breathed, thinking of the many wonderful hours she'd spent with her parents at the Malone home. "Please, Nicholas. Can't we find a spot for the painting?"

He sighed deeply, then a warm smile spread over his face. "To see you this happy, I'd almost leave a sack of seed corn." Then he laughed. "Well, almost."

Betsy clapped her hands. Elation made her want to dance and shout. "I'm so thrilled. When I'm lonesome, I'll just gaze into it and envision Mother and Father sitting on the front porch with you. It will be so grand."

Phillip ran his fingers through his blond and silver hair, then scanned the length of the wagon until he saw where he could slip the painting between a trunk and two boxes. He wrapped it tightly with an additional quilt before he and Nicholas anchored it in place.

343

"And I know a perfect place for it in our new home," Nicholas said, reaching around Betsy's waist.

"That's right," Deborah replied. "You've seen the house, but she hasn't. For a moment I'd forgotten the two months you were gone last fall tending to the property."

"And you'll see it, too," Nicholas said. "Father tells me you plan to visit us next spring."

"With the Wingerts," she added.

Betsy beamed. Now, she really had something to look forward to. A year seemed endless, but things could change. Her heart could soften and she could become the wife Nicholas deserved. She stole a look at him. He tried so hard, just like he'd always done.

"Then I'll plant half the tillable soil in wheat and the other half in corn. And we'll have plenty of good spring water. Why the place is overfilling with them, and a creek flows through the middle. It makes for great picnics and good pasture for the cows." Nicholas rattled on as the horses ambled down the road.

"What cows?" Betsy interrupted.

He leaned over and lightly kissed her cheek. "Oh, I bought three good Holsteins last fall. Willy Barrett, a neighbor, is feeding them for me."

"Milk cows?" she asked hesitantly, wondering if he'd already told her this.

"Yes," he replied, a dimple in his cheek deepening. "Didn't I tell you?"

She cringed. "Maybe, I'm sorry but I don't remember."

"You, Mrs. Malone, were too busy planning our wedding. Some days you were so distracted, that I worried you might have another fella." He laughed.

Betsy felt the all too familiar churning in the pit of her stomach. "Oh, you silly man. Just when would I have seen someone else?"

"Don't know. Don't matter now, anyhow, 'cause you're mine."

"That's right," she said with a nod, pulling her woolen coat closer around her shoulders. When the clouds covered the sun, a biting chill remained. "There's never been anyone else." And those words were true.

"Can I name the cows?"

"Of course."

She thought for a moment, biting her lip.

Nicholas laughed. "Don't work too hard at it. They're only cows."

She joined in his mirth. "Guess I need to see them first, but you can tell me all about the neighbors."

"The Barretts live about three miles from us on a farm with about the same amount of acreage—eighty in case you forgot. Willy and Ella are their names, and she's very nice. And they have seven or eight kids. I think she'll be a good friend to you."

"I hope so," she whispered as he squeezed her hand. She couldn't imagine filling her days with nothing but chores while he worked the fields.

Betsy listened to Nicholas talk about the farm. He'd told her so many times about the house and barn that she had the layout permanently engraved in her mind. They'd have a kitchen parlor, bedroom, and back porch with a root cellar for storing vegetables in the winter. She knew they would never run out of things to talk about because Nicholas always had a topic floating about in his head. Not like her, where too often melancholia set in and left her all too willing to shut herself away from the world. Mother said that wasn't good and to ask God's help in overcoming it. Once she did, but her moods didn't seem so terrible to her.

"And there's a church right down the road from us," Nicholas continued.

"What's it called?"

"Loss Creek Church, just like the name of the road we'll live on. I attended there last fall, good people, good minister. He preached the word unashamedly."

She nodded, making sure she remembered everything he'd just told her. "How far is the nearest town? I know you told me before, but I'm asking again."

"Seven miles, and it's called Crestline, a railroad town. Seems like a growing community to me. Bucyrus is about fourteen miles away, and it's bigger, right on the banks of the Sandusky River."

Betsy sighed. *Heavenly Father, I want to feel the same expectations as Nicholas. I hate pretending every moment of the day. If it all could be real.*

Perhaps someday it will. I want so to find myself loving him and the life he's chosen for us. Lord, only you can do miracles, and I desperately need one.

The first night Betsy and Nicholas slept at a cousin's home about twenty miles east of Eau Claire. Sore and aching all over from jostling in the wagon, she welcomed a hot bath and a comfortable bed. For the most part, the two would be spending their evenings in hotels and boardinghouses, but he'd prepared her for the times when they might need to sleep under the stars. She hoped the snow and ice had finished, but with the unpredictability of weather in March, it was hard to tell.

The two planned to cover nearly four hundred and twenty-four miles before reaching their destination—approximately three weeks of travel, barring any severe weather changes. By the time they reached Ohio and finally turned onto Loss Creek Road, Betsy believed every muscle in her body ached, yet she sensed an eagerness to see her new home.

Nicholas pulled the wagon to a halt.

"Why are we stopping?" she asked puzzled, especially since he'd been in such a hurry to reach the farm before dark.

"For you to close your eyes," he grinned, his blond hair picking up highlights from the late afternoon sun.

Obediently, she shut them tightly and hooked her arm into his as the horses meandered ahead.

"We just passed the Barretts'," he informed her. "But don't open your eyes. There's plenty of time for you to see their farm later."

"Nicholas, this is taking forever," she claimed, wanting desperately to view the countryside.

"Patience," he soothed. "I can see our house now."

"Can't I see, too?"

"No, this is my surprise. When I first saw the house, I could see you planting flowers and me working the land."

With nothing to see but blackness, her other senses became more acute. She heard the calling of a bobwhite and detected the scent of dark, rich soil. "Now?" she asked. "I can't wait much longer."

"Just a moment more. I may need a kiss first before I can give my consent," he teased.

"You can have two."

He laughed, and Betsy did love to hear him laugh. "Whoa," he shouted to the horses.

She felt his nearness and smiled. Sometimes Nicholas made life so much fun. He kissed her tenderly. "One," he whispered. His arms gathered her close and this time he lingered on her lips, making her feel warm...and loved. "All right, you paid the price. Open your eyes and welcome to the Malone farm."

Immediately her gaze flew to a small white frame home resting on a hill, nestled between two large maple trees. Peering closer, she saw it looked in much better condition than she'd ever envisioned.

Her hand flew to her mouth. "Nicholas, it looks very nice—not at all what I expected." She grimaced. "I mean, I didn't know what our home would look like."

He chuckled, seemingly delighted in her response. "Well, I did repair the roof and add the porch when I arrived last fall."

"That's why you were gone two months. Please, I want down from this wagon," she said, clasping her hands. "I want to see the inside, and, oh, is that a lilac bush I see?"

He jumped to the ground and turned to grasp her waist, lifting her gently down to the soft, green earth. "I understand the blooms are purple, the kind you like."

"I can almost smell them now—well, in a couple of months for sure."

He laughed and took her hand. "I can see you can't wait a minute more. Let's go inside." Once they climbed the hill and then the porch steps, he hesitated. "Now, Betsy, I need to build us some furniture. There's not much inside, 'cept a table, two chairs, a cookstove, and I built you a cupboard for your dishes. We have a bed and dresser in the wagon—"

"Nonsense, Nicholas. It will be fine. I'm simply glad to finally be here." She gazed up at him shyly, and he touched her nose with a kiss.

He opened the door and ushered her inside. Although small and very old, it looked in excellent condition. In the dim light, she saw he must have done a considerable amount of work during his previous visit. A red brick fireplace took in the entire wall of a rectangular parlor. As she gazed above a cherry mantel, he whispered, "For the painting."

Betsy nodded and saw the kitchen looked sufficiently roomy. "The cupboard is beautiful," she breathed, touching its oaken sides. He'd carved a scroll-like leaf pattern across the very top. "This took time," she said, gingerly fingering the engraving. "You're definitely a gifted carpenter. We'll be the envy of all the neighbors."

He slipped his arm around her waist. "I have so many plans, Betsy. Someday I'll build you a big, beautiful house full of fine things. But for now, we have to settle for being poor farmers."

She felt her emotions rise and fall. She'd never gone without in her life, yet this was where her new husband had brought her. Forcing an encouraging smile, she elected to search about the small home. After all, Nicholas deserved a devoted, loving wife, not what he'd gotten. "You're a fine man. I'm very fortunate to have you," Betsy said sincerely. Things could be much worse.

Hand in hand they walked into the bedroom. It looked bare and plain, but of course when their things were unloaded she'd make it quite homey. Mother had given her yard goods to sew curtains, and she'd packed a number of colorful quilts, along with a rug to keep their feet warm in winter.

Feeling both relief to be at the farm and gratitude for Nicholas's preparing the home, she faced him and lifted his other hand from his side. "I do want to be a good wife to you."

"All I ever want is your love," he replied. "Without that, I have nothing."

Chapter 3

The following morning before breakfast, Betsy and Nicholas walked out over their farm. He pointed out the many bubbling springs and skipped stones across a shady creek. In a shallow part, they crossed over on moss-covered rocks with Nicholas steadying her balance.

"This will be a perfect picnic spot," she said, glancing about her. "I can bring you lunch when you're working near here in the fields. It will be delightful."

"Delightful? I imagine I'll be plenty sweaty and smelly."

She feigned annoyance but burst into laughter. "Then you can wash up and dangle your feet in the water."

Hand in hand they strode on toward the fields where he planned to grow corn. "Over there's the cows." He gestured. "Want to see them so you can give them a proper name?" He grinned, and she poked his ribs.

"All right," she replied a few moments later when they reached the grazing animals. "See the one that keeps tossing her head?"

"Yes, she's practicing for the flies this summer."

She rolled her eyes. "Maybe so, but she's Bossy. I think the smaller one should be Prudence, and the medium one that keeps backing away from me, ah, well, Miss Skittish."

Nicholas roared, his blue eyes dancing. "Miss Skittish?"

She nodded and tried unsuccessfully to pat the cow. "She deserves special treatment until she feels comfortable."

He grimaced. "If she doesn't kick me when I try to milk her."

On they walked, and he pointed out moist areas in the woods where sponge mushrooms would most likely come up in April or early May after a good rain. The smell of fresh earth teased her nostrils, and the colorful signs of spring were a welcome sight.

"This is beautiful," she murmured.

He replied with a long, lingering kiss. Breaking away, Betsy swore she could eat a loaf of bread by herself so they ventured back to the house for breakfast. Nicholas dug through the wagon for the coffeepot while Betsy mixed up flour, lard, baking powder, and salt for biscuits. A bit of smoked ham and a jar of apple butter made for a tasty meal. While she cleaned up the kitchen, he hung the painting.

"Come see, Betsy," he called when the hammering ceased.

He had it centered above the mantle. "It's perfect," she complimented, drying her hands on her apron. "Some day you must tell me the story about the painting."

"I will," he said, "but not now. Too much to do."

Slowly the wagon shed its heavy load, or rather it shifted to the kitchen floor until Betsy could go through their belongings. He put together the black iron bed and she made it up with new sheets, embroidered pillowcases from her hope chest, and a quilt her mother had pieced from scraps of Betsy's childhood dresses.

That evening Willy and Ella Barrett stopped in for a visit, bringing a jar of rhubarb preserves and a loaf of freshly baked bread. They'd left their eight children at home, and Betsy saw they were expecting another.

Willy, a rather squarely built fellow, spoke softly and looked very strong. He had small, dark eyes that seemed to disappear into his round face when he laughed—and he did that a lot.

Ella, a tiny woman, had the most flaming red hair Betsy had ever seen. A patch of tan freckles dotted her nose, and sky blue eyes twinkled mischievously. She hardly looked like the mother of so many children.

Betsy put on coffee for them all before they moved outside to the porch steps, since they had only two chairs. She felt a bit uncomfortable about the seating arrangement, but the Barretts didn't seem to mind.

"What can I do for you?" Ella asked. "I know you must be tired from riding all this way."

"I am," Betsy admitted, "mostly sore, but it's exciting to finally be here. We unloaded everything today, and both of us worked inside and out, putting things in order."

"I do want to help in some way," Ella said, with a tilt of her head.

"You can be my friend," she replied gently. "Nothing else would make me happier." Nicholas reached for her hand and squeezed it lightly. She'd pleased him, but her reasons for friendship were selfish.

"Your husband and I plan to help each other off and on," Willy announced. "Sharing in some of the hard work makes it easier."

"Especially for one like me who needs to learn more about farming." Nicholas chuckled. "Starting tomorrow I milk my own cows."

Betsy felt a warm sensation growing inside her at the knowledge of finding such good friends near her new home. She excused herself to pour the fresh coffee, and Ella followed. "I can really get this. You most likely have your share of serving others," Betsy said.

Ella picked up two cups and held them out. "This is my ninth baby, and I feel fine. If I allowed myself to slow down, I'd get lazy." She glanced around and saw the yard goods piled in the corner of the kitchen. "Curtains?"

"Yes, hopefully I can get started on them after Sunday."

"We could get them done in one afternoon," Ella offered. "My two older girls are good seamstresses." In the lamplight, her hair looked like spun fire.

Betsy bit her lip in anticipation. "Are you sure you'd want to spend the time sewing my curtains?"

"Of course. We could come Monday right after lunch, and by suppertime we'll be finished."

"That would be wonderful."

Long after the Barretts left, Nicholas talked about the farms, their plans, and all the other things he desired until Betsy began nodding off to sleep. She didn't want to hear anymore about his dreams. For that's all they were—his dreams.

The next morning, Nicholas woke before dawn and milked the cows while Betsy sleepily made breakfast after he brought the milk to the house. He left right after sunrise and returned at noon, starved, yet eager to continue. Betsy warmed him ham and bread along with some of Ella's rhubarb preserves.

"I sure could have used a dipper of water about mid-morning," he said, slightly irritated.

She looked up startled. "I'm sorry. I did not know to bring you any." Silence followed. "I will remember tomorrow."

"So what did you do all morning?" he finally asked.

"Washed dishes and the other things we unpacked from the wagon," she replied, staring into his slightly reddened face. "I also cleaned and dried our clothes and put away the supplies we purchased in Bucyrus."

Again quiet prevailed.

"I'm sorry I was short with you," he finally said. "I just expected more things to be done."

"What else would you have me do?" Her voice rose, unfairness showering over her like the dirty laundry water from the morning.

Concern etched across his brow. "Not you, Betsy, me. I wanted more accomplished this morning. I must work faster if I'm to be a good farmer."

Wringing her hands in her lap, she wanted to speak fitting words that a good wife would use to encourage her husband. "You're simply learning, Nicholas. It will get faster."

He combed his fingers through his blond hair. "Yes, you're right." For the first time, he smiled and reached up to stroke her cheek with his thumb. "I love you."

"I know you do," she replied, wishing she could return the same affectionate words.

A few moments later he left for the fields, leaving Betsy waving good-bye from the porch.

"I'll bring you a jar of cool spring water during mid-afternoon," she called from the front porch.

He turned and eyed her curiously, almost suspiciously. "I love you," he called.

She blew him a kiss.

On Sunday morning Nicholas proudly drove the wagon for their first visit to Loss Creek Church. It was a smaller church than the one in Eau Claire, but the people welcomed them, most of whom remembered him from the previous fall. Many church members introduced themselves to Betsy, and he watched her graciously return their greetings.

The Barretts attended, and for the first time she met all eight children. They looked like an army of red hair and sky blue eyes. Betsy looked a bit overwhelmed at the brood and rightfully so. That many children meant a lot of mouths to feed.

Nicholas enjoyed Pastor Johnson's sermon on the first three Beatitudes and looked forward to hearing him in weeks to come. Observing his wife, he felt proud of the way she responded to the church folk. People took to Betsy easily. Her sweet and sometimes shy disposition seemed to bring out the best in them. Of course, he didn't think she realized her own capabilities and talents. He'd seen her teach a children's Bible study class, silently commanding even the rowdiest little boy's attention. Other times he watched her heart melt at the sight of an injured bird or animal, nursing it back to health.

And Betsy always told the truth, which accounted for why her lack of affection plagued him. He knew she feigned sleep at night to discourage him. It hurt and alarmed him. Yesterday morning while plowing, he tried to remember the last time she'd said "I love you." It must have been her fifteenth birthday.

They were seated in her mother's gazebo amidst bushes of red roses, and he'd brought her ribbons for her hair along with special words from his heart.

"These are lovely," she said, carefully removing them from the box. "And you remembered lavender is my favorite color."

Nicholas stammered and looked down at his freshly shined boots. He felt extremely awkward, not at all like the man of eighteen that he professed to be. "I. . .I thought they'd look pretty with your dark hair. . .and I want to tell you something." He met her wide smile and perfectly straight white teeth.

"Tell me what?" she asked innocently.

He picked up her hand as though she were made of the most delicate porcelain. Wetting his lips and staring into her beloved face, he suddenly forgot everything he'd planned to say. His face warmed and his hands dampened. "Betsy," he slowly began. "I. . .I want you to know that you are the most beautiful girl in all the world. . .and I love you."

Tears formed in her blue-green eyes, causing them to look even more green. She tilted her head slightly and the smile never left her. "And I love you, too," she whispered.

Standing in the midst of his partially plowed field, Nicholas took a ragged breath. Guess he'd simply took it for granted she'd meant those words to last a lifetime. Nevertheless, he needed to hear them soon or he'd explode.

On Monday morning, Nicholas left for the fields, taking with him a jar to fill with cool, sparkling spring water whenever he needed it. He appreciated the spring air, still crisp before the heat of summer set in. At noontime Betsy brought their lunch, and beside the rippling creek, they ate fried chicken and green beans from the night before and biscuits from breakfast. He simply didn't have much to say, especially with the worrisome thoughts rolling around in his head about Betsy.

"You've gotten a lot done this morning," she commented, handing him a generous portion of chicken. "When do you think the plowing will be done?"

"Probably the end of next week."

Setting aside her plate, she eyed him curiously. "Is something wrong?"

He shook his head, feeling lonelier than he could remember. "Should there be?"

Betsy stiffened, then smoothed the skirt of her green-flowered dress. She plucked a blade of grass and studied it. "I don't really know. Did I not pack enough food for your lunch? Is it that Ella and her girls are coming this afternoon?"

For a moment he pushed the nagging thought from his head. Gazing out over the creek bank, so placid—unaffected by human emotions and turmoil—Nicholas wondered if he'd been wrong.

She grasped his hand resting across his lap. "Is all this too much work?" she asked softly. "Do you want me to help you in the fields or take over milking the cows?"

His agitation dissipated at the sound of her voice. He couldn't resist stroking a loose strand of walnut-colored hair that she'd elected to wear down about her shoulders. His precious Betsy, so much a child and yet his wife. Of course nothing was amiss. She only needed time to adjust to the farm, Ohio. . .and to him.

"I'm sorry," he said. "You already do more than enough to help me. I didn't expect the plowing to take this long, even though Willy told me otherwise."

"You've been terribly tired."

He smiled sadly. "And a bear. I'll toughen up to this real soon. It's not like working at the lumber mill. I worked hard there, but I saw the fruits of my labor faster."

"You'll be just fine," she soothed, avoiding his eyes. "And I'll cook you a wonderful dinner tonight. Is there something special you'd like to have?"

He shook his head and hesitated. "I love you, Betsy Malone."

"I know," she whispered. "God and you, what more could I ask?"

Betsy hurried back to the house, realizing the time neared of Ella's arrival. The expectation of spending the afternoon with her new friend made her feel a bit giddy.

Without warning, a slow, mounting fear seized her as though threatening to choke the life out of her resolve. Nicholas knew. She couldn't hide it from him much longer. He almost asked her about it today.

Oh, God, what is wrong with me? I want to tell him I love him, but not unless I mean it. Help me be the woman You desire of me. She remembered the verses from Ephesians that her mother had given and repeated them in her mind. *Now unto him that is able to do exceeding abundantly above all that we ask or think, according to the power that worketh in us, Unto him be glory in the church by Christ Jesus throughout all ages, world without end. Amen.*

It will happen, she told herself firmly. *I simply need faith.*

Inside her home, Betsy glanced up at the painting of Laurelwood. Her eyes took it in at least a dozen times a day. Nicholas still hadn't shared the story behind it. She needed to ask, to know if the love behind his grandparents and parents came from a deep secret hidden within the home.

Her guests soon arrived. Ella and her two daughters, Belle and Verna, quickly set to task helping Betsy cut out and stitch curtains for the kitchen, parlor, and bedroom windows. A third daughter, Marie, stayed behind to tend to the younger children. After much deliberation, Betsy decided to embroider lilac and yellow flowers on the ones in the bedroom to match the pillowcases she'd done before the wedding. The afternoon sped by, much faster than any of them had anticipated.

"Mercy, look at the time," Ella said with a start.

Betsy glanced up at the clock sitting on the parlor mantle. "Oh, my, it is getting late. Our men will be wanting dinner before we know it."

"And we're not quite finished," Ella continued.

"Mama, we can hurry home and cook," Belle offered, a pretty young girl with a flawless complexion and the same shade of red hair as her mother.

"Yes, Mama, you can stay and finish with Mrs. Malone," Verna added, complete with freckles and strawberry-blonde hair.

Ella appeared to ponder the matter. "All right. I think that would be a fine idea."

Betsy checked on her own roast and potatoes simmering on the stove and returned to help her friend. The curtains looked beautiful, and she could do the embroidering in the evenings while Nicholas read from his Bible.

"You and Nicholas look so happy," Ella commented, after her daughters had left.

"He is a very good man," she said. A nudging at her mind prompted her to seek answers from her new friend. "Tell me, when did you first realize that you loved Willy?"

Ella laughed lightly. "Well, we married when I was barely sixteen years old, scarcely old enough for a girl to know what love really is or means."

Betsy nodded and smiled. "So you just always knew?"

"Oh, no. When I first met Willy, he impressed me with his calm ways and good nature. I felt a tremendous amount of respect for him—the way he worked hard and loved the Lord. When he did ask my father for my hand, I felt really confused. I didn't love him, but I sensed God leading me to take the step."

"Without reservation?" Betsy felt her heart pound against her chest.

Ella leaned into her. "I had never been so scared in my entire life." She sat back and a faint smile played upon her upturned lips. "But God is faithful. I prayed that I would be the wife God desired of me, and it happened!"

"When? How long did you have to wait?"

Ella sewed a few more stitches before replying, then she rested the fabric in her lap. "During the eighth month of my first baby, it all happened. Goodness, I felt like I carried a bushel basket of potatoes inside me."

Both women laughed, and Betsy attempted to relax.

"Well, one summer evening I saw Willy heading up from the fields. He always went straight to the well to wash up a bit, so I stood at the kitchen window and watched him. Suddenly, a strange feeling came over me. It seemed like I was looking at him for the first time. He stood erect, the muscles bulging from his tanned neck, grinning to himself. Later, he told me that he secretly hoped our first baby would be a girl. Anyway, a feeling of love spilled out over me like the water gushing out of the bucket rising from the well."

A faraway look settled in her blue eyes. "Poor Willy. I ran outside and threw my arms around his neck, laughing and crying at the same time. He didn't know what to think. I must have told him a hundred times I loved him." She glanced over at Betsy. "And everyday I love him more. We've had some rough times, but God molds us through adversity."

"Thank you," Betsy managed. "It's a beautiful story." Unfortunately she hadn't felt like that around Nicholas since they were much younger.

With the curtains completed, Ella gathered up her sewing basket, and the two hugged good-bye.

"This has been such a perfect afternoon," Betsy said. "I praise God for you, Ella."

Her friend smiled. "He put us together for a reason. I'll pray for you and Nicholas—that God will bless you richly with His unfailing love."

For a moment, Betsy feared even Ella knew her darkest secret.

Chapter 4

S everal long, lonely weeks slipped by, turning into months. One morning Betsy woke up, missing home more than ever—and everything about it. A lump formed in her throat, and tears leaked out each time she contemplated her dire circumstances. She felt miserable, alone, and afraid that the rest of her life would be no better than this. Praying didn't seem to help—neither did reading her Bible. The blackness persisted for three days until she no longer felt like talking to Nicholas in the early mornings or evenings. All she wanted was her mother and home, not the lonely existence of Nicholas's farm.

A few nights later, she attempted to mend his socks, although depression threatened to suffocate her.

"It's been three days, Betsy. What can I do to help you out of this?" Nicholas asked, closing his Bible.

She shook her head, fighting the melancholy and not wanting him to see her misery. In one breath, she felt ashamed of her gloom, and in the next she wanted desperately to blame him.

"Nothing? You're unhappy about something." He spoke kindly, making her feel like a child. "Is it me?" His blond hair fell across his forehead, and when he brushed it away she saw the concern in his eyes.

Betsy blinked away the tears, giving her attention to darning his socks. "I'll be all right. It's nothing, really."

"You can't keep things from me, Betsy. You've never been able to." He pulled his chair closer to hers. She almost reached out and touched him, wanting him to draw her close for a few minutes so she could close her eyes and wish the awfulness away. Except she didn't want to pretend any longer. God hadn't answered her prayers. She was forever stuck on this forsaken piece of land—away from home and family with a man she didn't love. What bothered her the most was the haunting realization that she would soon come to despise him for everything. If she hadn't already.

"I'm lonely," she finally said. "I miss home."

"What about Ella?"

Betsy swallowed hard. "Ella is a wonderful friend, but I'm still having a difficult time."

He nodded thoughtfully. "Willy offered me a puppy a few days ago. I could get it for you."

She wanted to scream at him, tell him that nothing would help short of going home, but she knew Nicholas's heart. "A puppy sounds nice," she said forcing a smile.

"All right," he said standing. "I'll go get it now. The mother only had one, so there's not several to choose from."

"You don't need to go now," she protested, sensing the lateness of the hour. "Wait until tomorrow."

He bent down to her. "No, I want you happy, and I'll do anything to make sure of it." He stepped out into the night with a look of weariness upon his handsome features.

Betsy stared after the door, deep in thought, feeling utter guilt for her behavior and feelings. How long before Nicholas decided to quit? He'd always done everything within his power to make her happy. Her recollections of his selfless giving and generosity pulled at her heartstrings. He deserved more than a child-bride brooding over pangs of homesickness. She wanted a marriage where both the husband and wife gave to the other, like she'd seen in her parents' relationship. But then she continued in her selfishness, brought down by black moods. When would it change? Why hadn't God answered her prayers?

In less than an hour, Nicholas carried in a yellowish brown, yapping puppy. Betsy laughed at the sight of him. "He needs to grow into his feet and ears," she giggled, taking him from Nicholas's arms. "What shall we call him?"

"You name him. He's your dog," he replied, scratching beneath the puppy's chin.

"Well, he kind of reminds me of Father's old yellow dog, Jasper. Do you remember him when we were children?"

"Sure do. He had the longest tongue of any dog I'd ever seen."

Betsy held him close. "Maybe I could call him Jasper. What do you think?" She glanced up into Nicholas's face and saw the fatigue creasing his brow and etching tiny lines under his eyes. "Oh, Nicholas. You do need to go to bed. You look so tired."

"First, let's get the puppy situated for the night."

"No, I will fix him a spot by the stove. You go on to bed." She smiled and shooed him on. "Go on now. I'll be there in a little bit."

Betsy waited until she heard his even breathing before snatching up the puppy. With one hand on the lantern, she headed to the barn. She remembered a wooden crate that would make a perfect bed for Jasper. It also gave her time to think.

She simply needed more things to keep her occupied. A garden needed planting—Nicholas had already worked the spot and purchased additional seeds to go with the tiny plants flourishing under his care. She loved flowers, and the lilac bush would be blooming in May, but she'd like more. Ella had plenty of peonies to share, and Mother had given her seeds for petunias and geraniums. A moment later, Betsy remembered one of Ella's daughters, Verna, wanted to learn embroidery. She could teach her. But most of all, she wanted to do more for Nicholas. And starting in the morning, she'd begin anew.

❧

The following morning when he stirred before dawn, Betsy lay still until he left. Every morning she stayed in bed until the very last minute before rising to prepare his breakfast, but not today.

Flinging back the covers, she hurried into the kitchen and added wood to the cookstove. Striking a match against the cast iron side, she lit some dry kindling. The flame rose and danced, slightly igniting the wood around it. A short while later, the nutty aroma of fresh coffee filled the kitchen.

While the coffee brewed, Betsy dressed and allowed her hair to cascade down her back. Nicholas liked it that way. She fed and petted Jasper, then poured her husband a steaming mug of coffee. Humming a tune, she opened the door to a still-darkened morning and cast her eyes in the direction of a flickering lantern where she knew Nicholas did his chores.

Stepping into the barn, she saw Nicholas bent beneath Bossy and heard the *swish swish* sound of his milking.

"Good morning," she called softly.

Startled, he glanced up. "Why Betsy, what are you doing out here?"

She knelt at his side and handed him the coffee. He smiled and it warmed her heart. "I thought you might enjoy this before breakfast."

"Thank you, sweetheart," he managed, taking the mug and abandoning his work. "You look beautiful. I thought you were an angel."

"No," she said softly. "Just your wife, but thank you for the compliment."

He reached for her hand, paused, then spoke. "You would tell me if you regretted marrying me, wouldn't you?"

She stifled a gasp. "You are my best friend, the one I've always told my dreams and secrets. You taught me how to fish and whistle, even when Mother said it was unladylike. Nicholas, you know me better than I know myself. How could I be discontent with such a wonderful man?"

He squeezed her hand gently but said nothing.

Longing to free herself of the awkwardness, she kissed his nose, then rose from the barn floor. "Now, Mr. Malone, you finish your chores so you can enjoy a long breakfast with your wife."

Outside, she lifted her head and inhaled deeply. She could do this, and she did care about Nicholas—in a brotherly way. He'd been her companion forever. Hopefully her answer had set his mind at ease, but a strange chill tormented her. He'd always understood her actions and words, and even saw through any lies or deception. Had he already guessed the truth? *Oh, Lord, help me. I'm so scared.*

She lived in anticipation that one day she might look outside her window and feel the tingly sensation of love just as Ella had. She had to believe it. No more melancholy or regrets, she'd simply concentrate on making Nicholas happy.

Out in the barn, Nicholas wanted to kick over the bucket of milk, punch the cow, and then for good measure set fire to the barn. What he'd feared for so long had just hit him in the bottom of his stomach. Pounding his fist into his hand, he fought the hurt and devastation whirling like a twister inside him.

Betsy didn't love him. He couldn't deny it any longer. They were simply childhood playmates who had grown up together and married out of convenience and a desire to please their parents—at least that's how she must surely view their wedded state.

Burning tears filled his eyes and he roughly brushed them away. Ever since he could remember, he'd loved Betsy with a fervor so strong that he failed to understand the depth of it. He'd done everything within his power and leaned on God's strength to make her life peaceful and happy. What he'd seen in her eyes and neglected to hear from her lips had stabbed him and wrenched out his heart.

Wondering if he should confront her or continue to ignore her lack of caring, Nicholas sought a place to kneel on the fresh hay. *Oh, heavenly Father, Creator of the universe, giver of love, I confess I am a sinful man, and I humbly ask You for guidance. Betsy is not a cruel woman. You know her heart, Lord. She wants to do all the right things, and I find no fault with her as my wife. She tries so hard. Look at how she just now brought me coffee. But I love her, and I know she doesn't feel the same. What am I supposed to do? Keep hoping and praying things will change. . .or send her back to Wisconsin?*

The idea of living without Betsy had not occurred to him before, and he paled at the thought of living without her. *Lord, I couldn't send her away! I'd rather she never love me than to be separated.*

Aren't I sufficient? came that still small voice.

Yes, Lord, You are my portion and my strength.

Don't you want her to be happy? Is love selfish?

You know I want the best for Betsy, but to live without her? The words of Psalm 34:8 raced across his mind: *Oh, taste and see that the Lord is good;*

blessed is the man that trusteth in him.

Nicholas blinked away the moisture filling his eyes. He'd obey. His wife had not been given to him as a pet, like he'd given her the puppy. She must choose to stay, or he must send her back to the family she loved. Struggling to regain his composure, he finished milking and made his way to the house for breakfast.

The wounds of rejection still churned inside him, fresh and bleeding. His whole life had been centered around God and Betsy. Now he'd seen the truth about his wife, and God wanted him to set her free.

Why had she consented to marry him if she felt nothing? Anger quelled the hurt, and he clenched his fists. Their marriage, their relationship meant nothing but a game to her. He felt like such a fool. How could she live a lie?

How long could he continue the masquerade?

He trudged up the hill and climbed the back porch steps, but surprisingly enough, the aroma of bacon and eggs greeted his nostrils. Betsy never cooked breakfast this early, and certainly nothing more than bread and jam from the night before. Startled, he entered the kitchen and eyed the table overflowing with butter, honey, biscuits, and oatmeal in addition to what had already tantalized his taste buds.

"Are you pleased?" Betsy asked, setting a skillet of bacon and eggs onto the table. Her face flushed from the heat of the stove, and she smiled sweetly.

Frustration settled upon him at the sight of the food. Was this supposed to soothe his hurt feelings? Jasper scampered beneath his feet, causing him to nearly trip and aggravating him even more. He could already see the dog was a mistake. She scooped up the puppy and placed him in a box near the cookstove.

"Nicholas?" she questioned, wringing her hands. "Is there something wrong?"

Avoiding her gaze, he clamped his jaw and brushed past her to refill his coffee. Nicholas didn't need her breakfast—or guilt sacrifice. "I'm not hungry," he grumbled. "I've got work to do."

"But. . .but you should eat."

He snatched up a strip of bacon and two biscuits on his way out. "This is enough," he muttered, slamming the door.

Strange, he ought to feel better not giving into her trickery—her "playing house" game, but instead a sick feeling swirled around in his stomach. He lifted his chin and looked up into the early morning sky breaking into shades of pink and orange. *Lord, she deserves to be shunned for what she's done.*

He walked into the barn and lifted the halter from the peg near the horses' stall. Usually he experienced a sense of joy in preparing to till the earth, but not today. A part of him wanted to turn and apologize for his rudeness, but the biggest part wanted to punish her for breaking his heart. He wanted her to feel the same gut-piercing pain.

Chapter 5

Bewildered, Betsy glared at the door. Her hand flew to her mouth as she shrunk into a chair. He knew the truth! What she'd dreaded for so long had happened. Any other time, he'd have been happy to see the spread of food so early in the morning. Instead he acted angry and couldn't wait to leave the house. How could she blame him? The realization had no doubt devastated him.

Liquid emotion spilled down her cheeks as she looked helplessly about her. Shame needled at her. Nicholas had seen through her attempt at portraying the perfect wife. Her gaze swept over the table. Steam rose and disappeared from the oatmeal and eggs, just like his dreams of their marriage.

Jasper yelped, seizing her attention. Through misty eyes, she held him to her bosom, clinging to the puppy as though the warm body could coax things right in her world. The longer she held him, the more tears welled up in her eyes. What a mess she'd made of her and Nicholas's life. She'd hurt the gentlest of all men.

Inhaling deeply, she searched for the words to pray. She still wanted to love him, but it might be too late. Betsy had a terrible thought that even if she ran after him shouting words of endearment, he wouldn't believe her. *God, I don't know how to fix this. I know You can. Help me, I beg of You.*

The morning dragged. She ironed and then checked on the tiny sprouting tomatoes and other vegetables growing in a corner of the kitchen. Sensing a warm spring day, she carried them outside to the rear of the house. Soon they'd mature enough to transplant outdoors. Yesterday the prospect sounded exciting, but not today.

Watching Jasper play sparked an occasional smile. The puppy barked at a family of sparrows and pulled at a stubborn weed.

She longed to see Ella and her family. The sight of her friend's smiling face and sparkling eyes always lifted her spirits. Ella's time fast approached, and in these last days before the new baby, she stayed close to home.

Betsy considered walking the three miles to the Barrett farm after delivering Nicholas's noon meal. Mother always said visiting with other folks helped a person forget their own problems. She also remembered her mother saying all anybody ever needed was the Lord. She spoke words of wisdom, even when Betsy didn't want to hear them. Remembering the verses from Ephesians tucked away in her Bible, Betsy called the Scripture to mind. *Now unto him that is able to do exceeding abundantly above all that we ask or think, according to the power that worketh in us, Unto him be glory in the church by Christ Jesus throughout all ages, world without end. Amen.*

As the morning wore on, she tried to focus on her relationship with God and not on the problems in her marriage. Each time she felt a fresh sprinkling of tears or shame creep across her mind, she prayed for answers. Begrudgingly she admitted she couldn't fix anything in her life; only God could do those things. In short, Betsy Malone needed a touch from the Father.

When the sun peaked high in the sky, she toted Nicholas's lunch in a wooden pail toward a far field. She'd covered it with a red checkered cloth and packed plenty of food, knowing he'd be hungry. Hopefully he had calmed down a bit. Maybe today, she'd see him and feel that peculiar twinge of love that Ella spoke about.

Jasper trailed after her, running and scampering about, exploring his new world. He chased a butterfly and scared up a rabbit. His antics made her laugh, and for a brief moment she forgot the earlier unpleasantness.

In the distance Betsy spied Nicholas driving the horse and plow toward her and she waved. She remembered tomorrow he wanted to plant the last of the corn. He lifted his head, but instantly cast his gaze back to the ground. Nibbling at her lip and wearing a shaky smile, she sauntered his way.

"I'll be at the creek bank when you're ready," she managed.

"All right," he muttered and continued down to the end of the row.

Without glancing behind her, Betsy headed in the direction of their familiar picnic spot. Setting down the lunch pail, she walked to the water's edge and listened to it gurgle over and around the rocks. It sounded so peaceful, not at all like the turmoil raging inside her. Nicholas's shadow fell across the water, and with a deep breath she turned to face him.

"You don't have to stay and eat with me," he said impassively.

Her heart pounded against her chest. "I'd like to, if you don't mind."

"I'm not in a good mood."

"I can see that. . .I'm sorry."

He lifted a brow and frowned. "Sorry about what?"

She swallowed hard. "For upsetting you."

"Who said you did?"

She stared into his clear blue eyes, dark and forbidding. "I don't want to play games, Nicholas."

"And who are you to accuse me of such nonsense?" he shouted, his voice echoing about them.

She trembled, not recognizing the stranger before her. "I want us to work this out and go on with our lives," she said.

"Why don't you tell me what we need to work out?"

"Our differences—the things separating us," she replied. "Can we sit down and talk about it?"

He chuckled sardonically. "And what exactly is our problem?"

Betsy knew she neared tears. This was her fault, and now she'd damaged their marriage, possibly beyond repair. "I'm not a good wife," she whispered.

"And why is that?" he demanded.

Lifting watery eyes to meet his gaze, she silently pleaded for understanding. Angry eyes met hers.

"Betsy, answer me."

She felt so ashamed. "I don't love you as I should."

"Oh?" he questioned harshly. "When did you come to this conclusion?"

Silence.

"When?"

"While planning our wedding day."

Nicholas still stood on the hill of the creek, glaring down at her like a furious giant. "Did you think I'd never find out? Am I stupid?"

She shook her head and wrung her hands. "I didn't want to hurt you."

He pointed to his heart. "And what do you call this?

"I'm sorry," she mumbled. "I've been praying. . . ."

"Praying? For what, that I'd never find out?"

Regret squeezed from her eyes. "No, Nicholas, for God. . . ."

"I've heard enough," he interrupted. "I think you should go on back to the house while I decide what's best."

She wanted to argue and tell him that they needed to talk right then— pray about the problem together, but instead she acquiesced to his request. Sensing his wrath would not dissipate in a moment's time, she nodded and climbed the hill, brushing past him on the path home.

Too shaken to cry, Betsy concentrated on Nicholas's final statement. She spun on her heels and saw his back. Obviously he was too provoked to watch her leave. With reluctant steps, she plodded on toward the house. Jasper yapped at her heels, causing her to remember when as a child, she'd trailed after Nicholas, begging to tag along no matter what he had planned to do.

Those days were gone. She could no longer invite the frivolous antics of a child or the impetuous temperament of a young girl. She must commit to the responsibilities of a wife, if she still had that role.

Betsy dreaded the afternoon, realizing it would be dark before Nicholas returned from the fields. She had to find something to occupy the empty hours. Perhaps visiting Ella would help, but she didn't dare confess her failing marriage. No one need know her misery.

Chewing on her lip, she glanced up into a cloudless sky. *Oh, Lord, I've made such a mess of things. Help me. I don't know what to do.*

🌿

Once he finished with his noon meal, Nicholas stuffed the checkered cloth into the wooden pail. He leaned back on the soft grass and clasped his hands behind his neck. The food sat heavily on his stomach just like the weight on his mind. He really should get back to work, but he had no desire to do so. The farm, his life, held no meaning without Betsy. He never should have brought her to Ohio. At least in Wisconsin she had her family to give her some sort of meaning to her loveless marriage. She would have been happy and content there.

His heart ached with the acknowledgment. *Betsy didn't love him.* Before he'd suspected it; now he'd heard it from her own lips. A tear trickled down his cheek. He shouldn't have been so harsh. Perhaps talking about it might bring about an end to it all—and get it over with.

For the next hour, Nicholas closed his eyes and fought the memories of Betsy plaguing his mind, from the time she was a little girl of six and he a boy of nine. He'd watched her grow into a woman. His Betsy. His love. His wife.

If he really loved her, he would send her back to Wisconsin.

Finally rising to his feet, he shuffled back to the fields, feeling too miserable to pray.

Midafternoon, Betsy decided she'd visit Ella after all. Anything had to be better than watching for Nicholas or crying. She washed her face, hoping her swollen eyes and blotchy skin didn't give away her anguish.

Leaving Jasper at home, she treaded down the road toward the Barrett farm. Just the sight of the farmhouse lifted her spirits. One of the younger boys spied her and raced her way.

"Hallo, Miz Malone. How do you like the puppy?" Boyd asked, a red-haired, freckle-faced boy with a toothless grin.

"Just fine. He wanted his mama pretty bad last night, but he'll be fine."

The boy frowned. "Papa said he'd do fine."

"Oh, he will. It takes time for him to get adjusted to his new home." *Just like me,* she thought sadly.

He nodded, apparently satisfied with her reply. "What did you name him?"

"Jasper."

He paused a moment. "That's a good name."

By now they were nearing the house. "How's your mama feeling?"

"All right, as far as I know. She's been doing all kinds of things today—washing, baking pies, and planting the garden."

Betsy smiled and ruffled his hair. "Guess she'll keep me busy while we visit."

She found Ella taking down clothes with little Audrey hanging onto her skirt. Betsy immediately began helping her. "Don't you think you should be resting?" she asked.

"Not when I don't feel like it," Ella replied with a smile. "This baby isn't ready to come, and I'm not slowing down a bit until I have to." She glanced at Betsy and frowned. "What's the matter?"

"Why, nothing."

"Nonsense. Your eyes are red and you're pale." Still staring, she waited for Betsy to reply.

Swallowing another onslaught of emotion, she shook her head in denial.

"You and Nicholas have a spat?"

Betsy reluctantly nodded, losing the battle against tears. "I didn't really come here to burden you with my troubles."

Ella smiled and placed a hand on her rounded stomach. "That's not what the Bible says. We're supposed to share in each other's problems. Now, I might not be able to help, but I sure can listen. Let's take a little walk and tell me what happened."

In the next several minutes, Betsy explained it all, even confessing her lack of affection for Nicholas. "I've prayed, but nothing's changed."

"And he found this out today?"

Betsy fought the tears. "Well, I think he suspected it before."

"And what are you willing to do about it?"

Ella's question stunned her. "I don't understand. I mean. . .I intend to keep the promises I made to God when we married."

"What about honesty between you and Nicholas?"

"You mean talking about it, instead of covering it up?"

Ella nodded. "Remember the truth sets you free."

Betsy sighed. "I tried today, but he's pretty angry."

"Most likely more hurt than anything. A man has an awful lot of pride and Nicholas's has been crushed. But he seems to be a sensible, God-fearing man. Give him a little time to sort things out."

"I hope you're right." She hesitated and looked beyond Ella to the older girls taking down the remainder of the laundry and the younger ones playing. "I wonder if a child would make things right," she said wistfully.

Ella studied her and tilted her head. "Babies are a miracle—they don't cause them. Only God does that."

Betsy sighed deeply, feeling her eyes moisten. She blinked back the tears, not wanting her friend to see any more weeping.

"Are you expecting?" Ella asked softly, compassion lacing her words.

Betsy could only nod. "It's been over two months, but I don't want to tell him when he's already upset."

"How do you feel about a baby?"

"I don't know for sure," she honestly replied. "I'm a little frightened, and I don't know what Nicholas will say about it."

Ella's hand slipped into hers. "I think this is a matter for the Lord. Let's take a moment and ask Him to direct you and your husband." When Betsy silently agreed, Ella began. "Oh heavenly Father, You know all things and You know us better than we know ourselves. Betsy and Nicholas need a touch from You to restore their marriage and have their relationship glorify You. Oh, Father, You are love, and You bestow it lavishly upon us. Help them to find joy in You and in each other. Thank You for the gift of this precious child, and give Betsy wisdom in telling Nicholas about the baby. In Jesus' name, Amen."

"Thank you," Betsy whispered, reaching to give her friend a hug.

"You're welcome." Ella smiled. "How about a cup of coffee and a piece of sugar cake? Belle just made it this afternoon and it smells delicious."

The two wrapped their arms around each other's waists and strolled across the yard past the children and on to the house.

For the first time, Betsy felt a little better, but how would she ever tell Nicholas about the baby?

He might decide he didn't want either of them.

Chapter 6

Nicholas finished the milking and glanced around the barn for more chores. He'd purposely dawdled, finding all sorts of things to do rather than head to the house. With a heavy sigh, he shut and latched the barn door. Leaning his back against it, he prayed for strength and control. He watched the smoke curl up the chimney of the house and disappear into the shadowed sky—a sight that usually warmed his spirit. And normally the lantern glowing from the kitchen looked cozy and inviting, but not tonight. Distrust and heartbreaking conclusions lay behind those doors.

He still radiated anger—hot, intense, and dangerously quiet. Peering up at the starless sky, he remembered his earlier resolve. He had a job to do, and he'd best tell Betsy his decision tonight.

The closer he walked to the door, the harder it was to put one foot in front of the other. He wanted her to think he didn't care about her rejection, but he feared his heavy heart would shatter into irreparable pieces.

Smelling his favorite meal of chicken and dumplings furthered his resentment. He didn't want special food or a neat, clean house. What he craved rested in what Betsy couldn't give. His large hand turned the knob on the door, and he stepped inside, avoiding the one he loved more than anyone else on earth.

Refusing to meet her gaze, he headed directly to the water-filled basin and washed up. All the while, her puppy played at his heels.

"I have your supper ready," Betsy said barely above a whisper, reaching down to gather up Jasper. "I'm sorry he worries you so." She placed him in a box near the stove before setting the pot of chicken and dumplings on the table.

She sat across from him with her hands clasped firmly in her lap. He ladled the steamy food into his plate and immediately scooped up a mouthful, burning his tongue.

"Nicholas, aren't you going to ask the blessing?"

He felt a twinge of guilt. "No," he replied.

Lowering her head, she closed her eyes for a few moments. For the first time, he stole a look at her. Her face pale and splotchy, he saw she'd been crying for quite a while. When she opened her eyes, he saw they were red and swollen. Hastily he looked away and forked another dumpling and bite of chicken. Betsy wouldn't get any sympathy from him.

She didn't eat, but he ignored her empty plate.

"Nicholas, can we talk?" she finally asked.

Finished with the hearty meal, he pushed back his plate. "I believe so."

Betsy sighed. "Can we pray first?"

He hadn't talked to God since that morning in the barn. Why start now? "That's not necessary," he grumbled, finding the courage to stare into her face.

She drew in a deep breath. "May I?"

Leaning back on the chair, he thought she didn't look very well at all. Good. She deserved a miserable day. "Go ahead, if it makes you feel any better."

Her lips quivered as she lowered her head and folded her hands. "Dear Lord, I've hurt my husband badly today."

"Betsy, please," he interrupted.

She continued praying. "But I want to work this out. It can't be done, unless You touch our hearts with love and understanding. Give us wisdom and patience in dealing with the problems between us. In Jesus' name, Amen."

He rubbed his whiskered jaw. "Before you say anything, I'd like for you to hear me out."

"All right," she replied, her hands still primly folded.

"I've thought all day about us and how you don't have feelings for me." He hesitated, fearing if she broke into sobs he'd be tempted to take her into his arms. Lifting his coffee cup to his lips, he maintained his stand. "Because of all this, I'm riding into Crestline first thing in the morning and purchasing a ticket for you—back to Wisconsin."

Her face blanched and the dreaded tears rolled swiftly down her cheeks. "I don't think that would solve anything," she said, dabbing her eyes with her apron.

"Yes, it does," he replied with a determined shake of his head. "You don't love me, so there's no reason for you to live here as my wife. You just go on home and carry on your life as though we were never married."

"No, please, Nicholas!" she protested. "We made a promise to God. . ."

"You lied!" He pounded the table with his fist. Startled, she rose from her chair and hurried to the door. "Where are you going?" he demanded.

"Outside," she managed. "I'm. . .I'm sick."

Nicholas paced the floor until she returned. He said nothing while she bathed her face but stood and watched her try to calm down. Knowing Betsy, she'd be upset for hours, and he didn't want to see or hear it.

"Are you in control of yourself now?" he demanded.

Her eyes looked incredibly green, and their haunting gaze bore into his—accusing, hurtful. "Yes," she whispered.

"Now, I don't want to hear you sniffling about." Never had he been so harsh with her, but he couldn't stop himself. If he stopped for one minute, he'd be apologizing for his cruelty.

"I'll be quiet."

"And put that dog in the barn. I don't want him yapping all night again."

"I will."

With her reply, he stepped outside to get a breath of fresh air. Seating himself on the porch step, he took a ragged breath. There, he'd done it.

He'd been mean and hateful so she'd think he no longer cared for her. After purchasing the train ticket tomorrow, she'd be on her way home. Guess he'd been pretty stupid right from the start.

A little girl's voice echoed in his mind. She was nine years old, and she'd just flung her arms around his neck when he consented to let her tag along to the fishing hole. "Oh, Nicholas, I'll always love you. You're better than a big brother 'cause you make me so happy."

I'm a fool, he told himself, *time to grow up and act like a man.*

Setting the teakettle on to boil water for dishes, Betsy felt her emotions vacillate from raw and bleeding to numb. She'd never imagined Nicholas would send her away—back to Wisconsin. As badly as she missed her old home, she detested the thought of returning there without him. Her parents, his parents. . .they'd be utterly disappointed. Now, even more shame settled upon her.

Lord, this isn't what I prayed for, she lamented. Her hand instantly covered her mouth to swallow the sobs threatening to escape. *I wanted You to show me how to love him, not drive me away from him! This can't be happening. Oh, Lord, please work this out.*

She cleared the table, waiting for the kettle to sing, waiting for Nicholas to come back inside, and waiting for God to answer her prayers. Only the water began to boil.

Much later she lifted Jasper into her arms for the trek to the barn. Nicholas had still not come inside, and she fretted over his state of mind. Only when his pony died one cold winter had she seen such fathomless despair. Passing through the parlor, shadows from her lantern lit up faint features of the painting above the fireplace. He'd never explained it to her. How, in nearly three months of marriage, had they not talked of his parents' home? Would he now? She doubted it, but perhaps it might help to discuss something other than their own private grief and disappointment.

The door creaked open, and she saw the outline of her husband standing in the grassy area between the house and barn. "Jasper, please be quiet," she whispered to the puppy. She had no reason to believe her husband would honor her request, but she had to try.

Upon the door opening, he walked in the opposite direction. "Nicholas," she called lightly.

Stopping, but not turning toward her, he replied simply, "Yes."

"Would you tell me the story of the painting?" She held her breath and nervously stroked the puppy, waiting for his answer.

"My mother can tell you when you get home."

"I'd hoped you'd tell me about it." Silence met her, as heavy as the blanket of black around them. "Please."

"It doesn't matter anymore," he claimed, jamming his hands inside his overall pockets.

"All right," she replied, resigned to the devastation of him sending her away. "I'm taking Jasper to the barn. If you change your mind, I'll be right back."

In the short time it took to settle in the puppy, Nicholas had already disappeared inside the house and gone to bed. He neither spoke nor moved when she joined him on the other side.

After a silent breakfast the following morning, Nicholas saddled up the dappled mare and rode off.

What do I do now? Betsy asked God, glancing up into the heavens. Looking about her she marveled at the beauty of life unfolding around her. Birds were pouring out their praises, and plants craned and arched their necks to get closer to the Creator. *How did Mother handle distress?*

Sitting on the front porch rocker, she deliberated those times at the Wingert household when the world cast them into ill fortune. *Mother and Father prayed,* she remembered. *Father read his Bible, and Mother busied herself and sang.* Retrieving her Bible, she elected to do the same.

Betsy prayed, then read through the book of Ephesians, her mother's favorite epistle. She dwelled a moment on chapter four, verse twenty-six and felt totally self-righteous about Nicholas's treatment of her. *Be ye angry, and sin not; let not the sun go down upon your wrath.* Then she read in chapter six how Nicholas had loved her exactly as God instructed, and she experienced true chastisement. Odd, Mother had told her those things, but she never knew they were a commandment of God. *Oh, Father, forgive me,* she prayed. *If given another chance, I'll put You first in my marriage and follow Your ways with Nicholas. I'll learn to love him. . . .* Whether or not her husband changed his mind, she meant to live every day for the Lord.

Nicholas lingered outside the train station for more than thirty minutes before he gained enough daring to step inside. Purchasing Betsy's ticket didn't sit well with him at all. But how could he continue living with a woman who admittedly shared no love for him, at least not the kind a wife should feel for her husband?

Things could change, he told himself. *She could grow to care for me. Ours wouldn't be the first marriage that started out this way.* Except he never thought about those circumstances for himself. Clenching his jaw, he stepped into the train station and bought the ticket.

Moments later, he walked back into the sunlight. "Hey, Nicholas," a familiar voice called.

Recognizing Willy, he waved and watched his neighbor cross the street to meet him. "Guess we're letting a good morning of work go by," his neighbor said with a lopsided grin.

"Suppose so," Nicholas replied, extending his hand to greet him.

Willy grasped it firmly. "Is something wrong? You look rather haggard."

He lifted his dusty hat and combed his fingers through his hair. "Oh, nothing to concern you about, just a few personal matters."

"I see," Willy said, his dark eyes studying Nicholas. "What brings you to town?"

"Oh, I needed to get something for Betsy," he replied with a sigh.

"At the train station?"

Nicholas sighed. "Yeah. . .I purchased a ticket back to Wisconsin for her."

Willy raised a brow and eyed him curiously. "Awfully soon to go sending her for a visit, isn't it? I mean with summer coming—the garden and the like. I'd think you'd wait till fall. Course it's none of my business."

He felt a tremendous need to tell Willy everything. This godly man, his neighbor and friend, might give him insight into his miserable problem. "I don't know what to do about Betsy," he finally blurted out.

"Would you like to get a cup of coffee and talk?"

Nicholas hesitated, then nodded. "Might as well. Don't feel much like ridin' home."

A couple hours later, he rode his horse beside Willy's wagon en route to their farms. The horses ambled on with Nicholas deep in thought. So far, his friend had only lent an ear—sometimes asking a question, but mostly listening.

"I hope I've done the right thing," Nicholas said, giving a heavy sigh.

"And you've already gotten the ticket?"

"Yeah, it's in my hip pocket."

"Nicholas, have you prayed about this?"

He shifted uneasily in the saddle. "Not since she confessed yesterday morning."

"Supposin' God wanted her to tell you the truth. Have you considered that for the first time since you were married, Betsy was honest? She could have lied, and you'd never have known the difference. What I'm saying is God brought you two together, and He wants you to stay together."

"Maybe so," Nicholas said. "But why would God have me choose a woman who didn't love me?"

Willy shook his head, then spoke softly. "We don't know God's plans and what He has in mind for us. What do you say we stop right here and pray?"

"Aw, you go right ahead. I'm not interested. Doesn't matter anyhow."

Willy pulled in the reins on his pair of horses and lowered his head. "Lord, we've got a big problem here with Nicholas and Betsy's marriage. He's hurting 'cause he loves her and wants her to feel the same. If he's not supposed to send her back to Wisconsin, would You kindly make it real clear to him? Thank You, Lord, for all Your many blessings. In Jesus' name, Amen."

Nicholas felt close to tears, and it embarrassed him. Hastily blinking them back, he chose to stare down the road. "Thanks," he mumbled. "I should be praying, but the words won't come."

"The Lord understands our hearts, and I'll be talking more to Him about you as the day goes on."

Nicholas nodded. "Appreciate it." Up ahead he could see the outline of his house and barn. Any other time, the sight would fill him with pride and anticipation of his dreams for him and Betsy. Now the thought of the days and weeks ahead without her grieved him. But he'd get used to it. Wouldn't he?

Chapter 7

Betsy watched the sun directly overhead and noted her growling stomach. She hadn't intended to be gone for so long, but the urge to walk and pray kept her away from home much longer than she expected. Most likely Nicholas would want his noon meal, and she wasn't there to prepare it. She'd left him a note explaining her desire to go for a walk.

She smiled and patted her stomach. Strange—but such a blessing, how spending a few hours with the Lord could fill her with such peace. . .and excitement for the new life growing inside her. She felt certain the problems between her and Nicholas would work out. Wonderfully contended, she hummed the hymn "Blessed Assurance."

I must not forget this glorious time with the Lord, she told herself. *I may need to remind myself of it later.* Shaking her head as though to dispel any unpleasant thoughts, she lifted her gaze to the cottony sky and sang. "This is my story, this is my song, praising my Savior all the day long."

Jasper barked, and she laughed. Surely a lovely morning like this meant Nicholas had changed his mind and wouldn't send her away.

By the time Betsy returned to the house, Nicholas had been there and gone. No doubt he'd hurried on to the fields, and she'd missed him on her way back. Glancing about the kitchen, she saw the remains of a ham sandwich, cold fried potatoes, and crumbs from a piece of chocolate cake. Her note had been moved, but he hadn't added anything to it. A big part of her wished he'd written something.

Rolling up the sleeves to her dress, she pulled out flour, salt, and yeast to make bread. Nicholas loved hot, fresh rolls, and she planned to churn butter as soon as the bread started to rise. While on her walk, she'd picked some fresh dandelion greens to add to the night's supper of pork chops and creamed corn. She prayed for a softening of his heart and the courage to tell him about the baby.

That evening when she heard the cow bells signaling time for the milking, she poured a dipper of cold water into a jar and walked it out to Nicholas. Nervous and trembling, she left Jasper inside the house so the puppy wouldn't get underfoot.

His back to her, he leaned into Prudence's side, and she heard the familiar *ping ping* hit the pail. "Good evening," she greeted, hoping her voice sounded more confident than she truly felt. "Thought you might enjoy a cool drink of water."

"Thank you. Just set it on that bail of hay," he said, without so much as a nod her way.

Setting it where he directed, Betsy drew a deep breath. "Mind if I stay? Supper is nearly done."

He sighed. "I'm not much company."

"Yes, you are. Even if you aren't in the mood to talk, I'd rather be here than alone in the house." And she sincerely meant it.

He stopped milking but still didn't give her any eye contact. "Don't say things you don't mean, Betsy," he muttered.

"I said exactly how I felt," she said. "And I'd like to talk after we eat. I have some things to say."

"All right," he replied, resuming milking the cow.

"Will you tell me about the painting tonight?" she hesitantly asked.

He paused for several long moments. "Guess it wouldn't hurt."

Betsy sat there beside him in silence until he completed the milking. Their dinner was finished except for putting it on the table, and she could do that while he washed up. All the while, her mind whirled, wondering how she'd tell him about the baby—and if it would make a difference in his wanting to send her back to Wisconsin.

At supper they ate without conversation until she elected to tell him about her walk, making certain she revealed all the fascinating little areas about the farm. She'd discovered marsh marigolds blooming above one of the springs and purple violets near the woods. While picking dandelion greens, she'd noted some large yellow blooms but discovered they were newly hatched baby chickens. Since they didn't own any chickens, she wondered where the hen belonged. Although Nicholas failed to respond, her chatter filled the quiet, empty moments.

Standing, Nicholas pulled something from his rear pocket and laid it on the table beside her. Instantly she recognized the train ticket. "I bought this today, just as I said I would. It's for the day after tomorrow, so you'll have time to pack your things."

She held her breath in horror. *Help me, Lord. Give me the right words to change his mind.* "Isn't it rather soon?" she asked, fighting the trepidation wreaking havoc through her body.

"No, considering the circumstances." He grasped his coffee cup and took a large gulp before continuing. "I want you to be happy, Betsy, and you aren't with me."

She wet her lips. "I don't want to go home. I belong here."

He lifted his chin and tightened his jaw. "It's settled. You can tell your folks, my folks, anything you like."

"That's not the point," she gently argued. "I made a commitment to be your wife—"

"And I'm releasing you of it."

Understanding their words weren't going anywhere, she prayed for a different topic and then struck upon an idea. "Would you tell me about the painting now?"

His ragged breath gave away his sentiments. "I suppose you will bother me until I do." He scooted his chair across the kitchen floor, scraping it along the way. "Let's go into the parlor and get this over with." He snatched up the lantern and carried it into the room.

Obediently she followed and carried her chair, but he chose to stand beside the fireplace. "Laurelwood is not a painting of my parents' home," he began. "It's of my grandmother's childhood home in Pennsylvania." He pointed to an apple tree. "You can see the landscaping is different from the one in Wisconsin. My grandparents moved there from Pennsylvania right after they married.

"Grandpa owned a lumber mill and worked so many long hours that my grandmother thought he didn't care about her. One day, she became so angry about him being gone so much that he promptly ushered her into a carriage and drove her to the home he'd just completed. It was identical to the one she'd left behind, and it was the real reason he'd spent time away from her." He shifted uncomfortably. "My father and I were born there, married there too."

"What a beautiful story," Betsy whispered. "So your grandparents had problems starting out in their marriage, too?"

He flashed her an angry scowl. "It's not the same."

"But still," she insisted. "They stayed together and worked it out."

"I'm not my grandfather, and you aren't my grandmother."

His words stung, but she knew he felt betrayed—and rightfully so. "I want to stay with you, Nicholas. I believe God will bless our marriage."

"I've given up on God," he fairly shouted, then his voice quieted. "I'm sorry to raise my voice. It's settled. Day after tomorrow you will board the train in Crestline and head back to Wisconsin." He walked toward the door.

"Wait," she urged. "Can we talk a little more? I have something important to tell you."

His shoulders slumped, and she felt like the most detestable creature God ever created. Without turning, he replied. "Tell me now. I have things to do."

Taking a deep breath and wetting her lips, she began. "I have wronged you terribly, Nicholas, and hurt you so deeply. Even now you can't look at me. It's my fault, and there is nothing I can do but beg your for-giveness. If you really want me to leave here after I finish, then I will go and not argue. But please understand this, I don't want to live anywhere except with you." She sighed and willed her queasy stomach to stop churning.

"I'm not sure what love is. You and I have been together since we were children. No one else has ever mattered or meant anything to me, but you.

You were my big brother, my hero, my teacher, and my husband. I may not know or comprehend exactly how I'm supposed to react as your wife, but we do have another reason to stay together."

He slowly turned to face her, frustration clearly written across his handsome features. "What's that?"

Someone pounded hard on the door, startling both of them. "Mr. Malone, Mrs. Malone, please open the door."

Nicholas flung it open wide to see Ed Barrett, Willy and Ella's eldest son, standing before them. He'd been running, and his efforts to talk were futile between his pants for air.

"Slow down, boy," Nicholas urged, grasping him gently by the shoulders. "What's wrong? Somebody hurt?"

Ed took a few deep breaths. "It's Mama," he finally said. "She's having the baby early. Pa went to get Mrs. Lanefield, the midwife, and sent me after you, Mrs. Malone. Can you come and help?"

"Of course," she replied and glanced hastily at Nicholas. "Would you come, too?"

He nodded. "Yes, I can keep the other children busy."

"I'm going back home," Ed announced, seemingly in more control.

"Wait, I'll get the buckboard," Nicholas said.

"No, I can run faster than it would take you to hitch it up." With those words, the boy took off in the shadows of night.

Betsy rose and touched Nicholas's arm. "Please, just saddle up the mare. We can ride together, and it'll be faster."

For the first time, he met her gaze. She saw the pained look in his blue eyes, the torment she'd caused. Instantly he looked the other way. "All right then, let's go."

The Barrett home looked quiet and peaceful when they arrived, but the moment Nicholas tied the mare to a post, Ed rushed to meet them.

"Thanks for coming," he breathed. "Papa's not back yet. Belle and Verna are with Mama, and Marie is tending to the others."

Betsy gave him a reassuring smile. She felt frightened and knew nothing about birthing a baby, unless Ella could talk her through it. Glancing up at Nicholas, she saw a worried frown pass over his face. "I'm going to her," she whispered, and he reached out and touched her hand.

"You'll be fine." For the first time since her early morning confession in the barn, he nodded encouragingly and revealed a glimpse of the Nicholas she knew. . .and loved.

She shook with the realization, except this wasn't the time or the place to tell him. "Pray for Ella," she said, passing through the door.

Verna directed Betsy to her mother's side where Belle dabbed the perspiration from Ella's forehead. At the sight of Betsy, the girl smiled weakly.

Betsy returned the gesture, but her gaze quickly rested upon her friend's face, pale and drawn. "I'll take over now," she whispered to Belle. "I'm sure your papa and Mrs. Lanefield will be here soon. Everything is going to be just fine."

The young girl kissed her mother's forehead, whisked away an errant tear, and disappeared. As soon as the door closed, Betsy took Ella's hand as she attempted to speak through a shallow breath. "This baby is coming fast, and it's much too soon."

Wetting her lips, Betsy vowed to stay calm and not reveal her fright. "Tell me what to do," she managed.

"Get the girls to boil water and fetch my sewing basket—oh," she moaned. "The pains are getting closer." Holding her breath, she squeezed Betsy's hand until the contraction subsided. "I'm glad you're with me."

"Does that mean the midwife might not arrive before the baby? I've never helped give birth before." Betsy felt herself shaking.

Ella smiled feebly. "I'll do all the work. You just follow my instructions. Giving birth is an opportunity to see one of God's special miracles." She squeezed Betsy's hand, perspiration beading on her forehead. When the contraction was over, Ella closed her eyes. "Are you ready for my ninth child?" she asked. Gripping Betsy's hand again, a faint groan escaped her lips. "Pray for my baby," she whispered.

"I will, I am," Betsy replied, wiping her damp brow.

"The girls. . ."

She nodded and turned to the door. "Belle, I need one of you girls to bring me your sewing basket—now!"

Within ten minutes, a tiny voice hailed his coming into the world.

"He's small," Ella whispered, crying, cradling the baby boy in her arms. "Dear God, he's much too small."

Chapter 8

"He's beautiful," Betsy soothed. Her ears perked at the sound of voices. "Willy and Mrs. Lanefield are here."

Ella glanced up through watery blue eyes. "Dear God, I'm afraid our little boy won't live. Betsy, get Willy for me, please."

A plump, matronly lady stole into the room with the most angelic smile that Betsy had ever seen. "Why, Ella, you've gone and had this baby without me."

"But he's too little," she cried. "Please, I've got to see Willy."

"Sure, honey." And she motioned to Betsy. "Let me look him over, Ella, clean him up. Goodness, he's got a good set of lungs."

Betsy found Willy and the children outside on the front porch, some talking, others silent in the lantern light, but they'd all heard the baby's cries and brimmed with excitement. Her gaze immediately went to Nicholas and silently pleaded for help. Smiling, she moved to Willy seated on the porch swing and kneeled in front of him. "Ella wants to see you," she whispered.

He fairly beamed. "The baby?"

"It's a boy," Betsy replied, then lowered her voice. "Willy, he's very small, and she's frightened. Please go to her, she needs you."

Immediately he stood, and his eyes clouded over. A worried frown replaced the laugh lines. "He was early," he reiterated.

"But Mrs. Lanefield says his lungs are good, and he certainly looks fine to me." She felt Nicholas's strong arms around her shoulders.

"You go on in," he urged. "Me and Betsy will have this group praying."

Willy nodded and stepped inside. Nicholas summoned the children's attention. "We need to pray for your mama and your new baby brother."

"Praise God," Ed said, with his father's same lopsided grin. "Now we've got another brother to help even the odds."

"That's wonderful," Nicholas continued and chuckled despite the grim circumstances. "But the baby is very small. We need to ask God to make him strong and healthy."

Instantly quietness fell, reminding Betsy of the dreadful stillness she'd experienced in the house when she realized Nicholas wanted to send her away. She didn't want the children to feel helpless; they needed the peace of God.

"Let's gather in a circle and hold hands," she suggested.

In moments, Nicholas stood with Betsy across from him and children on both sides. "I'm going to start praying," he said. "When I've finished, each one of you will have an opportunity to say something. Let's bow our heads and go to the Lord in prayer. Heavenly Father, we come to You right now thanking You for the gift of this new baby. We're real concerned, Lord, 'cause he came early and he's very little. We pray You'll place Your healing hand on him, making him strong and healthy. His mama is upset and she needs to hear from You that everything will be fine. Give her peace and courage in this time of trouble." He paused and waited for one of the children to begin.

"Help me to be a good big brother and help Papa more," Ed said.

"And Lord, I would really like to help Mama with this baby like I did with little Audrey," Belle added.

"And if you'll make this baby healthy, I won't ever grumble again about taking care of the younger ones," Marie vowed.

"I won't be pestering the others so much," Herbert promised.

A sob escaped from Verna. "I won't try to get out of helping with my chores."

Betsy took a deep breath. "Lord, you know the desires of my heart. I haven't served You as well as I should, but I want to be a better neighbor and not just lean on Ella. Please help the baby grow strong in health and in You." She paused. "And help me be the kind of wife that Nicholas deserves."

She wanted to raise her eyes to see if he responded, but in the dark, she wouldn't be able to see him.

"I'll share my mud pies with the new baby," Laura said softly.

Audrey and Boyd uttered a "please, Jesus" before Nicholas spoke a hearty "Amen." They raised their heads to find Willy observing them from the doorway.

"Mrs. Lanefield says he's strong and healthy," he called with a smile. "That was the sweetest prayer this side of heaven." With a deep sigh he walked toward them. "And it makes me proud of my family and my neighbors." Glancing about, he hugged his children. "Want to know what we've named him?"

"Yes," the children shouted.

"John," he stated. "Like the youngest of our Lord's disciples."

"Fine name," Nicholas complimented.

"Thanks, that's how we feel."

Shortly thereafter Mrs. Lanefield called from the doorway. "Here he is. Got him clean and wrapped up nice. Would you children like to take a peek?" She handed the tiny bundle to Willy, and the others took turns ooing and ahhing. Finally, he handed baby John to Nicholas. "Here, you two can have him for just a minute while we check on Ella. She said Betsy did a wonderful job during the birthing. I thank you, Betsy. We both are grateful for what you and Nicholas have done here tonight." Willy and his children filed into the house like an army on a mission, and Betsy laughed softly.

Nicholas sat in the porch swing and held the baby a bit awkwardly.

Betsy took a deep breath. "Isn't he beautiful?" she whispered, sitting down beside him.

"Yeah, a new little one sure is a blessing."

"Ella called them miracles."

"That, too." He hesitated, then looked into her face. "I've been thinking tonight, Betsy, about the painting and us. Well, as you said, my grandparents had it hard in the beginning—starting out in a strange place—but they ended up with a wonderful marriage. I know I already have the train ticket, but. . .but if you'd rather stay a little longer. . .well, I'd appreciate it. I don't really think God wants us apart."

Her eyes swelled with the liquid emotion filling her soul. "Oh, thank you, Nicholas. I don't want to leave you."

He cleared his throat. "I didn't treat you very good these last few days. I've asked God to forgive me for turning my back on Him, and now I'm asking if you will forgive me for being so cruel."

"But, I hurt you—deceived you," she insisted.

"That's no excuse for a man to act as I did toward the woman he loves. I think, Betsy. . ." He looked down at the baby, before glancing back at her. In the dim light, she could see a tear slip down his face, and she gently wiped it away with her finger. "I think I'd rather have you with me, even if you don't share in the same feelings, than live without you."

She tilted her head and swallowed hard. "I realized something tonight, too. Ever since I can remember, you've always been there for me—patching up my scrapes and bruises, playing house, listening to my girlish dreams, and most importantly loving me. You've been patient and kind, even when I acted horribly." She grasped his hand holding onto the baby blanket. "That's like God. All this time, you've loved me without asking anything in return. I took you for granted, just as I have our heavenly Father. Guess I just thought you'd always be there. Then, at the thought of losing you completely, I panicked. Facing the future without you caused me to see how much I really do love you—and always have. Please forgive me, Nicholas, for being such a child and not treasuring all the wonderful things you've done for me."

"Do you mean it?" he asked quietly, staring into her face.

"Oh, yes," she replied. Feeling a bit shy, she leaned over and brushed a kiss across his lips. "Nicholas Malone, I love you." She sat back on the swing and viewed the serene portrait he painted with the sleeping baby in his arms. A sweet little twinge danced across the bottom of her stomach, and she remembered Ella's words. "Oh, Nicholas, I want to be with you forever," she murmured, "until God sees fit to part us."

"That's my kind of wife," he said and entwined his fingers around hers. "Come back here," he ordered huskily and pulled her to him. When her face nearly touched his, he kissed her tenderly, and she longingly returned his kiss.

She leaned her head on his shoulder, and the swing slowly began to sway back and forth. "You're doing a great job with baby John," she noted, feeling happier than she could ever remember.

"Thank you, but I feel strange holding this little one."

"Do you think you could get over that feeling, say in the next six or so months?"

Stunned, he searched her face, but all she could do was smile in her excitement. "Am. . .am I going to be a father?" he stuttered.

"And a fine one you'll make, too," she replied, planting a kiss on his cheek. "Maybe for nine or ten."

"My grandparents didn't have nine or ten. They just had three. Why, I'll just have to start plans for a larger house, maybe bigger than the one in the painting."

"With God's help," she said.

"With God's help," he echoed. His lips found hers, sealing the commitment of husband and wife for a lifetime of love.

KIMBERLEY COMEAUX

Kimberley gets her inspiration from all sorts of places: travel, history, dreams and once over hearing (okay...eavesdropping on) a conversation between a couple arguing in the grocery store line. She not only is the author of 13 Inspirational romance books, but also writes and produces church musicals. She has been married for 28 years to her best friend, Brian, and has one son, Tyler, and a brand new daughter-in-law, Kellie! Kimberley resides with her family near New Orleans.

Susan K. Downs

Adoption has played a big part in Susan's life. She and her minister-husband adopted three of their five children. While missionaries to Korea, the Downs' family lovingly provided foster care for babies waiting to be adopted. Susan also performed many duties at the Korean social welfare agency that assisted their family with two of their three adoptions. As a licensed social worker, Susan served a number of years as the Eastern European adoption coordinator for a large adoption agency in Fort Worth, Texas. In this capacity, she helped many children find their Forever Families in homes across the United States. The adoption agency where Susan served got its start in 1887 by placing children from the orphan trains.

Currently, Susan resides in Texas and she is employed as a fiction editor for Guideposts Publications.

JoAnn A. Grote

JoAnn lives on the Minnesota prairie which is a setting for many of her stories. Once a full-time CPA, JoAnn now spends most of her time researching and writing. JoAnn has published historical nonfiction books for children and several novels with Barbour Publishing in the Heartsong Presents line as well as the American Adventure and Sisters in Time series for children. Several of her novellas are included in CBA best-selling anthologies by Barbour Publishing. JoAnn's love of history developed when she worked at an historical restoration in North Carolina for five years. She enjoys researching and weaving her fictional characters' lives into historical backgrounds and events. JoAnn believes that readers can receive a message of salvation and encouragement from well-crafted fiction. She captivates and addresses the deeper meaning between life and faith.

ELLEN EDWARDS KENNEDY

Ellen grew up in the Adirondack region of New York State where The Applesauce War takes place. A former award-winning advertising copywriter, she is the author Irregardless of Murder and Death Dangles a Participle, the first two books in the Miss Prentice Cozy mystery series from Sheaf House Publishers. She and her husband live in North Carolina, where they are the happy grandparents of five little answers to prayer.

Debby Mayne

Debby has been a freelance writer for as long as she can remember, starting with short slice-of-life stories in small newspapers, then moving on to parenting articles for regional publications and fiction stories for women and girls. She has been involved in all aspects of publishing, from the creative side, to editing a national health publication, to freelance proofreading for several book publishers. Her belief that all blessings come from the Lord has given her great comfort during trying times and gratitude for when she is rewarded for her efforts. She lives on the west coast of Florida with her husband and two daughters.

DiAnn Mills

Award-winning author DiAnn Mills is a fiction writer who combines an adventuresome spirit with unforgettable characters to create action-packed, suspense-filled novels. DiAnn's first book was published in 1998. She currently has more than fifty books published.

Her titles have appeared on the CBA and ECPA bestseller lists and have won placements through the American Christian Fiction Writer's Carol Awards and Inspirational Reader's Choice awards. DiAnn won the Christy Award in 2010 and 2011.

DiAnn is a founding board member for American Christian Fiction Writers and a member of Inspirational Writers Alive, Romance Writers of America, and Advanced Writers and Speakers Association. She speaks to various groups and teaches writing workshops around the country. DiAnn is also the Craftsman mentor for the Jerry B. Jenkins Christian Writers Guild.

She and her husband live in sunny Houston, Texas.

If you enjoyed
The Farmer's Bride Collection
Look for

The Immigrant Brides Collection

The Prairie Romance Collection

The Bartered Bride Collection

The Stitched with Love Collection

The Texas Brides Collection

Available wherever books are sold.